TARA GUHA

UNTOUCHABLE THINGS

05075996

Legend Press Ltd, The Old Fire Station,
140 Tabernacle Street, London, EC2A 4SD
info@legend-paperbooks.co.uk | www.legendpress.co.uk

Print ISBN 978-1-7850799-4-8
Ebook ISBN 978-1-7850799-5-5
Set in Times. Printed in the United Kingdom by Clays Ltd.
Cover design by Simon Levy www.simonlevyassociates.co.uk

Tara Guha was born to an Indian father and English mother and spent her childhood in the Ribble Valley, passing many a wet day writing poetry and music. After studying English at Cambridge she embarked on a career in the classical music industry in London, promoting artists including Placido Domingo, Paul McCartney and Dudley Moore.

Over the years she has also been a freelance journalist, charity worker and has trained as a counsellor. Tara is a keen amateur pianist, singer and songwriter and lives in the hills of West Yorkshire with her partner and two daughters.

Untouchable Things is Tara's first novel.

Follow Tara @taraguha

For my family, who believed.
And for my younger self, who didn't.

PROLOGUE

For the third time this week he is watching her scream.

Watching, not listening.

After the first time he tunes out of the less interesting part, the sound. The vibrato is uneven, the pitch wavering, the timbre too harsh. But the face is mesmeric, eyes contracted to penny slots while the mouth gapes to spew its cheap auditory prize. Munch, of course, is behind some of the distortion, stamping *The Scream* all over anyone who expresses horror. Even the pretty ones.

But the scream is hers too, and his by default. Not that she knows he is here, not as such. The invitation is tacit, a door left ajar. A paying peephole where he ogles with the others.

She has it down to a fine art, that slight shake of her head, almost a nervous tic, sending a ripple effect down the length of her hair until marigold tresses swing around her like the arms of twirling children. People approach at their peril. She likes it that way: look but don't touch. All her power wound into her hair, like Samson.

Her body holds no fear as it ripples through a series of postures designed to tantalise. Virgin, whore, mother, lover, a sequence choreographed especially for him. And it works. It works as she knows it will and she thrills in his powerlessness to do anything but watch.

His hand twitches and he stretches it slowly so the knuckles crack. Quick glances of disapproval: the watchers must stay silent. They must abide by the protocols of the genre, contain themselves until a glorious ovational climax.

It costs him nothing to wait.

For the fourth time this week he is watching her scream. Watching, not listening. Watching with the mute button on, pressing pause here and there to savour a particular expression, a line of her body. She moves like a dancer. Her hair is a responsive partner but a limelight stealer, forever trying to pirouette off but dragged back, like a recalcitrant Siamese twin. It shimmers in a weightless red-gold haze but he knows its truth, how it slumps into his hands hot and heavy and sticky.

You're staring at my hair.

Who goes here? Witch, spirit, dream? Curls converge to make a veil, darkened to rust and hiding her face.

You remind me of someone.

Do I?

Perhaps there is no face. Perhaps it's just bones under there, freckled skin peeled away to leave the gasp of eye sockets and a toothless grin. He hears rustling, the squirming of caged limbs and realises it's him, writhing, palpitating so that people are craning their heads to look. His neighbour shuffles away a little, crosses her leg with some difficulty so that her booted foot points passive-aggressively, Britishly, in the other direction. He thinks about crossing his own leg and sending one pristine Italian shoe in to remonstrate. He laughs, possibly aloud, and refocuses his gaze.

She has a face, he can see that now, but he can't tell which one. Her hair has fallen back into rank, a mutinous army ready to surge, jostling on her back, a teaming mass, a plural. Flickering memories project onto the exposed visage: Abigail. Ophelia. Julia. Rebecca. He can channel surf, one jab of his thumb to flick between them. But he can't be sure they're not in cahoots to confuse him, the mouth of one with the eyes of another, a high stakes game of *Guess Who?* He narrows his eyes to focus but the effect is to separate them, to see double, quadruple, until they have claimed the stage and evaded his remote control. His head throbs and his vision pixelates, spilling them – her – into patterns of dancing dots.

Flies crawl down from his hairline and when he dashes them, his hand comes away wet. The sucked taste is salt, and it soothes him.

For the fifth time this week he is watching her scream.

ACT 1 - SCENE 1

When she bows she lets the roar of the audience fall on her like a wave.

Tonight it's a tidal wave, pressing down on her head, booming in her ears until she wonders if she'll ever fight her way up again. She must. She has something left to deliver.

She raises her head, stands tall, stares out at them. She feels the ripples of shock spreading up from the ground to the gallery to the upper circle and back through her body. She is dripping and shivering, her hair matted into dark soaked tresses trickling a thin stream across the stage. The director's idea, reminding the room that Ophelia is dead, drowned, done. Blurring the line between art and life. The clapping shudders and stills, people horrified to find themselves applauding a suicide. She forces herself to stay with it, letting them feast on the sight of her, her nakedness skimmed with sopping white cotton, medusa coils of thick red hair slapped to her breasts. The classic male fantasy of Ophelia as neurotic virgin, laid out to arouse and shame the paying voyeurs. She shudders and it's not for effect. She is being sacrificed for a higher purpose.

The silence is louder than the applause, pulsating like a giant heart in her ears as she stands. But she is not done. She is in the round, heated by the gaze of those behind her waiting for their turn. Slowly she pivots, rotating like a ballerina impaled in a musical box. Swathes of gasps follow her round as she is revealed to each section of the house. She turns again into blinding lights. Squinting would spoil the effect so she suffers the white beams that will imprint purple circles on her vision for the next half-hour. She turns and lets them gawp, crane their heads, clench their fists. Then one voice cries out from the front of the stalls and the floodgates reopen, the audience bellows and she is felled once more.

Goodnight, ladies; goodnight, sweet ladies; goodnight, goodnight.

Thank you, Miss Laurence. To clarify, you met Seth Gardner on September 27th 1996 after a performance of *Hamlet*?

Yes, in the pub.

Which pub would that be?

The usual.

The Red Lion off Hanover Street. It was a favourite. She knew the landlord, Des. That night her hair was still damp, glowing like embers as Seth would tell her later. She was first in, first to the bar, looking to numb the places where so many eyes had burned.

Clunk. Eyes slotted into the gaze of another, a jigsaw completed, freeze frame of a shutter coming down. A dark-haired man sitting at a table is watching her. A moment stretched.

Then, turning back, her friends, the post-mortem, the babbled deconstruction and congratulations. A quick glance over her shoulder, the table now empty. A casting director? The usual chit-chat. *My agent isn't returning my calls. Is yours any good? Have you got anything lined up afterwards?* The older contingent banging on about the demise of rep.

She doesn't want to do this, not tonight. Instead she plies people with drinks, makes them laugh, reminds them it's a day off tomorrow. But by pint number three people are making their excuses. Drastic tactics are needed. She sways to the bar and orders three tequila slammers.

How now, fair Ophelia? The voice pours deep into her ear

like warm water. She turns and he is right there, next to her, the dark-haired man from across the room. Close up she sees that his eyes are the wrong shade of green and she can't look away from them. They drip amusement.

"It looks as though Rosencrantz has just exited pub left. So might I avail myself of one of these?" She's vaguely surprised at his cut-glass English accent. The hair, the eyes, suggest something other. She sees the curve of his mouth, plush as a woman's. Then a hand reaching, she's transfixed for a second before her ears pop and she grasps both his drift and the glass.

"No, you may not. I don't generally buy drinks for strange men." If he is a casting director she's blown it now.

"Not even a strange man who loves Shakespeare? You were amazing tonight."

A laugh, her laugh. Too far gone for self-deprecation. "Thank you. I was, wasn't I?"

His laugh, louder, more sonorous. "And modest too. It gets better." He stretches a serious hand out to her hair. "You must have been cold though. Look at you. You're still wet."

She is wet, suddenly, but not in the places he means. He has her hair in his fingers. If she tried to leave now, would he stop her?

There's a commotion to her right and an inebriated Hamlet, risen from the dead, lurches forwards.

"Becs, I gotta go. Lucy'll kill me if I'm late again. Oh... hello." He smiles at the man, tries to stand upright.

He thinks it's a casting director.

"Jez, meet..."

The man's lips stretch and curve. "Seth."

"Seth thought we were wonderful tonight. Isn't that right?" She giggles, her grip a little too tight on Jez's arm.

"Indeed I did. An electrifying performance."

Jez shoots a quizzical glance at Rebecca and she shakes her head. Then he grins and slaps the man on the back. "Cheers, mate, glad you enjoyed it. Here, have my drink. I've

13

really got to go, Becs – will you be all right?"

"Maybe I should come with you." The pub chatter is swelling, filling her head, and the faintly stubbled cleft on the man's chin is an unknown quantity. Jez winks and bends to kiss her cheeks.

"Nah, stay, you look like you're having fun. Be a good girl, eh? Call you tomorrow, darling."

You left the pub with him?
Yes. Yes, it was stupid and the only thing I could have done. I don't expect you to understand.
You had a boyfriend, Miss Laurence?
Rebecca, please. Yes, I did. What difference does that make? Nothing happened.
Could I take your boyfriend's details?
Is this relevant? We're not together now. And why all the sudden questions? Has something else happened? Is there something you're not telling me?
Your ex-boyfriend's details?
I'll fetch my address book. Here. (Jason Fletcher, 116a Reynolds Road, perfect boyfriend material.) We'd been together two years I think at that point.
Thank you, Miss Laurence. Was there anything else about the earlier part of that evening that stands out in your mind? Before you went on your way with Mr Gardner?
Not that I can remember. It was the third night of the run, we knew what we were doing. Oh yes – I'd forgotten. Backstage before the show. Some flowers...

It was impossible not to smile at her own reflection. Each red-gold tendril coiled softly and separately over her shoulders like a pre-Raphaelite painting. Her face, pale at the best of times, bleached translucent under the lights, but tonight it didn't matter. For the first time she felt perfectly physically matched to a character.

She stepped back in case anyone was watching but couldn't resist another furtive primp. People were milling about chatting, adjusting each other's costumes; comfortable background noise like a distant radio. In general her unusual – some said startling – look gave directors a headache casting her. Blondes and Mediterranean types always did better. On too many occasions she'd been told that her appearance would distract from the part, that she wasn't how they imagined a character to look. She wore more wigs than a drag queen, and of course there was stage make-up, but this time – she *was* Ophelia, simple as that.

Unsettling, given that Ophelia's life consisted of being screwed around by men and then going mad. Not quite the script Rebecca had in mind for herself. But she had to acknowledge some kind of affinity that went beyond looks. Getting into the role was no more challenging than slipping on a favourite dress.

What did that say about her? She wanted to follow the thought but that feeling ambushed her, the one that buckled her legs like being kicked in the back of the knees. She leant on a chair for a second. Here she was, twenty-eight years old and playing Ophelia. Her whole intestine seemed to straighten and re-coil at the thought. On Tuesday, her parents would be in the audience, holding each other's hands as they watched her take the stage. They hadn't always been sure about her choice of career, but they had supported her through it all, the big parts in student productions, the bit parts in fringe productions, the tears and the nearly giving up and the lack of anything approaching an income.

"Ten minutes, boys and girls."

The scene around her exploded into action. She had to jump back to avoid the sharp lip of a passing shovel; the gravediggers meant business. Intonations of lines started up around her like a sudden burst of prayer. She closed her eyes, waiting for her body's response.

Here it was, the surge of giddiness on the in-breath, held... held some more, then rushing out like tiny waves to her fingertips. Eyes blinked open like a doll. In front of her was Ophelia's fragile face, attempting, but not quite pulling off a smile. And then a beep from the table, making them both jump. She frowned. Ophelia would not be answering a mobile phone. But she couldn't help herself, moist fingers sliding over still unfamiliar keys.

BREAK A LEG, DARLING. I LOVE YOU. J XXX

Jason. Her frown deepened before smoothing into the wisp of a smile. Ever since she'd jumped on the mobile phone bandwagon he'd sent her the same message before every performance, capitals bellowing at her. It had become part of her pre-performance ritual; not as extreme as many – she liked to think she was pretty rational, for an actor – but it soothed her as it irritated her, the sameness of the message, night after night.

The rustle of plastic and Leah appears from nowhere, face almost hidden by a huge bouquet of flowers. She doesn't want to talk to Leah now, she needs to focus.

"For you-hoo!"

"What?"

"You're supposed to say *'For me?'* Look. Aren't they amazing?"

She half takes the flowers from Leah but she's not ready for their weight one-handed and they nearly fall between them. Leah makes a grab.

"Hey. Be careful. These are mega bucks."

Rebecca puts down her mobile, takes them properly this time and sees a blur of colours bleeding into each other. The smell is like a punch in the face. "Who are they from?"

"Dunno. There's no note." Of course Leah would have already checked. "Not exactly Jason's style, innit?"

Not exactly. And now Rebecca is irritated with the flowers, wants them to go away, and she knows it's just nerves but she actually wants to shout *fuck the flowers* and throw them across the room, but there's Leah to appease so she smiles, says "I wonder," and places them with exaggerated care on her bag. "Sorry, I need to…"

"I know, babe. See you in the pub."

She closes her eyes against the waves of lily sweetness, wonders if she might fall asleep like Dorothy in the poppy field. Breathe. She shuffles away a bit and a *boom* rushes up from her stomach, like she's falling upwards. She clutches the back of a chair and her eyes open on Anthony Lambury doing Tai Chi across the room, left leg wobbling precariously under purple robes, arms flailing like a puppet and it breaks the fall and she can smile, and then start over. When she looks back towards the mirror she is relieved to see Ophelia gazing at her through glassy eyes.

There was magic on stage. She always loved acting with Jez but the connection between them was like a power line tonight, fizzing and sparking. Ophelia barely spoke in the first two acts but Rebecca knew how to reel the audience in, draw every eye to her so that each person was implicated in what was to follow.

It's only now she thinks, *I never found out who sent the flowers.*

SCENE 2

Why would a sparrow be hovering by the large, glass doors of Draper & Sons if not to buy a piano?

Or to play one. The sparrow, who also went by the name of Catherine, hopped a little on twig-like legs made twiggier by tan tights and tried to summon the *chutzpah* to go in. The wind teased her mousy, shoulder-length hair like a curious kitten. Mist clung in droplets to the slightly oversized, red wool coat, a cast-off from her extravagant sister and the only possible entry permit she had. She fluttered along the glassed length of the building, a sparrow with a death wish, twittering ever so quietly to herself: "I can do this. I can play this role."

She needed to look serious. In this coat she could be a peacock, strutting disdainfully around the instruments, even preening. No, not preening. Preening might draw attention to her scuffed boots and shapeless jeans. Instead she should move swiftly, a hawk swooping down on its prey, seizing it before anyone had time to challenge her. Even if she was pulled off she would have filled her mouth by then, the taste dripping out of her, ravaged hunks to take home.

With a haughty inclination of her head she spins on her heel and collides with a woman behind her. Instant apologies, retreat, the gathering of resolve over again. A tide rising inside her, threatening to cut off her ability to act.

In the end it was the rain, swinging in from the West, from a tourist-soaked Carnaby Street, that drove the sparrow to seek shelter in an unfamiliar habitat. It paused briefly in the entrance, considering hurling itself back at the double doors, and then found it surprisingly easy to hop forward, avoiding the brazen overtures of electric guitars and drum kits, until it arrived at the foot of the curved central staircase.

Heel-toe, heel-toe, with a little hamstring tensing thrown in, is all it takes to mount the stairs, slowly like a queen, all poise and gravitas. She knows it's important to get into role early, lest a jittery entrance reveals her imposture.

I'd like to buy a piano.

Can you show me your best pianos?

I'm in the market for a top-of-the-range grand piano.

She scratches the last one – too American, new money, all show. This establishment values modest understatement. Though not in matters of footwear. She hopes no one looks at her feet.

She's reached the halfway point and there it is, the first gleam of ebony. Keep going. Heel-toe, the thrusting young uprights materialise first, bit by shiny bit, top down, coffins that turn into keyboards, perched, finally, on three funny little feet. Heel-toe and the veterans appear, the grands, grumbling away at the back.

She halts. Row upon row of pianos basking in the lights, a colour swatch of browns and blacks. Rosewood, mahogany, ebony, maple: a blinding mass of perfection. She feels herself growing smaller, as in the face of the sea. Breathe. Look at ease. You are at home with expensive pianos. You know that under their dazzling veneer all they want is to be touched properly, responsively. And you know how to do that.

She emerges as a child reaching the top of a fairy tale tree, stepping out into a different land. A tang of woodiness cools her nostrils and the hush that ghosts over her face is not a silence but a breathing presence. A piano choir watches her, waiting for her next move. For a second she breathes with them. And then the jolt of eye contact with a dark-haired man smiling at her next to a black Yamaha upright. Tall, polished, intimidating, looking disconcertingly like his product. If she's a sparrow, this one, under his sober suit, is a jay. Do jays eat sparrows? His feathers puff out as he strolls towards her, smiling.

"You look like the proverbial child in the sweet shop."

And you look like... but his words goad her and she lifts her chin. "I'm here to buy a piano."

"Well, you've made it to the right place." Something untrustworthy – sarcasm, perhaps – glitters green in his eyes. It's as if he has seen into her, watched her halting progress outside the shop. Has he? He's talking again. "Anything particular in mind?"

"Well..." she flicks her eyes as if to survey the room. "I'm after a grand. Something with a big bass."

"I see." His eyebrows arch into inverted smiles and she clenches her fist against a rising blush. "I presume it's okay to try one or two out?" Stand still. Mirror his self-assurance. Ignore the fact that he's just glanced at your shoes.

"I can't see that being a problem. It's the back right-hand corner you need, if I'm not mistaken."

You're not. She nods thanks and reins in her legs to walking pace. Is it still there? Why is he following her?

Stretched out in the corner she spots the focal point of her dreams for the past three months. Steinway Model B, Hamburg 1928. She wants to run her hands down its length, lay her cheek on its cool mottled surface. And she wants to be alone.

"Ah, the Steinway." The salesman looks at her as if she has answered a question correctly.

"Yes, I – I tried it once before and I guess I fell in love." She can't quite meet his gaze.

"Well, be my guest."

She pulls out the leather stool, adjusts the height slightly and is still. Her fingers strain towards the keyboard but her mind is negotiating enormity, the need to do the instrument justice. What is most fitting? Bach, to show off the clarity? Beethoven, for the brazen power of the thing? Or Chopin for both? Chopin it is. She dives in, finds herself in the slow movement of the E minor concerto, fingers plucking out the notes even though she hasn't looked at it for more than a year. She watches herself play a little slower, more indulgently, than she might have done in front of her teacher, lets herself soak in the sound.

Feather touch on the right hand runs, hear that crispness, each melody singing out like ice-cold champagne on a hot day. Notes rush up to meet her fingers, ripple through them leaving a river of sound. And sweeping her to the big chords, increase pressure, bigger, bigger... the whole world is resonating with E major and she's no longer in control, she could stay there, wants to stay, but cool keys caress her right hand and gently guide her down. It wasn't exactly what Chopin had written but it told his story.

At the final chord she finds she can't lift her head, can't emerge, won't emerge, even as she remembers her surroundings, the salesman. Perhaps he's wandered off. But when she raises her face, there he is, sitting on one of the nearby stools, staring out of the window with his back to her.

Without warning he snaps round and gets to his feet. The movement shocks her, an expletive in church, and she raises a hand to protect herself. He is moving in on her with a brisk sense of purpose. About to start the sales pitch, no doubt. Her game is up.

"Well, you've made up my mind for me."

"Sorry?" She tries to stand, foggily, stumbling as she pushes back the stool. Always the same after a moment like that, when the music passes through her, like she's forgotten how to use her limbs. Fluidly he reaches over to move the stool away.

"I feel like we've had sex. Even though I was just watching."

She feels her eyes expand into outrage. And then another suited man appears from nowhere, clutching some sort of pamphlet.

"I'm terribly sorry to keep you waiting, sir. Here's the updated catalogue." A quick disapproving glance at her as he holds out his hand.

The man smiles but doesn't accept the catalogue. "I won't be needing it now. I've decided to take this one." His vague wave of the hand could have been meant for Catherine or the piano.

"Sorry, sir, I'm not sure I understand." The second man's face is elongating in wonder, prompting Catherine to shut her own mouth. What is going on? She ducks her head against the barrage of sales patter – excellent choice, methods of payment, delivery dates – peppering her like hailstones. A name, spoken and then spelled: Seth Gardner, without the 'e'. The ground is swaying slightly and the top of the stairway urges her to get out of this strange land before it moves on and leaves her stranded. The two men are so busy with each other it will be easy to slip away unnoticed.

"Excuse me!" At the ground floor exit she hears a shout. A hand on her arm. She turns into the green-eyed piano purchaser, lit with the shop lights and a smile that is more

21

mischief than apology. She pulls away her arm, surprised at the sudden rush of anger. He moderates his smile. "Look, I'm sorry for that. You just seemed to assume I was a salesman so I, er, carried on the role play." It isn't much of an explanation. She moves toward the darkness behind the doors where umbrellas are hurrying past. "But then I heard you play and, well, I just had to take the piano. I wasn't that serious about buying, but what you did in there... it was one of the most beautiful things I've ever heard."

A smile is worming its way through the seal of her lips. She tries to check it. "Thank you. It's an amazing piano. I hope you enjoy it."

A muscle twitches on his barely stubbled cheek. "I shall certainly enjoy listening to it. I don't play myself, never taken the trouble to learn."

Words are sucked from her mouth. He's buying a £70,000 piano and doesn't play? "Well, I hope others enjoy it then." She means to be cutting but it comes out wobbly, tear-tinged. "I've got to go."

Once again a hand on her arm. "Don't go yet. Come back into the warm and give me a chance to explain. I just need to finish the paperwork upstairs but why don't you let me buy you a coffee afterwards? There's a great little place round the corner."

And that was the first time you met Seth Gardner?
Yes. Sorry, I know I've probably given you more detail than you need. It's just... I remember everything like it was a film.
Could you speak up, Miss Jarret?
Sorry, it's nothing. I just miss him, that's all. I – sorry...
Do you need to take a break?
No. No, I'll be fine. I know this is important. I'll try again.

SCENE 3

Can you tell us about the rest of the evening, Miss Laurence?

Now, there's a question. It would be nice if she could. It was certainly a night to remember, she's sure of that, but remembering is the problem. The shape of it was there, later, to admire, but the little details, whole hours in fact, were smudged and indecipherable. There was another round of tequilas, almost certainly. Then Seth's suggestion of taking a taxi to his club in Soho, which had made her laugh as she pictured leather armchairs and cigars. Of course, she'd got into the taxi anyhow, which made her laugh again as she imagined the disapproving tug of Jason's eyebrows. He never got cabs, insisting on consulting his *A to Z* at every opportunity to work out a walking route, even when her shoes were killing her.

One street blurring into the other, no idea where they were. It didn't matter. Seth was talking to the cabbie about which roads were best at this time of night and she leaned back into the seat, content to let the men blabber on about one-way streets and no left turns. His voice rose and fell like a babbling brook of her childhood. *Mellifluous.* The word surprises her. She tries it out in her mouth, savouring the effect on her tongue. At some point after that she may have drifted off.

"... are you?"

She judders, comes to, and looks across, reaching for an expression of alertness. The taxi has stopped. Seth's eyebrows are raised.

"Sorry?"

"I said, you're not going to bail on me, are you?"

She sits up. "Not me! Are we here?"

He grins and jumps out, appearing at her side like a magician to open her door and bowing as she makes a less-than-dignified exit.

"And put that away, please." It's a good job. She doesn't have more than a tenner on her. He offers her his arm, this man she's just met, and she takes it, regretting the tequila and her shoes, cursing the cobbles. She inches forwards like a geriatric.

"Lucky we don't have far to walk, eh?" He leads her to a black door with a gold knob. No number. No sign. He knocks twice, heavily. "*Now* why are you laughing?"

She bites her lip. "Because we're knocking on a random door in the middle of Soho. Part of me expects a mad hatter to open it."

"Ah, the magic threshold. You could have a point. Follow me, Alice."

A suited man was holding the door open and smiling. Other men seemed to appear from behind him like a cabaret trick, taking their coats and offering drinks. "You know I don't play cards?" she hissed as she followed Seth upstairs.

"Shame." He pushed open a heavy double door and blaring house music almost knocked her backwards.

Rebecca blinked. Shadowy bodies gyrated in the smoke and she smelled dry ice. She turned to Seth; his mouth was moving but she couldn't make out the words over the music. He smiled and let the door close. Abruptly the sound was sucked away.

"Later, perhaps?"

She shook her head and followed him upstairs into a lounge area replete with sofas, soft lighting and jazz. Rebecca felt her senses sharpening.

"You like?"

They were sitting next to a window that stretched the length of the room, like a giant spy hole over the city. Blue-black sky and swirls of smoky cloud gave way to jagged rooftops and, below those, silent traffic and moving figures. Neon flashes lit the glass.

"It's amazing. I've never been anywhere like this."

"Welcome to Wonderland. I'll tell you if you start shrinking. Mind if I smoke?"

She shook her head as he took out a silver cigarette box from his jacket. She had never seen anyone use a cigarette box. She was going to ask about it but he tucked it away again quickly. She looked around, wondering how many places like this were hiding in plain sight alongside the London she knew. The waft of burning as he lit his cigarette smelled of danger and possibilities.

"The Singapore Slings are excellent."

She dragged her gaze away from the window, towards the drinks menu and instantly gave up. "Suits me. Sorry, I just can't stop looking. It's like we're suspended in our own little bubble, but right in the middle of everything."

Seth exhaled a thin stream of smoke, signalled for the drinks and leaned in. The lights caught his eyes and they gleamed. "Exactly. Look, we're sitting here sipping our cocktails, having a private conversation, but any time we want we can jump down into the melee."

For a second she actually wanted to jump, could imagine the arc her body would make against the night sky as it leapt and fell. She gripped the table edge with tingling fingers. He looked at her as if he could read her mind.

"I think we're going to have a lot of fun, Ophelia."

"Me too." But something clanged inside and she dropped her gaze.

"Ah, don't tell me. You have a boyfriend."

She looked up with a wooden smile. "Ten out of ten." Her energy levels were sinking.

"Well, don't look like that about it. Isn't that supposed to be my reaction rather than yours?" Seth tapped his cigarette.

"I suppose so. I…"

"Look." His touch on her hand made her start. "I never expected a woman like you to be single. Believe it or not, I'm not here to seduce you, I'm just enjoying your company. Not that you're not a tempting proposition, of course."

"Thanks… I think." She knew she was blushing and hoped the candlelight would mask it. *A woman like you.* She felt about fifteen.

"Look, here come our drinks. We'll have one and then I insist on taking you downstairs."

It was two in the end – a mojito to follow – and she had time to examine him as sips of swanky cocktails flamed her insides. He was easily the best-dressed man she'd ever seen. Everything – navy blazer, lilac shirt, even his jeans, even his shoes, for God's sake – looked made for him. Perhaps they were.

"You're looking at my shoes, Rebecca."

"Sorry. How do you keep suede so pristine?"

He laughed but flicked his hand as if casting aside her question. "Let's go and dance."

And that was where the evening became blurred. He sends her spinning like a top and whips her back with a flick of his wrist. She is squealing like a child wanting more, wanting him to stop, sometimes graceful, sometimes stumbling into his arms. Each time she completes a revolution his face is there, steady, two cat's eyes guiding her home. She knows he is a good dancer and that she must yield to him as he throws her back over his arm, trust that he will hold her up. Sometimes his lips move and although he is looking at her she can't be sure that he is talking to her. She wants to dance a tango with him, to grasp his face in her hands then pull away, but she is at his mercy, spinning around him and finally, now, begging him to stop.

Then they are outside again on stripped streets. He squeezes her hand. "Back to reality." A group of men rounds the corner, shouting. One of them waits behind to vomit into a bin. "But any time you fancy, the portal is there."

"Thank you. It's been amazing." She throws back her head and lets sticky hair trickle down her back. Clouds sail hurriedly through a starless sky. Lit by a streetlamp a single leaf is wheeling and swirling, hurtling in the wind. She sighs as she watches it disappear. "What time is it?"

"Oh, you know. Early."

She grabs his hand and squints at an expensive watch. "God, it's not really 3.15 is it? I have to get home. Do you think I can get a cab around here?"

"Don't worry about that." He turns to face her. "There's something I wanted to ask you first."

She steadies herself. "Go on."

"How do you fancy joining a group?"

"A group? What sort of group?"

"I suppose you could call it a creative arts group."

"What?" She laughs. "Down at the community centre, that sort of thing? I didn't have you down as the type."

"Not exactly." And he's not smiling now. "Meetings are at my place. Friday nights usually. The Friday Folly, we call ourselves." He looks so serious that she squeezes the smile from her face like a naughty child.

"Sorry, I shouldn't have laughed. What happens at these… meetings?"

"Oh, someone shows a painting, someone reads a poem, that sort of thing. You could sing us some songs of madness. Then we get drunk and feast on home-cooked food. Of course, if it sounds a bit too odd for you…"

"I didn't say that." They size each other up, two gladiators in a ring. A smile starts on his face and passes over to hers. "Okay, sounds as crazy as the rest of this night, so yes, I'll come to your Friday Frolic."

"Folly." He kisses her, leaving a cool spot on her right cheek that she wants to touch. "Good. I'll be in touch. Now, I think your carriage may be arriving." He puts his foot into the road and waves at the yellow light. "Unless I can tempt you with further frolics?"

"No, thank you, I've been tempted enough already." She didn't mean that quite as it came out. The cab pulls up as she tries to explain and Seth puts his finger on her lips.

"Goodnight, sweet Ophelia."

And then he is gone and she is staring at the space he has left.

27

SCENE 4

Did you initiate further contact with Mr Gardner, Miss Jarret?

Catherine looked at the sheet music, waiting for hush. It was a strange thing, performing at the piano. There was no other instrument where you'd have your back to the audience, all straight spine and elevated chin. She couldn't see the eyes on her but it was almost worse to imagine them. She breathed twice as her teacher had instructed and placed her hands above the keys.

The loud squelch of a fart bubbled into the silence. Catherine didn't move but closed her eyes against a swell of titters and tuts.

"Him again."

"It's disgraceful. They should take him out."

"Look at her, poor love. Don't you take no notice, dear."

Catherine half turned, half smiled, hands now sinking to her lap. She saw the red face of Fred Worthington lean out towards the ladies.

"It's not my bloody fault, it's the food they give you in 'ere." He jabbed his walking stick at them, to a chorus of Oof!s and Oh!s.

"Quiet, now." Mrs Pratt's terrier-like bark cut through the racket. Gradually the room stilled and Catherine listened for the pulsing rhythm of the funeral march before putting her hands to the keyboard. Beethoven's Piano Sonata no. 12: not his best known but the slow movement offered intensity, drama and, foremost in her teacher's mind, the opportunity to practise playing in seven flats. She paced her way up to the climax and brought them down like a pilot smoothly landing a plane.

A small flurry of applause, which she turned to acknowledge. Rose Dowling was asleep, a droplet of drool quivering on the end of her chin. Another lady leaned over to her neighbour with a loud stage whisper.

"Bit boring, wasn't it?"

"Shhh, Mary."

"You what?"

"Turn your hearing aid up, you're shouting in my ear."

Catherine caught sight of Fred Worthington, face like a skinned tomato, muttering in the corner.

"What the fuck was that?"

"Fred Worthington!"

"Well, what am I supposed to say? It's miserable enough here without having to sit and listen to my own funeral. Might as well just choke myself in this fucking chair now." He grabbed his throat and made graphic retching sounds.

Mrs Pratt moved in. "Right, Fred – out. Now."

"Don't worry, I'm not bloody staying here." He banged his stick past the line of old ladies shaking their heads.

"What are you looking at, you frigid old…"

"Fred! Out." Mrs Pratt grabbed his arm and escorted him from the room. Catherine felt like a beacon pulsing with shame, marooned on the piano stool.

A bony finger touched her shoulder. "Don't you worry yourself about him. He's just a nasty piece of work with too much brandy inside him." It was Ada Hartley, her 'friend' on the inside. "I thought you played that wonderfully."

Catherine smiled. "Thank you."

The old lady winked a crinkly blue eye. "Mind you, you might want to do something a bit more lively next. Funeral marches are a bit too close to the bone for some of us, you know."

Catherine's face flared pink. "I'm sorry. I didn't think of it like that – I just thought it was a beautiful piece of music."

Ada patted her knee. "I know, dear, and why should you?" The lady in the next chair was craning forwards, trying to listen.

"Have you asked her for 'Roll Out the Barrel', Ada?"

"Shut up, Jean. You know that's not the kind of thing she plays."

Another woman put her hand to her ear. "Are we doing 'Roll Out the Barrel'? Do you know 'We'll Meet Again' as well, dear?"

A barrage of song requests buffeted her. Catherine shook her head. She had a Chopin prelude lined up as an encore; this was a disaster. Mrs Pratt stuck her head round the door and snarled.

"Mary, go and sit down. Now, Cath just plays the classics, don't you, love?" Catherine stiffened at the abbreviation of her name. "Besides, you know we're not having sing-songs after what happened last time." She looked around and let her words hang in the air. "Now, settle down and let Cath finish off."

When it was over she had a cup of tea with Ada in the lounge as usual. Ada had played the violin as a child and seemed to appreciate these visits the most. Sometimes, on days like this, Catherine wondered why she bothered. She'd started doing it as a teenager; one of their neighbours was a nurse in a care home and thought the residents would appreciate a bit of music. And they did, some of them. Others snored or chatted through the slow bits, but a few were entranced. One of them, a lady called Polly with severe dementia, sang and rocked through everything. On one occasion, when Catherine had just finished the first movement of the Moonlight Sonata, Polly looked at her with tears in her eyes and said, "That was beautiful." Apparently it was the first coherent sentence anyone had heard her utter in years.

Catherine knew she was no good at small talk and never knew what to say to cheer people up, but she did believe that music could reach out and say something better than any words. In that sense it was the music, not her, that was helping. The distinction helped her feel less presumptuous, less of a do-gooder. So when she moved to London and realised there was a care home on her road she'd offered her services. She came every other Saturday, alternating with bingo.

Ada was looking closely at her and Catherine realised she hadn't been listening properly. The old lady squeezed her upper arm. "Thin as a rake, you young girls. When did you last see a proper hot dinner?"

"Um… does a baked potato count?"

Ada shook her head and tutted. Then she narrowed her eyes. "Not got a young man distracting you, have you?"

"I'm afraid not," Catherine replied, but her rising colour whispered otherwise. It was stupid but she hadn't been able to stop thinking about Seth, that crazy encounter in Draper & Sons and the coffee afterwards. The way they'd talked.

"Now there's a blush if I ever did see one."

Flashes of their conversation. *My parents are dead.* (The reason he had money to burn.) *My parents are dead inside.* (The reason she had a 'safe' career.) She shouldn't have said that. But he drew things out of her, listening with his gaze combing the contours of her face.

"Leave the poor girl alone, Ada." Edna Haworth parked her zimmer frame in front of them. "I'm sure she's got better places to be."

Catherine tipped the last of her tea into her mouth. "I should be going."

Ada squeezed her hand. "Look after yourself, love. Make sure he treats you well."

Catherine shook her head, smiled and gathered up her music. "I'll see you in a fortnight."

She stepped out into premature December darkness and the usual blur of feelings. Old people lumped together with little dignity and less stimulation, waiting to die. Fred Worthington, rude though he was, had only put into words the truth of their situation. Catherine shivered, not wanting to dwell on this. And today there was another feeling, wriggling around to create space for itself. She smiled as she remembered Ada's teasing. Seth had given her his card, told her to call him to book 'first play' on the piano. A week had passed and she'd lost her nerve. Meeting him had been like peeping into a room filled with sunshine and laughter. The people in her life, herself included, seemed suddenly grey whereas he was… luminescent. Her heart craved the light but her head warned her off. They didn't belong in the same worlds.

She walked briskly, London style, towards the empty weekend ahead.

Miss Jarret, I appreciate your level of detail but if we could get to the point here?
Of course, I'm sorry. I'll speed things up.

[Twilight. A woman walks along a tree-lined street. Suddenly a rain-coated man emerges from the shadows and takes her arm. The woman screams.]

CATHERINE: Oh, it's you. What on earth?
SETH: Relax, my jittery little sparrow. You didn't call.
CATHERINE: I – meant to.
SETH: He's waiting for you, you know.
CATHERINE: Sorry?
SETH: Mr Steinway. Feeling lonely, no one to play with him.
CATHERINE: Oh. You must know others…
SETH: No one like you.
CATHERINE: Oh! I'm not sure. How did you find me?
SETH: The florid scent of Chopin follows you around. Come on, take a risk in your dull accountant's life and make an orphan boy happy.
CATHERINE: Maybe next week.
SETH: Mr Steinway is growing impatient. And as luck would have it, my car is right here. Hop in, little sparrow.

SCENE 5

I assume you joined his group, Miss Laurence?

32

She stumbled into the theatre late the next morning wearing sunglasses. No performance that evening but the director had called an extra rehearsal to iron out one or two 'niggly things'. Jason had already been on the phone, quizzing her because she'd not taken his calls after the show. Scenes from the rest of the night were bursting into her head like fireworks.

First she needed to get some water. But there was Jez, smirking at her and barring her way.

"Whoa, girl, slow down. Someone looks a little peaky." He gave her one of his winks. "Have a good time, did we?"

She tried to look cool. "Yes, it was okay. Didn't stay out long. Sorry Jason called you, by the way. You know how he is." She wrinkled her nose. "And thanks for, er..."

"Covering for you? Well, I didn't want to worry the poor boy, did I?" His words were obscured by sudden gales of laughter across the foyer. "Oh yes, Greg has something for you. You'd better go and collect it."

"What?" Rebecca looked at the group in the corner, heads bent over something. "A review?"

"I think you might have to answer that one. I'm going to grab a coffee before we start."

She walked over to a chorus of cheers and wolf whistles.

"The *lady* herself," said Greg.

"What are you talking about?"

"Think this might be for you." He was waving some sort of card in front of her. She grabbed for it but he pulled his hand away. "Not unless you ask nicely."

"Ask for what? Is it a review?"

"Come on Greg, let her see. Let her explain herself."

With a leering look, Greg handed her a postcard, which on first glance appeared to be a drawing of a man performing oral sex on a woman. She turned it over, mouth open in shock. On the back, in an unfamiliar, sloping hand, was scrawled *Lady, shall I lie on your lap?*

"What the…"

Roars of laughter surrounded her.

"So come on, fess up. Who's the guy? Not our Jason, methinks."

"I've no idea." Her heart was beating fast. She tried to think above the clamour.

"You don't expect us to believe that." Simon knelt in front of her and put his arms round her waist. "Lady, lady, shall I lie in your lap?"

"Fuck off, Si." She pulled herself free. Nothing made sense. Who would send her something like this? Obviously someone who knew the line in *Hamlet*, knew she was in it. Would Seth do this? It didn't seem to fit. But what did she know about him anyway?

"Jez reckons you were getting quite friendly with some bloke in the pub last night."

"Bullshit. Jez was off his head."

"He sounded pretty sure of his facts. Come on, spill. You *know* you can trust us, darling." Greg batted his eyelashes.

"There's nothing to spill. I bumped into someone. Someone from school."

"Look, there's a date and address too." Simon lifted the card out of her hand.

"What?" She snatched it back, saw the small block capitals at the bottom.

FRIDAY 18TH, 8PM, 15B LINFIELD GARDENS, NOTTING HILL.

"No prizes for guessing what he's got lined up for the evening. Make sure you have a good all-over wash, darling."

The crowd exploded and Rebecca couldn't help smiling, dealing Greg a mock blow. He put his arm round her and gave her a squeeze.

"I'm just jealous, you know."

"Hang on a minute, it was you, wasn't it? One of you?" Hope and disappointment battled it out.

Greg shook his head and folded his arms. "Uh-uh. You're

not getting off the hook that easily, young lady. Come on, Jez is calling us in. I'll deal with you later."

It wasn't even a temporary reprieve. The director started with the middle act, which led up to the line from the postcard. Jez's voice wobbled and the director looked baffled by the sniggers around her. She knew better than to let the joke take hold and called a break. Rebecca was sneaking out for a few minutes quiet when Leah rushed over and dragged her into a corner.

"A man's been here asking for you."

"What man?"

"Tall, dark and handsome with the most intense eyes."

Seth. Rebecca ran a hand through her hair. "Sounds like one of my school friends. I ran into him last night."

"You went to school with someone like that! Is he single? Can you introduce me?"

"Um, maybe. Did he say what he wanted?"

"No, he said he'll pop back later. I told him when you'd be done."

"Cool." Rebecca tried to look neutral.

"And don't worry." Leah squeezed her arm. "I've got some lippy in my bag."

The rehearsal finished with a few scenes from Act IV. After one of his entrances, Jez whispered in her ear, "There's a tall, dark stranger waiting for you at reception."

They carried on their stage dialogue, with Hamlet's *Get thee to a nunnery* sounding a little more emphatic than usual.

"Stop!" The director cut through the famous speech with a gesture of irritation. "I don't know what's wrong with you all again. Jeremy, I presume you were whispering to Rebecca to alert her to the fact that she's standing slightly too far to the left?" Her eyebrows were raised.

"Yes, sorry I was."

"Very helpful of you but save it in future. We'll leave it there. See you all tomorrow."

SCENE 6

So you are… one moment while I check your details… Michael Stanley, school teacher, Flat 6, 47 Hill Lane, N4 3JQ?

That's correct. Could I ask how long this will last?

I can't say at this stage, Mr Stanley. We'll be as quick as we can. I'm sure you appreciate the seriousness of the situation.

Possibly.

Possibly, Mr Stanley?

I mean it's possibly a serious situation and possibly not. I take it you have no more news?

We'll get to that. First of all I need you to tell me how you met Seth Gardner. Mr Stanley, could you please sit down?

Is it really necessary to rehash all this? I mean, shouldn't you be asking me about the last three months?

As I said, we will come to that. You seem rather agitated, Mr Stanley. Rather… angry, if I might say. I thought we were talking about a friend of yours?

Ex-friend would be closer.

But you were in a group together?

Yes.

Good, well I'd like you to take me through how you met and how you ended up becoming part of this group. Details that may seem unimportant to you may help us more than you realise.

Fine. We met three years ago. March 1994. I don't know the exact date but it was a Friday night.

Go on.

I was doing this thing, a collaboration, with the Barbican. An exhibition of the kids' work in response to a piece of classical music. We had a stand in the foyer and the press officer had organised a bit of a reception.

His latest attempt to build a link between the cloistered world of classical music and the chaotic lives of the kids at St Mary's. Only a handful of parents bothered to turn up but it was better than nothing. And there were some positives to take. There, rooted by the white wine, was the Barker kids' dad, last spotted at a parents' evening five years ago. His shirt was clearly borrowed, gaped into an O above the belt. But he'd made the effort. Maybe they should try free booze at parents' evenings in future. His son stood with a couple of his year at the far side of the stand, pocketed hands jiggling imaginary change, mouth curled slightly to indicate he was there under duress.

It was quite a coup that the Barbican had agreed to show the exhibition. And here came braying Briony, the Barbican press officer, greeting him as if he were the last person on earth she'd expected to see.

"*Michael*, hello!" He felt a squeeze on his tricep as she tiptoed to kiss his cheek. Background sniggers of teenage girls. "The exhibition looks *amazing!*"

"Hi, Briony." She seemed oblivious to the whispers and snorts behind them. Her round face beamed up at him and he took half a step backwards.

"All the locals are covering it. We'll take a few snaps in a minute for our newsletter. And David Baines, y'know the chief exec, said he might pop down."

"Fantastic," Michael replied.

Briony looked at her watch. "Didn't you say your headmaster was coming? It's quarter to already."

Michael shifted his feet. "I'm sure he'll be here any moment now."

"It's just – y'know, if we are planning to take this further, work together again…"

"Of course. He's very supportive of the whole thing, he must have just got tied up at school, you know how it is."

A slight frown to indicate she didn't know how it was. "Okay, well I'll pop back in a wee while then." Her face perked up. "Ciao."

Ciao? He watched her clipping off, giving little waves left and right like Princess Anne on happy pills. The snorts behind him became peals of laughter. "Ciao, Mr Stanley."

Michael tried to get his smile under control before turning round. "That's enough, Lauren. In terms of this project, Briony is a Very Important Person. We need to keep her sweet."

"We'll leave that to you sir, eh? Sir? No one's drinking that wine. Seems a shame to waste it." Her friends giggled.

"Nice try, you lot. The orange juice is a fine vintage. Now, can you at least pretend to look interested?"

"But we've seen the exhibition at school, sir. Can't we go and have a look round? We've never been anywhere like this." Her face was smooth, all innocence. Michael tried to think.

"Ok, you've got fifteen minutes to look round the foyer. Go and collect some fliers, have a look what sort of concerts are coming up. There's a good shop too. I want you back here by seven on the dot. Remember – you are in uniform and representing St Mary's."

"Yes, sir, thanks, sir." The girls rushed off, tittering in their non-regulation shoes and hitched-up skirts. Michael felt his stomach clench. Where the hell was Trelawny? What was the point in setting up things like this if your own Head didn't back you up?

He caught the eye of one of the mothers and saw his own awkwardness mirrored. Standing around in the Barbican foyer, sipping wine and making arts-related small talk was probably just a regular day in the lives of most of the people here. He watched the pre-concert bustle unfolding. Well-heeled spouses greeted each other, reunited after his day at the office and her shopping spree. Friends kissed on both cheeks. No wonder classical music was a middle-class hobby.

His mind drifts to that T.S. Eliot poem they'd done at school:

In the room the women come and go
Talking of Michelangelo.

Daniel Barenboim. A new gallery opening. Where to have supper. Hairdressers. Personal trainers. Minor marital irritations. Children's achievements... Words break like waves over his head, keeping him down, the working-class lad from West Yorkshire.

He knows he must tread water, keep his head lifted, or he'll be swept away on a tide of RP chit chat, clinging in vain to a stand of What's On leaflets until he's finally found washed up outside a kebab house still clutching *Fire and Water: a musical Odyssey with Mark Elder.*

He allows himself a slight smile. On one level he does belong here, at sea level where music is pure and belongs to anyone who dives down far enough to find it. But it percolates to many other levels, slippery ledges of education and privilege and old school ties. He will never stand on those strata nor does he want to.

Bloody London. He breathes deeply into lifeless air that smells of school coach trips. His eyes seek out the door, his nearest emergency exit, but he knows that all it opens onto is the growl of enraged rush-hour traffic. Sometimes he has a physical craving for Yorkshire air. Wind and wet hedgerows as he walks Bess along the top path. Tramping down thistles and running to keep up with her.

Mr Stanley?
Sorry, I got distracted.

Automatically he smoothed the back of his hair, which always looked windblown anyway, and turned his attention back to the garish panels behind him: *Responses to Beethoven's 9th,* standing out like a strumpet against their sober surroundings. Then, a familiar profile weaving his way. Catherine. At least he could rely on her support. It looked as though she was chatting to someone. He took off his glasses and gave them a quick rub. As she approached he saw that her arm was linked with that of her companion's, a tall, dark-haired man.

They strolled up like an item. Catherine looked different somehow. She kissed him on both cheeks, taking in the pictures.

"This looks wonderful. I've brought Seth – we were going to a concert here anyway. Michael and I were at university together."

She didn't quite meet his eyes. Seth leaned in to shake hands, as at ease with his surroundings as Michael was not. "Congratulations. The Barbican foyer certainly needs brightening up. Dreadful building, but what can you do?"

Michael stiffened, hearing condescension and public school vowels. "Have a drink, both of you." He picked up a couple of glasses.

"Sir?" It was the aptly named Robert Bedlam, looking shifty as ever, flanked by a couple of henchmen.

"Yes, Bedlam?" He could feel Catherine's friend's smile even though he didn't make eye contact as he passed the drinks over.

"Can we go off too, like the girls?"

It was like being observed in a lesson when things are starting to slip out of control. Michael swallowed. "You've got ten minutes. Back here by seven. Now move it."

"Rather you than me," murmured the man, Seth, taking a sip of his wine. The boys scarpered, elbowing each other, already removing their school blazers.

"They're not bad kids."

"No?" Seth raised a lazy eyebrow as he watched them go. Michael realised his grip had clenched around the wine glass it held with a tell-tale tremble. "Excuse me, I have things to do." He stepped back, batting away a brief urge to kick over the drinks stand and tell them all to go fuck themselves.

"Michael?" A touch on his hand and Catherine's fluttering, concerned voice. He located a smile before turning to look at her. "Are you okay?"

"I'm fine." He walked to the end of the stand under the pretext of straightening a panel. She followed him, pointed at a huge collage of tinfoil and crisp packets. "This one's interesting."

"Yes."

Her fingers played on the stem of her glass. "I hope you don't mind me bringing Seth." She lowered her voice. "He's the one – you know – from the piano shop."

Christ. Him. The nutter. That would explain a lot. Michael frowned. "Catherine…"

"Michael!"

Tinkling soprano tones called out from a few feet away. Catherine's eyebrows arched. Michael swivelled and saw Briony approaching, accompanied by a suited man in his fifties.

"Michael, meet David Baines, the Chief Executive. David, this is Michael Stanley, the music teacher who put the exhibition together." Michael fumbled to put his wine glass down, finding the edge of the table, and reached to shake hands.

"Marvellous, just the kind of thing we like to do. A creative bunch of pupils, eh?" He looked round. "None of them here?"

"They're, um, looking round, getting a sense of what goes on here."

"Ah, marvellous, marvellous. Catch 'em young, I always say. Well, well, look who it is." Catherine's friend was walking over with a broad smile. Michael watched the two men shake hands and pat each other on the back.

"David." Seth inclined his head. "And Briony, looking as

lovely as ever."

Briony smiled coyly and inclined her head in turn. "Your tickets are at the front desk, Mr Gardner. There's a drinks reception in the interval."

"Perfect." He looked around. "I'm just admiring this unusual exhibition." He pointed at the picture behind Michael's head. "I'm delighted to see a connection between the Choral Symphony and Walker's Cheese and Onion. Everyone's favourite symphony and everyone's favourite crisp – well, until Kettle Chips came along."

Polite chuckles and a hoot from Briony. Michael smiled through his teeth. "We wanted the children to express how they felt about the music using everyday objects." Even to him it sounded sanctimonious, defensive.

David Baines nodded. "Absolutely. Out of the mouths of babes and all that."

Seth grimaced. "A rather unsavoury image given that we're talking about crisps…"

"Rather savoury, I should say!" Both men boomed with laughter. Michael watched the puns pinging back and forth with no idea of how to get into the conversation. This was his moment to sound out some of his ideas for future collaborations, but Seth stood as a wall between them.

"Going back to that picture, Michael." Seth pointed and Michael swivelled. He felt the back of his jacket swish against something on the edge of the table, knew exactly what was going to happen a split second before the tinkle and crash of the glass hitting the floor. A reflex action to bend down, sending more glasses toppling behind him, dropping to the floor one after another like a fugue. A cold, wet seeping down the back of his trousers. Catherine was at his side, kneeling and fussing, and animated voices closed in over his head. In a flurry of words and hands he looked up to see a brown tweed jacket approaching. Of course. The Head arriving to complete his humiliation. He straightened up, shaking slightly.

"I'm…"

"So sorry, everyone. Are you okay, Michael? Let the bar staff do that." Seth was batting his jacket and shaking his head with a rueful smile. "My apologies, David. You'd think I'd be used to negotiating your trays of glasses by now."

The two men laughed. Martin Trelawny hovered in front of them, awkward and bemused. Michael cleared his throat. "Mr Baines, could I introduce our Head Teacher, Martin Trelawny?"

Introductions were completed as Briony appeared with two women bearing mops. Seth's eyes twinkled. "This might be a good moment to take my leave and get cleaned up. David – always a pleasure. Bill me for the damages. Michael – sorry for causing chaos on your big night." They shook hands and Michael wondered if he saw the dart of wink. "Catherine, shall we?"

They moved away and Michael took a deep breath, keeping the back of his trousers against the table. "Mr Baines, I wondered if I might throw a couple of ideas your way?"

So, Mr Gardner saved your bacon, so to speak, that night?
That's one way of putting it.
Is there another way of putting it, Mr Stanley?
Well, it could be seen as a display of power. To make me indebted to him. Or…
Or?
Nothing. It was just about manipulation. It always was.

SCENE 7

Seth was standing with his back to her when Rebecca came into the foyer, idling through some flyers and holding a dark Fedora hat. Ignoring the theatrical pointing from Greg and Simon who were lounging against the front desk, she approached him with a hesitant hello. He turned and gave her a huge smile, which she found herself returning.

"Ophelia!" They did the London double kiss.

"Actually, I prefer Rebecca."

"Well, Rebecca, shall we go?"

"Go?"

"I assumed we were going somewhere. Or we could just stay here under the formidable gaze of Rosencrantz and Guildenstern."

She looked at Greg and Simon who grinned and waved. This was absurd.

"No, let's go. I'm following you."

"A brave woman."

They stepped into light drizzle and sweating streets. Seth offered his arm as he put on his hat and steered her down the high street. Cars hummed noisily in the spray and black umbrellas sprang up to poke them in the face. It was almost impossible to talk. Rebecca pictured her hair growing frizzier by the second. Seth took her arm and pulled her under a red-and-white-striped canopy. "Do you fancy some lunch?"

He led her into a cosy Italian restaurant with bread baskets on checked paper table cloths.

"Table for two, please." Rebecca inhaled Seth's proximity as he took her coat. She was only wearing jeans and a shirt but she suddenly felt sexy. Or maybe that was just him. They sat across from each other and the leftover rain on their hair and faces shimmered intimacy.

"I love your hat."

He bowed slightly as he removed it. "Rather practical for days like today." He smiled. "Rain suits you, you know."

She fingered her hair and smiled back. "I'm not so sure about that."

"Trust me."

She looked down to break some bread.

"So, Rebecca. What have you been doing since last night?"

"Oh, you know, this and that. Receiving explicit postcards at work." She had to know. He laughed. "Yes, that's partly why I'm here. I realise I owe you an explanation."

"You certainly do."

"I only realised later how it must have looked. But I assure you there's an innocent explanation. Do you remember I mentioned that creative arts group?"

"Ye-es."

"Well, I added you to the mailing list and asked Anna to drop your card as she was going that way this morning. She grabbed all the cards and I forgot I needed to put a covering note in with yours."

She struggled to make sense of it. "So – that was an invitation to this group?"

"Yes." He took out the silver box that she'd seen last night and removed a cigarette. "Can you make it?"

She laughed, bewildered. "Exactly what sort of group are we talking about here?"

He smiled and took a long first drag of the cigarette. As he exhaled from the corner of his mouth she looked at the cigarette box, tarnished and slightly dented. Probably an antique. He slipped it back into his pocket and smiled. "Ah – the drawing? Don't take any notice of that – I just use whatever stimulus is in my mind at the time to theme the invitations. On Monday I was thinking about *Hamlet*, and you, and thought I'd do something a little provocative."

"Oh, I see." She had no idea what to say.

"*Lady, shall I lie in your lap?* Such a great line – classic bawdy Shakespeare. I think it could spark some great things." He was grinning at her mischievously. "Seriously. It's a cool group of people, you'll love them. And, more to the point, they will love you."

A petite, dark-haired waitress comes over to take their drinks order. Seth scans the menu. "White okay?"

She opens her mouth to say no she shouldn't, but words of assent spill out instead. *Go on. Just a drop.*

"I was thinking it might be a rather nice come-down after *Hamlet*. You'll have just finished, won't you?"

She is flattered that he knows her schedule, has even arranged this group around her. "That's true."

"But?"

"It all sounds a bit – strange."

"Is that such a bad thing? Don't you ever want to try something different?" His eyes challenge hers, tug her into their strange green. She opens her mouth to answer, realises the trap and breaks into a smile.

"Great, that's settled then. As a first-timer you can just sit and observe." He holds her gaze. "What is it?"

She takes a risk. "Your eyes. I've never seen a colour like them. What would you call them – sage?"

"Whatever you would like to call them." They stare at each other.

He taps his cigarette and to her relief looks away. "When I was in India I found people with the same colour eyes. Dark skin, much darker than mine, but with these eyes." He laughs. "My parents always denied the existence of any *exotic* genes in our family. So that leaves the possibility that I'm a gypsy, a changeling. A Heathcliff."

She laughs too. "Heathcliff in an Armani blazer. I can't see it."

"Jean Paul Gaultier, for the record. What you forget, my dear Ophelia, sorry, *Rebecca*, is that Heathcliff reinvented himself as the archetypal English gentleman. Externally, that is. Except for when he was hanging puppies."

"I see. So underneath this suave exterior lurks…"

"A wolf." He grabs her hand and makes her jump. "Come on, let's order. Or I might indeed turn into a wolf and swallow you whole."

Long lunch, was it?
You could say. Three courses and two bottles of wine. And I was working the next day.

Can you remember what you talked about?
Oh - food, music, theatre, poetry. That
sort of stuff. Mornington Crescent, how I
don't listen to enough Radio 4. And… other
recreational activities.

"So how do you spend your weekends now? Getting high or
getting laid?"

"Neither?" Another small betrayal of Jason. "Sorry – I
didn't mean that. Jason lives in Milton Keynes at the moment
so we sort of shuttle back and forth on the train. In a way
it should be ideal – someone in your life without being
suffocated – but the pressure to have a perfect weekend can
make everything fuck up." Is that what she thought? It wasn't
a conversation she'd had with anyone before.

"Tell me to butt out, but it sounds like you're suffocating
anyway. Do you love him?"

She sighed. "I… don't know. He's a lovely guy, takes care
of me. But…"

"You want more."

Her averted eyes blinked agreement. "Maybe. Sometimes
I think there must be more, sometimes I think I've watched
too many soppy films." She looked up. "What about you?"

He took a slow drag on his cigarette "Oh, I know there's
more. For people like us, people who know how to feel,
people who wring every last drop from life instead of running
away from it." He chuckled. "I'll be breaking into *To His Coy
Mistress* in a second."

She laughed, wanting to show she got the reference. He
watched her. "Recite it to me."

"God, I can't, I've forgotten half of it."

"I'll prompt you."

Greedy, glittering eyes pinned hers in the fading afternoon
light and her outer vision darkened, as though she was going
blind. She breathed, trying to focus.

"Had we but world enough, and time

This coyness, lady, were no crime."

He held her eyes, mouthing words when she faltered, as she took the part of the poet attempting to seduce his muse.

"But at my back I always hear
Time's winged chariot hurrying near..."

She knew it from here, the shift of gears so that hedonism became something profound, triumphal, death-defying.

"Let us roll all our strength, and all
Our sweetness up into one ball;
And tear our pleasures with rough strife
Through the iron gates of life.
Thus, though we cannot make our sun
Stand still, yet we will make him run."

Her eyes swam: her tears or his? Her breathing stopped and started in shudders as they regarded each other. She had never known such desire. Not just for him, maybe not even for him, but for his words and his gaze and the possibilities that simmered between them.

And then?
Then...
Are you okay, Miss Laurence?

She went home reeling, metallic, jangling inside. Thank God she had the house to herself. She flung herself on her bed, dropping her keys to the floor, pushing down her jeans, stroking and groaning to a shivery orgasm. Afterwards she lay curled up on her side clutching the pillow, wondering what on earth she had met.

SCENE 8

I believe Michael Stanley is an old friend of yours, Miss Jarret?
Michael? Yes, since university.
And how does he get on with the rest of the group?

48

Um – well, on the whole. He's honest and principled, people respect him.

Honest and principled. Could you describe his relationship with Mr Gardner?

Seth? It's… they're sparring partners, I suppose. Seth used to tease Michael and Michael would put him in his place… it was all good humoured. Mostly.

You see, that's not exactly what I've been hearing, Miss Jarret. It would seem that there's a certain amount of antipathy towards Michael from some quarters. Would that be fair to say?

Look, Michael's stressed right now, we all are. Sometimes he goes too far.

Too far?

I mean, he says what he thinks. But what you've got to remember is, unlike some people, he doesn't gossip. He's straight up. I'd trust him completely and he's a brilliant friend. He drove me up to see my parents last year because he knew I was anxious about it…

The summons. Her mother was having a clear-out and now that Catherine was in a place of her own, surely she could take some of her stuff away, which they'd kindly been storing for her but was now rather cluttering the place up. She knew she would leave a little less of a person, some of her newly expanded horizon cordoned off. So Michael had come for moral support. And Seth had so kindly lent his car.

…I believe Mr Gardner lent you his car that weekend, Mr Stanley?

Not me, he lent it to Catherine. She was nervous of pranging it so I drove.

49

Nice car, was it?

A Jaguar: what else would Seth drive? Pale blue, an extension of the April sky, shimmering in front of Catherine's front door like a mirage.

> If you like that sort of thing.
> **And you don't, of course, Mr Stanley.**
> So just because I'm a man I'm some sort of petrolhead? You lot are all the same. I've never owned a car, nor do I want to.

But it didn't take him long to start enjoying it. The give of the leather around his thighs, the purr of the motor, the responsiveness of the wheel. He felt Seth all around them, the cool, woody scent of his aftershave still hanging in the air, the driver's seat still weighted and warm. And his laughter, as Michael put his foot down in the fast lane and felt the engine kick...

> **So you drove out of the goodness of your heart to help an old friend. You and Catherine Jarret were at university together?**
> Yes. Nottingham.

He found her in the practice rooms one day playing the Schubert B flat sonata. A skittish little Maths stowaway, scared of being chucked back into a sea of algebra. Not like his fellow music students, pissheads with a sense of entitlement inversely proportional to their talent.

> **And your friendship remained… platonic?**
> Yes. Believe it or not, a man and a woman can have a friendship without… sex coming into it. Catherine and I, we look out for each other.

50

I see. Was there anything noteworthy about the weekend? Perhaps something connected to Mr Gardner and the loan of the car?

All that springs to mind, quite frankly, is Catherine's mother, making sure the neighbours got a good look at the Jag.

Pouring out cups of tea for him and put-downs for her daughter. 'Don't you ever want to wear colour, darling? You'll never stand out from the crowd in neutrals.'

We packed up Catherine's stuff and left the next day.

It was an insight into her home life, though. He was even privy to a family argument, when Catherine discovered they'd sold her old piano. A proper middle-class argument, where nobody swore and people clenched their jaws instead of their fists. Wine was produced over tea, dinner as they called it, whereupon Sylvia Jarret's merciless hospitality became open flirtation. Catherine stared at her strawberry gateau, her face reflecting its colour, while her dad tried in vain to cork the wine. Poor chap. He'd been a musician, first violin for the CBSO, until Mrs Jarret had put her foot down and insisted he did something more ambitious. Apparently the subject was off-limits now.

Later, all tucked up in Catherine's sister's old room, staring at posters of black-clad rock bands and, bizzarely, Boris Becker, Michael thought about meals in his own family home. Meat, potatoes and two veg, delivered onto a scrubbed table at five on the dot or else there was trouble. No conversation he could recall, unless the meat was overcooked. Then *I wouldn't feed this to the fuckin' dog*, a meal shoved in the bin, a slammed door and his mother's face pulled taut like the skin of a drum. *I don't know what you're staring at. Finish your carrots, else there's no pudding.*

There was no love that he could remember. He and his brother and sister were fed and clothed in a cramped but pristine home environment. There was no connection between them all. They rolled around each other like different-sized marbles on a tray. Thank God for his Walkman, drowning out the arguments between his parents when his dad had stayed too late at the pub. No jaw-clenching restraint there.

And thank God for... but it's hard to say his name, even in his head, even after all this time. The person who'd saved him, put something inside him that he would always have, something of beauty that lay apart from the shittiness of the world. The person who'd done too much, gone too far and ruined everything.

Mr Stanley?
I had a bad night. It happens to me sometimes.

He'd had flashbacks before, but this was different. This wasn't moments, this was the whole scene on playback, his own childhood made viscerally real again by stepping back into Catherine's.

The top sheet of the single bed becomes the brush of velvet on his bare forearms. He's back there, fifteen years old, concealed behind the curtains of the practice room where his music teacher, Mr Fleming, lets him stay after school. He can't have a piano at home so this is the next best thing. Mr Fleming teaches him in his lunch hour and he practises here after school. But he's just heard footsteps and instinct has told him to hide. Through a frayed hole in the fabric he sees Mr Johnson and Mr Crane enter the room.

"No one in here today. Thought I might find that fifth year, what's his name? Stevens... Stanley, Michael Stanley. Fleming seems to let him practise piano after school. All a bit non-regulation."

"Oh yes, the boy he's mentoring. I must say he's

52

blossoming with it."

"Yes, apparently he has real talent."

"Not the boy – I mean old Fleming! You must have noticed. He used to walk around all hunched up…" Mr Crane stoops and pulls a face and both teachers snigger. Michael finds he has a handful of velvet tight in his fist. "Kids giving him a hard time, I think. But now he's swaggering around with a twinkle in his eye, if you know what I mean. Given him a reason to keep going, poor bugger."

What sort of bad night?

Michael threw back the covers, wincing at the boom of the teachers' laughter in his head, torched all over again with that strange feeling of shame. Despite the assault of floral fabric softener he could still catch a whiff of the musty damp of the practice room where he'd waited the next day for his lunch hour lesson, staring at cobwebs he'd never noticed before, the yellow-toothed grin of the keyboard. The door opening and Mr Fleming's eyes lighting up at the sight of Michael. The grotesque image of a dog bounding over to its master.

Michael sat up. He switched on the bedside light, but he knew it was too late. The scene played out in front of his eyes like a film.

Sorry, I got distracted. I couldn't sleep, that's all.
You look a little pale, Mr Stanley. Is there anything else of note from that weekend?
Only… no. Nothing of note.

SCENE 9

So you drove home, Miss Jarret?
Yes.

It's hard not to tremble and look down as she says it. She

knew from the beginning she shouldn't be in charge of that car. But when she saw Michael's face at the breakfast table what could she do? He hardly looked like he should be behind a wheel either. His eyes were bloodshot behind his glasses. Said he'd had a bad night. She insisted on driving.

At first it was a relief to be leaving the labyrinth of identical tree-lined suburban roads. Leaving her mother, her hen-pecked father, that house of disappointments where the music had been snuffed out. The car was straining towards London, mirroring her energy. She started to relax as they hit the motorway and she got the hang of power steering. Michael was already asleep, or at least his eyes were closed, frowning under a thatch of wayward hair. She was glad they didn't have to talk. A squeeze of tenderness made her smile. He was always there when she needed him. He was a good-looking guy, intelligent, musical but somehow she'd never felt like *that* about him.

A pulse started inside her as she pictured Seth, green eyes teasing. He had exploded into her life like a firework, a Catherine wheel, turning and spinning and lighting her with energy. She struggled to remember a time before she knew him.

She breathed slower and deeper.

She is a concert pianist, making a name. She has a gig at the Wigmore Hall. Her dress, long and burgundy, her hair swept off her neck. She is playing Bach. No, she is at the Festival Hall performing the E minor Chopin piano concerto. Her hair is loose, her body a conduit for the music. She is playing how she has always wanted to play. He is watching her, transfixed by her, eyes spilling tears. The audience bellows and stamps when she finishes, the conductor takes her hand as if in shock, hardened orchestral players wipe their eyes. She goes to her dressing room for a few minutes alone. There is a hesitant knock at the door. He stands at the threshold, unable to speak. Slowly he reaches out a hand...

"*Catherine!*" Michael's voice is a roar, a scream, a sound

she has never heard before. And there's another scream from the wheels as they leave their lane and she sees the barriers rushing up to meet them. One of them twists the wheel, sends them ricocheting back into lane but they don't stop there and a horn bays like a wolf at their heels. Then they're over in the next lane and she waits for the bang but Michael is holding the wheel with her, and together they steady the panicked car.

"Oh my God, I'm so sorry." Every part of her is shaking.

"Pull over."

"But you're not allowed…"

"Pull over now!"

She turns the car onto the hard shoulder and brings them to a stop. For a whole minute they sit in silence, panting like they've been sprinting. Catherine lays her head on the steering wheel and her shoulders heave. His voice, that cry, seems to echo round and round them. She feels a hand on her shoulder.

"Did you fall asleep?"

"I – no – I just…" She doesn't know what to say. She nearly killed them. She's never gone that far before, lost herself so completely.

Miss Jarret?
Sorry. Yes, I drove. The journey was fine, from what I remember.
We haven't yet located Mr Gardner's car. Do you know where he kept it?
Oh. No, he dropped it off at mine and picked it up on Sunday. I think he rented a garage somewhere.
And you have no idea where?
Sorry, no. Do you think…?
Let's leave it there for now.

SCENE 10
And so your first meeting of the — what was

55

it? — Friday Folly. Was it what you were
expecting, Miss Laurence?

Expecting? She had no idea what to expect. Up until an hour
before she was still considering a tub of ice cream and an
episode of *Friends* as a safer alternative. *Hamlet* had just
finished and she could feel the downer hovering over her like
a cloud, looking for a point of entry. Something out of the
ordinary would be more likely to fend it off.

So she went, as Seth knew she would. Her newly washed
hair had dried into soft spirals with no hint of frizz: a good
omen. She arrived outside 15 Linfield Gardens at just gone
eight – too eager, too early. It was one of those majestic rows
of white, Regency houses where London showed its best side.
She walked on for a few more minutes and stopped in the
shadows to prepare, closing her eyes and breathing slowly
as if she were going on stage. A lone breath of wind found
its way down the neckline of her coat and made her shiver.
Her cue.

As she approached the house she heard voices from an
open balcony door on the first floor. She buzzed Flat B. For
a second nothing happened. Then the intercom blared into
life with the sound of raucous laughter and a man shouting,
"Hello?"

"It's Rebecca." Now she wanted to go home.

"Come in, first floor." She was buzzed into a grand old
hallway with a marbled staircase and shiny black bannisters.
She mounted slowly, admiring the carved cornices but in
reality buying herself a little time. Chatter swirled above her
head, increasing in volume as she climbed. And then there
was Seth in a white shirt and jeans, smiling and holding open
a black door.

"I wasn't sure you'd come."

"Me neither." She was held by his eyes, which caught the
hallway light like algae on a sunlit pond. Waist down she was
jelly already.

"Don't worry, I'll hold your hand." And he did, gently squeezing heat into her palm as he led her into a white hallway. The first thing she saw was her own face smiling nervously into a huge mirror panel. She followed Seth down the passageway, which abruptly gave into an expanse of twinkling lights, people and laughter.

She blinked and wolf-whistled under her breath; she couldn't help it. Seth was enjoying her reaction. "Does the lady Ophelia approve?"

How could she not? The room was at least forty feet long, hung with gilt-framed oil paintings, mirrors and a chandelier glimmering in the candlelight. Near her was a dining table set for dinner; at the other end she could see a blazing fire and dark wood furnishings. The back wall seemed to be one huge window where the brooding night sky provided a panoramic frieze. As she took it in her eyes fell on the painting nearest to her, showing a howling man on his knees.

"Oedipus." He was following her gaze.

"Wow." She couldn't think of anything else to say. The other side of the room seemed to be teeming with people, voices interwoven as they clustered round the fire. Set back a little, as though snoozing in the corner, was a grand piano.

"I didn't know you were a pianist."

"I'm not." Before she had chance to ask more she realised the room had hushed and everyone had turned to look at them. Now she could focus, Rebecca was surprised to see how few people there were – maybe half a dozen. Still holding her hand, Seth led her towards the fire. "Ladies and gentlemen, meet the lovely Ophelia, who also goes by the name Rebecca."

She felt like a child allowed into an adults' party. There was a general murmur of hellos. She felt the heat from the fire seeping into her cheeks. The woman nearest to her, blonde and curly haired, flicked her eyes towards Rebecca and Seth's joined hands before a kind-faced, bearded man came over and kissed her on both cheeks.

"Delighted to meet you. I'm Charles. We've heard all about your amazing portrayal of Ophelia from Seth. He hasn't shut up about you, in fact."

"And who can blame him?" A huge hulk of a man with a skunk-like stripe of blonde in his light brown hair grinned down at her. "I'm Jake. I'll be your chef tonight. I 'ope you 'ave a good appetite." Rebecca wasn't sure if he was hamming up the strong cockney accent. He winked and she smiled back easily. Noticing neither of the women had approached her she moved towards the tall blonde as the others melted away. "Hi there."

Seth stepped in. "Rebecca, this is Anna, the grande dame of the group. How's life as a thirty-something, sweetheart?"

Anna pulled a face. "Ya cheeky fucker. Actually it's fine now the hangover's fading." She spoke with a Northern Irish burr.

Seth dropped Rebecca's hand to brush what looked like a sliver of potato crisp from Anna's hair. "Anna's a marketing whiz who likes to spend her free time with a bunch of no-hope creatives."

"Ah there's always hope – even for you, Seth Gardner." She cocked her head and her smile passed over Rebecca as if accidentally. They were a similar height but Anna was considerably broader, with a huge bob of curly blonde hair and unmissable cleavage. Rebecca turned towards a third man, a mad professor type as her mother would say, with wiry hair and glasses, his eyes hidden as they caught the candlelight.

"I'm Michael." He grasped her hand and a static shock ran through her, causing them both to jump back a bit.

They shared an embarrassed smile.

"Even his handshake is over-flowing with good intentions." Seth's voice was smooth, hard to read. "Michael keeps us on the moral straight and narrow. Unlike José."

A short Mediterranean-looking man with closely cropped hair, neatly trimmed goatee and a tight T-shirt grinned and kissed her. "Welcome to the madhouse, darling."

"Aww, he had to get up on his toes." It was Anna to her left. "You'll have to get your high heels out, José."

"Stilettos or wedges, darling?"

"Enough, you two." Seth waggled a finger. "Now, are we done? Ah, no, Rebecca, this is my Catherine." Seth had put his arm round a mousy-haired young woman who leaned into it. Rebecca stuck out a hand pointedly. My Catherine? A sister perhaps? Her fringe grazed the top of her eyebrows like a child's. A small, cool hand was offered and almost immediately withdrawn. They said a guarded hello.

"Now, who's going to get Rebecca a drink?" Considering this was Seth's house, he didn't seem inclined to play host. The big man, Jake, put a hand on her back. "What d'ya fancy, Rebecca? I can do most things." Clearly the accent was real.

"And he makes great drinks too." Anna, it seemed, was always ready with a quip. Rebecca joined in the laughter, while peeking at the glasses around her. It looked like they were on cocktails but she played safe and asked for white wine.

"Anyway, this gallery is really worth checking out. They like taking stuff from virgin artists." A previous conversation resumed to her right.

"I can't imagine José fits either criteria then," cackled Anna.

"Criterion," muttered the bearded man, almost to himself, and then turned to Rebecca. "So, is *Hamlet* still showing? I might try to catch it."

They talked theatre and before long Rebecca felt comfortable enough to ask his name again – Charles – and to run through the others. He had a slightly odd, asymmetrical face and she found herself studying it: his nose was flat-nostrilled on one side and flared on the other. She suspected the beard, which had a hint of red, softened the overall effect considerably, and his eyes were chocolate and gentle. At one point he sucked on a blue asthma inhaler, waving his hand at the stream of smoke snaking from Seth's cigarette. Then Jake brought her drink, at which point Seth tapped the side of his glass with a spoon.

"Time for the main feature, ladies and gents." There were mutterings of dissent.

"Do we have to?"

"Can't we have another drink?"

Seth raised his voice. "Quiet, philistines, and take your seats."

People moved towards an assortment of chairs and sofas, arranged in a rough circle near the fire. Rebecca noticed Catherine gathering up their empty glasses and putting them on a tray. Charles gestured towards the largest sofa – "You ladies may be more comfortable here" – and Rebecca sank down, grateful to take the weight off her heels. Still muttering and giggling, people found themselves a seat. Only Seth remained standing.

"Now, as it's Rebecca's first week she's just going to observe, as she has understandably expressed the concern that we're a bunch of psychopaths."

Rebecca looked down and smiled over the cat calls.

"So, to put her mind at rest, or perhaps not, would anyone like to explain to her what this group is and what we do?"

"We fall on our knees to worship the God of Art. Naked, of course."

"Thank you, José. Glad you'll be putting on your usual show. Anyone got anything useful to say?"

Anna raised her hand. "Please, sir."

"Anna?"

"We're your trusted prodigies, brought together to entertain you through dark winter nights with sumptuous artistic delights."

Seth smiled. "I think the word you're looking for is protégés, though I do feel like I'm in a room full of children sometimes."

"Ooh, sorry sir."

Ignoring the sniggers, Seth turned to Rebecca. "It's probably better to say as little as possible and leave it up to you to judge. Call it an open mic session without the mic. We might have a theme to get us started, hence the unusual postcard you were sent at work." Various heckling. "I was rather pleased with it myself. A picture from Pompeii, a quote from *Hamlet*, with an overarching theme of female pleasure. Plenty to get us going. So to speak."

Pretentious *and* weird, thought Rebecca. Seth turned to her as if reading her mind. "This isn't a group for everyone and some people might see us as a bunch of luvvies – though I doubt that would bother you." Rebecca smiled. "But I like to think everyone here has a passion for the arts and believes there's a bit more to life than the nine-to-five and *EastEnders*. That we can articulate our feelings about life and death and love and everything in the middle instead of sticking our fingers in our ears and pretending it's not happening." The room had gone quiet. The thread of magic that wrapped itself round Rebecca seemed to embrace them all.

"As far as I see it, the Friday Folly gives us two extra things we wouldn't have if left to our own devices: a deadline and an audience. The deadline provides the kick up the arse we all need at times," a ripple of acknowledgement, "and then showing our work in front of an audience makes it real, helps it to come to life – which of course you of all people understand." She smiled and nodded. "And having dealt with cerebral matters we can then stuff ourselves with fine food and get extremely drunk."

There was a release of laughter as Seth settled down on an ornate gold armchair that seemed to have been left for him. He leaned over the coffee table and opened the silver cigarette box. "Let me introduce you to the players. Charles is an architect with a divine bass voice. José is a graphic designer who may yet become a proper artist."

"Hey!"

"I just think you're good, that's all. Michael is a teacher dedicated to relieving the misery of under-privileged hooligans through the gift of music."

"Change the record, Seth."

"He's also our composer in residence. Anna, well why are you here, Anna?"

"For my supportive comments and pertinent feedback, darling."

"Anna has somehow admitted herself to the group without any credentials except the ability to drink insane amounts of Guinness. Not that you're a walking stereotype or anything, sweetheart."

Anna smiled and gave him the finger. "As I keep saying to you, give the next one a dressing-up theme and I'd be happy to participate."

"She would too. You should see her dressing-up box." José put a finger to the side of his head. "Crazy."

"And as I keep saying to you, my dear Anna, you are welcome to dress up for us any time. But, yes, I have taken your comments on board." He looked back to Rebecca. "Continuing our role call, Jake, as you may have gathered, is taking a break from the stress of cooking for the rich and famous to tickle our culinary pallets."

José turned to Rebecca. "In other words, he's on the dole and can cook."

Rebecca smiled, trying to keep up.

"And Catherine – what can I say?" What indeed? She had barely uttered a word. Rebecca struggled to see how she could fit with a group like this. All she seemed to do was flank Seth like a bodyguard.

"Well, you'll see about Catherine later. It's customary for her to round off proceedings. Now," looking round, "who's going to kick off?"

"Don't forget yourself, Seth."

"Sorry? Oh yes – I write. Poetry mainly. Some academic stuff. Now, Charles, why don't you start for a change?"

Rebecca felt the mood of the room change as Charles and Michael got to their feet. People shifted round, snuggled in, practically rubbed their hands with glee. Seth lit his cigarette, leaned back and crossed his legs. For the first time there was silence. Michael took out a small guitar-type instrument that Rebecca recognised as a lute.

"Don't even ask how I got hold of this."

Charles cleared his throat. "In the spirit of the postcard we've gone for a 15th century bawdy lovesong."

A smattering of appreciation, then Charles' enormous bass voice filled the room with a surprisingly catchy, cheeky little ditty. Several times the audience erupted with laughter at the punchlines and Charles' innocent *fa la las*. Rebecca had to admit it was a great performance. As she clapped she wondered at the bizarreness of life, that she was spending her Friday night in what looked like a 19th century drawing room surrounded by mad people with lutes and grand pianos. And it wasn't just that she was having fun… she felt excited, curious, alive. She thought of the Italian restaurant and the conversation they'd had. *People like us. People who wring every last drop from life instead of running away from it.* Is that what she was doing?

José was next. "As you can imagine, I'm not really an expert on this week's subject matter."

Anna sliced through the sniggers: "I doubt many of the men in this room are, darling." Rebecca noticed Michael tighten his lips and look away.

"But," José was struggling to make himself heard above guffaws and wolf whistles, "I've done my own take on it. Here." He put a piece of paper on Anna's knee. She looked down for a second then laughed.

"Aw, that's dead on. Look at this, Rebecca." It was the first time Anna had addressed her directly, and Rebecca felt suddenly at ease as Anna leaned over to put the paper down on her knee. It was a drawing of a curled-up baby with a grown man's features who seemed to be looking right up into her eyes. The title was *Lady, shall I lie in your lap?* The man-baby gazed at her with a mixture of neediness and suggestiveness – she found it hard to drag her eyes away.

"That's great." She looked down again and shivered. "And creepy."

Charles laughed. "Let me see." He frowned at the paper and Anna laughed.

"You'd have to be a woman to get this one, I'd say. Check it out, Catherine."

Catherine reddened and took the picture hesitantly. "Yes, that's definitely… different." She smiled but sounded unsure.

Jake put out his hand. "Give us a butchers." He was chewing gum and Rebecca noticed the glint of an earring in his left ear.

"A *butchers*?" José looked puzzled. Everyone laughed.

Seth put a hand on her arm. "He's from Barcelona."

"Really? Oh I love…" and then she got the *Fawlty Towers* reference.

José shook his head. "Siguenza actually, darling. Or near enough."

Seth gave him a mock duff round the head. "But he's still our resident Manuel."

By now the rest of the room was vying to look at José's picture. Anna said she wanted the 'maby' on her knee for the rest of the night. "Can you make me one for my next birthday?"

"You can have me instead, darling." Jake put his head on Anna's lap and batted his eyelashes up at her, still chewing gum. She gave him a quick stroke then shoved him away.

"Sorry, but you're a bit *too* creepy."

A drinks break was declared, and Rebecca succumbed to the pull of the red umbrella. She sipped her Screaming Orgasm carefully, reminding herself that cocktails tended to make her very drunk very fast. Jake asked her to hand round a tray of the first of his 'themed culinary contributions' to the evening, little oysters to slurp and swallow. He winked at her as he passed the tray. "We have mini ice cream cornets to lick for dessert. But I'm afraid the fish main course will make me unpopular." Anna was on hand with a wooden spoon to field that one.

She found herself once more on the periphery of conversations she didn't really understand and drew closer to the fire instead, admiring its white marble surrounds and carved green panels which complemented floor-length velvet curtains across the room. Anna joined her. "He's chosen all the trimmings to match his eyes. See?" She waved her hand. "Curtains, cushion covers, piano stool. But this is my favourite." She threw herself on a pale green chaise longue behind the circle of chairs and stuck her tongue out lewdly at Seth, who had stopped talking to Catherine and was looking over. "I'm all yours, darling."

"Later, wench." He grinned at Rebecca. "Whatever she's telling you, just remember the Irish and their tall tales."

After a while they settled down again. Seth put down his drink and turned to her. "As I said, Catherine tends to round things off in these groups, but tonight I'm using host's prerogative to take that spot. So, over to you, Catherine."

Catherine moved towards the piano, clutching some sheet music.

"Ah, so someone can play the piano." Rebecca smiled, making an effort to be friendly.

Seth grinned. "Oh, she can play all right. You'll see."

Catherine shook her head as she fiddled with the stool. "Don't get too excited. I really didn't know what to do this week."

"She always says this," whispered José, seated next to her. Rebecca smiled, feeling much more a part of things. Hopefully it wasn't just the cocktail.

"This may be familiar," said Catherine, striking up a soft chord. It was slow and beautiful, and then the penny dropped. The theme to the Hamlet cigars advert, one of the few pieces of classical music Rebecca knew. A ripple of chuckles.

"I'll name that tune in one."

"Nice one, Catherine."

The voices died away as the music continued. Rebecca noticed how much straighter and stronger Catherine looked at the piano, holding the attention of the room effortlessly. Before long she had forgotten the advert connection and closed her eyes, letting the delicate notes ripple over her. She could tell the piece wasn't difficult but there was something in the way Catherine delivered it that made it completely spellbinding. There was clearly more to her than met the eye.

Warm applause as Catherine took her seat.

"Ah, the old Hair on a G String, always a winner." Rebecca stared as Charles and Michael started chortling like a couple of school boys. Charles looked like he might be getting tipsy. She noticed Catherine shift ever so slightly away from him on the sofa.

"Follow that, as they say." Seth was on his feet. "I know you're all hungry and you'll be glad to know I won't take long. I was, let's say, inspired to write poetry on today's theme."

"This should be good." The mood had got a bit raucous now.

Seth looked at Rebecca. "It's called *My Lady's Pleasure*."

Her heart throbbed as the room quietened and Seth's voice softly filled the space, rising and falling with lingering cadences.

"My lady lies a-waiting
Reclined on golden pillows,
Her ruby hair stretched out in waves
Where're my fingers follow.

My lady lies a-sighing
With eyelids drawn for dreams,
The ruffles of her white lace gown
Cascading o'er her knees.

My lady lies a-gasping
With twisting bosom wild,
Her fingers spread to grasp the air
Her cry is like a child.

66

My lady lies a-weeping
Her head drawn into mine,
Our bodies merge in silent prayer
As distant noon bells chime."

As the last vibrations of his voice drifted away, Rebecca felt rooted to the spot, unable to look up. She had found it deeply erotic. Was 'ruby hair' a reference to her? Were the others wondering the same thing? A second of stillness gave way to whistles and murmurs of approval.

"Raunchy but restrained – like it, buddy."

"Lucky lady is all I can say."

"I thought the end was moving. Hmmmm." Everyone laughed at José's wistful voice and Rebecca started to relax; no one seemed to be thinking about ruby hair. But as she glanced to her left she caught Catherine watching her. The eye contact was blinked away immediately, and later Rebecca wondered what she had really seen.

What did it look like?
Hatred, I suppose.

SCENE 11

I'm getting the impression that things changed in your group when Rebecca Laurence came on the scene?

It was twilight and the trees outside the window blackened. Catherine took her hands off the keys for a minute to watch the cityscape's geometric certainty erode to shadows. Her favourite time of day. Or was it just that she was here, at Seth's, with this piano and this view? In her little flat in Queen's Park the drawing in of night could feel oppressive, frightening even. That London could squeeze the breath out of you. This London you could inhale like pure oxygen.

Could I ask where Seth Gardner was at the time?

Oh – sorry, he was out. At an auction.

He'd left you alone in his flat?

No, I'd let myself in. I had a key. He used to let me play the Steinway.

Did other people have a key to his flat?

No, not as far as I know. They do now. But at the time it was just me.

I see. Go on.

I didn't abuse it, you know. I always checked first if it was okay. And I only played the piano.

Of course, Miss Jarret. Do go on. We were talking about Rebecca Laurence.

She continued sitting, treasuring the silence and the space. The sky was deep blue but not yet navy. Lights from the street were appearing like stars. If she were Michael she would paint the scene with music, but the idea of plucking notes at random panicked her. Other people's music she could play, play well even, but she had no idea how to write her own.

She checked her watch: just gone seven. If Seth came back now he might find it strange that she was sitting here in the dark. But she felt rooted to the stool. She looked up and saw herself peeping over the music stand like a child. That bloody mirror. She hated the way she could see herself playing, still hadn't learned to fully switch off from it. Mawkish and plain, poor little Jane.

She ran a hand through her drab bob and thought of Rebecca, the beautiful creature who had appeared on Friday, here in this room, all legs and hair and self-assurance.

Seth had seemed protective towards Rebecca, like he was with her. With Anna he bantered hard, flirted openly, but in a playful sort of way. With her, Catherine, he was different, softer. She had seen his eyes fill with tears as she played for him. He hugged her when she did things for him, sometimes stroked her hair.

She imagined him stroking Rebecca's lustrous tresses and felt tight. Soon there would be no room for her. Could she crawl back under that stone, the life from which he had pulled her? Could she survive that darkness again, having felt the warmth of the sun on her face? She knew the answer. The advancing night had become menacing, the trees reaching out thin black arms to coil around her. She shivered, leaned to press the lamp switch. Now she would be illuminated to the outside world. What would passers-by make of the solitary figure motionless at the piano? Perhaps they would see straight through her like a ghost. Perhaps she would blend in with the surroundings.

Blending in, that's her trademark. Where Michael is the corner piece of a jigsaw, angled, rigid, crucial, she's amorphous and shape-shifting, moulding herself to the situation and making herself invisible or at least unnoticed. She can cling around Michael's sharp corner or slink away to fit somewhere else. Fitting but not fitting in. Like a dog that nestles around its owner's feet at night, making itself as small as possible to avoid discovery, and then in the glare of morning is kicked out, chastised, discarded.

But not when she plays. Then she's solid, she impacts on people. The music gives her conviction, fills her with it. Each press of the foot pedal pumps her fuller, but when the music stops she can't hold her shape. However hard she tries, the hissing of release begins, accelerates, and then it's all over.

Rebecca, she suspects, may be a bit of a chameleon too; she's an actress after all. But she's beautiful so it doesn't matter. No one would look through her. Their eyes would snag on the curve of her cheekbones, the line of her leg, get caught up in the autumn forest of her hair.

A memory attacks her from nowhere. Blood on the floor of this room and a cascade of red hair falling to the ground. She clasps hands over her mouth and stifles the scream like she did the first time. She can't think of this now. She promised to forget. They all did.

She can feel the night behind her, sweeping its gaze over her shoulders and back like a hostile audience. She knows it's unlikely that anyone will raise their gaze above their own shoes, their own thoughts of reports to finish and supper to make. But she has an urgent need to close the curtains over her vulnerability. She walks towards the window.

Curtains still closed at midday. Something must be wrong. No, she won't think of this.

Don't open them yet, for God's sake.

As her hand tugs harder at the fabric she hears the key in the lock.

"Hey honey, I'm home." This is Seth's usual return call. Normally it makes her feel safe, like they're a family. Today she starts and trembles like a trapped bird.

"Hello." She is flushed, guilty, caught fumbling at the window. He stops in the doorway and his eyes narrow. "Now what is my little Catherine up to over there?"

"Sorry, I was just closing the curtains, I know you don't like it though…" Her voice trails off.

"I certainly don't like it if you don't use the cord."

"Oh dear, sorry, I forgot." She perches on the piano stool, slowing her breathing.

"Nothing broken. But can we keep them open? You know I feel penned in if I can't see out."

"Of course, sorry, it was just being on my own." She sits on her hands, which are suddenly cold.

He walks over to her. "Now what have I told you about constant apologising?"

"I know, sorry – God…"

He grins. "How about you pour us a nice glass of wine and we'll say no more about it?"

She smiles relief, gets to her feet. "Red or white?"

"White. There's a Sancerre chilling in the door of the fridge. And you'll find some cashews in the cupboard."

70

She set to, suddenly peckish and hoping they might pop out for pizza soon. Seth was in high spirits, having spent the afternoon at an auction in Hampstead out-manoeuvring a 'crusty old twerp' who was bidding, like him, for an Italianate sideboard, which would look divine next to the armchair and would be delivered tomorrow. He leaned back for a second, crossed his legs and sighed with satisfaction.

"Isn't it wonderful to win?" As she watched him, Catherine thought she felt as a mother must feel. All her earlier jumpiness had passed. He looked up, caught her eye. "Dear little Catherine. Now, what naughty things have you been up to while I've been away?" She quietly told him what she'd been practising, but he was barely listening. "You know, I'm absolutely starving. What would you say to Thai takeaway?"

She smiled. "Sounds great."

SCENE 12

I've yet to understand, Mr Stanley, why you became involved with Seth Gardner.
Involved?
Friends with him. From what you've told me he doesn't exactly strike me as your type.
He isn't. Wasn't.

But there were moments.

Simon Rattle and the CBSO, Royal Festival Hall, May 1994. The whole place chattering with excitement. All the musos out in force, a constant process of ducking and weaving to avoid being seen by teaching contacts and ex-choir associates. He is here alone. Mahler's second symphony, the Resurrection. No Marcus, his singing buddy, no Catherine, no need for conversation. Just him and the music. Until the distinction erodes.

We share a love of music.

Catherine always claims that he and Seth are 'more similar than you realise. You talk about music in a similar way. If you could just look past him having a different background from you...' He doesn't care what Catherine thinks. Tonight all he cares about is this moment, this music, the first shivers of violins and rumbling basses as the funeral march begins. This time there will be no escape, no pity. He closes his eyes and is flooded by the old feeling, the one he craves.

This is why I'm here, only this. This is enough.

It affected me a great deal. It's hard to explain.

He is thrown backwards and forwards, propelled through trumpet cries and ambushed by violent drum bursts. Waltzed to an old world of innocence where things makes sense, then abandoned again as the ground shifts beneath him. He should expect her by now but when she comes, the Voice, she is a quiet shock, lightly soaring above his head like a guardian angel, telling him things he doesn't understand but wants to hear.

One day I will understand.

But the death march returns and hauls him before It, the Terror, the rage that splits his head and leaves him breathless, judged and found wanting. He cringes, cowers before it but there is no mercy. Here is where he must stay.

But... look... no. Yes. A pinprick of light in front of him, then a small hole, slowly expanding. He is reaching the end of the tunnel. As he emerges a mass of people in turquoise are standing waiting for him. In deep throbbing hushed song they open their arms to him and he goes to them, tears flooding his face. Here are cool hands to soothe him, loving words to forgive him; here at last there is a place saved for him. He takes it and his heart explodes with joy.

The clapping thunders around him, overwhelming, so many people celebrating his deliverance. And then he comes back to himself and his body, picks up clenched hands from his lap and joins them, clapping like he will never stop. But he must. He must get out before he is noticed. He knows exactly where to find the toilets and reaches them before the third ovation, locking himself in a cubicle where he can let the sobs come hard. He has traversed a whole lifetime of despair and euphoria in eighty minutes. Now he has nothing left.

He hears the room getting busy, people chattering about the performance. How can they speak? Make dinner plans, laugh, wash the music away under the hot tap. He must wait till they have all gone.

A long time later it is quiet. Michael unlocks the door and sees just one other person leaning over the basin. As he approaches, the man looks up into the mirror and their eyes lock and spring away in shock. It's Catherine's friend Seth. Of all the people on the planet there isn't anyone he wants to see less at this moment. He keeps his eyes down as he washes his hands at the next sink.

"Quite something wasn't it?"

"Yes."

"It's Michael, isn't it?"

He is forced to look across at Seth in the mirror. He looks terrible. Ashen, bloodshot eyes like his own. He has clearly been crying too. Seth half smiles.

"It always does this to me."

"Me too."

"I never know what to do with myself afterwards."

"I know what you mean." Suddenly Michael feels appalled by the thought of going back to his empty flat. They both dry their hands silently on the pull-down towel and step out into the foyer.

"Did you come on your own?"

"Yes. You?"

"Always. I don't generally like people seeing me like this." Michael smiles.

Seth pauses and then, "Do you fancy doing something now? I don't really know what because neither of us is probably in the mood for talking."

Michael looks outside. "What about a walk?" He stops, shocked by his own words. But in Seth's face, the last place he would have looked for understanding, he has seen his own feelings reflected. Perhaps this is the only person he can be with tonight.

They walk slowly along the Embankment, watching the river's ethereal distortion of the city lights. A sniff of summer over the cool tang of the water. Even the traffic noise is a lullaby tonight. At moments like this, Michael can love London, appreciate its beauty. These are the times that make up for the rest, the nights spent with a pillow over his head because he can't bear the constant intrusion of noise, other people. The longing for the heady, empty hills of his childhood where he used to walk for hours, until even Bess the family Labrador protested.

They stop and look back along the river. "Even the South Bank looks pretty tonight."

Seth glances over, lighting a cigarette. "You don't much like London, do you?"

"Not really."

"So why do you stay?"

It's not an easy one to answer without sounding self-righteous. He stays because there's good that he can do, because the people he's trying to reach out to can't leave themselves. But would they want to? Sometimes it seems that it's only him with the problem.

"I don't know really. Obviously there's a lot of music here. But I'll leave one day." He catches the first smoky whiff of Seth's cigarette and even that melds in with the rightness of the moment. "I can't imagine you'd ever think of leaving."

Seth pauses to take a drag. "London sustains me. I feed on its energy. Every corner of the globe is here, every experience. Galleries, museums, restaurants, theatres… all that is best in mankind is showcased here."

"And all the worst."

"You're right. Perhaps that's why it appeals so much." He flashes over a wicked grin and Michael is annoyed to feel himself smiling back.

They resume walking. Talk of themselves, music, moments from the concert he would normally tuck away for private savouring. Their worlds are so different and yet there's an ease of communication he has rarely found with anyone. Seth quizzes him hungrily about music and composing. Few people have ever done that. Only one, in fact.

At London Bridge station they said goodbye. Seth held out his hand and then they were hugging each other. Michael couldn't remember when he had last hugged a man. Had he ever? They swapped numbers and Michael agreed to come along to the musical evening Catherine had been badgering him about. His life up in Finsbury Park had fallen into a rut. Perhaps it was time to allow more people in.

And if they were arseholes he could just go home.

SCENE 13

José's leather jacket was scuffing hard against the wall and his head kept catching on a metal sign as the man's tongue plunged into his mouth. This one was desperate. Must be married, probably a kid or two waiting for him at home. Kissing like this was not José's style, but what did that have to do with anything? He kissed back harder, squeezed the man's arse and slipped a knee between his legs. The man groaned and started pulling at José's belt. José pushed him backwards – a little rough was clearly called for – and yanked down his own trousers and boxers. The man looked at his erect cock, gasping. It was pretty impressive, José knew. Impressive enough to have half a town full of regular clients.

He rubbed himself salaciously, avoiding eye contact, before releasing the man's belt one-handed and stripping him down. Gasping in return would have required better acting skills than he could muster, so he went for the grope. The man made a guttural noise and turned him round; here came the wall again.

"Not so fast."

José held the condom he had ready behind him, looking to check the man put it on. Two minutes later he was whistling down the street with 50 quid chafing his pocket.

He went dancing. He always went dancing afterwards – maybe to lose the encounter in a room crammed with people, maybe to sweat off his feelings, whatever they were. Did he even have feelings anymore? He used to. The first time he'd puked into the canal afterwards. But he'd got used to it now, didn't ever look at their faces – that way it was only about his cock and their cock, it didn't need to concern his mind. Sometimes he even enjoyed it, if the waist-down package was good.

He danced, letting his body wriggle to the slowed tempo. Something a bit reggae-ish. It didn't really matter, he could dance to anything, loved it all. A tickle of sweat brushed his nose, then his mouth. His eyes were half closed as he gyrated his hips, raised his arms. He loved the blackness of the room and the way the neon beams darted and dazzled, making everyone the same flashing no one. The problem was that no one was getting rather close to him. Between the splashes of white light he could see legs moving too near his own. He felt irritated, then irritated with his reaction. He wanted to feel nothing. Without looking up he pivoted an obvious message of rejection. But now the man was pushing his hips into José's arse, grinding with him to the music. And it clearly wasn't just the music he was interested in. José was about to elbow him away when a raised voice right against his ear said, "Two hundred for a night at your place." José jolted. How did he know? Had he been followed? Was it a copper? He started walking off the dance floor, but a hand on his arm pulled him towards the toilets. He whirled to see the most beautiful face he had ever seen looking down at him. "I've been watching you for weeks. You're worth more than a quick fuck under the arches, José. Let me treat you."

José stared, unable to think, unable to tear himself away from the eyes caressing him. Before he could act the man took his face in his hands and kissed him on the mouth, achingly lightly, so their lips just brushed, and brushed again. He felt like he had been pulled underwater. Abruptly the man drew back.

"Is that a yes?"

José swallowed and tried to collect himself. "Three hundred. A night is a long time."

"Oh, I think this one will be." The man looked him up and down. "I could haggle you down... but I think you'll be worth every penny. Three hundred it is."

Could I check again... it's just if anything came out I'd be finished.

I assure you, Mr Sanchez, that everything you tell me here will remain confidential and no further action will be taken. Please go on.

He was regretting it as soon as he was in the taxi. What if this man was crazy? He'd heard the tales of boys being beaten to pulp, or even killed. And now the man would know where he lived. But three hundred pounds... what he could do with it. And that kiss, the memory still throbbing on his lips. Which got him worrying again. His first rule was already broken. Not only had he seen the client's face but he'd fallen in love with it.

They went back to his place, his tiny bedsit, and José lit candles and put on some music. They danced. Not like in the club. Tenderly, like lovers, touching their way over each other. The sex was like nothing José had ever known.

Afterwards they held each other in bed and José had assumed they'd go to sleep, but the man wanted to talk. He said his name was Seth but in José's experience, people were rarely honest about their names. Their bodies, sometimes their lives, but never their names.

"What do you want to talk about?"

"What do you like talking about?" That was a good question. What did he talk about these days, since he'd started selling himself? Good patches. Bad clients. The fucking weather. He turned away slightly.

"Oh – you know, interest rates, the economy." The bitterness in the echo surprised him. He felt a hand stroking his hair.

"What did you do before this?"

José sighed. "I – I was an art student."

"In Spain?"

"Yes, in Siguenza." His throat constricted at the vision of colourful houses on sunny streets.

"You miss it."

"Not really." He got up abruptly, slamming his hand on the bedside table without really knowing why. Great rent boy he was proving to be. The man would probably want half his money back. He leant over the sink and gulped down a glass of water. When he turned round, Seth was watching him from the bed.

"Have you ever thought of doing something artistic?" Just his luck to have shagged a career counsellor.

"No money in it." What he meant was he'd come to London with dreams of doing just that. Something artistic. Wasn't London bulging with artists? He had a vague notion of a studio shared with a few friends, nothing grand but something satisfying, a life worth leading. When he arrived he'd bunked down on a Spanish friend's floor amidst cigarette packets and beer stains. He didn't have a place to paint and quickly realised he couldn't afford a flat on his own. He got by for a while doing crappy temping jobs, trying to save money. One night in Soho he'd been mooching around, unable to afford the bar prices, when a middle-aged suited man had sidled up to him and asked how much for a hand job. At first he had started to protest and explain, but the man seemed to think it was part of the act. Five minutes later he'd walked away with a sticky hand and twenty pounds.

Initially he was buoyed by the possibilities. How many men could he wank in a night? Five? Ten? More? The dream of the flat and the studio leapt into focus again. If he did this for a year, say, what did it matter anyway? It was no different from the saunas or the toilets or Hampstead Heath really. With so many bodily fluids being exchanged amongst strangers, what was a little cash?

And so he started his life as a rent boy. He planned to stick to hand jobs as they were easier, less messy, less intimate. But he quickly found that wasn't going to work. His first client seemed to be an exception – most people wanted blow jobs or full sex. He wasn't stupid, insisted on condoms and found he could expand his repertoire. The artistic dream shimmered in front of him, the eternal carrot, and kept him trotting along in his blinkers.

That was two years ago. He hadn't thought about art or studios for at least half of that, not even when he looked at exhibitions in the trendy coffee bars where he spent his takings. He now had his own place on the edge of Soho, but he needed to work every night to pay the rent and then slept most of the day – so where was the time or money to paint? That was what he told himself. That dream seemed to belong to another him, a naïve boy with no clue about the real world.

Of course he wouldn't be doing this forever, at some level he assumed that. But how he would stop or what he'd do next – these were questions he was always too tired or busy to answer. To ask.

And yet here was a complete stranger asking him. Why? London, or maybe his occupation, had taught José cynicism: as far as he could see, self-interest was the bedrock of all communication.

"You haven't answered. What if it was an artistic pursuit that brought in money?"

"What if? What if there was a tree outside my window that grew £50 notes, what if this tap poured with wine, what if you shut the fuck up and left me alone?" He waved his hands and waited for the man to get angry, to leave without paying him. He didn't care about the money now, he just wanted to be alone. But instead the man reached out his hand. "Come back to bed." And José found himself walking towards the compassion in a stranger's eyes.

He went pretty crazy. He was rough. The man not only let him but matched him, gave it back. It was if they had swapped roles and José was calling the shots, demanding his needs be met. They grabbed, tussled, bit. José growled and howled like a cornered animal. After coming he pushed the man to the bed and locked himself in the bathroom where he crouched and sobbed and sobbed. Something had woken up, something that made him retch with grief for what he had lost. He heard a door closing, footsteps disappearing, but he stayed on the floor until his tears and feelings had died down.

Painfully he straightened up, opened the door onto the emptiness of his room, the day ahead. No money had been left. He hugged himself, shivering. He couldn't deal with this now. He needed to sleep, to blot himself out for as long as his body allowed. A sudden chirp from the door buzzer made him jump. Probably some drunk who hadn't made it to bed – it wouldn't be the first time. He caught sight of himself in the full-length mirror, clutching his nakedness like a madman. The door buzzed again, and then continually for five seconds. Wearily he picked up the receiver. "Hello?"

The answering voice was both strange and familiar. "Your coffee's getting cold."

Seth stayed for the whole day. José was scared by his rising feelings of neediness towards this person, this client. He didn't know how he could have got through the day alone. He found himself talking, opening up, about the dreams he'd had and the decisions he'd made that had left him pinned in a trap. No one from his old life visited him, not even his parents, because he had told too many lies. They all believed he was in sales. Which he was, but the product would have appalled them. His only friends, such as they were, were fellow street workers. Even his Spanish friend Carlos had thrown him out of his flat when he'd found out what José was doing. With no one to hold a mirror to him he lost sight of himself.

Who could have imagined that one of his clients would provide the mirror? The reflection was not pretty. Part of him wanted to smash the glass but it was too late, he had seen himself. This was not who he was supposed to be. This face belonged to a nightmare.

"You should go. You must have things to do." He tried to throw a veil of lightness over his terror of being abandoned now.

"I've got a better idea. Why don't we go out for some food and a bottle of wine?"

José recoiled at the thought of stepping outside, his rubbed-raw face on view to a city of watchful strangers.

"Come on, it'll do you good. You've been hiding away in here for long enough. I'll look after you."

José managed a wan smile and shook his head. "It's okay, you go. I have some thinking to do."

"Then let's think together." Seth took his hand and squeezed it, almost tenderly. "Whoever managed to do any decent thinking on an empty stomach?"

José squeezed back and then, like a little miracle, he felt a bubbling of hunger in his belly. "Well, there is a little place round the corner ..."

He took you out for a meal. Did that not strike you as a little unusual, given the circumstances?
Of course. But everything about Seth was unusual. That was the attraction.

81

They drank wine and ate paninis. José felt like something had lifted. He had stopped wondering why Seth was still there and was just enjoying this moment, two lovers – or two people who had made love, he corrected himself – sharing a meal. He sat back, looking around at the familiar space.

"Very bad décor in here, isn't it?"

Seth looked surprised. "You don't like the minimalist look."

"Minimalism without soul is empty, just for effect. See, if you splashed some colour on the walls, got rid of these ridiculous hard chairs, put hand-written menu boards up it would start to feel human. Every time I come here I think this place is trying too hard to be 'modern'." He shrugged. "I guess I keep coming though."

Seth was leaning in, looking alert. "What else would you do?"

"Oh, don't get me started. Wooden table and chairs with funky coloured cushions. Big bright painted blocks on the wall. Soft side lighting instead of these Nazi spotlights. It would still be modern but it would be…"

"Welcoming." Seth looked round, nodding in slow motion. "Do you regularly sit in restaurants mentally improving them?"

"I suppose I do. I'd never really thought about it. It's something I've always done."

"And you never thought about being a designer?"

José laughed. "Not seriously. It seemed a bit – ambitious maybe? Like I'd have to be a young, thrusting – what's the word? Gobshite. I only thought about the studio thing really."

"And is that still your dream?"

José spoke slowly, thinking his words out. "It seems far away, a dream I had when I was someone else. I don't feel the same desire or connection. It doesn't seem very practical."

They were both silent.

"José, I think I have a proposition for you."

"Does it involve another night at my place? Because you still haven't paid me for the first one."

They both laughed. "Well, actually it could involve quite

a few nights at *my* place."

José raised his eyebrows.

"Here's the thing." Seth looked excited, spoke quickly. "I have a couple of other flats in London. I'm one of those revolting rich people everyone despises."

"I couldn't have guessed."

Seth smiled. "Anyway, I rent one of them out, in Shepherd's Bush, and the last tenants trashed it. It's not the most amazing flat in the world but I've always thought I could do more with it."

José nodded, no idea what was coming next.

"It's obvious. You need somewhere to live to get off the game. You also need an income and to develop a career in something else. Yes?"

"Ye-es." It was all true but José felt odd having someone else articulate it so matter-of-factly.

"Well, how about this, you come and live in the flat, rent free of course, and at the same time use your creativity to give it a makeover – no, a full facelift. I'll pay you for that and at the end of the day you might find yourself on a new career path." He stopped, keeping his eyes on José's face.

José almost laughed. How could this man, this stranger, make him an offer like that? How could he accept? It was wine and sexual attraction talking and he'd retract tomorrow.

He shook his head. "It's an amazing offer. But I can't accept."

"Because?"

"You don't know me. It's crazy. I would never be able to pay you back."

Seth pulled a cigarette out of a tarnished silver box. "Okay, number one, I don't know you well but I never know my tenants or the people who do work for me. What's the difference? Number two, it may be impetuous but it's not crazy – it's actually a divinely logical solution. Number three, you would have nothing to pay back in either the financial or moral sense. I don't hand out charity. I always make sure there's something in it for me."

The last sentence hung in the air as José tried to think. Seth had been following him around, had wanted something from him from the beginning. What was he getting involved with? But to say no, to turn down this opportunity... What was it the British said, something about horses?

"Don't look a gift horse in the mouth, José," said Seth softly, causing him to jerk his head up and stare. "And don't think I'd be looking for payment in kind. In fact, if you say yes, I think we should agree that there will be nothing more physical between us. Keeps it cleaner."

"Of course." José had to work to keep his face neutral. The man had made him the offer of a lifetime and yet he still felt rejected. Seth put a hand over his. "Not that I wouldn't like to. But I've been in this situation before and it can get messy."

José squeezed the hand lightly before removing his. "Okay, you're the boss. I think I should be getting home now – I need to think this through."

Seth nodded. "Think away but don't take too long. In my experience your first instinct is always the right one."

José slept for eleven hours that night and in the morning rang Seth and said yes.

You're telling us that Seth Gardner helped you when he barely knew you?
He didn't help me. Let's get that straight. He saved me.

SCENE 14
Did you feel accepted as part of the Friday Folly, Miss Laurence?

Rebecca munched at another cold piece of toast and marmite. Richard and Judy were looking in wonder at a pork chop that had been marinated in balsamic vinegar. Rebecca hadn't eaten meat since 1987 and still she didn't turn it off. She flicked crumbs off her dressing gown onto the floor, where they'd show up less. Her flatmate, Shazia, was due back tomorrow and even that hadn't motivated her to clean the house. She'd have to do something today. Even Shaz had her standards.

It was always hard after a show had finished, but this was worse than usual. Her agent had gone quiet, always a bad sign. She still hadn't managed to get a voice-over agent; a couple of radio ads a month would give her a financial cushion for times like these. Her allowance from her parents – her guilty secret that she told no one about – wouldn't last to the end of the month. She should get off her backside and phone the temp agency. And not just for the money. Even updating the filing system of a freight company, as she'd done last time, would be more rewarding than this.

She sighed and watched Richard and Judy make their way – he bounding, she plodding – to the fashion area. Hell, she even knew it was the fashion area with the sound turned down. A model, not paid to speak, smiled and rotated like a musical box fairy, displaying a grim red PVC skirt with a black zipped jacket. Richard leaned his head to one side and talked animatedly. Judy was probably saying 'Yes, Richard' in that slightly schoolmarmish way.

With no warning, Rebecca hurled the remote control across the room. It didn't seem to bother Richard and Judy but she looked down at her hand, surprised. There was nothing to feel bad about really. *Hamlet* was over but had got some great reviews; so had she. It didn't seem to help. She and Jason had been tetchy with each other all weekend and he'd admitted he felt jealous of her new friends.

The new friends who had gone very quiet. This, she hated to admit, was the real problem. Anna had mentioned some girls' lunch at the end of the group and said she'd get in touch. Nothing. Then there was Seth. She hadn't expected to hear from him, at least so quickly, but she still felt his absence like a door swinging in the wind.

She stood up slowly, batting more crumbs onto the floor.

And then her phone pinged into life.

* * * * *

The next morning, Shazia found Rebecca singing over a sink of washing-up.

"Bloody hell, mate. You almost look like you're enjoying yourself. Careful now."

Rebecca laughed. "I'm just trying to be a better flatmate. I've got to go out in an hour so I thought I'd surprise you."

"You have. Where are you off?"

"A girly lunch in Covent Garden."

"What better plan for a sunny Saturday morning, I say. I'm going back to bed."

Rebecca grinned and moved onto the frying pan.

Two hours later she found Anna and José huddled over a bottle of wine in the corner of a busy bistro.

"Hey, is this the girly lunch table?"

"Girls and honorary girls. And dishonourable girls. All welcome here."

God, Anna was sharp. She'd need her wits about her. "Well, I'm sure I fit one of those categories – just not sure which."

She sat down and Anna slid a wine glass towards her. Rebecca looked round. "No Catherine?"

Anna and José raised eyebrows at each other. "The Andersen's android is indisposed." Said in a sort of dalek voice.

"Oh, she's an accountant?" It fitted.

"Accountant-cum-housekeeper. She's probably ironing Seth's shirts as we speak."

"Anna!" José shook a finger at her, but Rebecca laughed. She felt no particular loyalty to Catherine.

Anna poured the wine. "You think I jest?"

"You're not serious?"

Anna nodded, smirking. "Quite the little maid. José caught her in the act, so to speak, *dashing away with the smoothing iron.*" She slurped her drink and laughed at

Rebecca's expression. "After he bought her that piano she'll do anything for him."

Rebecca shook her head, confused. "Sorry…?"

"Ah, there's so much you don't know yet." The two of them laughed, not unkindly. Rebecca took a gulp of wine. A full-blooded Chardonnay.

"So Seth bought a piano for Catherine?"

"Not just any piano. A grand piano, which is housed at his place just to confuse matters."

"The *Steinway*?" Rebecca puckered up her face in disbelief. "Are they… together?"

"Yes and no." Anna laughed again. "As in, yes he bought the Steinway for her – well, pretty much, though he knew it would look good in the flat – and no, they're not together. Much as she'd like to be."

"I see – I think." She looked at José, who shrugged.

"It's true. Seth was in a piano shop one day, heard Catherine play that piano, bought it and gave her a spare set of keys. Bish bosh."

"It's Friday Folly folklore now." They both smiled broadly.

"Wow, that's so… generous." Rebecca summoned a return smile to hide the seething in her gut.

Anna winked. "That's our Seth. Generous to a fault with his parents' money. And he gets nothing in return except a lifetime of devotion from the Little Maid and all his cleaning needs taken care of."

"So he's got rich parents?" Rebecca couldn't help the direct question. She needed to know more, to understand.

"Had, darling. I doubt they need the money much now."

"What, they're dead?"

Anna nodded.

Seth, an orphan. "I had no idea." She swallowed, realising how little she knew about him.

"Yeah, it's not something he talks about much. Car crash, apparently. When he was eighteen." Anna's tone had softened as she played with a breadstick. There was a brief pause.

"Anyway, enough of that. We're here to find out all about you." They both leaned in, theatrically.

"Well, what can I tell you?" The abrupt change of subject was disorientating. Everything was disorientating.

"Ooh, you name it, darling. We've got all day."

"Anna usually starts with general questions like what knickers you wear before moving to the more personal stuff. Say, your favourite vibrator. In case she's missed one." Anna and José giggled.

Rebecca thought quickly. "*Knickers*? How very quaint." A split second's silence then guffaws from both of them. At least she'd sidestepped the vibrator question.

Anna raised her glass. "Very good. I can see we'll have to watch you. Like Seth does."

"Seth?" It was a reasonable attempt at nonchalance.

"Come on, don't pretend you haven't noticed. You're his latest crush. He's captivated by that translucent skin and that abundant red hair…"

"And those long, slim legs and feline eyes. *Rrrrrr*." José imitated a cat stretching its claws.

Rebecca laughed. She was dying to know more but sensed a trap. "Well, thank you kindly, ladies, but he hasn't bought me a piano yet."

"Oh, you'll probably be in line for a small theatre if you play your cards right."

Rebecca took a slug of wine and grinned. She needed to change the subject.

"So, how did you all meet? How did the Friday Folly come to be?"

"Dreadful name," muttered José, shaking his head. "Seth's choice, of course."

"Well it is his group. Seth has a recruitment programme. Meets someone, takes a shine to them, finds out they're artistic in some way and lures them in with sweet talking and the odd gift."

"You make him sound predatory."

"Predatory." Anna swilled the word round in her mouth. "That's probably about right."

"But that's awful."

"Awful? God, no. Seth's a one-off. He makes things happen. Meet him once and you can't stay away – you know that. And why would you want to when you have so much damn fun hanging out with him."

"True enough," said José, getting up. "Sorry – weak bladder."

Rebecca turned back to Anna as José headed towards the gents. "Was that how you met him?"

Anna took another breadstick. "We should order soon. I met him through José. He and I became friends a few years ago, when he was involved with Seth. Naturally I wanted to meet this amazing person he talked about all the time."

Rebecca jolted. Involved? "So – he and Seth…?"

Anna laughed. "Once upon a time, honey. Seth doesn't limit himself to one particular flavour, if you see what I mean. Not that he talks about it much."

"Right." Rebecca's mind was fizzing. So Seth was bisexual. It fitted somehow. Thank God she hadn't made a fool of herself, burned her bridges with Jason. She couldn't imagine being with a bisexual man.

Anna was looking at her with narrowed eyes. "Shocked you, hasn't it?"

"No…"

"Come on, you're that not good an actress. You'll get used to it. It sort of makes him who he is. Hey, José. I was just telling Rebecca about Seth swinging both ways. She seems to like it as much as you do."

José sat down heavily. "Can we change the subject?"

José Sanchez doesn't like the fact that Mr Gardner is bisexual?
I suppose not. We've never really talked about it.

89

Did he seem jealous of you?
José? No, not at all. Well, not then. He's
a sweetie.
What about Anna Carmel?
That's a tougher one. Not jealous, exactly,
but wary. I think I offended her a bit.

It was well-intended. She asked her a question about Northern Ireland, referring to it as 'home'. She knew immediately that she'd made a faux pas as she watched Anna's face stiffen and turn away.

"It's not my home anymore."

There was silence, all the more awkward for it being the first one of the lunch. Rebecca flicked her hair off her face. "Sorry."

"Take no notice of Anna, she's just jealous because you get to dress up for a living." Rebecca laughed, a little too eagerly, and as they discussed Anna's dressing-up fetish, Anna re-established eye contact and Rebecca's breathing relaxed. Despite the awkward moment, she went home feeling she'd passed some sort of test.

SCENE 15
**Mr Gardner's plan to get you off the streets
and into employment – did it work?**

Yes, on the whole. Certainly the first part. He spent six arduous months doing up Seth's flat in Shepherd's Bush, sleeping on a mattress surrounded by takeaway trays and empty beer cans. It was easy to give up the hustling but he missed his street buddies, the gossip and camaraderie. Shepherd's Bush might have been the Australian outback for all the connection he felt to the place. But whenever his feet itched to go dancing he'd imagine bumping into old colleagues or, worse, clients. Better to be a Cinderella at the moment. Seth provided the odd Fairy Godmother visit, waving his wallet to take José out to dinner, always returning him untouched by midnight. A mixed blessing.

The final *ta-da* moment was nerve-wracking. José hid up in the newly built mezzanine during the inspection, waiting to be redeemed or cast out. Footsteps slowly approached, mounting the spiral staircase onerously.

The footsteps stopped. "José."

He stood up. "I'm sorry, I..."

"José, look at me." He raised his head and saw Seth's eyes were shining. "I love it. I bloody love it."

So you were well set on your path as an interior designer...
Not exactly.

Dinner afterwards, a trendy new place in Hammersmith, and a confession to make.

"I don't want to be an interior designer."

Seth's eyes widening, José's hands shaking to the point that he sat on them.

"It's been an amazing experience." José groped for the right words. "I've learned so much. But it's too lonely for me. I want – I need to work with people." A silence, broken only by Seth reaching for a cigarette. "I've been thinking that I could try to get into graphic design. There are loads of small companies in Soho." Managing to meet Seth's eye, hating how much he wanted his approval.

Seth blew smoke out of the side of his mouth and nodded. "Well, it's all design, isn't it? So, where do you go from here?"

A flame leaping in his belly. "Work experience, I reckon. There's a consultancy on Frith Street I've got my eye on." He used to watch them from his flat, a group of young men in black jeans leaving the office at lunch time just as he was getting up, laughing and heading to a wine bar. This was what he craved. A structure, a group of colleagues, a shared identity.

Seth nodded again. "Well, go for it then. You can carry on living in the flat while you're doing work experience, then you're on your own, kid."

José's eyes filled up as he went to give Seth a hug that was partly returned. "I can't thank you enough."

Seth smiled. "Well, there is something else I'd like from you."

José reclaimed his seat, heart pumping. "What's that?"

"I'd like you to help me redesign my own flat. Obviously I'll get someone in to do the work but I'd like you to advise me."

José's smile barely faltered. "It would be a pleasure."

And you succeeded with the work experience and getting a job?
I did.

He often gives thanks on the way into work. Lifts his face to the tickle of rain, takes a drag on the smoggy air. Looking, no doubt, like a crazy man, a nutter as they put it here. Breaking the rule of no stopping in the morning rush hour. He doesn't mind the angry elbows barging him from both sides. He's just happy to be here and needs to absorb it for a second. It didn't take him long to make himself indispensable to Brand X, a team of seven men, some gay, some straight, having fun about their business in their regulation white shirt and jeans with optional jacket and man bag. They gave him a permanent contract within three months. He has Seth to thank, Seth who's meeting him after work. A change of top, deodorant and hair gel are safely tucked away in his black leather satchel.

Before that he's meeting Anna Carmel from Remus for lunch. Theoretically to talk shop, but really to drink and gossip. They've become great friends in that gay man/straight woman way. He loves her outrageousness and the fact that she doesn't give a shit. They compare notes on sexual conquests in lurid detail. She's never short of things to tell; privately José is amazed that there are men brave enough to go near her. Not only is she physically imposing but she has a tongue that can slice you in two. With a broad Northern Irish burr.

He sighs slightly as he arrives at her restaurant of choice. Another new Conran place, indistinguishable from all the others. Deep breath before plunging down into a huge, echoing cavern where clattering cutlery puts paid to meaningful conversation. He winces as he takes his seat. Anna is late, of course. José watches her make her way towards him, broad shouldered and beaming, already talking before she is properly in earshot. Cheeks are kissed, wine poured, contents of bag spilled, cigarette lit, 'only while I'm cutting out carbs,' olives requested. Her maroon blouse gapes when she sits, revealing a fold of midriff over her skirt waistband. José sits up straighter, can't help feeling smug about his own flat stomach. For such an irresistible person she's terrible with clothes, tries to dress 'corporate' without any instinct about what suits her. Maybe he'll take her shopping one day, tactfully of course. He smiles and lets himself get swallowed up in her energy, her complaints about 'bastard' colleagues and the rules of her new diet. Halfway through the main course she starts to slow down, as she always does. Today it's partly to do with the thickness of the steak she's devouring. José eyes his own pious plate of chickpeas and couscous with relief.

"So, darling," she sputters through a mouthful of food, "how are things with you? What gorgeous men have you been seeing?"

"Nothing much to report from the weekend. Bit of a quiet one."

Anna snorts. "Not allowed. You gay young things have to have enough fun to compensate for the rest of the population's heterosexual misery."

"Sorry not to be able to amuse you. What?"

She is looking at him through narrowed eyes, waving a

bloody, serrated knife at him.

"It's him, isn't it?"

"Who?"

"Who? The man you're besotted with. Mr Two-houses."

"Seth. What about him?"

"That's why you're not seeing anyone else, isn't it? You still want him."

He can't help looking down for a fraction of a second, then back up at Anna's face which is now triumphant. "Look, it's not going to happen. Yes, I might want it to but it's clear he doesn't." Even since getting his own flat, when everything between them was straightforward again, Seth has given no sign of wanting more than the friendship they have crafted.

"When are you seeing him again?"

"Tonight, as it happens."

"Perfect. Keeley just cancelled on me, silly bitch. I'll join yous. I need to meet him. Then I can tell you what his game is. If there's any hope or if you should cast your wand in another direction, so to speak."

He tries to protest but he knows the game is up.

"Look, if I stay in I'll only eat a bag of Kettle Chips and a pizza and then I'll have to phone you to confess and I'll ruin your night anyway."

He smiles, beaten. Maybe it's a good thing anyway. If anyone can figure Seth out, it's Anna.

Tell me about that meeting.

They took an instant shine to each other. Anna was her no-holds-barred self, surprised and then delighted by her new sparring partner. They argued, bantered and shouted each other down, attracting disapproving glances for Anna's volley of 'fuck you's across the table.

After a couple of hours he switched to vodka mixers while Anna and Seth matched each other on pints. Anna was in her element, holding forth about the conflict in Ireland with copious mentions of 'terrorist Catholic bastards'. José was far from being an IRA sympathiser, but having been raised a Catholic he found himself looking round and motioning for her to keep her voice down, as if God might be sitting in the alcove behind them. Seth threw in the odd question or observation like a missile, looking delighted when the inevitable explosion came. José tuned out and started eyeing the surrounding talent, or lack of it. He didn't know the details of the Irish situation and, frankly, couldn't be bothered just now.

When he tuned back in they were talking about sex, which was no real surprise. At least he might have a chance of contributing to the conversation. They were debating sex in fiction: who did it best. Anna was jabbering about a new series of erotic novels aimed at women and how they had become 'more fingered than her vibrator'. Anna had to mention her vibrator at least once over the course of an evening. José now knew more about it than he did her family. Or anything else in her past.

`Sorry to cut over you, but we're running a`
`little short of time. Did Miss Carmel give`
`her verdict on what she thought of Seth`
`Gardner?`

Even now he winces at the memory.

"He's straight, José." This was after an emotional scene the next day.

José had scoffed at first. "Don't be ridiculous. Do you think I wouldn't know? I've had crushes on straight men before but this was different. We had sex, for a start."

Anna pointed her fork at him. Roast potatoes today. "I'm telling you, he was flirting with me. Not just me, every female he came into contact with."

"Anna, Anna, what kind of fag hag are you if you don't know that all gay men flirt with all straight women?"

"Not that sort of flirting. The real sort. Where you feel

stripped down to your underwear."

José laughed. "Do you mean he was looking at your tits? He's gay, of course he was. And it's hard to avoid it with you."

For once she shunned the bait. "Listen, José, I'm telling you there's something strange going on with him. How much do you know about him? How do you know he's not into women too?"

Was it possible? Would that explain his hot-cold behaviour?

"Watch him next time you're out. I'm never wrong about these things."

SCENE 16

Would you like to tell us how you first met Seth Gardner, Miss Carmel?

Just a second while I fetch my coffee. Okay, but I'm not sure it'll help you much. I'd rather talk about now. Is there any news?

We'll get to that. Please answer the question.

Okay. Let me think. I've known Seth for three years so it must have been 1994. It was cold. February, I reckon. It was just a few drinks. Well, quite a few. My friend José was infatuated with Seth and I wanted to check him out.

Poor José, he'd looked lost as she and Seth went off on their own tangent. He wasn't at all what she'd expected. She'd let him have it with both barrels, expecting to send him scuttling, but he'd laughed and come back for more. She hadn't had such a kick out of meeting someone in a long time. But, Seth and José? She couldn't see it, somehow. There was something jarring. She usually had a sense for these things.

What did you make of Seth Gardner?

The friendship equivalent of love at first sight. She lay in the bath the next morning giggling like a naughty toddler, dialogue from their night out floating piecemeal into her head. She'd even gone for a swim afterwards, 40 lengths straight. Afterwards the café and a post-exercise glow she'd always pooh-poohed as a figment of deluded imaginations. The tingle of coffee on her tongue. She sat back and sighed, wondering when she'd last had such a perfect Saturday.

By the time she got back home she was shaking with hunger, cursing herself for not having a snack in the café. She fell on the new loaf of bread, cutting a thick slice and smearing it with butter and Marmite. She knew she should sit at the table so that her body registered what it was eating (according to something she'd read in some tabloid newspaper), but it would hardly be worth it before she'd have to get up again to cut another slice.

Then the phone started up. No question of answering it; she was still way too hungry. Her older brother's voice. Gentle, sounding hesitant to leave a message. Saying he knew how she'd be feeling and wishing she could be with them today. She stopped mid-chew, cheeks stuffed like a hamster's. What was the date? All the energy drained from her so rapidly she thought she might faint. March 12th. Her ma's birthday. For the first time she'd forgotten.

Miss Carmel?
It was March, actually. I've just remembered.

She was seventeen when her mother died. She knew she was ill, but not that ill. Her fathers and brothers protecting her from the truth so that when it happened she was stupefied. How could her ma no longer be there? Standing over the cooker in a frilly white apron; speaking to someone in soft, soothing cadences; saying grace before the meal. A quiet and

97

constant backdrop, a canvas for the rest of them as they played out their noisy dramas. Her mind is awash with technicolour memories of her father: making them cry with laughter at the dinner table; roaring through a megaphone at some rally or other; flying kites with them on Sunday morning. But when she thinks of her mother it's just gentle, wordless murmuring. And a feeling: a feeling of being safe. A feeling she had lost thirteen years ago.

Anna sank onto one of her new Ikea chairs. The day had been blown apart. She yearned for the warmth of her brother's voice but couldn't face the inevitable questions about going home. Her pa had betrayed her, betrayed them all and, as far as she was concerned, that was that.

The phone trilled again, each blast drilling into her skull. In the end she picked up. It was only fair to speak to Conor.

"Anna! Can't believe you're out of bed already. So, what did you think?"

José. "I, yeah, I really like him." Her mind felt blank.

"Are you okay?" José's tone switched to concern. Anna felt something loosening inside her. Her shoulders started shaking with mute sobs.

"It's my ma's birthday. I forgot." The last word was almost shouted as a sob forced its way out.

"I'm coming over."

* * * * *

They sat on the sofa drinking hot chocolate – Anna's idea, something her ma made her as a child. Anna's legs were tucked under her and she held the mug with both hands as if it were a baby animal. Now that José was here the tears seemed to have dried up. She felt a bit of a fraud for bringing him over.

"So, Mr Two-houses."

José shook his head. "Not now. That stuff doesn't matter. Have you spoken to your brother yet?"

Anna shook her head.

"Why don't you ring him now? I'll pop out and get some stuff for dinner."

Anna sighed. "Later. He's okay, he's with his family."

José touched her hand. "You're his family, Anna."

She nodded, looked at the photo above the fireplace. Conor and Daniel, her adored older brothers. Nothing could ever touch her with them around. They felt half a world away now.

"You all look so close." José had followed her gaze, watching Conor and Daniel waving to camera while an eight-year-old Anna nestled between them, showing off a missing front tooth.

"We were. We fought amongst ourselves but if anyone gave me grief at school, I'd just threaten to get my brothers on them."

José smiled. "Handy."

"Yeah, I strutted round that playground like I owned the place. Thought I was so cool, so tough." It seemed to her now that she'd spent her childhood under a giant canopy, sheltered by her family without even noticing. She pointed at the photograph. "At that age I had my own business. Selling set squares and stuff."

"Selling what?"

"Maths stuff we needed for school – rulers, compasses, that sort of thing. If anyone lost theirs and didn't want to tell their parents, then I was your man."

José laughed. "Why doesn't that surprise me? Where did you get your…"

"Supply? My brothers, of course. I never asked where it came from. Gave them a cut. They always said I had the real business head. That's why pa pushed me to come over here. Said Ireland was a mess and I had the 'ability to make something of myself'." She boomed the last bit in a Northern Irish accent more pronounced than her own.

"Your dad sounds like quite a character."

"Ah, that he was. A local councillor. We'd go and watch

him speak. He could turn a room full of men into jabbering wrecks. Ma used to say he should have been a priest."

José snorted. "She's right there."

"She also said he could charm the birds from the trees when it suited him."

"Could?"

Anna twitched her eyebrow. She did talk about her father almost as if he was dead. "Can, I suppose. He certainly charmed Mrs Warwick out of hers." She laughed without humour. The first time she'd come home after her ma had died, maybe three months after the funeral, there she was, Mrs Warwick, sitting in her house, making tea, doing the things her ma should have been doing. For some reason her brothers seemed to go along with it, saying it had given Pa back the glint in his eye. Anna had hardly been home since.

"Is that your father's new wife?"

"Yes." She hadn't gone to the wedding, claimed a last-minute work crisis. "She was a neighbour from a few doors down. Gave Pa a shoulder to cry on, very kindly." She chewed her bottom lip, looked out of the window. "It's history now. I was just caught off guard today." She sat up straighter. "Let's go to the pub. Come on, it's Saturday afternoon. What the hell else is there to do?"

José raised his eyebrows. "I had planned to go to the gym."

"Gym-shmym. Come on, let me sink a couple of pints and you can nurse your half a shandy and we'll dissect the life and times of Lord Setheric Two-houses."

José shook his head and reached for his coat. "Sometimes, woman, there's no arguing with you."

Are you okay, Miss Carmel?
Sorry, yes. Can you repeat the question?

SCENE 17
When did you first notice something odd in Seth Gardner's behaviour?

Three days into her new temping job, Rebecca came home to find a large white envelope in the mailbox, hand-addressed in loopy, sloping writing that looked familiar. She dropped her bags in the hallway and ripped open the envelope. It was an invitation to dinner from Seth, addressed to *The lovely Ophelia and her lucky suitor*. She found herself wanting to squeal with delight – apart from the fact that Jason was invited too and would no doubt hate the whole thing.

She spent a long time getting ready, Jason sticking his head in from time to time with silent disapproval. Up until five o'clock the day had gone well: a lazy Saturday of coffee, sex and shopping. But as their dinner date loomed closer, Jason had got tetchy. Going to dinner parties wasn't his thing, still less with a bunch of strangers who talked about art. He subsided in front of the TV as she contemplated her wardrobe. The invitation simply said *Dress for dinner*. What did that mean? Evening dress? Seth moved in a different world from her, no doubt with its own protocols that she knew nothing about. In the end she opted for a strappy black top and pinstriped trousers that made her legs look as long as Naomi Campbell's – according to Des in the Red Lion. Then she spent the best part of forty minutes wrestling her hair with grips, bobbles and hairspray to create her own interpretation of a French pleat, complete with stray tresses spiralling to her shoulders. She found Jason sulking in front of *Blind Date*.

"What do you think?" The 'aren't I gorgeous?' pirouette was pushing it but she wasn't going to let him spoil her night.

He muttered something sarcastic about bridesmaids.

"For God's sake." She stopped herself, turned away. Now was not the time to get into an argument. "We should get going. Are you ready? Shouldn't you put a shirt on?"

* * * * *

It went well, mostly, until dinner was over. Seth had greeted her with a compliment and a kiss and shaken Jason's hand warmly. The room looked wonderful, red tea lights winking and extra lighting provided by the full moon gazing on through the back window. Jason looked a little awed despite himself. Seth checked his watch a couple of times until Anna and José arrived, late, bitching about the Circle and Northern line respectively, which led into one of those inevitable London conversations about the Tube. Seth listened with the twitch of a smile on his face.

"Funnily enough I find it perfectly possible to avoid all that by never taking the Tube."

José snorted. "You avoid all that by never leaving your flat."

"*Au contraire*, my dear José. I spend many a day when the rest of you are beavering away in your offices, or whatever it is you do, pacing the streets of London. Know it like the back of my 'and, I do." He had switched to a Cockney accent. "I could be a cabbie in my next life."

A gale of laughter. "Yes, I can really see that."

Rebecca sensed Jason bristling beside her.

Anna scooped up a mound of hummus onto a Kettle Chip and turned to Seth. "So what is it exactly you do all day then? I've often wondered."

Seth raised an eyebrow. "Well, I walk, like I said. Go to galleries, afternoon concerts, matinees. Pay for sex now and again."

He was almost certainly joking but Rebecca felt uncomfortable and saw her feelings mirrored on José's face. Jason was muttering under his breath next to her.

Anna snorted. "I've never had to pay, myself." The banter continued.

Jake had done the food again, veggie moussaka for José and Rebecca, steak for the rest, Catherine ferrying things backwards and forwards like a waitress. Rebecca wondered if it provided her with a purpose and an excuse not to join in the conversation. Seth was an accomplished host, tossing in conversational bones, which he unobtrusively withdrew if people started tussling over them. That only happened once, when Michael and Anna got a little heated on the subject of the Iraq war. Rebecca was glad to see the subject changed; politics secretly bored her and she didn't want her lack of current affairs knowledge exposed. She was flattered to be seated next to Seth, who was at the head of the table. Jason, to her right, chatted a lot to Charles, who was customarily solicitous to both of them, while José kept up the repartee.

Before dessert they braved the patio where a November wind was gusting across shivery gardens. Anna shivered too. "What are we doing here? Since when do you bother to smoke outside?"

Seth wrapped his free arm round her shoulder, flicking cigarette ash with his other hand. "We're trying to get a flavour of autumn. See – trees, darling." They looked across to where clusters of skinny branches waved back in response. "I must say it's the one season where I'm not fully satisfied with London. I'm sure Michael would agree with me."

Michael was leaning over the railings, his Roman profile silhouetted against the glow, hair flapping about madly. "For once I do agree with you, Seth." He turned and smiled, a softness around his face that Rebecca hadn't seen before.

"Ah well. I shall just have to gaze upon Rebecca's hair and let my imagination do the rest." Seth sighed dreamily and Jason tightened his grip on her arm. Catherine turned away so her face was hidden, but Rebecca could read the tension in her stance.

Charles smoothed things over, as ever. "Have you got anything new lined up, Rebecca?"

She laughed. "You sound like a casting director. Actually, I have." It was fresh off the press, a bit part in a TV serial drama. Her first telly.

"So we'll see you on Tuesday nights?"

"For a couple of episodes. Not until after Christmas."

"Crikey. Are you excited?"

She laughed. "Not as much as my mum. To be honest I think I prefer theatre but I'll give it a go and see what happens."

Seth stubbed out his cigarette on the railing. "And what do you make of our own Hugh Grant here? Rocking the floppy-haired look, Charlie boy."

Rebecca bit her lip. With his concave chest, beard and crew neck jumper, Charles bore little resemblance to his *Four Weddings and a Funeral* alter ego, bar perhaps the hair. He coughed and gave a little bow. "I try my best."

The light kiss of rain in the air drove them inside to huddle round the fire, while Anna raided Seth's music collection. "Still plenty of vinyl I see. Hmmm. Classical. Classical. More classical. Don't you ever listen to anything else?"

"There's some jazz on the right-hand shelf."

Anna screwed up her face. "You need your music updating, my son. I'll tell you who you'd like, Divine Comedy."

"I presume we're not talking Dante?"

"Well, not exactly, but there are enough literary references and classical music influences to keep even *you* happy." Anna twiddled with the stem of her glass. "I met the lead singer, Neil Hannon, way before he got famous."

"Ooh, get you."

José winked at Seth. "Northern Irish."

"Ah," a knowing nod, "enough said. Does he play the fiddle and dance a reel?"

Cue raised voices, mostly Anna's, and more laughter, while Catherine scurried around clearing the table. Rebecca felt a brief prod of guilt, which she shrugged off fairly easily. Why should she offer to help just because she was female? She didn't want to miss a second, and besides, Catherine was probably happier being a martyr about it. She smiled quickly at Jason who was reaching for the bottle of wine on the coffee table to top up his glass. He was knocking it back.

They subsided onto comfy chairs, watching the fire. Seth suggested making some stove-top coffee.

"One of your coffees at this time? You must be kidding." There were general murmurings about herbal tea, which Seth derided.

"You won't find any of that gubbins in my cupboard. Come on, Rebecca, be my partner in crime. I know what you're like for a good strong espresso."

She accepted, of course, excusing herself so she could head to the loo first. It was gleaming white with an old fashioned pull-chain that took her back to childhood. A sprawling corner bath, which she briefly pictured sharing with Seth. When she returned, Seth handed her the coffee in a tiny, colourful cup. "Miro. Gorgeous, aren't they?" He looked at his watch. "I think it must be time for a little after-dinner entertainment."

From nowhere came the rasp of Jason's voice, slurred and suggestive. "Got some strippers booked, mate?"

The room fell totally, utterly silent. Rebecca saw now that Jason was as drunk as she'd ever seen him. It wasn't even the kind of thing he approved of. She wanted to die.

Jake boomed with laughter. Everyone else looked at Seth, who was smirking.

"Actually, *mate*, we thought you could do the honours." Over more laughter it flashed into her mind that Seth was bisexual. Was he attracted to Jason? The thought was too disturbing to pursue. Luckily Jason wasn't quick enough to flick back a reply and conversation moved on. Everyone was pressing Catherine to play, who protested that she couldn't possibly after drinking. Had she even had a full glass? Rebecca deliberately looked away, didn't add her voice.

Naturally, Catherine demurred and everyone took their seats for the grand performance. Seth requested 'something dark to match the night'. Catherine took a breath. Deep black chords moved into swelling rumbling runs down the bass of the piano. It was impossible not to be captivated. Like the rest of the room, Rebecca stared at the slight figure creating such a vast, restless energy. Where did it come from? Anna leaned her head back, Jason sipped his wine, Michael looked like he'd found God. And Seth – Seth was gazing at Catherine as if she were an angel and Rebecca felt the exiled fury of the dark angel fly off the keys and seize her.

The mood of the evening was transformed. Whisky replaced wine, soul searching bypassed small talk. People were curled up, lying back, sitting on the floor. Jake and Seth were smoking. José had his arm round Anna, who was resting against Charles' legs. Michael and Catherine's arms were touching on the sofa. Rebecca could almost taste the intimacy. Jason put a hand on her knee. They were the only couple in the room. She put her hand over his, wishing she could push it away.

"Of course you know what we need now." Seth blew his smoke thoughtfully upwards.

"What?"

"Someone to read to us." He eyed Rebecca. "Someone to tell us our dreams and desires. Someone, perhaps, with a background in theatre."

"No way!" But she couldn't help a smile. She had the sudden urge to perform.

"Yes, come on Rebecca. For all of us who didn't see *Hamlet*."

"What would I read?"

Seth shrugged. "Whatever you like. Either something you know by heart, or you're very welcome to come and browse my bookshelves for inspiration."

"What if she doesn't want to? I'm sure you want a break, darling – it is Friday night."

Bloody Jason. Now she'd have to pretend she didn't want to, or look like a total show-off. But Seth stepped in, literally, coming over to pull her up.

"You were allowed to say no the first time but not tonight. Get thee to a library!"

She giggled as he pulled her towards the door, feeling Jason's eyes on them.

"Here." They were in the adjoining room, made up as a bedroom but with floor-to-ceiling shelves crammed full of books. Library was not far off the mark.

"Wow." She exhaled slowly and grabbed hold of the door frame. "Oh!"

"What is it?"

"The books are dancing in front of my eyes – optical illusion or too much whisky?"

"Just clever books, darling." They laughed and looped their arms round each other. Seth straightened. "Look. I've got something to show you." He led her into the room and turned her round.

She was gazing at a huge picture of a woman lying under water, hands open as if in prayer, hair streaming like a sea creature.

"Just a print, I'm afraid. Millais' *Ophelia*. Thought you'd like it."

"Of course! I love it."

"What I wouldn't give to own the original. I must admit to a certain weakness for the pre-Raphs. Not at all the done thing, of course." He turned suddenly and took her face in his right hand, hard enough for her to feel his thumb digging into her cheek. "There's a look of you, though you're a little more – how shall I say – feline." She could hear her own breathing in the short silence as she met his eyes.

"Those delicately upturned eyes," she barely dared to blink, "and those cheekbones." He skated his thumb along the line of the left one. She waited for him to reach her lips, eyes already closing. But he released her face and brushed a spiralled curl with his index finger. "I suppose you've got your hair up just to torment me."

She smiled, didn't trust her voice to sound.

"Well, it's worked. I keep wondering what it would look like if I suddenly made it spill around your shoulders." He threaded his fingers into the hair swept up at the bottom of her neck. Voices sounded from the next room. She arched her spine, a silent invitation. What was she doing? Jason was there, everyone waiting for them. But she stayed, as though spooled in threads of a dream as his thumbs brushed the back

107

of her neck. He tugged at her hair and she felt the bottom grips begin to loosen.

"I want it to look like hers." A whisper that she barely caught. Then without warning he swivelled back towards the painting, letting go of her so that she staggered. "Sorry, are you okay?" His voice smooth and charming again. They both stared at the painting, though Rebecca could barely see.

"Was there ever a better capturing of female perfection?"

She needed to pull herself together, find her voice. She cleared her throat. "I didn't know you had necrophiliac tendencies."

He continued to gaze at *Ophelia*. "I have a great many tendencies, Rebecca, but I don't want to give away all my secrets in the first month."

She chuckled, took a deep breath and turned towards the books. "So, how on earth am I going to find something amongst all these?"

He said goodbye to the painting with a final glance and walked towards the back wall. "What kind of thing are you after?"

"Am *I* after? Remember this was *your* idea."

"Oh yes, you needed to be forced into it."

"Hey!" She mock-slapped him.

"Why? What's wrong in performing to the audience now and then? Feeling the heat of adulation and awe upon you. It's what you do for a living, is it not?"

"Well, I don't…"

"Oh don't give me that crap that you just do it for the joy of literature. The performing is the main thing, you love it, remember I've seen you post-coital as it were, high as a kite." He was looking at her with an intensity that made her insides churn. She was sure he was going to kiss her. She didn't look away.

"You've got me there. Yes, it's the best feeling. I can't get enough."

"Enough of what?" Jason was standing in the doorway

behind them.

"Bloody hell, Jason, you made me jump."

"We were just talking about the interplay between audience and actors in a theatre. Interesting subject, don't you think?" Seth eyed Jason inscrutably.

"If you say so. I was just going to see if anyone wanted another drink."

"Not for me."

"No thanks."

"Right, well everyone's waiting for you in there."

"Tell them we won't be long."

Rebecca grimaced as Jason skulked off. "I'm really sorry, he's not normally like this. I think he feels a bit, well, threatened."

"He's defending his corner, you mean. Against the foreign invaders."

"Something like that."

"And what do you think about being invaded?"

She eyeballed him. "I'm rather enjoying it."

* * * * *

Catherine watched the two empty seats with growing angst. What was taking them so long? It was embarrassing. Rebecca's poor boyfriend looked humiliated and they could all hear the titters coming from next door. What was she doing behaving like that when she had a boyfriend? Catherine ground her teeth and crossed her legs again. Conversation had become stuttering and eyes kept glancing to the open door, until Jake called out, "Oi, you two. Sometime today would be nice."

"Sorry, this is taking longer than expected. Rebecca seems a bit overwhelmed," Seth called back. More tittering. "Talk amongst yourselves, we'll be out shortly."

* * * * *

109

They went for T.S. Eliot's *The Waste Land* in the end, partly because Rebecca knew it well and partly because it was the nearest thing to drama in Seth's glut of poetry volumes. Apart from Shakespeare, of course, whose best soliloquies were all for men. She just read the first part, enjoying the different voices and the bleak comedy they created. As she finished there was nervous laughter.

"Wow – you read it beautifully but I don't have a clue what it meant."

"That's a relief – I thought it was because I'm Spanish…"

"Any chance you could explain it, Rebecca?"

She laughed. "Not without the help of the Mr Eliot's notes, which are nearly as long as the poem – which is about half a day long!"

Charles stroked his beard. "I seem to remember lots of references to vegetation ceremonies and impotent fishermen." He had a twinkle in his eye. "It was one of our A-Level set texts."

Michael nodded. "And the disjointed structure reflecting the fractured state of society after the First World War, right?"

Instinctively everyone turned towards Seth, whose eyes were in shadow.

"'What is that noise?'
The wind under the door.
'What is that noise now? What is the wind doing?'
Nothing again nothing."

No one spoke. Rebecca heard Jason shift in his seat and sigh a little too loudly.

"'*Do*
You know nothing? Do you see nothing? Do you remember
Nothing?'"

His voice spat scorn and anger. Rebecca saw Anna and José exchange a look; Catherine put her hand briefly on Seth's inert arm. The room hummed with tension. Jason took a slug of brandy.

"Well then." Jake got briskly to his feet. "Time for another drink I think. Rebecca, what're you 'aving?"

Seth remained motionless. *"Now when we look to him we are all afraid. He's pilot of our ship and he is frightened."*

What was he quoting from now? Anna and José frowned at Charles, gesturing for him to do something. He coughed uncertainly. "Yes, definitely time for a break. I, for one, could do with a glass of water."

As if he hadn't spoken, Seth continued intoning the words of *The Waste Land*, staring past everyone towards the window.

"'What shall I do now? What shall I do?
I shall rush out as I am, and walk the street
With my hair down, so. What shall we do tomorrow?
What shall we ever do?'"

Everyone looked alarmed now, Jake frozen like a self-conscious statue with his hands in his pockets. But Rebecca had an instinct; she also had the poem in front of her.

"The hot water at ten.
And if it rains, a closed car at four.
And we shall play a game of chess,
Pressing lidless eyes and waiting for a knock upon the door."

Slowly Seth looked up at her and their eyes locked. As the connection was made he started to look more like himself. Quickly Rebecca hurried into the East End pub scene that followed, hamming up her cockney wench bit to get people laughing. She looked to Seth for the last line of the section which he delivered in sonorous but no longer brooding tones.

"'Good night, ladies, good night, sweet ladies, good night, good night.'"

"Oi – are you trying to get rid of us? I thought I was getting a refill!" There was laughter at José's bad cockney accent and people starting moving, talking, drinking again like someone had pushed the Play button. Rebecca noticed Charles with his arm round Seth by the window. She made her excuses shortly afterwards, sensing that the sands of

Jason's self-control were about to trickle away. As she went to look for their coats she passed Anna and José talking in low voices in the study. Then Seth appeared behind her. His eyes were bloodshot and he seemed unsteady on his feet. He took her hand and gripped it hard. "Goodnight, sweet lady."

"Are you okay?"

"I'm fine. More to the point, are you? I don't think your beloved enjoyed himself too much."

"Oh – " but at this point Jason had returned and they said their goodbyes.

"Bloody hell." Jason couldn't even wait until they'd reached the bottom step.

"He wasn't himself. I don't know what happened."

"You can say that again. Come on, let's walk." He had sobered up and had a spring in his step as he gleefully dissected Seth and his hang-ups. "And did you notice? No photos. Not a single one. Don't you think that's a bit odd? Especially if he's lost his parents."

"Maybe the memories are too painful."

"And all those mirrors. I've never seen so much of myself."

Lacking encouragement, he finally ran out of steam and they walked the rest of the way home in silence. Passing neon-lit kebab shops and boarded-up flats, the words of *The Waste Land* circled Rebecca like vultures.

"*'What shall we do tomorrow? What shall we ever do?'*"

SCENE 18

And you are...?
Charles Maslowe.
Ah yes. Could you tell me, Mr Maslowe, how you first met Seth Gardner?
We were in the same year at St John's College, Cambridge.

He'd gone up to Cambridge because his sister was there.

Most younger siblings he knew tried to break away, go somewhere different, but then their sisters weren't ill. He was at a different college from Sarah, but he could still keep an eye on her and reassure their parents.

It was at a tutor's drinks party in Freshers' Week.

Everyone trying to impress, trying so hard to be liked. Braying voices talking about rugger. Some good-looking girls. Ladies, rather. He felt no need to join in the scrum. A dark-haired chap in a well-cut blazer accosted him by the drinks table.

"I'd go for the red. It's French and quaffable. The sparkling stuff is nasty."

Charles was in the mood for white but felt it would be rude to ignore the advice. He took a sip. "Not bad." What did he know? He'd barely touched the stuff before.

The man extended his arm. "Seth Basildon."

"Charles Maslowe." They shook hands.

"You look like a man who might know something about music."

"Um…"

"I'm after something dark and apocalyptic from his collection." Seth pointed at Dr Cheetham's shelves of records. "You've heard the Wagner rumours?"

Charles smiled. "Do you think it's true?" It was being passed round that Dr Cheetham would signal it was time to clear off by blasting them with Wagner.

"If it is it's predictable. I was wondering if we might offer him another choice. Frankly I'm desperate for any distraction." He made a face in the direction of a couple of young men with bushy hair and suits that hung off them. 'Mathmos'. The plural of Mathmo. Even to Charles they looked like people to avoid.

"Gives us a chance to check out his record collection,

113

anyway. Excuse me." He leaned over towards the tutor and indicated the shelves. "May we?"

Charles started rifling the record sleeves nearest to him, quickly becoming engrossed. Saint-Saëns, Schubert, Schumann, all alphabeticised. When he looked up, his supposed partner in crime was over by the door chatting to two attractive girls. Ladies. Charles felt his face grow a little warmer. He put his hands in his pockets and went back to the drinks table. He'd bloody well have the sparkling this time.

"Don't say I didn't warn you." The glass nearly jumped out of his hand. Seth was back, smiling a little sheepishly. "Sorry about that, I got distracted at Fauré. So then, what's your verdict?

Charles made a non-committal face. "I only had a quick flip. *A Space Odyssey* would seem to fit the bill, though." He spoke casually to show it was of no consequence to him.

The other man nodded slowly, eyes narrowing. "Richard Strauss. An excellent choice. Well, Charles, my instinct wasn't wrong. I was rather hoping you'd pick that one."

Before Charles had a chance to process his words, Seth strode over to the record player and the first blasting chords of *A Space Odyssey* sounded at top volume. Students looked at each other in confusion. Was this their cue to leave? Most of them headed for the door immediately, causing a small crush. By the time Dr Cheetham had spluttered his way to the record player there was almost no one left. The tutor turned to Seth in bewilderment.

"What do you think you're doing?"

Seth was waiting with a million dollar smile. "I didn't want you to waste your wine on people who don't know their Wagner from their Strauss."

They'd ended up drinking port with Dr Cheetham until 3am.

So you became friends.

Yes, he'd clearly passed some kind of test at that moment. Occasionally he wondered how his Cambridge experience might have turned out if he'd failed, gone for Beethoven's 5th or something. More recently, he had taken to wondering how his life might have turned out without Seth in it. Best not to think of that now.

Close friends?
Well, yes, we shared a set in the second year.
A what?
A sort of, ahem, suite. Obviously with two beds. And a shared space.
Good room mate, was he?
Well...

Charles was in the library trying to finish his dissertation. The deadline was in a fortnight and he only had two thousand decent words. Panic simmered as he jotted down notes and tried to focus. For some reason a section of the room had been set up as a dining hall, where a group of first years sat banging their cutlery on the table. He recognised one of them as somebody he'd been at Scouts with as a boy, and wondered if he should say hello. But then a strange alarm began to sound intermittently. It didn't sound like a fire alarm. No one else seemed to take much notice of it. Charles knew that if the alarm didn't stop he would never finish his dissertation. And then he would probably be sent down.

He woke to a terrible piercing ringing in the darkness. It took him a second to reach clumsily for the lamp switch and another to identify the source of the racket – a shiny red telephone newly installed on the coffee table. Why the hell wasn't Seth answering it? He dropped his feet onto cold floor and lunged for the receiver, desperate for the screeching to stop. "Hello?"

"Charlie, you godda help me."

It sounded like Seth but it couldn't be. Seth was in bed in the next room.

"Who is this?"

"You godda help me. I'm in trouble."

"Seth?"

"Come and get me."

He sounded blind drunk. Again. Charles sighed deeply and slumped to perch on the edge of the coffee table.

"Where are you?"

"In Ely."

"*Ely?*"

"I need you to come and get me. Can't stay here."

Charles frowned at the phone. "I can't come and get you from Ely."

"Take my car."

"Don't be stupid, I'm not insured…"

"Please. I need to get home."

"Just get a taxi." He moved to hang up the phone.

"No taxis. I have to get out of here. Car's on Silver Street. Keys are… oh God."

"Seth? Are you okay? What's going on? Seth!" He could hear distant echoes of traffic but nothing else. He must be in a phone box.

"Seth, are you there?"

There was a loud bump in his ear then a slurred whisper, "I don't know what I'm going to do."

He folded. "Look, it's okay, don't worry, just tell me where you are and I'll come and get you."

I, er, well I didn't know what to do for the best.

Rest assured, Mr Maslowe, that driving uninsured is of no interest to us at the moment.

Ah. I see. Well, I got directions from a girl who was at the party.

116

By the time Charles had pulled on yesterday's clothes, found Seth's car keys and persuaded a very grumpy night porter that he had a good reason for leaving college at 3a.m, he'd already wasted twenty minutes. The silver Audi was in its usual place. His hand paused on the handle. But the strangeness of Seth's voice was in his head. The sound of it made him press his foot on the accelerator, checking mirrors and praying there were no police around.

```
It's just... I'd never heard him afraid
before.
```

Good old law-abiding Charles zipping through residential streets at 3am in a car he shouldn't be driving. He knew it made no sense, he and Seth, that it took the cliché of opposites attracting to a new dimension. But it worked, mostly. His parents had told him to have some fun, not to worry about Sarah too much, and fun was something Seth did in style. On some level it thrilled him to be hanging out with the bad boy instead of the swots. In return he supposed he provided some sort of anchor for Seth in the absence of family.

He squinted at the scribbled notes resting on the passenger seat. Left after the pub on the corner. As predicted, he heard music blaring as he pulled up into Wharf Villas. The front door of number three was slightly ajar; since no one stood a chance of hearing his knock, he pushed it open. A bare light bulb blared down on a tangle of semi-clothed limbs and discarded clothes on the stairs. Charles shuddered slightly. Averting his eyes, he followed the hall and turned into the first room he found. Thumping bass and near-darkness stopped him in his tracks; then, as his eyes and ears relaxed, he saw a familiar figure propped against the sofa holding a thin, misshapen cigarette.

"Charlie boy! You made it! Hang on a tick." The figure leaned over to his left making jabbing motions. Without warning the music slammed to a halt.

Whatever Charles had expected, it was not this. Seth had his free hand around a bobbed brunette who looked up at him with unconvincing head control.

"Oi, what you doing? Put the music back." She turned a slack face towards Charles. "Is this your friend then?"

"It certainly is. Charles – get yourself a drink, old chap. There's beer in the kitchen – unless we've drunk it – oops." The two of them started giggling.

Charles stared, feeling jarringly displaced and sober.

"Are you okay, Seth?"

"Okay? I'm fucking fantastic. Must be the weed this charming lady has served me. Did you get a drink?"

"I thought I was supposed to be driving you home."

"But you've only just arrived. Besides I'm – um – starting to enjoy myself." He winked as the woman's head slumped towards his shoulder.

Charles felt an unfamiliar surge of fury. "Fine, well I'm off anyway. Have a good night." His legs shook as he strode towards the door.

"Hey, hey, wait – what the hell's wrong with you?" Seth came lurching after him and flung an arm over his shoulder.

"Fuck!" Something moved and groaned on the floor. Charles threw off Seth's arm and stepped away from the body at his feet, which appeared to be trying to sleep. He faced Seth.

"What's wrong with me? You wake me in the middle of the night, tell me you're in trouble, I drive over without fucking insurance and then you just say 'Hi Charles, want a drink?' Work it out." The expletive registered more than the words. Charles never swore. Seth opened his eyes wider and tottered like a discarded beer bottle.

"Sorry, I'm a twat." Then his face changed. "Poor little Charlie boy, all tucked up in his little bed in his jim jams when along comes the big, bad wolf... oh God..." He made a sudden zig-zag stagger, shoving Charles out of the way and diving towards the door. Bursts of violent hawking from the back of his throat intermingled with the splattering of liquid hitting the ground.

"Fuck, man." The figure from the floor began to crawl towards the lounge. Charles stood with his face turned away as Seth continued to gag and moan.

"God, I feel terrible. Need to go home. Sorry." Seth put his head in his hands and began to cry.

Charles went to pull him up like so many times before. "It's okay. We'll get you home now."

SCENE 19

Such an idiot. Such a bloody idiot. He might just as well have the words 'gullible fool' tattooed onto his forehead.

Safe in the privacy of his room, Michael clenched his fists, letting his frustration explode loudly and wordlessly from the back of his throat. Like a child having a tantrum. A child who didn't like the magic show.

A fucking magic show. That was what happened when you tried to have a serious conversation with Seth. He'd turned up on Saturday all set to have a heart-to-heart, assure himself about Seth's state of mind, and then the doorbell had rung not once but twice more. Catherine, Jose and him, all expecting a private audience with Seth, all worried about him after that strange business with *The Waste Land*. Instead of which it was literally smoke and mirrors and Jake dancing around in that ridiculous costume as he and Seth put on their show. Seth, giddy as a goat, delighted with the way his little surprise had turned out, the others humouring him as per. Exposed as rivals, beneath the banter and bonhomie, all vying to be Seth's number one.

I will not be that person. I will draw back. But I don't know if I can. Or if I can afford to.

Mr Stanley? My colleague asked how the Friday Folly came about. We already have accounts from some of the others but we'd

119

like to hear your perspective.
I'm sorry, I skipped ahead. It was at the
musical evening that Seth hosted. June 1994.
At the time it seemed like a spontaneous
idea. Now, of course, I'm not so sure.

All it needed was a stag's head hanging over the doorway to complete the scene. Oil paintings, period furnishings, chandeliers, chaise longue; the man was a living relic. Every one of Michael's worst fears brought to life like a nightmare. Canapés, old school tie, the hum of polite chit-chat. And here came the orchestrator, clad in black tie and about to pump Michael's hand.

"Delighted you could make it. Are you a purist or will you have a drink?" At the flick of his fingers Catherine appeared with a drinks tray. "Champagne okay? Let me take that from you." Michael relinquished his £3.99 bottle of plonk he now saw was a mistake. Seth glanced at it and deposited it somewhere in the kitchen. Catherine raised her eyebrows as Michael lifted a glass from the tray and took a sizeable swig.

"Dutch courage?"

He laughed without humour. "I can't believe you persuaded me to come. How are you?" She was pale under her smile.

"Oh, you know, terrified. Handing out drinks gives me something to do."

"You'll be fantastic, you always are. Do you know anyone else here?"

She made a face. "I've met some of them."

"Anna – over here." A short Mediterranean-looking man was approaching, with a tall blonde woman behind him. He grinned at them. "So this is where the champagne is hiding."

Michael noticed the flush seeping over Catherine's cheeks as she greeted him.

"Hi, José."

"How are you, Catherine? I see Seth's got you working

120

again." Both he and the blonde woman gave her broad smiles. Catherine wouldn't meet their eyes.

"I'm Michael." He stepped forward to take the attention away from Catherine. The blonde woman gave him a handshake that wouldn't have been out of place in a boardroom. They all talked for a few minutes while Catherine moved away with the drinks tray. They seemed okay, not stuffy and not in black tie. Very loud, especially in the woman's case. Another man joined them, Charles, had been at Cambridge with Seth, but after a few minutes Michael didn't hold it against him. He spoke thoughtfully, although Michael couldn't catch everything he said; some of his words seemed to get lost in his beard. Not the type of friends he'd expected Seth to attract.

Some of the others were, though. By now Michael had nearly finished his glass of champagne and didn't care so much. A vile cellist, Camilla, who called everyone 'darling', kept throwing her head back and whinnying like a horse. He could see Anna and José sniggering at her in the corner. There was a Chinese-looking girl, surely no older than seventeen, and a whole clique of the usual concert-going crowd that Michael avoided. Also a petite, incredibly pretty brunette called Penny who said she was just there because Seth had invited her and didn't know anything about music. Michael tried to get her into proper conversation but whenever he was talking her eyes would drift over towards Seth, like their old family Renault that always pulled to the left.

Seth's introductory address anticipated an evening of shared music-making rather than a recital or competition. Michael felt himself relax a bit. Whatever you thought of Seth he was seductively articulate. And the musical part did turn out to be very enjoyable. The bearded man, Charles, opened with a gorgeous Brahms *lied* – song – that was new to Michael, accompanied by Catherine – so those two must have met before. The Chinese girl got up next, amid whispers that she was some sort of prodigy. She performed an incredibly difficult Rachmaninov Étude, fingers moving almost comically fast while her upper body remained ramrod straight. She bowed to acknowledge the extravagant applause, but didn't smile.

Just his luck to follow that. He had lost concentration on the last part of the Étude and now regretted the champagne as he walked to the piano. He'd chosen Schubert's *An Die Musik* – 'To Music' – because it was short and had a gorgeous piano line. And there was Catherine smiling at him and actually it was fine, all over in a couple of minutes. He even remembered to reach down to the top note in the way his college singing tutor had shown him to avoid the classic tenor yelp. It was slightly uncomfortable performing to such a small audience, though. He knew the received wisdom: look round the room and make as much eye contact as possible to draw people in. The trouble was that Seth was looking at him with an intensity that made it hard to look away. He was also mouthing the words – probably unconsciously, though God knows how, unless he was a German-speaker – but the effect was unsettling, as if they were having a private conversation over other people's heads.

Camilla the cellist's contribution turned out to be as vile as her laugh. Her tuning meandered and her timing departed altogether; Michael started to feel seasick. Some of his kids could have done better. But she still took her bows as if she were Slava Rostropovich himself, reluctant to relinquish the spotlight to Catherine, the last performer. Michael had a suspicion that the whole evening was really an opportunity to showcase Catherine – for motives he didn't fully understand.

She was amazing. It made you realise what you'd been missing with the Chinese girl, whose technique far outclassed Catherine's. Soul. Her fingers gave this shy, self-deprecating woman an eloquence he had never encountered in poetry, an insight he had never found in philosophy. As his tear ducts started itching he caught Seth's eye again. They both looked quickly back at Catherine.

* * * * *

The applause had been far more than she'd deserved, especially with that blunder in the middle section, but Catherine had to admit it felt good. She'd been terrified of showing herself up after the Chinese student's incredible performance. Seth should have told her he was inviting a pianist of that calibre. Of course she'd never have agreed to play, and he knew that. And now she was so glad she had, and he probably knew that too.

People were coming up and saying lovely things. Anna, who never bothered with her much, looked a bit stunned as she congratulated her. Good. She knew Anna and José thought she was Seth's doormat and she was pleased to show there was more to her than handing round canapés or doing his ironing. Michael gave her a big hug and Seth got down on his knees and kissed her hand. That gave Anna something to look at.

* * * * *

Okay, the woman was good, but did he really need to make such a fuss of her? She'd played the piano, not had his baby. To be honest this whole music thing was a bit much. Anna looked at her watch. Would it be sacrilege to suggest going clubbing?

* * * * *

José couldn't help watching Seth differently now he knew the truth. Watching him around women. He was suddenly jealous of their accentuated breasts and curvy backsides. Not that there were many curves going on with Catherine. He saw Anna watching too.

"Bit over the top, don't you think? I mean I know she was good…"

"Come on, you've got to admit, she plays piano like an angel."

Anna shrugged. "You wouldn't want to have a beer with an angel, though, would you? Let alone shag her."

"An-na. Do I detect a note of jealousy?" He asked lightly but there was a catch in his voice. God forbid they should end up chasing the same man.

"Don't be ridiculous. There's just something about her that I don't trust, I suppose. All this butter wouldn't melt stuff, but I've caught a look on her face."

"You women – it's always so complicated between you." They were interrupted by Seth, bringing Charles, Catherine and her friend Michael over.

"Fantastic evening, Seth. Well done."

"Well, don't thank me, thank our three artistes here. I had a good feeling about tonight." He surveyed the small group of them. "You know, I think we might be ready for the next level up."

Charles chuckled. "The next level up? I'm afraid I'm as far up that ladder as I'm ever likely to get."

Seth looked thoughtful. "I don't mean standard. Something else. A regular group, doing this sort of thing – but not just music. Poetry, art – you could bring your paintings, José."

José blinked.

"We could meet here on Fridays. The Friday Group. The Friday… Folly. That's it, the Friday Folly!"

"Folly? You mean silliness? I'm all for that." Anna was starting to slur her words.

"In a way. I'm thinking architectural follies." Seth pointed at Charles. "Ask the expert here."

Charles coughed. "Not exactly much call for follies these days. More offices and shopping malls. Dull though it may sound." He looked at José's blank face. "Sorry. A folly is a building that looks functional but is in fact purely decorative. You see them quite a lot in the gardens of stately homes. Bit of a nineteenth-century fixation."

Seth grinned. "There you go – perfect for our purposes. Give it some thought. I'll be right back." He ushered his protégés on to the next group, Charles calling back over his shoulder something about a giant pineapple in Scotland.

José and Anna looked at each other and giggled. Anna shook her head. "Barking, the lot of them." They watched Seth making more introductions. "What d'you think of Catherine's friend? He looks like he'd rather be somewhere else."

Michael had excused himself and was standing near the French windows, rubbing his glasses on a handkerchief. He pinched the bridge of his nose and closed his eyes for a second.

"Yeah, talked to him a bit. Tall, dark, sexy little glasses too. Just up your street, I would have thought."

Anna narrowed her eyes. "Hmm, I'm not sure I'm up his, if you see what I mean. Hard to make him out. Does something terribly worthy for a living. Made me feel quite superficial."

"Surely not." They shared a complicit laugh. José followed Michael's gaze to a swirly grey-black sky. "Hey, you don't fancy heading into town, do you?"

* * * * *

He leaves as the headache starts. Looking for his coat, he opens a door at the far end of the hall and walks in. A four-poster bed, beautifully made up, is lofting up from the middle of an immaculate room. A hotel room, you might say, but for the huge ceiling mirror glimmering above. Michael flinches like he's been bitten, closes the door on his confusion and leaves less politely than he might.

Outside it is little better. Long, leafy streets speckled with BMW soft-tops stretch in every direction. An unnatural silence hangs over them, not the restful quiet of the countryside but the suffocation of city life with the damper pedal on. The canopy of trees overhead absorbs the sound of his footsteps, making him invisible, a ghost, nothing. He inhales hard, searching for oxygen in the humid air. Why does he feel so much more threatened here than amongst the muggers and joyriders of Finsbury Park? What is he afraid of – someone stepping out of a doorway and offering him a sherry?

He knows that what he is afraid of lies inside him, skulking like a nervous animal, and that something has made it skittish tonight.

He doesn't want to give it wriggle room. He doesn't want to taste its fetid breath in his mouth. He doesn't want to watch the show. But tonight he may have no choice.

SCENE 20

Your friend Anna Carmel tells me you didn't realise that Seth Gardner was bisexual at first. Did it come as a shock, Mr Sanchez?

If the sudden rush of bile into his mouth means shock, then yes. If his legs no longer wanting to support him, the ground no longer wanting to support them, holds significance, then yes. If a casual wink from a face he thought he knew, a face tongue deep in a drunk woman, can bring tears to his eyes, then what do you think? It was a fucking gay bar and he still found a woman to snog.

Later, a text. *So now you know. Hope it doesn't change anything.*

It changed everything and nothing. It changed his understanding of Seth but didn't change his feelings for him.

Next time they met he probed a bit; he'd known gay men who snogged women to throw a smokescreen over their sexuality. Seth evaded his questions for a while and then said quietly, "Judge not, that ye be not judged." José blushed. He knew Seth had never judged him for the way they met. Two piercing eyes were fixed on him.

"I like to fuck who I like to fuck. I don't set limits on it the way you and everyone else does. Cocks and cunts, it's all the same to me, only it's not, of course, it's infinite variety and I never get bored. I love a man's tight butt and a woman's

126

fleshy arse. Rippling pecs one night, quivering tits the next. Is that so hard to understand? Do I need people like you telling me what I really want, who I really am?"

The laser beam of his gaze made José look down, ashamed. "I'm sorry. It's none of my business anyway."

Seth relaxed, reached for a cigarette. "Good. Glad we sorted that out. Bit of an old wound you scratched. Let's go dancing."

Were you angry with him?
Yes, at first. But how can you be angry with someone for what they are? What they are they can't help. What they do, that's another matter.

SCENE 21

The boy with the bogbrush hair sits alone at the piano. Piles of sheet music, three stacked chairs, a metronome and a battered box of descant recorders supervise him. A clock he has never heard before ticks inside his head. The boy notices the cobwebs for the first time, adorning the eaves and crevices like insipid bunting. He inspects his shoes, their scuff marks, the place where the heel is starting to come away from the sole. He sees that the white keys are jaundiced, failing through age and lack of care. He can't bring himself to play a note. He thinks of Mr Johnson and Mr Crane and their jokes, the tone of insinuation, the shame of hearing it all from behind stale, fraying curtains.

He lifts his head at the creak of the door and there he is, Mr Fleming, the light in his eyes that has become a fixture of their lessons, the spring in his step that the whole school has noticed.

"Michael! Not like you to be sitting here quietly. What about a run of E major to get us going? Definitely an E major day!" Mr Fleming chuckles and pulls up a chair to sit next to him.

"Okay, sir." The scale collapses into a fumble of fingers

halfway down. "Sorry." Michael bows his head.

Mr Fleming laughs nervously. "Not such an E major day, eh? Never mind, let's try it again more slowly."

After a third tangle with the scale, Mr Fleming leans over the keyboard to demonstrate. Michael sees chipped fingernails and long, black hairs on the back of pallid fingers. He twists slightly, away from the warm, sour breath brushing his face. The teacher speaks and Michael has to turn towards him, confronting constellations of scattered red pores joined by lined skin, inches from his face. Spectacle lenses flash and take the place of eyes. Michael is breathing through his mouth and hears nothing but he can feel. He feels the hand on his back, a gentle stroke. It's the same hand that moves round to squeeze his thigh. His upper thigh.

Michael starts and pushes back the stool, jumps to his feet. "I – I'm sorry, sir, I don't feel very well." He faces the wall with his hands in his pockets as if he's being punished, trying not to cry. Stifling intimacy throbs in his ears. Then a voice, different from normal, more a husky whisper.

"It's all right, Michael, we'll finish the lesson if you're not feeling well. I'll see you at choir practice on Thursday."

A flash of the teacher's haggard face leaving the room.

He has never known what to think, how to process what happened. Of all the badness surrounding it, the worst is that along with shock at the teacher's touch, he had felt arousal. The part of him that had responded was the part of him he'd recently started touching, at night, when his brother was asleep. His dick, no longer just something to pee with, something that could shoot out another type of deposit, slimy and hot and shameful. Did Mr Fleming know? Was it some sort of test? A warning?

Of course he knew now that it wasn't, but he still couldn't be sure if Mr Fleming had been comforting him... or something more. Now he's a teacher himself he sees the pure vulnerability of the kids, even the mouthy ones. How easy it would be to take advantage of that.

Things had changed between him and his teacher after that day. The teacher who had given him the gift of music, who had believed in him, nurtured him, helped him to rise like scum from the slurry of his youth to be skimmed off into university and a different life. It was not so much a bubble that burst as a balloon that started losing air, leaking trust and easiness until all that was left was a sad, shrivelled scrap. After O-Levels he defied the huffing and puffing of his parents and transferred to a nearby sixth-form college to do A-Levels. He came back in to collect his results, an A in music, of course. Mr Fleming came over to congratulate him. An awkward handshake, churn of feelings. He wanted to say sorry and he wanted to flee from the sadness he glimpsed behind the glasses. That was the last time he saw him.

It was his mother who'd written to tell him, during his second year at Nottingham. He was amazed to see her handwriting on a small brown envelope in his pigeon hole. The first time he'd ever had a letter from her. Inside was the *Yorkshire Post* cutting, *Local teacher found dead in home.* She'd written:

I know you liked him Michael and I thought you'd want to know. Apparently, he was dead for three weeks before anyone found him poor man. People are saying he was lonely and there's talk of some kids picking on him though it was in the holidays so I don't know. Me and your father are well and Mrs Butler across the road, well her daughter Shirley has just had a baby girl. She was in your class I think. I hope you are well. Love Mum.

At the time he'd ripped the letter into shreds and gone running, sopping with sweat and rain, until long after dark. In bed, next to the discarded fragments, the familiar mulch of anger, guilt and shame sucked him down, but this time he allowed himself to cry.

SCENE 22

Were you worried about Seth Gardner after

Worried, disturbed, a strange feeling of impending doom. Like her mind had been taken over by a pack of demons, chuckling and chanting from *The Waste Land* to keep her awake. Even when she touched the edge of sleep they stabbed at her with little pitchforks, invading her dreams so that she woke gasping, over and over again. She saw Seth, his hooded eyes, heard his voice with its empty resonance and the tremor of something that frightened her. She'd rebuffed Jason's advances pretty savagely and in the morning they fought. About Seth. She used his jealousy to beat him, knowing he had every right to it. They made up in the end, but she was glad when he left her earlier than usual on Sunday. She had a phone call to make.

"Hello?" The voice was abrupt, irritable even. She knew immediately she'd made a mistake.

"Oh, hi Seth, it's Rebecca."

"Rebecca, hi." His voice stayed level, registering neither surprise nor pleasure.

"I was just ringing to thank you for a great night on Friday."

"Not at all. I'm glad you enjoyed it."

"Felt a bit rough yesterday, though." Now she sounded like a teenager.

"Then you didn't drink enough to spend the day in a comatose stupor like me. Much the best solution. Before you know it, it's Sunday."

She laughed, relieved at his arch tone. "I'll remember that. So, what are you up to today?"

"Oh, nothing much, hanging out really, as they say over the pond. What about you?"

"Same. Jason's just gone so I've got a bit of time to myself."

"Ah." There was a pause. "And how are things there?" Rebecca had the feeling that he didn't really want to ask but felt he should.

"Oh, you know – a bit up and down. We had a nice brunch today, though." She rushed on, not wanting him to think she'd phoned for a whinge. "I would have phoned yesterday but didn't have the chance. I just wanted to check you were okay – you know, after Friday." She picked at something sticky embedded in the carpet and held her breath.

"Sorry?"

So he was going to make this difficult. "It's just, you seemed a bit – quiet – at one point, and I just wondered if you were all right."

"Ah. To be honest my memory of the evening is a little hazy. I'd probably been deprived of the power of speech by too much whisky. That does happen to me sometimes."

"Oh, well that would explain it." She made her tone bright. It sounded like there was a male voice in the background.

"Look, I'll let you get on with your Sunday – I just wanted to say thanks, really."

"Okay, well hope to see you soon. I'll let you know about the next group."

"Great, see you then."

His end clicked before hers did. She sat with her head between her knees for a minute before thumping the carpet until the side of her hand was red. The dull thuds faded into emptiness as hours till bedtime gaped ahead of her. Jason might be home already. She picked up the phone again and dialled his number.

SCENE 23

So Mr Gardner denied that anything had been wrong when he had you all over to dinner.

Yes. But he did talk to me in the end.

Rebecca's phone pinged in her pocket as she leant over the photocopier. A text from Anna. *drinks thurs 7pm bar retro piccadilly. Ax* Getting a text from anyone other than Jason was still a novelty. She typed *cool see you there. Rx* then changed it to *great*, then back to *cool* and sent it. At least there was something to look forward to this week. Would Seth be there? She wasn't sure if she wanted him to see him or not. Moments from their excruciating phone call plagued her, popping up like leering little imps to ruin her tea break or spoil the taste of her Marks and Spencer's ready meal.

In her lunch hour she rang Leah, who knew where all the trendiest bars were.

"Bar Retro – yeah, it's just off Piccadilly – what's that little street called?" They caught up on what they'd been doing, agreed they must get the cast together again for drinks.

"Hey, have you seen that school friend again? The yummy one."

Rebecca cleared her throat. "Oh – no, not recently."

"Well, do put a word in for me. He's not going along to Bar Retro, is he? I might find myself just passing."

Rebecca mouthed an expletive. "Sorry, love, it's a different crowd."

She arrived at 7.30 and was glad she'd waited. Anna and José had just arrived. Apparently there'd been some sort of drama with a client. She let them whitter on about it, smiling and saying 'shit' and 'thank God' at appropriate moments. Then they wanted to hear about the filming and when she'd be on telly. Anna was warming to her more and more, and she already felt like she'd known José for years. The three of them sank a bottle of wine in fifteen minutes, by which time Michael had arrived. Rebecca asked casually if anyone else was coming.

"Seth might join us later if he's not got lucky. Charles and Catherine are at some recital at the Wigmore Hall."

Rebecca noticed Michael's face tighten. Did he have something for Catherine? Out of the whole group she'd talked to him and Catherine least. As he was sitting next to her she decided to rectify that.

Twenty minutes later she knew all about the social problems in North East London. He was clearly passionate about what he did but she couldn't escape the feeling of being lectured. Maybe that's what being a teacher did to you. Still, he was intelligent and interested in theatre. They talked for a while about using drama to help socially deprived kids, and Rebecca found herself agreeing to run some workshops for him later in the term. Why not, it was probably that or more temping and here was the chance to do something useful.

Every now and then she noticed Michael glance towards the door. Was he hoping Catherine and Charles might come on after their concert? Once again she pushed Seth from her head. She needed to use the opportunity to get to know the others. She and Michael were running out of conversational steam and started to tune into the surrounding chit-chat. Everyone was knocking back the wine, even Michael, whom she had down as a lightweight. Anna was enthusing about her car, a soft-top MG, while José shook his head and Michael shifted pointedly in his seat. Then she stopped mid-sentence and pulled out her phone with a flourish.

"Aha."

"What?"

"New message. Bet it's from Seth."

"What does it say?" Rebecca noticed José check his phone too while Michael muttered about mobiles.

"On my way."

She could almost taste the change in energy. José went to the bar, saying Seth would want a bottle of beer. Michael's restless glances at the door increased. Rebecca ran a hand through her hair and took a slug of wine.

Half an hour later and Seth hadn't arrived. His bottle of beer stood in the middle of the table like a totem of his absence. Everyone kept checking their phone. Another half hour went by. In the end, Anna rang his mobile but it was switched off.

"Maybe he's run out of battery and has got held up."

"You mean he's got a better offer. Typical Seth, doesn't even let us know." Michael's lips were tight.

133

Anna glared. "Why don't you get off his case? We don't even know what's happened." There was a brief, tense silence where everyone listened to 'Pump up the Jam' with unprecedented concentration.

"Anyone for another drink? My shout," offered José. Various murmurs of acceptance; Michael stood up.

"Well, I'm off. You're all mad to wait for him."

"We're not waiting for him, Michael. It's called having a night out." Even José sounded riled. Rebecca looked down at her drink, feeling the hum of group tensions that were new to her. At that moment her phone pinged in her pocket. Frowning, she pulled it out.

Meet me in All Bar One round corner. Don't tell others. S.

She assumed a neutral face as she pocketed the phone, heart thumping.

"Message?"

"Yeah, just Jason."

"Another drink, Becca?" José had stood up.

"Rebecca, I'm off, I'll call you about those sessions." Michael lifted his hand as he left.

"Great, see you soon."

Anna raised her eyebrows. "Date with Michael?"

"Yeah, right. I'm doing some workshops for him. Sorry José, no, I'm heading too, I think."

Anna pulled a face. "Don't mind her, mine's a large glass of white. Catch you later, Becs."

Rebecca said her goodbyes in a flurry, having to turn back for her bag before stepping out onto the street. The air felt sharp in its purity after the dense smoke of the bar and her chest tightened as she strode out towards Soho. Twice she looked over her shoulder like a spy in a James Bond film. Who did she think might be following her? Life had got weird.

As she entered the bar she saw him smiling at her from a free table, the post-work drinks crowd starting to thin. Rebecca opted for a semi-smile as she sat down. He handed her a glass of white wine and moved his Fedora hat from the table to the seat next to him.

"Did anyone see you come here?"

She laughed drily. "Sorry, have I just stepped into a John Grisham novel? Why the secrecy?" She felt spikier towards him after their last phone conversation.

He smiled. "Touché. I was heading over to meet you all when I suddenly thought, 'I'd much rather see Rebecca on her own.' Didn't feel like doing the whole big group thing. So that's why I sent the message. And you came."

She looked down at her glass. "Yeah, I felt strange slipping away like that." She wasn't going to be won over quite so easily.

"Well, thank you anyway. No one would dream of looking for me here, amongst all these working types. How was the evening?"

She nodded. "Pretty good."

"Just pretty good? Any domestics?"

Rebecca couldn't help a smile. "Well, Anna and José got a bit annoyed with Michael."

Seth made his eyes wide. "Why?"

Too late, she realised her mistake. "Oh – I'm not really sure. I thought there was probably some sort of history there. But you'd know more about that than me." She took a sip of her wine.

He gave her a searching look for a second then chuckled. "Fine, I'll get it out of Anna. But let's not talk about all of them now."

Rebecca leaned back. "So what do you want to talk about?"

He fished a cigarette out of the silver box and spent a few seconds lighting it. Finally he sat back too and looked at her. "I think I owe you an apology. Well, I know I owe you an apology."

Rebecca raised her eyebrows. "Why's that?"

"The other day when you phoned and I played dumb... I was a bit taken aback, to be honest. That you asked. But I do know what you were referring to."

She took a sip of wine. "Oh. I'm sorry if I put you on the spot. I just felt a bit concerned afterwards."

Neither of them spoke for half a minute. Seth tapped his cigarette over a thick glass ashtray.

"Rebecca, do you know what I mean by the black bird?"

"Blackbird?"

"No, the black bird. Churchill called it the Black Dog. To me it's a bird that swoops down and hovers over your head."

She had no idea what he was talking about. "I think so."

"Do you? At the time I thought you did, you seemed to know how to respond to me, but later I wasn't sure."

It was her turn to struggle to explain herself. "I did know how to respond, I just had an instinct what to do – it was weird. But I'm not sure I've experienced the black bird myself."

Seth exhaled smoke slowly. "You'd know if you had. One flap of its wings can snuff out all the joy in the world."

Jack Chisholm, she thought, her first heartbreak, those nightmarish few months before her parents packed her off to Cornwall. And something else, blurry and indistinct at the edge of her memory. She ran her finger around the rim of her wine glass. "Or maybe I do know. It's a time in my life I try not to think about."

He nodded. "The poem you read, *The Waste Land* – well, it has some particular associations for me. I thought I could handle it but clearly I couldn't."

She put her hand over his. "I'm sorry. You shouldn't have let me read it."

"No, I wanted you to – after all it's an incredible poem. Eliot's masterpiece. Far better than all the other stuff after he'd found God."

She understood the squeeze of her hand was also a cue to let go; they both took a sip of wine. Seth leaned back. "I mean, why is it that angst and pain and despair makes so much better art than peace and hope and happiness?"

She thought about it. "Well, comedy can be a wonderful thing too."

"Can it? Does anyone really prefer *A Midsummer Night's Dream* to *Lear*?"

"Maybe not to *Lear* but certainly to *Hamlet*." They both laughed.

"It's the same in music. Mozart – well, I just can't get worked up about him. Give me a bit of Beethoven or Tchaikovsky any day. Composers who knew about suffering." She nodded, not sure she'd be able to tell any of them apart. Something crossed his face.

"What is it?"

His eyes trawled her face. "Nothing. You remind me of someone, that's all."

"Dare I ask who?"

He smiled. "My fingers are itching for untouchable things, Rebecca."

Was he quoting something? She remembered his hands in her hair last time they met.

He stubbed out his cigarette. "You stir up embers I thought had long settled. And I find they're still hot." Watery lights came on, making them blink. He shook his head, breaking her trance. "God, is that the time already?"

"Drink up please, ladies and gents."

"Hurry up please, it's time," she quoted, remembering *The Waste Land*, in her best Peggy Mitchell voice. Seth chuckled.

"This bloody country and its licensing laws. This wouldn't be happening to us if we were sitting in a bar in Madrid now."

"Well, there are plenty of other places we could go. If…"

He reached for his jacket. "Hmmm, tempting but I should probably shoot. Quit while I'm ahead." Disappointment clanged hollow in her belly.

He touched her arm. "But Cinderella shall go to the ball. Special Christmas edition of the Friday Folly a week on Friday. I know it's a bit early but it can get us all feeling festive."

It was her turn to go to Milton Keynes that weekend. "Sounds good. Dare I ask what the theme is this time?"

He held open her coat for her. "Well, the theme is

Christmas but there's nothing to prepare. All will be revealed on the night."

She laughed. "So once again I turn up at your house with no idea what I'm letting myself in for."

He kissed her goodnight and stroked a strand of hair away from her face.

"You've got it."

ACT 2 - PROLOGUE

Time for a quick refresher while we reintroduce the players. Take your seats, here they come.

First up, it's *Michael*, looking like he just got out of bed, but of course we know he's doubly cursed with wild hair and a mind that rests on higher things. That gesture – taking his glasses off and squinting – is a bit of a trademark and not just because of the lights.

Following him is *Catherine*, or Cath-in-a-cardy as Anna might say. Mousy bob and an eye colour you won't remember, she hates the spotlight. See her shrinking into Michael?

Approaching with something of a proprietorial air is *Charles*. He's reaching for Catherine's hand but it's too early to bow so he just stands there looking a bit awkward. Coughing, probably, it's too far away to tell.

Now *José* comes running up, nimble on his toes, big smile, no doubt wearing some shade of green. Yes, it's his trainers tonight, he might be off clubbing afterwards. And where there's José there's *Anna*, striding forward, bouncing from her hair downwards, sounding off about something or other and laughing with a Northern Irish accent.

No need to tell you to look at the sashaying siren now claiming the stage. It's *Rebecca*, the only pro, as if you couldn't tell. Come on, you would if you looked as good as her. You'd certainly swish your hair over your shoulders like that if it shone like fire opal under the lights.

The group is parting now to let someone through. You know this one. Dark haired, moves like an assassin, face in

139

shadow. But they're all watching him so intently that they don't notice the last person join the line. *Jake*. He's hard to miss really. A blonde-streaked bear, if you can imagine such a thing. Chewing gum, as ever. It's probably about time we heard from him.

SCENE 1

The missing jigsaw piece. Thank you for coming in. Could you tell me how you met Seth Gardner? Sit back, Mr Etheridge. You look uncomfortable.

That obvious, is it? Yep, 1995 it was. May.

Tip-top morning, one of those days where summer suddenly arrives and people slide pasty legs into creased shorts. Everyone was out. There couldn't be a better day to run a waterside restaurant. Of course Jake didn't own the restaurant, but with the way he was bringing in the punters he hoped he might get a share in it soon. Today he'd do a couple of salad specials for the ladies and a barbeque for the blokes. A barbeque was perfect because it meant he could be outside, doing the hospitality stuff as well as the cooking. People loved that. It was his chance to show the front of house staff how charm was really done.

"Oi, Warren. Rise and shine, my lad. Them peppers ain't about to peel themselves." His eighteen-year-old sous chef was shaping wooden as ever, gazing vacantly through eyes that had clearly seen a lot of pints the night before. Kids today had no staying power. One night on the town and they felt they were owed a day off, probably with their mum's cooking them a nice fry-up and wiping their runny arses.

Warren grunted and made towards the pile of peppers.

"Look sharp, they ain't gonna bite you. And when you've done them there's a load of mushrooms in the fridge that need chopping."

140

Jake went over to the meat board, whistling. He resisted the urge to give a sharp pinch to Emma's arse as it bustled past him. Not the done thing these days. Instead he tipped her a wink.

"Awright, darling?"

She grinned. Gloria, senior waitress and resident sourpuss, tutted at both of them. "There's tables need setting out there, Emma."

Emma saluted. "Yes, ma'am." She winked back at Jake as she strolled towards the dining room.

By one o'clock the garden was packed with his target group: yuppies. High disposable income, no responsibilities, planning to stay in their twenties forever. Jake's experience of his twenties could not have been more different. From having it all at twenty-six – wife, flash car, big house in the suburbs – to losing it all a year later, along with his freedom. Now at thirty-five and on his third lifetime, he was going to get it right.

A crowd was gathering round the barbeque, watching him whip fish kebabs, Texan steaks and veggie skewers on and off the hot plate, all the while delivering a running patter of what he was doing and how he'd prepared them. Better than Anthony Worrall Thompson or whatever his name was. Sweat ran down his hairline as he joked with his customers but the cheeky boy smile didn't desert him once. 'Cheeky boy' was one of a number of labels that followed him around, along with 'chancer', 'barrow boy' and 'gift of the gab'. It didn't bother him; people could make him fit whatever stereotype they liked as long as he got what he wanted from them in the end. As Lester used to say, life was just a series of transactions – and he'd learned the hard way that staying in credit was the only thing that mattered.

The punters were in high spirits but there was one table making twice as much noise as the others. Jake glanced over a few times, wondering if they would come to the barbeque. There was nothing particularly remarkable about them as a group, except that they had an obvious leader. The body language changed each time the man with the dark hair spoke. Everyone leaned in and listened, and invariably exploded with laughter when he finished. That was power. Jake felt a stirring of interest and self-interest. When the latest batch of fish kebabs was done he stuck his chewing gum behind his ear and headed over with a tray of bait.

"Afternoon, all." A sweet breeze of spring flowers tickled his nostrils and he squinted against the hazy sunshine. "Fancy a bit o' Lilian Gish?" No harm in hamming up the geezer bit.

A brief silence then the dark-haired man laughed and they seized on his tray, babbling with lager-fuelled delight and explaining the concept of Cockney rhyming slang to the small Spanish one while cracking 'Manuel' gags. Monkfish and prawns went down a treat. Jake slipped into conversation with them, making them laugh, completely comfortable despite the fact that they were all craning their necks to look up at him and he had the sun in his eyes. The blonde woman on the end even shuffled up and invited him to sit down. Jake had to decline, but made her promise that they would all head over to the barbeque. He returned just in time to rescue his steaks.

Half an hour later he had a new gang of groupies, munching and bantering around the grill. He didn't usually like his customers but there was something about this group that lit a flicker inside him. Yes, they were middle class, full of themselves, but there was something a bit different, even dangerous going on too. It stemmed from the ring leader, Seth. He looked like someone who lived life to the full – someone, maybe, a bit like him. Jake didn't hesitate to accept the invitation to join them after his shift.

I can understand that this meeting might not be particularly relaxing to you, Mr Etheridge, given your history, but I do need to ask you for some more details.
Fine. It's practically legal anyway.

"How did you know?" Seth was looking delightedly at the little pile of pills peeping out of Jake's curled palm. "Thought we'd left it too late tonight."

"Call it an educated guess." It was a big risk and he'd been lucky. If he'd called that one wrong he'd have been back at his flat in no time cooking corn beef hash for one. But something had told him this person would be a fellow boundary-pusher.

"How much?"

"How many do you need?"

Seth looked over his shoulder. "Me, José, Anna – just three, I think. We might forget to mention this to Michael and Charles."

"The two on the end?"

"That's right. Not really their scene."

"And what about the woman who was sitting next to you earlier?" The killjoy who'd scarcely given him eye contact.

"Catherine – she's gone home. Turns into a pumpkin at midnight. And doesn't do nightclubs."

"Gotcha." The group got more interesting. Factions and politics. Jake wondered what it was that pulled them all together. He counted four pills into Seth's hand. "Let's call it £30."

"Here's £40 for your trouble."

They smiled at each other. "Nice doing business with you. Now, shall I go distract the old codgers while you sort the others out?"

It was a cracking night. The pills were top notch and Jake tipped his head back to watch the crazy play of neon on the ceiling, laughing and loved-up with people he'd known for a few hours. This was what he'd been missing. He knew he had to play things straight for a while but it didn't need to be poker straight, did it? There hadn't exactly been a lot to laugh about recently; things had been tough since getting out, tougher than he'd expected, and maybe he deserved a bit of fun. Not everyone would see it that way, of course. Not the family of Charlie Piper. But he'd done his time, paid his debt, and there was no point flogging a dead horse.

He'd been staying away from his old mates for so long that he'd forgotten the gap they had left. Now, watching Seth and Anna bumping and grinding, watching José close his eyes and sway, even watching Michael and Charles doing dad dancing, he tasted the high of being part of a group. When he caught Seth's eye the smile seemed to break from inside him rather than being something he wore. It had been a long time.

SCENE 2

You don't much like Jake Etheridge, do you?
I   always   knew   there   was   something untrustworthy about him. And I was right, wasn't I?

Catherine slammed her fingers down on the piano keys as she used to do as a child when she couldn't get it right. She'd slept okay, it was Sunday, it wasn't raining and she had a good book on the go. So why was she stomping round her flat like a three-year-old? The others would still be bed-bound, no doubt, warding off the moment when they would have to sit up and acknowledge they'd drunk too much. Or worse. At least that wasn't her. But the thought gave her no relief, not even a sneaky smug smile. If anything she envied them. Later they'd all huddle up on Seth's sofa, groaning and sporting their hangovers like a badge of honour, membership to an exclusive club. While she would potter round doling out tea and sympathy. Usually she didn't mind – if anything it made her feel useful. Seth always called her his hangover angel, and she did enjoy looking after him when he was so sweet, feeble and grateful. But it would be nice sometimes to be part of the club.

She didn't know why she found it so hard to feel a part of things. Especially with women. There was a gene she didn't have, a gene for gossip and secrets and endless boyfriend analysis. That was why at work she preferred auditing a company to being in the office; at least in an unfamiliar organisation, no one would wonder at her eating her sandwich alone.

She's not a self-pitying person, she's sure she isn't, but she feels the cool slide of tears down her cheeks. A cup of camomile tea will help, it always does, and she takes it and sits on her bed, pristinely made up in white. Things aren't so bad. She's a London girl now, a professional with her own flat – rented, but still – and she's proud of herself. She doesn't want to be part of the hangover club, not really, not after all that Granny business. It would be enough to put anyone off booze for life. She shudders when she watches people get drunk, losing control of their movements, speech, emotions. She knows Seth drinks too much. It's the one subject she dare not raise with him. Instead she makes sure she's always there to pick up the pieces afterwards.

No doubt there will be several pieces to go at today. Catherine saw at a glance what sort of person Jake was. Not to be trusted. It was strange that the others gravitated to him like that. Smiles were cheap, and his face looked like it had done a lot of smiling over the years. The crinkly twinkliness of his eyes put her teeth on edge. It was a face too used to charming.

She drains her camomile tea and sighs. Seth loves Jake of course. He's so trusting, so generous, an overflowing honeypot to someone like that. She will need to be on her guard.

Only Mr Gardner did trust Jake Etheridge. He let him into his inner circle.
I know, you don't need to remind me.

"Honey, I'm home!" It was a week later and she'd had the Steinway to herself for most of the day. Seth banged the front door shut and dropped his keys on the table. Catherine broke off from a swirl of chromatic scales. "Hello. You look pleased with yourself."

"Indeed I am. What are you doing next Saturday?"

She pretended to think. "Nothing, as far as I know."

"Well, you are now."

"And what am I doing exactly?"

"Having dinner at mine."

"Great." She looked at him questioningly. There was clearly more to it. "Do you want me to cook?"

He tapped a dotted rhythm on the table. "That's the thing – Jake will be doing the cooking."

"Oh."

Seth lit a cigarette. "Isn't that nice of him?"

"He offered?"

"Yes, I said I loved holding dinner parties but found the whole cooking thing a bit of a bore, and he stepped in straight away. So I'm meeting him later to draw up a menu. He'll be ideal for the Friday Folly. I can't believe I've never thought of cultivating a friendship with a chef before." He settled onto the sofa and took a long drag of his cigarette. Then he saw Catherine's face. "Fuck, I've offended you. You know I love your food."

The piano felt like a barrier between them. "Of course you haven't – I mean, he's a proper chef and I would never compare my stuff to his. It's just, well, you don't exactly know him well, do you?"

Seth crossed his legs. "What do you mean?"

"I don't know… you just seem to be seeing a lot of him suddenly." She moved away from the piano and perched on the edge of an armchair. Seth tapped his cigarette over an ashtray.

"I like him. I act on impulse about these things. I didn't exactly know you well when I bought you your piano, now did I?" He folded his arms and an arrow of shame pierced her chest.

"I suppose not." She couldn't look at him, wanted to cry.

"Hey. Come here." He patted the sofa and she went to him like a puppy. He squeezed her hand. "I didn't mean to make you feel bad. I just think Jake will be a really fun person to have around."

She sniffed and tried to smile. "I'm sure you're right."

SCENE 3

Has there been any conflict between you and Seth Gardner? You're smiling, Mr Stanley.
Seth and I generally didn't agree on a great deal.
I'm talking major fallings out, not minor verbals. Does anything spring to mind?
It does. Glyndebourne.
Glyndebourne?
Three summers ago, I think. 19 - 94. Yes. August 1994.

Michael watches London backpedal in a soft-focus whirl, red brick houses blurring and melding as if in a dream. In this dream he's sitting in a soft-top Porsche, the wind doing crazy things to his hair, or rather his hair doing crazy things in the wind. He folds his chin down over his chest and realises that he's in full black tie regalia, down to a cummerbund. Next to him in the driver's seat is Seth. They are on their way to Glyndebourne, the privately owned opera house full of toffs drinking champagne.

The taste of the dusty wind was real enough. Perhaps he'd been spliced in two, leaving behind the 'killjoy'– Seth's label – to mutter about elitist bastions of privilege while his treacherous musical mojo hot-footed it into the car to catch Roger Norrington doing the *Magic Flute.*

The killjoy had insisted on jeans as a condition of release but Seth had seen straight through that one and instantly revoked the invitation. So here he was, dressed up like a dog's dinner with his hair providing the only slight subversion.

They were in the countryside now. Michael was no lover of the tame flatlands of the south but today the haziness of the light resting on the softness of the landscape created an ethereal beauty. Expanses of hay-baled fields yawned and stretched on all sides. It was the perfect night for Glyndebourne, picnic and all. Michael shifted in his seat, suddenly frivolous, a child on an adventure. He wanted to ask Seth to put his foot down.

Instead he leaned out slightly and closed his eyes as the wind rushed over his face. Seth glanced over.

"You okay?" He had to shout a bit, like a character in a sitcom.

"Enjoying the scenery. Ages since I've been in a car."

"I suppose it makes a change from pedalling. Nice to get out of the city, isn't it?"

"Yeah, I don't do it often enough."

The wind put paid to further conversation. It was odd seeing Seth drive – incongruous somehow, but it suited him. Turned out in addition to the Jaguar, he had this Porche stashed away in a garage somewhere. He looked gleeful behind the wheel, shirt sleeves rolled up, right elbow resting on the window frame. Michael looked away.

"Nearly there now. You'll see the house in a minute."

Ten minutes later they pulled up in the car park and Michael got his first proper view of the opera house. Nestling modestly yet modishly in the classic English country estate, it had won, so Seth told him, various design awards.

"I'm not always a fan of modernisation but the old house had more appendages than an Indian goddess – it just wasn't big enough." Seth sighed. "Although, sadly, this one does open things up more to the masses."

He laughed as he saw Michael's colour rising.

"Come on, enjoy being one of the elite for a day. You never know, you might like it. Or maybe that's what you're afraid of."

He got out of the car before Michael could put him right.

They had two hours to stroll around, or more precisely to scout and secure the best picnic spot. Michael found himself entering into it with an enthusiasm that amused his companion.

"You're like a German with a beach towel," Seth said, as they lugged an enormous picnic hamper to the chosen place, somewhere between the two ponds.

Michael ignored him. "Come on, it's just past the Ha Ha."

Seth grinned. "Words I'm sure you never thought you'd utter."

It was true. Michael stopped abruptly and put his end of the basket down.

"What's the matter? Hurting your back? Or your conscience?"

Michael took off his glasses and rubbed them on a hanky. It was like an out-of-body experience, the whole thing. What the hell was a Ha Ha anyway? "If my Year Nines could see me now." He shook his head.

Seth cackled theatrically. "You have sold your soul to the dark side, Doctor Faustus." They heaved up the picnic basket and carried on.

After a rip-roaring first half they opened the basket and Michael understood why it had felt like shifting a coffin. Seth coughed.

"I just told the guy at Selfridges food hall to give me a bit of everything."

They unloaded rows of plastic tubs with unlikely smells that tweaked at Michael's stomach, laid them on the red tartan picnic blanket. There wasn't much space left for sitting. Seth produced two dinner plates and grinned.

"The food may have travelled in plastic but we're sure as hell eating it from china. Grab the cutlery and I'll open the champers."

They clinked glasses. "Here's to your corruption."

Michael smiled. "You'll be lucky." But he drank anyway, with an eye on the tub of cockles. With any luck they were doused in vinegar, the northern way.

Later, when the encores and the hoorahs had faded into the night, Seth insisted on driving him all the way home.

He drove you home? Hadn't he been drinking?

Yes, but somehow that hadn't seemed important at the time. There was another reason why Michael had wanted dropping at the Tube.

Seth raised an eyebrow. "Come on, I do go to areas outside of West London, you know."

Michael scowled. "It's not that." But of course it was; he felt a twinge of embarrassment that Seth would see where he lived and his scowl deepened. Why should he be ashamed of who he was?

As the fields darkened, conversation flowed again. Seth sounded him out about the new group he wanted to form, the Friday Folly. Once again Michael felt a fault line opening inside him. He loved music, books, the arts. But something about this group whispered elitism. The more time he spent with Seth, the more blurred his own values and opinions became.

"You don't like the idea?"

"I'm not sure."

Seth shot him a glance. "You like the idea but you don't approve of it. Just like tonight. Christ, it must be hard work walking in your shoes."

"I just think there's more to life than pursuing one's own pleasure. Surely even you've heard of the concept of principles?"

His companion laughed. "Such a charming, archaic concept. The problem with principles is that not everything is black and white, good or bad. What do you do with all the stuff in the middle?"

Michael fiddled with his watch. "I think it mostly falls on one side or the other."

Seth looked at him. "But sometimes you don't know which until you try."

They pulled up outside the council flats next to his house. Two kids mooched over, checking out the car. Seth switched off the engine.

"Would you like me to go in with you?"

The kids swaggered off and Michael laughed. "Not so used to this end of town, after all? I'll be fine."

And then Seth was leaning over, and without thinking, Michael mirrored him. Their lips connected and for a second or two his thoughts stopped. Then blood rushed to his head and he shoved Seth's face away hard.

"What the hell are you doing?"

He grabbed the door handle, arm trembling. Seth was holding his left cheek and spoke quietly. "I could ask you the same question."

"So this was your plan, eh? Free opera tickets to suck me into your – debauchery?"

Seth gave him an acid smile, colour creeping back to his face. "Don't tell me you didn't want it."

Michael thought he would lunge then, throttle the mocking smile off that face, but through the driver's window he saw two sets of teenage eyes watching them. He wrenched open the door, struggling with his seat belt. Seth snorted.

"Go on – off you run."

Michael gave the door a slam it wouldn't forget, not looking back as he strode to his front door. Only as he twisted the key in the lock did he hear the car revving and setting off at speed. Once inside he smashed his fist on the wall and roared. Then he climbed the stairs and let himself into the warm, sour darkness of his flat.

Thank you, Mr Stanley. To clarify, Mr Gardner made unwelcome and entirely unreciprocated sexual advances to you that night?
Correct.

Michael slept in a web of ghoulish dreams where he was kissing Mr Fleming's corpse as it hung above his parents' kitchen table. His teacher's dry lips were crumbling like digestive biscuits and Michael couldn't help swallowing bits.

He woke gagging and spitting and stumbled to the bathroom, stuck his head under the tap. When he raised his head his eyes stared like the corpse of the dream and he unconsciously bit his lips. He saw the bath in the mirror and started running the taps, climbing in and letting the water rise around him until it was deep enough to submerge his head. He stayed there for an hour. When he got out he was cold and had to pad through to the bedroom to find a clean towel. The clock on the chest of drawers said 6.13am.

There was no point going back to sleep, so he sat in bed with a coffee listening to nameless objects providing rattling percussion to the rumble of the Tube. An almost forgotten sound joined them: rain pattering steadily against the window. The weather charm of the past few weeks had finally broken. He let his thoughts drift with the rain, splash across memory, until they alighted on Ursula, black and glowing and radiant. He wondered how she was doing in her West London girls' school. He wasn't sure if she had really wanted the job or had been driven away by the awkward silences and accidental eye contact in the staffroom. It was a relief when she left.

They had dated for nearly a year, Michael's first relationship, though she never knew that. He saw in her, at least at first, the heat and colour and intensity of his year in Tanzania. The vast mandarin sky. Caked mud in his hands, hands that were soiled and real for the first time in his life. Spontaneous eruptions of music that made him wish he could shed his English skin and writhe to the rhythms as Adin did. But Ursula was a South London girl with no interest in Africa. When he asked about her roots she grinned and said she had a hair appointment on Thursday. She was evasive about slavery, had no problem living amongst the colonial oppressors of her ancestors. She was beautiful and her taut black body drove him to premature ejaculation again and again. Over the year, shame turned to anger until eventually he blamed her though could not say why. She cried when she ended it.

Maybe he'd go back to Africa one day. He was still in

touch with Adin, whose latest letter lay tea-stained by his bedside. Adin taught too now, in the school they had built together that magical summer. He kept telling Michael to come over and see the fruits of their labour, hear the little ones sing "Twinkle, Twinkle" and the big ones talk of being engineers or doctors, even the girls. Michael had never gone. He told himself it was the money, but sitting here now, with the rain tapping at his subconscious, he knew there was more to it. Maybe he just wanted to keep that summer perfect, intact and tucked away.

Or maybe revisiting that time would throw too much relief onto what he was doing now: trying to change the world with one tinny piano and a few descant recorders. He was the anomaly in the staffroom, the one who didn't join in with the gags, the racism, the constant complaints about the kids and the area, the stream of applications to selective schools. And if friendships were thin on the ground, his romantic life was a desert.

There had been no one since Ursula. No one Michael had even been interested in. Sometimes he thought he was asexual. Sometimes he thought that would be easier. And now a memory made him flinch and clench his fists. He wasn't gay – he would have known. It wasn't that he had a problem with it; gay or straight, that wasn't the point. It was Seth. He was poison. But the harder Michael tried to run from him, the more he was yanked back like a tethered animal.

You must have been angry with Mr Gardner.
Yes. For a while.
You made up?
He sent a note.

Smooth, charming, apologetic. Hoping it wouldn't spoil anything between them.

And he never did it again.

SCENE 4

John Lennon was doing his usual end-of-year cameos, popping up like Banquo's ghost to deliver his vaguely ominous Christmas greeting. Rebecca hummed along with the radio, pleased to be able to give him a straight answer this time. She'd done plenty. She thought back over the year: *Hamlet*, meeting Seth and the group, even doing her workshops for Michael's school, which she'd enjoyed more than she'd expected. They'd gone so well that they invited her back for a second week and managed to find some money in the budget to pay her with. There was a buzz in doing something 'useful' for a change, a different sense of achievement.

Michael was worried that some of the kids would play up but she saw those lads on the back row looking at her legs and knew she'd be fine. Men were all the same. And the kids had really enjoyed themselves, once they'd stopped worrying about looking cool in front of their mates. Some of them gaped at her in awe after she delivered the Lady Macbeth soliloquy, throwing her voice as if she were in a theatre. It gave her a power, the same power she exploited night after night, but it felt good to be putting something back at the same time. Even if just one of those kids had their horizon widened as a result it would have been worth it.

Not a bad twelve months all in all. She settled back on the sofa with a coffee, pulling her knees under her and retying her faded, green dressing gown. Threadbare and coffee-stained as it was, she couldn't bring herself to throw it away. Partly her inherently slobbish nature, partly… well, she hadn't been that close to her grandma but it was a present from her, the last present, and her mum was pleased she still wore it. They almost never agreed on the subject of clothes. Rebecca put it down to her mother being older than other people's mothers. She'd had Rebecca in her forties after years of trying. There had been two of them, twins, but her sister had died at birth. It made her feel funny to think she was half of a whole and would never know her other half. She used to complain when she was little about everyone having brothers and sisters apart from her and her parents would look pained. They only told her the truth when she was thirteen.

She must have known something at the time. There's a shadowy memory of a big man in a grey room talking to her about wetting the bed, which she did until she was seven. She suspects she had some sort of counselling but she's never asked. When she hit adulthood she saw it suddenly from her parents' perspective, losing one of their children after a traumatic birth. Once, after a few drinks on her birthday, her mum said sorry to her about her early childhood. But all Rebecca remembered was love and attention, being the apple of their eye. She knew she was lucky in many ways. The only problem was that her parents were getting old. Maybe she was hanging onto the dressing gown to avoid facing the fact that things were changing.

But it did have a hood. On days like this, when the heating was still cranking up and a thieving draught rattled the single-glazed window panes it was comforting to put the hood up and hunch around like an old woman. Especially without Shaz around to take the piss.

She contemplated the night ahead, the mysterious Christmas group. The only clue she'd had from Seth, after much cajoling, was that, for one night only, the group would be the Friday Follies, as in the French word for cabaret. He seemed pretty pleased with his pun. Anna and José had been unable or unwilling to shed any light on it when she'd met them on Wednesday. Michael was grumpy about the whole thing but said he was going. It was odd that he was so openly hostile towards Seth but still turned up to everything. Maybe it was to see Catherine.

The sharp trill of the phone made her jump. She grabbed it to stop the noise.

"Becky?"

"Hi, Jason." A sigh inside her. "What's up?" She grabbed at the remote control and turned the radio down.

"Just wanted to check you hadn't changed your mind about coming tonight."

This time her sigh was audible. "You know I'm busy. I'll come as soon as I can in the morning."

"Okay. Look, I'd better go. See you tomorrow then."

He hung up to mask his hurt. She knew him, knew that he had a right to be hurt. She knew him better than she'd probably ever know Seth. And in the knowing was a security she couldn't give up. She was being unfair, hedging her bets, and he was letting her.

No. This wasn't a day for guilt. She thought about the dress she'd wear later, black and lacy and oh so short. An answering bolt of excitement. She got to her feet, caught sight of herself in the lounge mirror in her green hood and cackled.

SCENE 5

So we move to 6th December 1996 for your Christmas group. Could you talk me through the sequence of events?

Well… I mean, obviously I'll try, but, well, I did get a bit drunk later and I'm not sure I'll remember everything. You should talk to the others as well.

I assure you we are asking all members of the group for their own accounts of the evening.

Of course. Sorry. It would be interesting to know, you know, what the different perspectives are. What we remember of that evening… or not…

* * * * *

Bloody hell, the woman was gorgeous. Even more so than usual tonight. Jake struggled to keep his eyes on her face but gave up almost immediately, the old "Look at you!" line

156

legitimising a full head-to-toe appraisal. Patterned black stockings. High heels. Lacy black dress finishing mid thigh. It didn't get much better than that. Slipping a hand on her back he leaned into her, the way women liked. He caught Seth's eye and they both pursed their mouths expressively over her head. Christmas had come early this year.

* * * * *

One look at Jake's face told her how good she looked. When he put his arm round her, she leaned in, the way men liked, looking up at him as she laughed and chattered. Then she spotted Anna across the room hesitating just a fraction before coming over and greeting her. The second confirmation she was looking good. The push-up bra was helping her silhouette no end. She pretended not to notice Seth and Jake exchange a look. It was hardly something to be offended about. She dropped her cardigan at the door.

* * * * *

Rebecca caused a stir, of course, dressed to kill and didn't she know it. Even as a gay man José couldn't help appreciating the lacy undulations. He showered her with compliments and took care not to notice the way Seth was looking at her. Jake passed her a glass of champagne.

"For the gorgeous Ophelia. Or should I say, oh feel ya!" General groans. Rebecca didn't seem to mind as Jake squeezed her waist.

"You've been rehearsing that one."

"Maybe." Jake winked and looked around. "Who's for more champers? We're on Bolly for our jolly. Rather an upmarket jolly, of course, in our exclusive W2 surroundings."

Seth offered his cigarette box around. "I think edgy is the word you're looking for. If I wanted exclusive I'd be living in stuffy old South Ken like Charlie boy." He raised his eyebrows at the sniggers of dissent. "What? It's true. I'm much happier amongst the riff-raff of Notting Hill."

Anna roared with laughter as Michael shook his head. "Was there ever someone more cushioned from reality?"

"*Au contraire,* my dear Anna, I seek to embrace as much reality as life will allow me. You should know that."

Was Anna blushing? She recovered herself quickly. "It's just a different reality from those of us who have to work for a living."

Seth blew smoke upwards. "You're like a stuck record, darling. Like every working woman."

"Time, you two." José stepped in, before Anna's inevitable explosion. "Let's remember it's Christmas."

* * * * *

Rebecca could hear singing. Surely it was singing? The stereo was off. Seth watched her, smiling, as the room stilled. This must be the start of things. The singing was getting closer and she recognised the tune from school carol concerts and heard the words as they arrived at Seth's open door, "Here we come a-wassailing." Catherine, Michael and Charles entered the room, dressed in black surplices and singing in beautiful harmonies. She hadn't even realised they'd gone. Charles was carrying a large pot with some sort of liquid in. She backed towards the window to let them pass, wanting to giggle. At the fireplace they halted, looked at each other, then broke into another song about wassailing. She didn't know this one – it sounded like a folk song, darker, otherwordly. Jake leaned over and whispered something that sounded like "Steal I Spam" in her ear; she frowned slightly but he was already walking out of the room. They all clapped and whistled as Seth called out, "Now for the wassail!" and Jake returned with pint glasses into which he ladled the liquid from Charles' bowl, dark and murky with mysterious chunks floating on its surface. Rebecca sniffed cloves and hops and other flavours she couldn't immediately place.

"Is this *mould*?" Anna was looking down at her glass, unconvinced.

Seth winked. "Toast, actually. As in, let's make a toast." He raised his glass and the others followed.

"To a night of surprises." They drank, tentatively. It was some sort of mulled cider, dense and heavily spiced, and the topping did seem to be toast. Rebecca's gullet glowed after two mouthfuls.

"What is wassailing anyway?" asked Anna, who had overcome her initial reservations and was already making impressive progress on her grog.

Charles, still in a surplice, answered. "Isn't it just the old word for carol singing?" Everyone looked at Seth.

"Yes, but the wassail also referred to this splendid drink which the wassailers would bring in as they sang. Seemed like a good way to begin the festivities."

Rebecca remembered what Jake had said to her and turned to him. "Why were you whispering about stealing Spam? Don't tell me that's the secret ingredient."

Jake frowned before booming with laughter, creating more amusement as he repeated her comment loudly to the rest of the group.

"Steeleye Span, not stealing Spam," he expanded eventually, wiping his eyes. "As in the folk band."

"Strange 1970s bunch, period instruments, funny accents, hardcore fan base," said Seth, more gently. "And funny name too."

José touched her arm. "Don't worry, Rebecca, I haven't got a clue what they're on about either."

"That's a relief."

"Ladies and gentlemen, your attention please." Seth was brandishing sheets of white paper. Weren't they going to eat yet? The table was fully set and sumptuous in purple linen, and although tantalising cooking smells surrounded her, there was no sign of actual food. She should have snacked

159

before leaving the house.

"Continuing the wassailing theme, we will shortly enjoy a mummers' Christmas pageant to keep us mindful of the important things at this time of year."

"*Mummers*? I presume this is some more weird English shit?" Anna pinched an olive from a bowl Rebecca hadn't noticed.

"People shouldn't be allowed to live on islands. Except the Irish, of course," José added quickly, dodging a blow from Anna.

"Mummers, my dear ignorami, were a group of players, or actors, who would travel around from house to house at Christmas performing plays to entertain the household, usually about the trials of King George."

"As in the dragon?"

"Exactly."

José shook his head. "God, you British and your dragons. So we're going to watch a play about some king fighting dragons?"

"In a nutshell, yes. Mumming pageants were used at significant times of the year to draw out the populace's fears, give them some sort of voice and then dispel them. Keep the dark side under control and everyone on the moral straight and narrow. A sort of group therapy."

Charles raised his eyebrows. "I must say with all these knights and dragons it sounds more Monty Python to me."

"You're on the right lines, Charlie boy. I thought we could initiate our dear brethren José and Anna into the shadowy world of English panto."

Rebecca chuckled. "A word to strike fear into the heart of any actor. Mine starts in – shit, ten days." She had joined Anna at the olive bowl.

"Treat this as a warm-up, darling."

José leaned over to Anna. "What's panto?"

Anna winked. "Meester Fawlty, I know nothing. Where have you been for the last four years, Josie?" He shrugged.

"God – where do I start? We do have them in Ireland, you know, Seth. Fairy tales, stupid catch phrases, men in drag." She paused. "Actually, come to think of it, José, you'd love it."

Everyone laughed. Then Jake gasped and pointed at José. "Watch out – he's behind you!"

José whipped his head round to more guffaws. "What the…?"

Anna was spit-laughing a mouthful of grog and only half caught it in her glass.

Jake put an arm round José's shoulders. "One of the catch phrases, mate. He's behind you!"

Charles coughed. "Oh, no he isn't!"

"Oh yes he is!"

José's eyes widened at the group chorus. "That's it, you're all complete nutters. Let's get this panto mummy shit over with then we can get down to proper Christmas activities like eating. Where are the actors?"

Seth took a cloth from the sideboard and wiped away the grog spatters at Anna's feet. He replaced the cloth as Anna giggled an apology. "Well, here of course. I'm looking at them."

"No. No way."

Seth folded his arms. "Way. You've been invited to my house and now you need to earn your supper. I have parts, costumes, props. Here, take one each." He started handing out copies of the play.

"You want us to act out this play?"

"I can't even read this, let alone act it."

Seth shrugged. "Blame Anna if you must. This is entirely for her benefit."

"Mine?"

"Well, what does panto mean, in a nutshell?"

A grin broke over Anna's face. "Dressing up!"

Seth winked and turned to the others. "If it makes you feel any better, I've got a part too."

Rebecca scanned the list of characters. "What as?"

"Father Christmas, of course. He always introduced the pageant."

Anna snorted. The idea of Seth as Father Christmas was about as incongruous as it got. But, of course, that was the whole point of panto.

"Who's who then?"

"Well, I thought you could all read the play first before we sort that out. Maybe a certain part will jump out at you."

Not straightforward slapstick, then. This was Seth, of course. Amidst the mutterings. Rebecca took herself off to a corner armchair and tried to focus on the words in front of her.

Let's get this straight, Seth Gardner wrote a pantomime for you all to perform?

He did. I still have a copy, actually. Do you want to see it?

If you have it to hand.

Just a second... Sorry, that took longer than expected. Here it is.

Thank you. Please go on for now.

Well, I read it over and it did look as if certain parts matched certain people.

For example?

Well, King George sounded like Michael – a bit serious, you know. Moralistic and humourless. And Cinderella I assumed was Catherine.

Because?

Um – apparently she used to do Seth's ironing and stuff. According to Anna.

I see.

And there was an elf, who had to be José...

Because he's gay?

Er, yes. And Jake and the Beanstalk – Jake, of course – and the Princess in the land of theatre – well, me.

It says here, 'Dressed in sexy Santa suit.'
Um, yes. So I thought.
And Beauty and, let's see, Gretel?
I wasn't sure. Though Gretel bingeing on
gingerbread sounded a bit like Anna.
Oh?
Well, I don't mean literally… well, she
has food fads. And she loves sweet things.
Right. So once you'd worked out your parts…
No, that's just it. We weren't who we
thought we would be.

Seth stubbed out his cigarette. "All finished reading it through? Now, these are your parts. Based on her superior experience, Rebecca will take the part of King George."

Rebecca swallowed.

"Cinderella will be played by Michael," a small ripple, "Charles will be my elf," a louder ripple, "Jake will make an exquisite Beauty," a wink from the big man, "Anna can do her bawdy best as Jake and the Beanstalk, José can blow his weekly calorie count as Gretel and Catherine can be Princess for a day." Catherine's eyes grew wide.

A moment's silence and then Seth repeated the parts.

"Are these parts supposed to represent us? You've lost me." José's confusion was mirrored in the faces around him.

"Let's say you're not necessarily playing yourselves. Trust me, this will add to the fun. And in the true tradition of Christmas, I hope there'll be something for everyone to take home with them."

SCENE 6

**So he was deliberately confusing you. One
could say playing with you.**
Yes, but there was usually a point with
Seth.

Rebecca wished there was more food and less grog in her stomach. She was used to experimenting with roles in a theatre, but this multi-layering was messing with her mind. And she was the main part. Playing King George, aka Michael.

Seth stood up. "Now come and get your costumes."

She was covered head to toe in faux chainmail, hot and hard to move in, with a visored helmet over her head. What made it worse was that Catherine, in the sexy Santa suit that should have been hers, was exposing surprisingly good legs. She even got a wolf whistle from Jake. Catherine was one of those women who didn't know how to make the most of herself. Her hair hung around her shoulders, of nondescript colour and style. A few highlights, a haircut, and a new wardrobe would probably make her quite pretty.

Dressing the boys as girls was fun and recovered a bit of the jollity. Michael looked comically uncomfortable in his raggedy dress with thin hairy legs poking out the bottom. Jake was enjoying himself with her lipstick and José looked rather stunning with his eyes made up. Funniest of all was Charles in tights, lederhosen and a pointy hat.

Anna was pleased with her beanstalk, a giant phallic appendage, some sort of balloon. A hirsute, well-cushioned Seth summoned them back to the drawing room, which now had a cleared stage area with screens running down the sides. Miraculously, the space had been turned into a small theatre.

"Now, you should all sit in the audience until your character is about to enter, then slip behind the screen and come on. All the props you need should be tucked away back there. Shall we start?"

Everyone sat on the chairs in front of the 'stage' apart from Rebecca and Seth. Three booming knocks were heard from the wings and then Seth stepped forwards.

"In comes I, old Father Christmas,
Compere of the evening's games.
You may know my many faces,

But you may not know my name.
Some folk call me old Saint Nick,
Kris Kringle, sometimes Père Nöel;
Santa Claus across the water,
See Old Winter, hear his bell."

Only Seth could transform Father Christmas from a jolly old benefactor to a mysterious, even sinister enigma. Rebecca stepped forward to the sound of a bell.

"In comes I, your good King George
In search of monsters to be slain;
Fierce and green with tongue obscene
And preferably exhaling flames."

She looked around, waving her sword.

"None such here; a disappointment,
No fair maiden to be saved.
On I go with sword erect
To find the wicked dragon's cave."

She hammed up the *sword erect* gags: this was familiar panto territory. Father Christmas stepped forward again to three knocks.

"But who comes here? A ragamuffin!
Dirty hair and faded bloom.
A scully maid and yet a child,
She clutches to that witch's broom."

On walked Michael complete with hairnet and mop. The whole place fell about.

"Oh, woe is me! I never stop,
I have to clean and sweep and mop

Which leaves no time to find a fella –
Pity poor old Cinderella!"

Rebecca saw how clever Seth had been now. If Catherine had played Cinderella it would have been too close to the bone. This way, watching Michael in drag reaching for a feather duster, it was just pure comedy. It looked as though he was starting to enjoy himself, addressing the audience as she approached.

"But who comes here without a horse?
His upright sword is most disarming!
Makes me quite forget my chores –
Perhaps, at last, it's my Prince Charming!"

He batted his eyelashes in her direction. "Greetings, Sir Knight."

Rebecca faced Michael, trying to keep her face straight. "Greetings, fair maiden. What services may I perform for you?"

Michael raised his eyebrows to the audience. "What, already?" More titters.

Who knew Michael could do innuendo?

* * * * *

Catherine clapped with the rest. The forced smile was beginning to hurt and she bent over for her glass of water. Was that supposed to be her, then? Certainly that's what Anna and José thought. Was Seth making fun of her or was it just supposed to be a joke?

* * * * *

José folded his arms and prepared himself for the next section. Three loud knocks and the crimson beanbag that was

Seth stepped forward.

> "So onwards rides our steadfast knight
> With not a dragon's tail in sight
> Until he meets a little chappie,
> Short and sweet and gay and happy."

Anna dug him in the ribs as Charles skipped onto stage in his lederhosen, hands outstretched like a penguin's wings.

> "Here am I a merry elf,
> Never thinking of himself,
> Never low and never listless,
> Singing songs for Father Christmas."

Anna was nearly wetting herself. Even the professional, Rebecca, was hiding her chuckles behind the lid thing on her helmet as she looked down at her script for the next line. She asked if he'd seen any dragons.

Charles bowed. "Greetings, my Lord. I have not seen a dragon for many a year."

"Pity. Still, there must be one around here somewhere. You seem like a jolly chap. Do you want to help me in my search?"

Charles shook his head.

> "Sadly, Lord, my present contract
> Means I may serve but one master.
> Were I to renege on this
> It would spell sure career disaster."

Rebecca patted his arm. "Oh dear, bit of an ogre, your boss?"

Charles looked round in alarm. "An ogre? Where?"

"Hush, timid elf. Not a real ogre."

The elf wiped his brow. "Phew. I once sold myself to an

ogre. It wasn't pretty."

King George nodded. "Ugly creatures, so I've heard." A few chuckles. "But why sell yourself?"

Charles' eyes were wide. "How would I live otherwise? At least my current owner provides for me, stops me going back on the streets." He looked around nervously. "I must not say more. My master hears everything. Ernie must go. Good luck in your search."

The audience laughed and Anna leaned over. "Who would have thought Charles could be so camp?" José concentrated on trying to slow his breathing, realising his palms were clammy on his knees. How fucking dare he? Parade his knowledge like that, taunt him with it, shove it in his face. And that stuff about serving one master – Seth must know that he was still in love with him.

He closed his eyes. On the other hand, couldn't it apply to all of them? Wasn't that why they were all here – to serve one master? He opened his eyes to Jake mincing onstage in a yellow, frilly dress. He forced a smile back at Anna. Maybe it was just a bit of fun.

* * * * *

Charles took his seat back in the audience, slightly out of breath, and acknowledged the back slaps with a grin. He'd always wondered about amateur dramatics. Maybe he could join a group after Christmas. He looked around. Another group, God, he'd have to be mad.

Rebecca was brandishing her sword towards the weeping Jake.

> "Hail, good lady, good King George
> Who pays no court to fun or feast
> Will help you in your hour of need
> And hunt and slay the dreadful beast."

Jake swooned.

"Kill the beast? No, no, I beseech you, do not. He is a good beast, though he looks fearsome."

Jake continued in a squeaky voice.

"Good my knight, my name is Beauty,
Strive I to fulfil my duty
But now my heart doth bleed and blister
And I am torn 'tween love and sister."

Charles stiffened in his chair and frowned.

"Whatever do you mean? Take me to the dragon at once!"

"Dragon? There is no dragon, my Lord.
Only a beast so kind and tender
That with a smile he doth render
Himself a shining prince to me.
My sisters say I must leave him be."

Charles flicked his gaze towards Seth, inscrutable under his cotton wool beard. Was this supposed to be a dig, a reference to Sarah, the way he looked out for her? She'd not been well again lately. A couple of times he'd made soup and taken it over in portion-sized tupperwares. Sarah-sized portions. He hadn't mentioned anything to Seth, though. He never mentioned her name in front of Seth.

King George had ascertained that the Beast was no dragon and said his goodbyes to Beauty.

"How strange this quest is now becoming,
So many people in such strife,
Such tears and fears and lack of cheer
Without a dragon in their life!"

169

Charles shivered unexpectedly. It was a good time for Anna to enter, waving her inflated 'beanstalk' in front of her. Rebecca gasped.

"Saints alive, what travesty is this?"

Anna leered at her.

"Travesty? This ain't no travesty, mate." It was a pretty good Cockney accent. "But if it's a tapestry you're after I can get you one proper cheap, that big French one, top-class fake, no one would know."

"Not a tapestry, you fool, a trav – oh, it doesn't matter. Who are you and what is your business?"

"Jolly Jake it is my name
And jolly jape, it is my game.
I don't talk posh like kings and queens talk
But folks admire me for my beanstalk!"

Anna swung the beanstalk wildly. "Why, surely you've 'eard of Jake and the Beanstalk, guv'nor?"

* * * * *

It could have been Lester talking. Jake knew he was watching a portrayal of himself but he felt like he was watching his mum's old boyfriend, the only one who'd stuck around long enough to become a role model. It was like someone holding up a mirror, to show him how much he'd modelled himself on Lester – his patter, the dodgy buying and selling, the banter.

"Sold the owd lady's cow, din' I, in return for these beans. Magic beans, if you know what I mean, eh? Nudge nudge, wink wink."

Jake grinned at the obvious reference to the pills he scored for Seth from time to time. At least Lester had been kind. He'd taken Jake under his wing, even taught him to cook a bit. But this barrow boy stuff in Anna's terrible accent – was that really him? Was he just a walking cliché, a laughing stock? He tightened his hand on his glass and glanced over at the clock on the sideboard. Things were running to plan. Should be finished by 10, just as he'd said.

* * * * *

When could he take this ridiculous dress off? It felt about 100 degrees in the room with the fire still burning high. Michael's stomach tightened as he watched the stage. It had been okay for a while prancing around with cleaning equipment, he'd done his bit, but it appeared there was more sport to be had at his expense. Anna was talking about magic beans to Rebecca's King George – the character he assumed was modelled on him.

"Well, they growed me a bloody enormous beanstalk, didn't they? See for yourself. Have a feel, mate." Anna waved the ludicrously phallic beanstalk. Michael squirmed in his chair.

"I most certainly will not."

Anna-as-Jake moved closer to King George. "It's what's on the end that excites me most."

"What do you mean?"

"Well, I had a bit of an explore up there once and the whole thing starts shaking doesn' it, and there was 'eavy breathing, the lot!"

The audience chortled as King George's eyes lit up.

"Good heavens. Could it be – a dragon?"

"Don't think it was no dragon, though it did get pretty 'ot up there. Is that your thing then, dragons?"

King George waved his flag.

"Good King George will never tire
Till he's put out the dragon's fire.
Its teeth will shatter, its blood will splatter,
Its eyes will – oh, it doesn't matter."

Anna looked down at the script and then frowned. "Whatever's

171

wrong, Squire?"

King George had slumped. "Nothing. It's just, well, no one seems to care about dragons anymore and I can't find one anywhere. Maybe I just need to accept it isn't a job for life anymore and change field."

Anna put her hands on her hips. "Don't be downhearted now, sir. Why I 'eard only last week about a princess 'o'd been captured by a dragon."

"You did? Where? That's wonderful news. I mean, obviously…"

"Don't worry, I understand you, guv. But I'm afraid I don't know where the dragon is. You could always start by lookin' up this beanstalk, sir?"

Anna held out her beanstalk eagerly.

"I don't know… perhaps I should…" King George put out his hand tentatively. "No, I will venture east first. My dragon radar is starting to throb. Farewell, Jake with the Beanstalk."

Michael crossed his legs. It was bad enough being portrayed as a do-gooder with no sense of humour but this was taking it too far. Another dig from Seth to show that Glyndebourne night was not forgotten. Had anyone else caught onto the subtext? Did anyone else know?

* * * * *

Anna, minus beanstalk, flopped down on one of the chairs. Thank God her bit was over. Or was it? She laughed with everyone else as José entered as Gretel, stuffing a cake into his mouth, his words indistinguishable as crumbs flew everywhere. Cheeky swines, him and Seth. At least she could laugh at herself.

Rebecca as King George was looking appalled.

"I pray, dear lady, do not gorge
For I am abstinent King George.
It's hard for me to stay acetic

172

When I wish to have your cake and eat it."

Gretel handed King George a cake, who bit it and then spat it out. Gretel looked upset.

"Good my Lord, I beg your pardon
I did not mean to give you a hard one!"

In true panto spirit – she'd known this stuff would be up José's street – he looked around to get the laugh.

"My name is Gretel and, with my brother,
We're prisoners of a wicked other."

King George leaned in. "A dragon, perchance?"

"Witch, I'm afraid. Long nose, pointy hat, the works. She's forcing us to spend our days eating candy and gingerbread. It's terrible."

Gretel-José stuffed another cake in. Maybe he'd negotiated low-fat muffins with Seth.

"This truly is dreadful. Surely you can escape and return home?"

A shake of the head. "Never. My father married again and Hansel and I fled from our stepmother. Then the witch caught us. On balance I'd rather be with her."

Anna gulped her grog. Seth had made his point about her going home many times; now it was starting to feel like a lecture. Was it obvious to the others? Wicked stepmother, panto – perhaps not.

At last Gretel exited and three knocks heralded the return of Father Christmas, surely even hotter than Rebecca in his padded suit.

"For weeks and months our saintly king
Did tirelessly pursue his prey
Till word of mouth propelled him

To a gaudy kingdom far away."

King George entered. "Why, what land is this? Bedecked with tinsel and huge pink murals. Surely a dragon cannot be hiding here?"

Charles minced on, sporting a cravat and pink feather boa.

"Why surely 'tis Ernie the Elf? I scarely recognise him in this new attire. Ernie the Elf, is that you?"

Charles cleared his throat and flipped his hand in the age-old symbol of campness. "I go by the name Eduardo now." Anna sniggered, stepmothers receding from her mind. "'Tis the land of theatre, m'Lord."

She blinked as Jake and José skipped across the stage, arm in arm, saying "darling!"

King George looked severe. "And is there a poor princess here held captive by a dragon?"

Eduardo gestured to the audience. Catherine had just tiptoed on in her sexy santa suit. Anna joined the chorus –

"She's behind you!"

King George looked around vaguely. "Oh, no she isn't."

Anna leaned over to José, now back in his chair, but saw he didn't need prompting. "Oh, yes she is!" They grinned at each other.

Catherine came forward now, hips sashaying in a most un-Catherine like way. "Eduardo!" She and Charles air-kissed several times. On seeing King George, now looking distinctly tetchy, Princess Catherine swooned and started sobbing loudly.

"My lady."

Charles mopped her brow.

"Apologies, I am not well,
Dear knight, and live in daily hell.
This monster's aim is plain to see –
He seeks his wicked way with me!"

174

Catherine was really going for it, perhaps seeking revenge for the Cinderella connotations. Rebecca felt herself growing even hotter. She looked down at her script and saw that she, as King George, had the killer couplet to deliver:

"Is my lady's story clean
Or is she but a… drama queen?"

The audience clapped its appreciation and Rebecca had to acknowledge it. Was she damning Catherine or herself? Her legs ached and she felt slightly seasick.

"My lady, cease your weeping. And pray stand up."

Catherine rose, batting her eyelashes.

"Speak truly now. There is no dragon, is there?"

A slight pause. "No, my lord."

"You invented it?"

"I dreamt about one and it seemed to become real. Plus, everyone was so much nicer to me then. And my life seemed more real, somehow. You're not cross, are you?" Catherine's voice warmed as she spoke and her colour was up. She was actually acting rather well.

Rebecca slumped down, head in hands, giving Charles his cue.

"He's having a 'moment', my lady. Soliloquy will follow."

Thank God, the damn thing was nearly over.

* * * * *

Michael watched Rebecca deliver the soliloquy, the final puncturing of King George's pomposity.

"For years I've toiled with this great flag on,
Stung by jeers of "George with drag on!"

175

It took a second but then people got it and laughed.

"Fighting foes so Good may conquer
– And now I just feel such a plonker!"

Catherine and Charles tiptoed in with a tea tray and Rebecca
sighed.
"Oh, spare the big soliloquy – I could just have a cup of
tea."
They handed Rebecca a cup, which must have had
something nice in it as she downed the lot. Time for Seth to
finish off, with three ponderous knocks.

"And so our brave, distinguished knight
Learns that the world's not black nor white.
So may we bid you, sires and sisters
A grey, but very merry Christmas."

Michael clapped with the rest and then everyone got up and
made a bow to the empty chairs. Maybe they could figure out
how many subplots, revelations and emotional triggers were
lurking under that innocuous little farce, because he sure as
hell couldn't.

SCENE 7

We've read the transcript of the pantomime.
Clearly Mr Gardner was alluding to events
in your past you'd prefer to keep hidden.
In your position I think I'd be rather
angry, Mr Sanchez.
I was.
Could you tell me what happened next? We
have already heard the account from a
couple of the others.

They were having a drink, cooling off by the open patio

doors, when it happened. Three forceful knocks at Seth's door. Conversation stalled instantly.

"Aye aye, what's this then? Some grand finale?" Anna raised her eyebrows and they all looked at Seth.

"Perhaps the real Father Christmas, come to take an encore," he replied, but he looked puzzled as he headed to the door. Jake grabbed a jug of cocktails and started refilling glasses, talking loudly. Seconds later they heard raised voices.

"Jake, could you spare a second?" It was Seth calling from the hall. José made to go with him but Jake put out a hand.

"Won't be a tick." He pushed the door to as he left, leaving the others to exchange blank looks.

"What's going on?" José asked.

It had gone quiet from the hall so they carried on talking, until once again, voices reached them.

"I'm going to look." Anna put her drink down to a loud bang from the front door. As she opened the drawing room door, Seth and Jake re-entered, both smiling.

Jake batted his hands. "Well, we saw those twats off."

"What do you mean? Who were they?"

Jake shrugged. "Some local yobs. They must have taken offence at our theatrical activities. Wanted to put the frighteners up us."

"But why would they be here? How did they get into the building?"

"I told you about the local riff-raff. Maybe you'll believe me now." It was the first time Seth had spoken and he looked a bit pale under his half-smile.

"Are you okay?" Both Catherine and Rebecca moved towards him.

"Never better, my pretty little worriers. I could have probably handled it by myself but I thought a bit of muscle might do the job faster. Cheers, Jakey boy."

Jake slapped his back. "Any time, guv."

José saw Anna watching Jake. Statue still.

Only you were there at the door, Mr Etheridge. Your account is crucial.
It's just like I said. Some local meat heads wanting to dangle their cocks at us. So to speak.
How many were there?
Four or five? Five, I reckon – it was hard to tell.
Why do you think they knocked three times? Almost as if they'd been briefed to do so.
Search me. Must have been listening to us, like I said. Trying to be funny or something.
And you just told them to go away?
In so many words. They got the message soon enough. It's no big deal.
You don't think it could be connected with recent events?
Nah. Not that lot. Probably just ran 'ome to Mummy afterwards.

*****

Jake looked preoccupied, not his usual chit-chatty self. Not the wide boy she'd just portrayed. Anna was aware of him even as she bantered with José at the table. She watched him checking his phone. What had gone on just then, at the door? Seth had been rattled, she could tell. But Jake had been all shrugs and smiles. He'd said something once about being a bouncer – a bloody good one, she suspected. Under that boyish grin was someone you wouldn't mess with. He was watching Rebecca now, who was off her head. Who could blame her after suffocating all night under a suit of armour and weighty morals? The purple paper crown on her head tipped slightly over her eyes as she rested her head. Anna checked that José was still wearing his paper hat. He was upset that it clashed with his green shirt. Seth said that if you wanted to experience all the different shades of green that nature could provide you should spend an hour in José's wardrobe.

* * * * *

Rebecca was breathing out of every pore of her skin, or so it felt. The chainmail costume was in an ugly heap in the spare bedroom. She felt free in her limbs, light, agile, almost as if she'd traded in her old body for a new, streamlined version. Was it just the costume that had been oppressive or the persona too? She looked at Michael's face, drawn, watchful, and felt free all over again.

A huge roast goose was curled up in a hump in the middle of the table. Dribbles of fat glistened on its pale brown back. For the first time in a decade, Rebecca felt tempted to eat meat. There was something symbolic about it, a slaughtered animal, the celebration of the end of the quest. But having starved herself all day she knew it would be stupid. Besides, Jake had made a nut roast especially for her and José.

Wine was flowing and her glass never seemed to get empty; Jake and Seth saw to that. The mood was celebratory now, as if they had all endured and conquered some great challenge. Perhaps, like the people of old, they had aired their demons and could put them away for another year. Is that what Seth had planned? She watched him, the ripple of muscles on his forearms, the flash of the carving knife as he severed the legs and wings of the goose. He was telling an anecdote but it was as if someone had switched the sound off and all she could do was follow the shapes of his mouth and the play of his eyes.

By dessert she felt as if they were all flying through the air, holding hands, looking down on the table of dismembered

179

Christmas pudding and empty wine glasses. The panto felt an age ago, something in their past. She looked around the table, at these faces that had become so important to her, and felt something filling up inside her, something better than wine and roast potatoes and homemade rum sauce. Michael was throwing his head back and laughing with Seth, Charles and Catherine were making a toast, José and Anna were engaged in a typically smutty exchange. She sat back and allowed herself a Louis moment. It truly was a wonderful world.

* * * * *

Jake watched the delicate curve of Rebecca's neck as she tipped her head back. Another glass of dessert wine and she would struggle to sit up again. It was strange, but he didn't really feel pissed. He must have had at least three pints of grog in the kitchen, and the collection of empty wine bottles on the floor was now becoming scandalous. But he felt so sober that he'd have offered to drive a car. His business for the evening was done, but for some reason he couldn't switch off. Something was making him thoughtful, playing parts of his life back to him like a home movie. Maybe the something was Christmas.

Surrounded by all these people, these friends, in this beautiful room was not a good time to rewind to Christmases gone by. Yet he sat fixed, unable to stop. There he was, as a grubby-faced child, watching his mum giggling with some boyfriend or other on the sofa. They'd 'made an effort', got out the crap artificial tree with lights that constantly fused, bought a Bernard Matthews turkey roll. There were even mutilated crackers on the table. There went the two adults, giggling over to the bedroom while little Jake watched telly with the sound turned up. Some years it was better, when they invited his nan. She would do a proper roast turkey and his mum would have to stay up all afternoon.

Thank God for his nan. She'd been the most stable thing in his world until she died seven years ago. At least she'd never had to visit him *there*, at least he'd still been her golden boy when she shuddered and died on Ward 9.

And those years with Lester weren't so bad; in fact, they were pretty good times. Of course he'd known that Lester was ripping his mum off, that he was borrowing money from her to place doomed bets at the bookies – she'd caught him in the end – but he liked his attitude, his *joie de vivre* – as Seth would say. The bearded bloke from the off-licence who slipped him money was no substitute. Set against what happened later those were times of innocence. He should have appreciated them more.

He's already messed up once since getting out and it's cost him the job at the River. Shagging the boss' wife wasn't his cleverest move. Still, he's landed on his feet. He eyed Seth, opening a bottle of vintage port that probably cost more than his monthly rent. *Stick with me, kid.* He doesn't need to be asked twice.

He looked back at Rebecca, smudged eyelids pulled halfway over her eyes like blinds, and smiled. She would definitely need help getting home.

SCENE 8

I made a bit of a fool of myself.
You got drunk?
Very.

She hadn't drunk herself sick since – easily over three years ago. But here she was, worshipping a toilet she wouldn't like to observe at this range in the best of circumstances, let alone with a convulsing gut. Rebecca peeked into the bowl. There was something about the translucent shimmer on the water that made her judder. She remembered Seth tempting her with a slice of goose breast. Surely she hadn't?

She pressed the flush and ran her hands under the hot tap. At least the soured milk smell of vomit was disguising the usual eau de mildew. Only in London would you get windowless bathrooms. She splashed water on her face and groaned at her soft-focus reflection. No chance of lenses today after passing out in them last night. She leaned on the sink as her stomach lurched again. It wasn't what she had eaten, it was the amount she'd drunk. For a second she blamed Seth and Jake for constantly filling her glass and it felt good, a pleasant rush of indignation that even she could laugh at. She peeled off her dress, grabbed her specs from the windowsill and stepped onto the scales. Eight stone twelve – that's what a good puke did for you. Two cups of coffee and she'd be back to normal but there was still something satisfying about the needle dipping below the nine.

Back to bed. There was no chance she could make it to Milton Keynes, where Jason would be waiting. How would she get out of that one? Scenes from the evening whirled backwards and forwards in a haze. How had she got home? She had a vision of Jake driving her, which couldn't be right – he wouldn't have driven drunk, would he? She pulled the duvet over her legs. As it grazed the top of her thigh another image burst over her: a hand on her thigh in the car. Whose car? She hadn't been in a car. It must be a flashback to a drink-fuelled dream.

"God." She was talking to herself now. Who did she need to apologise to? A blurry memory of wayward dancing tapped her on the shoulder. Everyone, probably.

She needed to speak to somebody, exchange stories from the evening, find out they'd all been as drunk as her. Dare she ring Seth? Not after their last phone call. Oh God, that dancing. He'd probably been trying to get rid of her. She'd only known these people for a few months – it was like getting hammered at your first office party. How would she face them again?

On her way to fetch another glass of water the phone started ringing in the hall. She stared at it: friend or foe? Her hand grabbed at the receiver.

"Well, good morning." Someone was chuckling at her.

That ruled out Jason, at least. "You sound like a woman who's downed several bottles of wine and danced for three hours."

"Oh God. Don't talk about it." She was so glad she'd picked up. It was Seth and he didn't sound cross. She slumped to the floor leaning her ear on the receiver.

"I'm really sorry."

"Sorry? The video of you dancing has sorted out my Christmas shopping overnight."

"Video?"

"Joke, darling. But it did make rather fetching viewing."

"Oh no. I'm embarrassed to ask, but when did I leave? And how did I get home?"

"Ah, well, I was actually ringing to check that Jake had behaved honourably in the taxi and delivered you home safely. On the second point, I am assured but the first – it looks like we shall never know the answer."

"Taxi?" Rebecca screwed up her face. Was that the car in her flashback? "Oh. I know it's weird but I thought I remembered him driving me."

"Driving? I doubt he'd risk it with his track record. You both left together and he said he knew where to pick up a cab."

"Well, that's probably right then. What do I know?" But the memory continued to tickle her like an irritating fly and she pushed it away. What track record? "Anyway, it was a great night and great panto – really clever. Did you enjoy it?"

"Especially with a pro taking the central role. Hope there weren't too many theatre gags."

"No, we actors know how to rise above these things." A lurch of her belly warned her she wouldn't be able to sustain the banter for much longer.

"Now, I was also ringing to let you know your cardy is safe – it had got mixed up with the Cinderella costume."

"My cardy – oh, okay."

"Not going to rise to that one either?"

"Sorry?" She had to get back to bed.

"Oh dear, that bad? I'll be brief then. I wondered if you

wanted to collect it via a modest supper on your way back from Milton Keynes tomorrow. If you're still planning to go, of course."

Her stomach lurched – in a good way this time. "Yes please, that sounds great. I may not make it to Milton Keynes today, but – well, I'm sure I'll get there at some point." She wasn't going to turn down the offer of supper at Seth's.

"Super. Now get yourself in the shower, woman."

SCENE 9

The boy stared at the long, red-gold hair rippling over her shoulders and into the secret coves of her spine. It hovered about her as she moved around the kitchen, damp and shining beneath the overhead lights. It looked as though it had just been combed through, coaxed straight where it was wettest but starting to rebel at the ends into skittish curls. She hadn't got dressed yet. A rich purple towel skimmed the top of her breasts so that he could just see the gathering of flesh that hinted at unseen depths. She was making coffee, humming under her breath, her soles bare against the burgundy tiled floor. As she bent over to reach for the milk out of the fridge he glimpsed the very whitest, most hidden part of her legs, where the flesh swelled and bumped and changed texture. He felt funny. She turned and saw him sitting at the table.

"Hello, darling, I didn't see you there." She came over and swished her fingers along his face then leaned to kiss his cheek. Damp spirals of hair brushed his neck and he smelled her bath oil. His cock stiffened under his dressing gown as he gripped his glass of orange juice. She kissed him again, on the top of his head and tilted his chin up towards her.

"Now, I'll be out most of today – all sorts of people I need to catch up with, but Lucinda will look after you, of course. This evening we have an important associate of Daddy's coming over for dinner. I thought you could do your bit from *Hamlet*, like you did for Peter Bainbridge last week. He was most taken by you, you know."

The boy pulled his chin away and scowled at the table.

"Now, darling, don't be like that. You know how your father has to keep certain people sweet. And you're so good at it. Lord Ashburn nearly wet his pants over that Keats number – *Ode to a Skylark*, was it? He said later – "

"*Nightingale.*"

"Sorry?"

"It was *Ode to a Nightingale.*"

"Of course it was. He said – "

"Shelley wrote *Skylark.*"

She sighed and reached out a hand. "Come on, darling, don't be like this about it. You know you love to perform. Look, I'll tell you what, I'll just take your father his coffee up and then we can have breakfast together before I go out. How does that sound?"

He swallowed down stupid, pointless tears. "Okay." He knew what they were going to do upstairs. She'd come down later with flamy patches all over the creamy skin of her neck and shoulders. He looked up as she wafted towards the door. "Mama?"

"Yes, darling?"

"Don't be too long."

SCENE 10

So you saw your boyfriend the next day?
Yes. Is this relevant? It's just I'm running a little late.
There's no quick way to do this, Miss Laurence. I'm sure you appreciate we need to be thorough, given the circumstances.
Yes, of course. I'm afraid I just need to use the toilet first.

Jason was late. Not just a couple of minutes late – half an hour. Rebecca felt the glow of her eleven hours sleep start to flicker. She'd been standing outside the station so long peering into small black cars she probably looked like a prostitute. This was punishment. And, of course, she was really the late one – not just a day late, but two now. The wind whipped her hair across her face and burned the ends of her fingers. He'd made his point. Another five minutes… was that him? She held her hair away from her eyes and saw his face, fixed on the road. With barely a click of eye contact between them she got into the car and slammed the door.

"Where have you been? It's bloody freezing out there." She leaned over and cranked the heater up to max, holding her hands over the vent.

Silence. Just the hiss-hushing of the fan. "What's the matter?" She glanced over at bloodshot eyes and stubble. "Blimey, you look rough."

He stared ahead. "Thanks. You don't, though. Feeling better?"

"Yeah, must have been one of those twenty-four-hour things. I was in a right state yesterday."

He reached out his left hand and she thought he'd put it on her knee. Instead he turned the fan down and put his hand back on the wheel. Neither of them spoke as he turned the car this way and that. Outside his front door she recoiled from the stale beer breath she would usually have teased him about.

He brought two mugs of coffee to his room. Instant, in another deliberate gesture of neglect. Fuck, she'd even bought him a cafetiere so she didn't have to suffer Nescafé every weekend. No sign of creepy Carl. For the first time she wished his weirdo housemate was around to puncture the black cloud of silence that hung over them. She spotted the CD she'd left there last time. *Jagged Little Pill*. It would do.

He raised his eyebrows at her choice of music but said nothing. One of them had to bridge the gap. "So, big night last night?"

He shrugged. "Just a few pints with Tony and the boys from work."

She took a breath. "Are you going to say why you're

pissed off with me?"

He shrank from her directness, looked out of the window.

"Well, this is going to be a fun weekend."

He swivelled then, turned his eyes like weapons on her. "Weekend? More like a few hours."

Bugger. She'd walked straight into that one. "Sorry, I meant... come on, it's hardly my fault. Looks like you've been enjoying yourself, anyway."

He stared at her. "So, how was the audition?"

"Audition? Oh, the meeting with George Harrow." She wasn't quick enough. "Yeah, you know, nothing definite but he'll consider me for future things." Her excuse for not going over on Friday night sounded dubious enough without the clambering heat working its way up to her face.

"Why was your phone turned off afterwards?"

"Was it? I don't know – for God's sake, it's like the inquisition." Her voice was climbing higher in pitch to Alanis Morrisette's.

"That's because you're hiding things from me." Jason's voice rose too, not higher but louder. He hit the side of the desk with his palm. "Tell me the truth, Becky. And turn that ranting banshee off."

Rebecca opened her mouth into an outraged O. "That *ranting banshee* is one of the best-selling artists in the world." She was possibly dealing with things in the wrong order. Jason grabbed the remote control and jabbed the stop button. The room was suddenly quiet.

"I notice you haven't answered my other question. Tell me what you were doing on Friday night. I'm not stupid, Rebecca."

"Well, that's debatable." She muttered it under her breath but Jason sprang up and grabbed her arm. For a split second she was frightened; then he dropped it scathingly and turned away.

"Just tell me. Is it him? Seth? Are you having an affair?" He faced her again.

"What? Are you mad? Of course I'm not." She grasped the ammunition he'd just handed her, gratefully hauling herself back to the high ground. "Oh, I see. That's what you think of me, is it? Thanks a lot."

"I just needed to know." Jason's voice was softer. "I just don't know where you are and what you're doing any more."

"You're my boyfriend, not my bodyguard. You have to trust me. Which you clearly don't."

"Your story about the weekend just didn't seem to ring true."

Rebecca sighed and sat on the edge of the bed. "Look, if you must know I went out after the audition and had a few drinks and then felt really ill yesterday, which was definitely more than just a hangover."

He was staring at her again. "Why didn't you tell me you went out on Friday?"

"Because I knew I'd get the bloody inquisition."

"Who were you out with?"

She laughed humourlessly. "Oh, here we go. Thumbscrew time. I was out with the Friday Group people."

His turn to laugh. "What a surprise."

"What the hell is that supposed to mean?" She was on her feet, suddenly screaming. "I am absolutely sick of this shit. Either you start trusting me and let me live my life, or…"

"Or what?" They looked at each other from opposite sides of the room.

"Or this just isn't going to work." They held eye contact for another second before Rebecca turned away. She was panting, suddenly out of breath.

"Is that what you want? Is this what you've been trying to do? Break up with me?"

She wouldn't look at him. "No, of course not. But it's not really working right now, is it?" She felt unexpectedly exhilarated, buoyed with adrenaline, hovering on the brink of something momentous. Whether she jumped was up to her.

You broke up, I take it?

She caught a taxi to the station. Jason had his back to her as she left, shoulders hunched as if crying. She wanted to cry too, connect with him for one last time, but there was nothing inside her. On the train she stared out of the window, slumped and vacant as a rag doll. Two and a half years. She tried to summon the appropriate emotion, any emotion. Halfway home her phone buzzed in her pocket and she steeled herself for his pleas or accusations.

Are we still on for tonight? Do you like mushrooms?

The smile that spread across her face brought the appropriate emotion at last. Relief.

SCENE 11

So, Miss Laurence, you broke up with your boyfriend and ran straight to Mr Gardner?
I didn't run. Walked briskly, perhaps. Jogged up the odd escalator. He was waiting on the concourse. Of course I was touched. People don't pick each other up from the station in London.

An hour later she was sitting on Seth's sofa, legs curled under her, clutching a cup of rum-laced tea (for shock) and once again unable to deliver the tears that the scene might seem to call for. Seth was being a sweetheart, declared himself her agony uncle for the day, and put an eclectic selection of nibbles on the coffee table – Bombay Mix to Belgian truffles – to tempt her into eating. She had a troubling suspicion that she was enjoying herself more than might be appropriate. Conversation looped and glided like a dance, gradually opening out until they were sharing things from long ago. Or, as Rebecca realised later, she was. She hadn't talked about her first boyfriend, Jack Chisholm, in a long time. It must be the rum.

"I thought I was the bee's knees, as my mum said. Drainpipe jeans, green eyeshadow and an older boyfriend with a souped-up Ford Capri. God, imagine. Mum and Dad were out of their minds – I'd always been their little princess. And when they found a cigarette in my coat pocket, well Mum definitely cried."

"So the little princess tumbled off her pedestal?"

"In style. I didn't even have time to enjoy it before Chis dumped me for Felicity Mitchell, a scrawny cow in the Upper Sixth." She smiled but Seth was looking at her intently.

"Not funny at the time, I bet. What happened?"

She took a gulp of tea and raised her eyebrows. "I guess I had some sort of nervous breakdown. Went a bit gothy and flunked my O-Levels."

"Not part of the script."

"Not exactly." He took her hand and she was glad to feel tears not far away. It would be odd to look too composed today. "I suppose I *was* used to being treated like a princess, Mum was over forty when she had me and they'd almost given up on having kids. There was another one, another baby at the same time, but it died."

His eyes widened, drawing her in. "So you should have been one of twins?"

"Yes."

"Two of you?" He shook his head. "The mind boggles – in a very, very good way. Excuse the cliché of the male libido."

She laughed, squirmed away from his gaze. He took her hand and it was as if she was looking down on herself, waiting for his next move.

"But seriously." His voice had changed and she jolted as she found his eyes. "Do you feel it – inside? An emptiness? Something missing?" His eyes tugged on hers, dragging them down, down into their murky green depths.

"Yes." It came out as a whisper. It was true, she had always known it, but no one had said it to her before. She had never formed those words in her own head.

He put a finger under her chin. "Then that's another thing we share." They stared at each other and she waited for him to pull her to him but he spoke again. "I've heard that losing a twin can feel like an amputated limb."

She flinched and pulled back her hand, an instinct to protect herself. His words had triggered vibrations at the edge of her mind, a white noise that muted her thoughts and was somehow familiar. She looked up at him and found his eyes, searching still, and though she opened her mouth she knew no sound would come. A silent appeal... but what was she asking for? Seconds passed. Then, abruptly, he broke eye contact and reached for the cigarette box.

"Better get you some food in a minute."

For an instant she was in free fall, trying to adjust to the sudden shift in tone. Her fingers twisted at her hair, at the implicit question that still hung between them.

"I don't know about that – I mean it's not like I ever knew her. Well, not properly. Consciously." She wasn't even sure if he was listening now, intent on lighting a cigarette. She stumbled on. "There is that feeling, though, of something... absent." But she'd lost his interest, needed to lighten things up. "And I had a certain relationship with my parents that I wouldn't have had otherwise. I wasn't spoilt but – hey!"

Seth had turned and was grinning mischievously. The sands had shifted again. She smiled too. "I wasn't. But I guess they gave me whatever they could, and made me believe I could achieve what I wanted."

He exhaled smoke. "And now you find yourself stranded in adulthood with an inordinate sense of entitlement."

She wasn't sure what he meant and it didn't sound altogether complimentary. He read her expression and reached to squeeze her hand. "Don't worry, you're not the only one. I don't think it's possible to be an interesting or successful person without it. And you, my dear, are both of those."

Her smile hovered uncertainly as he released her hand. She thought how much smoking suited him.

191

"So how did the teenage Rebecca get herself back on track?"

She took a breath to focus. "Packed off to stay with goody-goody cousin Annabelle for the summer who turned out to be a complete party animal. Spent the summer surfing, playing volleyball and having a fling with a cute local lad, got back refreshed and ready to knuckle down for A-Levels."

Seth smiled. "Return of Alpha Daughter. I like it. And drama school after that?"

"Actually a year skiing in Val D'Isère. It was amazing – one of the best years of my life." Memories glowed on her face.

"Why?"

"Oh, everything. The people, the skiing, being outdoors all the time. God, I got a tan for the first and only time in my life." They both laughed. "Then Newcastle Uni, then Guildhall."

"Had you always wanted to act?"

He'd never asked her so many questions. It was sweet, he was clearly trying to take her mind off recent events. And succeeding.

"I don't know about always, but even as a child I used to put these performances on with my teddies and dolls. And when I was older I was always performing for Mum and Dad's friends, you know little ballet routines or songs. In fact, I wanted to be a ballerina before I got too tall. What is it?"

She watched his expression wipe clean. "Nothing. I can picture it well, little Rebecca enchanting all and sundry in a pink tutu. You must have been a beautiful child."

His eyes brushed over her and the child in her blushed. Then the woman. "I don't know about that. I used to be teased horribly about my freckles at school, all the usual ginger gags." *Rebecca Freckle-bum*. It was one of the main reasons she'd got a stage name, to get away from Featherstone and its associations. But she was hardly going to tell him that.

He rested his cigarette on the edge of the ashtray and

looked at her with an intensity that reminded her of their first meeting. "I've never understood that. A true redhead is something extraordinary, like a rare bird, something you don't see very often. Look at this." He lifted a handful of her hair. "It's exquisite."

"Thank you." She wasn't sure how to respond.

He mussed her hair round his fingers. "But beauty like this can make you seem a little aloof, unapproachable. I expect the local urchins were secretly besotted by you. And terrified."

She laughed and he dropped her hair.

"My mother was a redhead."

Rebecca nearly stopped breathing. He had never mentioned her before. "Was she?"

"She was so beautiful. Perhaps as beautiful as you." Rebecca tucked that one away for later because she needed to focus on his words. "Perhaps too beautiful. I don't think she ever saw herself as my mother. I had a nanny for that."

He picked up his cigarette box and ran his thumb across the embossed lid. "This was hers, you know."

It was the first time he'd let her look at it properly. She followed the movement of his thumb towards the initials *JG*, carved in the corner. He ran his thumbnail under them slowly. "Julia Gardner."

Rebecca let out a breath. "You must miss her."

He said nothing, running his thumb over and over the initials as if to erase them. Then he turned to her, smiling. "I had very ambitious parents, Rebecca."

"Ambitious?"

"Money, status, power, you name it. Most of the time I was packed off to school so I didn't get in the way."

He spoke lightly but the loneliness was almost tangible. She reached out her hand but he was already sitting forward to stub out his cigarette.

"Now, how's your appetite coming along, Ms Laurence?"

She reeled at the quick change of subject. "Um, I don't

know really. I'm fine for now."

"How about I serve up in half an hour?" He got to his feet.

"Sure." He wasn't going to say more. As Rebecca followed him into the kitchen she felt as though an opportunity had slipped through her fingers.

She tried to steer the subject back to him over dinner but never quite managed it. They drank two bottles of wine before the inevitable whisky appeared – tasters from several bottles, Seth having decided to educate her into the intricacies of single malt. She pulled her face at the peaty ones but fell for a golden, honey-edged liquor that turned out to be the most expensive of the lot. She felt swollen with blurry emotion, punch-drunk from a day she couldn't yet process.

"Can I have one of those?" Seth was lighting up again. Sod it, there was no Jason now to lecture her.

He raised his eyebrows. "Are you sure that's wise? No point in throwing the bathwater out with the boyfriend."

She laughed. "Maybe you're right." She straightened. "I should probably go home."

"Soon. Let's have some music first."

He pulled her to her feet and she didn't resist him – she couldn't, wasn't steady enough – and it was easier to lean into him and sway gently and then rest her head too and close her eyes. He was murmuring into the top of her head, something about the smell of her hair, and now his fingers were delving in, bringing handfuls to his face. In a second she would lift her eyes and discover what it was like to kiss him.

The phone trilled sharply, piercing the moment. Neither of them moved as the answering machine whirred up and a man's voice, drunk, berated Seth for being out and said he was missing him. The machine cut him off. Rebecca pushed back, keeping her eyes averted, and sat heavily on the sofa. Seth turned the music down and sat next to her.

Sorry to cut in – but did you recognise the voice on the machine?

Pardon? Oh - no. I don't think, no, I
didn't.

Okay, carry on.

Um, I need the bathroom again. Just a
minute.

Are you all right, Miss Laurence?

Yes, sorry, I've got a bit of a, you know,
infection, I'll be right back.

"Look at me, Rebecca."

She skimmed his face for a split second. "I'd better go
home."

He put a hand on her arm. "I know we haven't talked
about it but I was assuming that the others had filled you in on
my... extra-curricular activities. You do know I'm bisexual?"

She shrank at the word. "Yes, but I suppose it was a shock
just now."

"It wasn't the best timing, granted." He chuckled. "Or
maybe it saved us from doing something rash. You have had
a bit of a day, haven't you?"

She smiled, close to tears. "I suppose I have."

He put an arm round her and squeezed. "Well, why don't
we get you home now. I take it you're not working tomorrow?"

She shook her head, filled with sudden fear at the empty
day before her.

"Well, I'll give you a ring to see how you're doing. Let's
call you a cab. Oh, and by the way," he leant over and grabbed
a carrier bag from the side of the sofa, "here's your cardigan."

SCENE 12

**We have been talking to other people about
what happened at the Christmas group,
after the pantomime. When Seth Gardner was
called to the door. Do you have a take on
that, Mr Stanley?**

A take? Who knows what was going on? Sorry,

I'm not being difficult but I'd guess the only person who can answer that is Seth himself.

But did it worry you at the time?

I suppose I was a little concerned. If I remember rightly I took him out for a drink to check everything was okay. Don't remember getting very far, though.

That was putting it mildly. Seth had made him suffer from the beginning, the mumbled invitation to a gallery opening in Islington, the mockingly raised eyebrows in response: *Have I got this right, you're asking me out?* The lid lifted off Glyndebourne in one fell swoop and the stench of locked-up memories escaping. He needn't have worried. Seth behaved chivalrously throughout, just as he had ever since sending that note and Michael relenting to join the Friday Folly. In fact, conversation had flowed. Seth liked the exhibition and before long, Michael found himself knee-deep in a rather enjoyable debate about the accessibility of the arts. But that wasn't what the evening was for.

"So," a slight cough, "everything all right with you?"

Seth blinked at the abrupt change of tack. Then he threw his head back and laughed. "God, Michael, you sound exactly like Charles. Don't you start, please. I'm fine, everything's fine, the beer is a little warm but perfectly acceptable and please, for Christ's sake, can we just be blokes and talk about stuff rather than feelings?"

So that's what they did. At least for a while. But somehow the stuff became more personal until he was telling Seth about his family. How did that happen? He had the uncomfortable sense of Seth having turned the tables on him without having a clue of how it had happened or how to reverse it. When he almost mentioned Mr Fleming's name he realised it was time to leave. He refused the offer to share a cab. The goodbye was awkward, a flicker of a smile on Seth's face as he shook

Michael's hand. He strode off feeling thwarted and oddly buoyed.

SCENE 13

[Anna bursts onto stage and stops, blinking into the dark]

ANNA: Hey. Sorry for interrupting. But at this rate you'll all forget who I am. I feel like I'm being hidden away back there. It's all Rebecca, Rebecca, Rebecca. Don't get me wrong. I like her, I really do. I admit I wasn't sure at first. All that hair, you know. That actress thing. I mean, look at me in my civvies. Don't even get a costume.

I know, she's sound really. She was a good choice. But you need to hear from more than one person if you want to get the full picture. And something's changed since she arrived. Something's not right. I'm not saying it's her fault. But Seth – he's different. Everything feels a bit shaky. I don't like it.

Who's that?

[enter José, peering into the dark]

JOSÉ: Anna! What are you doing? You know you're not supposed to be here.

ANNA: Ah, give it a break, Josie. I just needed a bit of air.

JOSÉ: So what's up?

ANNA: I was just thinking about Becs, the way things have been since Seth met her.

JOSÉ: What do you mean?

ANNA: Ah, come on. You know something's going on. Something's been knocked out of kilter. I know we needed to bring someone in, you know, after last year...

JOSÉ: Anna! We can't talk about this.

ANNA: I know. But after that dinner – that heavy

	poem, the way he was acting – aren't you concerned?
JOSÉ:	Of course.
ANNA:	And then that weird thing after the panto. Do you think he's in some sort of trouble?
JOSÉ:	I hope not. I've been trying to get some time alone with him but he dances away from me.
ANNA:	If you ask me, Jake's involved somehow.
JOSÉ:	You mean those men at the door? I'm pretty sure Jake helped Seth out of a tricky situation.
ANNA:	Maybe. But what do we know about him?
JOSÉ:	What do we know about any of us?
ANNA:	Don't be like that. I know I'm right. From now on I'm watching him.
JOSÉ:	Anna…
ANNA:	Sorry, I'll loosen up. Christmas is coming and all that. Remember last year? That ridiculous game – what was it, where you had to be an animal?
JOSÉ:	[*laughs*] I've blotted it out. And you must admit Jake put on an amazing spread. Particularly if you like eating chunks of animal.
ANNA:	Oh, he can cook, I don't deny that. But as I pull my cracker and neck my fifth glass of wine, I'll still be watching him.

SCENE 14

Everyone was great when we split up.
Your friends in the group?
Yeah, some of them took me under their wing
a bit. I went Christmas shopping with José.

It was nice to have him to herself for once, away from Anna.
Linked arms, taking on the Kensington High Street crowds,
spending extravagantly and mostly on themselves. A brass

band playing carols as the light faded. The chance to probe a little, to learn about Anna's rift with her family and ask about Charles and Seth's friendship.

"They were room mates, weren't they, at university?"

José smiled. "Yes, imagine sharing a room with Seth. Especially someone like Charles. God knows how many times he bailed Seth out."

Rebecca raised her eyebrows. "Bless him. He's such a sweetheart." She took a sip of her sweet, eggnog-infused coffee. Normally she was a purist, but it was Christmas.

"I know. I think he's the closest thing Seth's got to family. They spend a lot of time together listening to music and stuff."

"It's surprising in a way. They seem so different."

José laughed. "They are. Did you know, Charles lives in an even swankier pad than Seth but he's so modest you'd never know it. He's an amazing architect."

"I'm surprised someone hasn't snapped him up."

"Oh, he's far too involved with his sister to look further."

"What?" Rebecca's eyes expanded and José laughed.

"I don't mean like that. I think she's unwell in some way and Charles looks after her a lot. Get the feeling it's a no-go subject so I've never really asked."

Rebecca pondered this. "So I guess Charles won't be at Seth's for Christmas." She'd been hearing about Christmas at Seth's. Just her luck to be away.

"No it's only for people who are avoiding their families – or who don't have any. Me, Jake, Anna and Michael, for the first time.

She stirred her coffee. "Poor Seth. Do you – do you know how his parents died? I don't like to ask."

"Car crash, I think, just before university. He never talks about it, though. Never mentions them at all."

Rebecca swallowed. "He mentioned his mother the other day."

"Did he?"

She knew immediately from the surprise in his voice

that she'd said the wrong thing. She tried to backtrack but saw the jealousy dance in his eyes like a flame. "Only in passing. He barely said anything."

José took a sip of coffee and when he looked back at her his eyes were matt brown again. "It's fine. I'm glad he's talking about it."

Did you meet up with any of the group over Christmas? Have I amused you, Miss Laurence?
No, it's just that about the only day you get off when you do panto is Christmas Day. No time to be popping down to London and hanging out with friends. It was sweet, though, the Christmas present from Seth. Perfume in an old-fashioned stoppered bottle, like the sort on my mum's dressing table I used to play with. It was musky, darkly floral, not my usual thing at all.
But presumably his. It sounds like you'd rather have been somewhere else, Miss Laurence.
And some.

Day after day of playing the fool, still dishing out gags when everyone else has taken down their decorations and is detoxing. And no hope of a casting director just popping into Cheltenham. Still, she was grateful of the distraction. Only a handful of hours a day left to deal with all the stuff in her head. Better to slap on the eye make-up and grin at family friends waving from the audience.

You didn't see your boyfriend?
Ex-boyfriend. No. He was supposed to be staying for a few days over Christmas but obviously that didn't happen. He might as

well have been, though, the amount people
went on about him.

She was like a cat on hot bricks, restless, locked full of
secrets like an adolescent. Everyone assumed it was because
of Jason, talked to her about Jason, but it wasn't Jason she
wanted to talk about. Her mind looped round Seth in ever-
decreasing circles while she answered unending questions
about Jason. She only cried once, on Christmas Day, after
too much red wine and an awkward phone call.

**So you were glad to get back to London.
With your friends.**
And out of drag. I was.

SCENE 15

January was Rebecca's least favourite month but the constant
hurry to get from A to B, now intensified by the cold, pinched
faces of passers-by, propelled her like a power surge. London
didn't die off in the winter; if anything it upped the ante, forced
the pace faster and more furious. This year that suited her.

Being back in contact with them all, pressing the Play
button again, was a relief. It was hard to imagine what her life
had been like before Seth, before the group. How empty it
must have been. She was in daily contact with Anna and José,
regularly thrilled by Seth's velvety voice on her landline and
the whole group met at least once a week, with infinite sub-
set possibilities in between. Rebecca started to initiate things
herself: a visit to the Sensations exhibition, which provoked
an hour of debate; a meal at the new South Indian restaurant
up near Euston; even rollerblading in Hyde Park in the
stripped winter sunshine. In return she was asked on Sunday
walks by Seth and Michael, taken to a concert by Charles and
asked to accompany Anna to a fancy dress party, with strict
instructions not to look sexy. Her Catwoman costume was
banned and Anna turned her into The Joker instead.

There was no work on the horizon but she wasn't going to worry about it. Her two episodes in the serial drama had aired but hadn't led to a deluge of other offers, despite her mum's prediction. Instead she was doing some more school stuff for Michael and getting expenses for it. Better than answering phones all day – or vegging out in her pyjamas. It was strange how little she missed Jason. The others seemed to have gushed into the void, maybe on purpose to keep her busy, or maybe it was always going to be that way when she had more space in her life. She missed him when the lights fused or the landlord announced he was putting up the rent. On Sunday mornings she missed sex. But other than that she pulsed with guilty relief, concealed under vague talk of 'getting over him'.

One sunny Saturday morning she had a crackly call from Anna.

"Fancy cruising the King's Road with me?"

"What?"

"I've got the hood down, shades on and I'm looking for talent."

Rebecca laughed. "In January? You're nuts."

"Well, wrap up warm because I'm picking you up in fifteen minutes."

Fourteen minutes later she was summoned to the door by an insistent horn.

"So this is the famous car." Anna's pride and joy, an old green MG. She and Seth liked to talk about cars but Rebecca sensed that it was a real passion for Anna, more a toy thing for Seth.

"This is the green goddess. Hop in."

They laughed and shivered all the way to Sloane Square, people staring as if they were mad. Just being around Anna was like having an adrenaline shot. When they finally parked they were so cold they headed straight for Anna's favourite patisserie and clutched hot chocolates, still giggling.

"As far as pick-up tactics go, this wasn't the most

successful I've come across."

"Don't write it off yet. We've still got the return journey."

"If that hood's still down, I'm on the Tube, mate." They grinned at each other. Anna glugged her drink and burped. Rebecca smiled to hide an involuntary wince. She'd been brought up to see farting and burping as 'unfeminine', not for public display. Anna did both with abandon. Still, there wasn't much conventionally feminine about Anna – least of all her sexual appetite. How strange and wonderful to have that comfort in your own skin without wondering how people perceived you.

"So, tell me about Christmas at Seth's. I've barely heard anything, except that Jake found several new uses for leftover turkey."

Anna grinned and shrugged. "The usual. Seth was sky high, you know how he can be."

A twist of jealousy in her gut. "Did Michael enjoy it?"

"Hard to tell with him. Always so watchful, you know? Sometimes I just want to slap him. But he loosened up in the end."

"And no surprises, à la panto?"

Anna chuckled. "Nothing quite as extreme as that. The odd game or two, if I recall, into the early hours."

Rebecca could tell there was more but she wasn't going to hear about it. She changed tack slightly.

"Wasn't it weird, by the way, the panto?" It was a while ago now, but she still hadn't dissected it properly with anyone.

"How do you mean?" Anna's face revealed nothing.

"Well, the whole stuff about who was who."

"Seth loves all that shit. Secrets, disguises, pretending. Confused identity."

"He's a hard person to get to know, isn't he?" Anna's eyes flicked over her and Rebecca had the feeling she'd just shown a card in her hand.

"Well we all are, aren't we? Maybe that's what the play was about."

"Maybe. And then those blokes at the door." Rebecca shuddered slightly. "That was weird."

"Yeah." Anna looked as if she was about to say more but seemed to change her mind. "Anyway." She shifted in her seat and Rebecca mirrored her. "What are you planning for the next group?"

"I'm not sure yet. Now I've finished panto I can give it some thought. It sounds very different from the last one."

The theme was 'Childhood [*cut short*]' and Seth's invitations had featured – shockingly – a newspaper cutting of the Dunblane massacre. He'd written:

Come to a tea party on Saturday. Do something different. Take a risk. Show us something of yourself.

"Yes, on a Saturday for a start. What does that make us, Saturday Sillybillies?" They laughed and Anna mopped up a biscotti crumb from the table with her finger. "I thought I'd join in this time." An unfamiliar expression of shyness hovered briefly over her face.

"Really? How come?"

Anna shrugged. "It's about time really. And I'm sure I'll find a way of lowering the tone, even with a childhood theme."

"I'm sure you will."

A clatter from the next table caught their attention. A baby covered in mustard-coloured goo grinned over at them while his mother fished around on the floor for the spoon he'd thrown.

Anna winked. "How's single life treating you?"

"Good, actually. It's been a while."

"Well, it'll probably be a while before you're attached again if you hang around with us for too long."

Rebecca smiled. "Yes, it's weird everyone being single."

"Tell me about it. Either the group is a hotbed of simmering sexual tensions or we're just a bunch of freaks. Or both. Come on – you're the new kid here – what do you think?" She leaned back. Rebecca felt at a sudden disadvantage.

"Well, I have wondered about Michael and Catherine.

Whether he's pissed off because she only has eyes for Seth."

Anna nodded slowly. "I see where you're coming from but I don't think so. They've been friends since university and he's protective of her but I don't think it goes further than that." She thought for a second. "Catherine seems to have some sort of effect on men. One look at her playing that bloody piano and they think she's the Angel Gabriel. Although he was a bloke, wasn't he?"

Rebecca grinned. "I know exactly what you mean, though. Even Seth."

"Seth most of all, I'd say."

Another twist of jealousy, burrowing into her like a corkscrew. Anna looked thoughtful. "Or maybe not, maybe Charles actually."

Just for a second it all felt too much, too intense, too bizarre, and Rebecca wondered what she was getting into. Then she took another sip of hot chocolate and happily let herself get sucked back in.

SCENE 16

Did you notice Seth Gardner behaving oddly around this time, Miss Jarret?
No, he was his normal self, I think. We saw each other every week, more or less. I'd make dinner for him, we'd chat.
So he regularly came to your flat?
No, I meant at his flat.
You'd make dinner for him at his home?
He didn't - doesn't - cook that much. It was just a habit we got into, I suppose.

"Catherine Jarret, you're an amazing woman. How on earth do you produce something like that from the contents, or non-contents, of my fridge? It smells divine."

No one called her amazing. No one except Seth. She smiled, as though cherishing a secret, as if she'd done

205

something more mysterious than frying up garlic, onions, anchovies and chilli. In some ways men, even this man, were easy to impress.

"I take it you're hungry?" She stood up to ladle spaghetti onto his plate, enjoying the way he was looking at her.

"You bet. Why don't you come and play piano here every day?"

"Well, apart from the fact that businesses everywhere would go bust without me..." She made her tone arch and her eyes, hopefully, teasing.

"You're a hard woman, Ms Jarret." Just for a second his eyes slipped over her and she felt aware of the pull of her ribbed sweater over her breasts.

"More, sir?" She was playing this just right.

He put his hand over his plate. "No, I think that will do me." Stupidly, she felt rebuffed.

They were part way through the meal when she saw his eyes widen and his face freeze. She was telling him about her sister, how she worried about her lifestyle with all those boyfriends, coming home late at night on her own. How she wondered if Suzanne would ever be responsible enough to start saving or buy a flat. She wasn't *judging* her, she was just worried. Then Seth stopped chewing and stared at something to her left with a mouth full of food.

"Are you okay?" He didn't reply but she was relieved to see him swallow and put down his cutlery. He reached over and plucked a long, ginger hair from one of the place mats, rolling it slightly between his thumb and forefinger as he held it up to the light.

Catherine pulled her mouth. "Ew – one of Rebecca's, I guess." She couldn't understand why women grew their hair so long; it was plainly unsanitary. But Seth showed no sign of throwing the hair in the bin, where it belonged. She felt slightly sick.

"Shall I get the bin for you?" It was as if he'd forgotten she was there. The hair wiggled like a caterpillar, catching the light.

Finally he looked at her. "Sorry – bit of a flashback." He looked pale. He was stroking the hair, holding it with one hand and running his index finger and thumb along it with the other. There was no way she could go back to her spaghetti now.

She swallowed garlicky saliva. "Do you want to talk about it?"

He smiled as his eyes left her face. "Talk about it. I could try." He looked back at her. "I don't suppose you ever caught your parents fucking on the dining room table?"

"What? No, I didn't. Did you?"

"Oh yes. They weren't particularly careful where they did it, my parents. Not too worried about privacy, let's say."

He looked at her. "Rather the opposite, in fact."

She found herself looking away as if it were her revelation.

Seth laughed. "I take it you don't have those sorts of parents."

"No, thank God. Mum wears sensible knee-length skirts and Dad gets undressed at night in the bathroom. Sex was never mentioned in our house."

He nodded. "Very nice and normal. My mother was more baby doll nightie than sensible skirt." He had started to curl the hair around his middle finger. Catherine wanted to grab it from him. They both watched as it entwined his finger like bindweed. She forced herself to look up.

"It must have been awful – seeing your parents like that. How old were you?"

"Old enough to know what was going on."

"God, I've have needed trauma counselling if it were me."

"Well, I've been through my fair share of therapists since." He continued to twist the hair round and round, smiling absentmindedly. "Of course, I generally end up sleeping with them."

She jolted again. Was he joking? Wasn't that abuse? His face gave nothing away. Suddenly he dropped his hands to his lap and smiled at her.

"Ignore me, my sweet Catherine. I seem to be in a funny

mood. And in the meantime your delicious spaghetti is going cold and I'm spoiling our dinner. Let's eat and talk about cheery things."

When he picked up his cutlery again the hair had gone. She would have been relieved, but for the suspicion that he had put it in his pocket.

SCENE 17

"Oh my God!"

It was all anyone could say as they walked in. Rebecca watched her friends' eyes widen with shock as they took in the balloons and streamers and were greeted by an unfolding paper trumpet blown in their ear. The same laughter, slightly anxious and high-pitched, the same question on their face: What the hell is going on? A tape of children's songs playing jarringly from a music system with flashing lights. Seth giddy and braying with laughter, grabbing people's hands and swinging them round. The table strewn with bowls of Smarties, Hula Hoops and mini cola bottles.

"It's party time! Get your orange squash from Jake."

"Go on," urged José to Rebecca. "It's mainly vodka. I think we'll need it."

They watched Seth grab a handful of Smarties and pour them down his throat. "Do you think he's had too many E numbers?"

"Yo, Smarties!" A large, curvaceous Wonder Woman bounded over to follow suit. Anna, about to burst out of her lycra by the look of things. "What's your favourite colour, Mikey boy?"

"Mmm?" Michael and Catherine were wide-eyed in the corner.

"Smarties – everyone had a favourite. Mine's orange. What about you, Cazza?"

"Jesus, she's as high as Seth," muttered José, as Catherine said something about never really liking them.

"In my opinion," Anna proclaimed, approaching Rebecca

and José and waving her cape like a matador, "the whole blue Smartie thing was a complete gimmick. Everyone knows they don't taste any different. It's only the orange ones that stand out. Hey, what do you think about my decorations?" She gestured at a selection of garish paper chains. "Pretty good, Mr Interior Designer, huh?"

"Dazzling, darling. Rather like you. Who knew that it was fancy dress?"

"It's a children's party, isn't it? Plus, you know I was born in Hollywood."

Rebecca put down her drink. "What, really?"

José sighed. "A small town in Northern Ireland near Belfast. Surely you've heard that one before?"

Charles popped up behind them, making Rebecca jump. "I suspect that Seth and Anna have spent a pleasant afternoon drinking orange squash and taking brightly coloured pills."

Seth turned round and grinned. "Indeed we have. I feel like I'm eight years old for the first time."

"The first time?"

"Well, we didn't have many parties at prep school."

Everyone held their smiles but Rebecca suspected that, like her, they were surprised at the leak of personal information. It made her realise how seldom it happened with Seth. Only that night at his flat… but it was better not to think about that now. She took another warming sip of squash and wondered what was going to happen.

"Now, here's the rough plan for the afternoon. First we play party games. Then we avail ourselves of the numerous activities strewn round the room." Rebecca followed the curve of his arm and took in the space for the first time. Seth's drawing room had been turned into a nursery. The two rugs were rolled back and chairs had been moved or pushed against the wall to make way for the activities.

Jake winked. "Who needs Persian rugs, eh?"

Half the room laughed. Anna translated the rhyming slang for the rest.

Er...

**Yes, Miss Laurence, I'm aware of the slang.
And the activity. No need to be coy.**

Of course. Sorry.

Near the piano was a toy chest, two tricycles, another box with bits of lace sticking out of it, a Twister mat and large pieces of blank paper. Seth continued. "Then we have our tea party. And finally we should be ready to share our impressions of childhood."

Anna made for a tricycle. "Well, I'm starting down here. Dodgems, anyone?"

"Not so fast." Seth put out a hand. "We'll save the full-on anarchy for later. Let's do party games. Musical bumps to kick off? I'm reliably informed this is a birthday party classic."

"Bugger." Everyone stared at Charles, who had his hand over his mouth. "It's your bloody birthday, isn't it?"

There was an instant outcry. Only Catherine was quiet, looking down.

Anna slapped Seth lightly on the cheek. "So finally you tell us. Don't think you're keeping that quiet in future."

He flinched. "Something tells me I might regret this."

"Too right." She turned to Catherine. "Did *you* know?" There was a note of aggression.

"Yes, but I..."

"Catherine knew I didn't want a fuss made and tactfully kept mum. Besides, we're all gathered together, it's a party, so what am I missing? Some badly chosen presents?" Seth's voice skimmed lightly over the tension.

Anna pouted.

"Look, if it makes you feel better, anyone who wants to can make me a present in the arts and crafts corner later. I'd like that far more than a pair of Gap socks."

* * * * *

"I bet she made a right fuss of his birthday, without telling us." Anna had briefly cheered up through winning musical bumps but seemed determined to hold onto her grudge. José and Rebecca were with her in the kitchen and caught each other's eye over the bowls of nibbles.

"Let it drop, Anna. What difference would it have made?"

"I don't know, it's just typical of her not to share the information. She's a bloody snake in the grass." Anna snapped a Twiglet.

Rebecca raised her eyebrows. "It does seem funny she didn't tell us."

José sighed. "Is it really such a big deal? We all know now."

Anna scowled. "But now it's too late to do anything. We could have planned a surprise."

"And perhaps that's what Seth was worried about. Have you thought of that?"

Anna's scowl darkened.

"Seriously. I know birthdays are a big deal to you but that's not how everyone sees them. You know Seth likes to control things. He'd probably hate a surprise. Anyway, the best birthday present you could give him would be cheering up and enjoying the party."

Rebecca sucked her breath in silently but as Anna smiled sarcastically at him, she realised he knew how to handle her.

"I shall do exactly that," she said, downing her plastic cup.

"And now I feel even more worried," muttered José as she left. "Pass the Twiglets, Becs."

* * * * *

Rebecca couldn't believe how much fun she was having making her picture. There was a whole box of paints, crayons, glue, glitter, beads, sequins, flower petals and fluorescent stickers. It was helping to take her mind off what would come next, the scribbled monologue folded up in her bag that she'd written herself. Her stomach turned over. *Show us something of yourself...* a bloody strip-tease at this moment would be preferable. What if she'd pitched it wrong, taken him too much at his word?

She took a handful of petals and a couple of feathers as her mind drifted to the audition she had this week. A new play, young director, and the press would definitely come. But it was at the West Yorkshire Playhouse, followed by a long tour. She'd be away for months. For the first time she wished she had a normal life, and a normal, settled job.

Now was not the time to worry about that. As the music looped on and the teddy bears had yet another picnic she turned her attention back to licking and sticking and spilling and splodging.

It didn't matter about the audition. She'd never get it anyway.

* * * * *

José had been roped into a game of Twister with Seth and Anna. He'd never played before and it was hard to get any real idea of how it worked because a sumo wrestling Wonder Woman kept toppling over and landing heavily and, apparently, hilariously on some part of his anatomy. Or maybe that was exactly how it was supposed to work. Seth was busy making every position as suggestive as possible, even if that meant performing ludicrous contortions to hook a leg between his or Anna's thighs. The British were so weird, constitutionally uptight about most things, especially sex, and yet prone to a sudden, embarrassing reversal at moments like this. Maybe that's what repression did to you.

He tumbled to the side and let Seth and Anna continue with their contortions. There was something brittle in Seth's giddiness, like he was at Christmas. Brittle and impenetrable. It put José on edge.

* * * * *

Catherine had taken over from the music tape now, playing from a children's piano book. She should be able to play this stuff by ear really, but that was more Michael's domain. She was glad to find an excuse to retire to the outskirts. This kind of party filled her with horror as a child and seemed to have got no better after twenty years. All those clashing colours, the shrieking and squabbling like a cage of agitated parrots. And the games – everyone desperate to win. She remembered trying so hard to make sure she was in the middle so that no one would notice her; not rushing for that spare chair as hard as she might, feigning an unavoidable twitch when she looked in danger of winning musical statues. And now there was Anna giving her dead eyes, having a go at her in front of everyone just because she was organised and thoughtful. She reached the last chord of *I'm forever blowing bubbles* and paused. Maybe she shouldn't have kept Seth's birthday to herself. It was true she wanted to be the one to do something special for him, to have him squeeze his arm around her and call her his lovely Catherine. But it was their fault if they couldn't be bothered to find out things like that. And Seth had loved the shirt and CD.

* * * * *

Michael sat fiddling with the Rubik's cube. He'd spent hours with it as a child until one day, by sheer persistence rather than logic, solid blocks of colour had materialised on all six sides. He rushed downstairs clutching the cube over his head like a victorious athlete. His siblings were impressed enough but his mum muttered that now he could stop wasting his time on silly puzzles. His dad barely looked up from the telly where he was swearing at picketing miners, saying they'd bring the country to ruin. Michael stood there, letting the triumph drain away through his feet and into the thick,

213

swirling carpet, ready to be hoovered away. He put the cube carefully back on his bedroom shelf and never really looked at it again.

* * * * *

Charles wandered over to the piano and leant over the music so he could sing along. Catherine half turned and flashed him a slight smile. She looked as if she'd been crying. She seemed out on a limb in the corner, engulfed by expanses of mahogany, and he wanted to show her some moral support. He wished he'd said something when Anna snapped at her, but Seth had stepped in so smoothly that any further comment would have made things worse. Most of the time, Anna's directness rather thrilled him, a flash of how you could communicate if you weren't buttoned up like him, but tonight it had felt like bullying. Dynamics between women were complicated. He spent a lot of time listening to Sarah and the things she worried about. Left to himself his lens onto the world was on a panoramic setting whereas Sarah's was in permanent zoom mode, trying to figure out the subtext of every conversation. It seemed harder for women somehow.

Unable to articulate this to Catherine, he sang a particularly gusty rendition of 'Nelly the Elephant'.

* * * * *

It was ironic, really, preparing the kind of birthday tea he'd always had at other people's houses but never his own. Jake remembered the component items photographically, having wished so hard for them for himself. His mum scorned the whole party thing, claiming it was boring and clichéd, but really she couldn't be bothered. She always gave him a present and once or twice she bought a sponge cake too, but she never let him have a party.

Cheese and pineapple on sticks, crisps called French Fries,

little egg and fish paste sandwiches, sausages on sticks, even vol-au-vents as people grew more sophisticated. Then jelly and blancmange along with those chocolate marshmallow teacakes. And a big birthday cake, homemade with an iced tractor or dartboard or kitten and *Happy Birthday Bobby/ Kevin/Wayne/Janet*. Candles to blow out in one breath. The first time Jake got to do that was on his twenty-first birthday.

Seth never had that kind of party either. He was touchingly ignorant of chocolate teacakes and cheese on sticks, didn't believe Jake at first when he said that's what children ate. Of course Seth probably had caviar and tarte tatin instead, but you could see he'd missed out just as much.

* * * * *

Anna was rooting through the toy chest like a terrier digging in a sandpit. Then she squeaked. "Fuzzy felts! I fuckin' loved these. I used to steal them from school."

José and Seth were leaning against each other on the floor, exhausted from Twister.

"So your criminal days began early."

"Yeah, I used to stuff them down my tights and when mam undressed me in the evenings they'd all come tumbling out. Look at this, it's the farmyard one. I'm sure I used to have this."

The men watched as she unearthed more fuzzy felt boxes.

"Right, I'm sorted for your birthday present now. Give me a few minutes and I'll amaze you."

Seth sighed. "I can hardly wait."

Twenty minutes later she put the final touches to her artwork, wrapped it up with a convenient length of red ribbon and handed it to Seth with a flourish. The felt letters read Happy 8th Birthday.

SCENE 18

Tea descended into an enormous food fight. Rebecca was

shocked to see Seth's designer home turned into a scene from Happy Eater on Sunday afternoon. But, if anything, he was the ringleader, flicking squares of cheese across the table and ducking the debris that boomeranged back. The polished floorboards squelched with squashed sausages, crunched with Monster Munch.

Cigarette smoke sketched spirals around streams of glittering bubbles that popped on their plates. Oedipus had been turned to the wall so as not to cast a shadow over proceedings. Rebecca pictured the flat in its usual pristine state and felt a rush of giddy glee. Scooping out a wobbling pink blob of jelly she pulled back her spoon, and lobbed it straight at Seth.

It was war then. Seth grabbed a fistful of blancmange and chased her round the room as she shrieked, eventually begging and covering her head with her hands as he shampooed her with it. Vol-au-vents and sausages continued assailing them from the table. In the mayhem she saw Michael lobbing bread rolls and Charles ducking. She couldn't breathe, she was laughing so much.

A truce was called and after fifteen minutes it actually held. Jake cleared the table while everyone else got down on their knees, scraping up food. Rebecca showered her hair over the side of the bath trying to avoid the inevitable cascade of mascara. Several others needed strip washes. By the time they'd all convened in the drawing room, now mostly tidy but looking as though it had seen off an invasion, it was eight o'clock.

In her damp shirt and wet hair, Rebecca was aware of Seth and Jake looking at her. Jake had lit a fire and Seth sat her next to it. Was it just her or did he feel this bubbling tide between them? His eyes shone dewy green with his hair black wet on his face. She wanted to run her hand through it and pull his face to hers, finish what they had started last time she was in this room. No, not finish; plunge headfirst into the wave of longing that had been rolling inside her since they first met.

He caught her eye and she let her thoughts splay across her face. The sides of her ribs burned where he'd tickled them and her cheeks ached from laughing. He held her gaze while people handed out cups of tea and slumped down into chairs, giving her the tiniest smile before accepting his mug from Catherine.

Jake held out a packet of chewing gum. "To take away the taste of all those sweets." Rebecca shook her head, thinking Jake looked better dressed these days. He was in a brightly striped shirt today, almost like something Seth would wear.

"So, I think it's time." Seth paused for effect and surveyed the room. "I wanted to do something different today, experiment, engage us more with the theme. I think you'll all agree we make pretty good children." He let the giggles subside. "I also thought it might help us to be creative, a bit more subversive, saying fuck you instead of better not. Strange that children might have something to teach us about rebelling, but there it is."

Michael smiled. "At the risk of belying my role as a world-weary, inner-city school teacher, children can teach you pretty much anything."

Seth nodded. "Anyway, there's another part of the experiment too, but it won't be clear if it's worked until we've shared our stuff."

Charles coughed. "Are we being monitored by Nestlé to see how much sugar a human being can tolerate before ripping its own head off?" He had a gleam in his eye, as he often did after a couple of drinks.

Seth reached for a cigarette. "Nope, Anna's already been paid and had reconstructive surgery for that one." Anna threatened to recommence confectionery hurling but was restrained by José. "So I think we should see what happens. Who wants to go first?"

The usual silence. Anna, standing by the fireplace, ran her hand over the green marble frieze. "Perhaps the fat cherubs here could kick off."

"*Bacchic putti*, if you don't mind."

"Even better, bet they could tell a story or two between them."

Catherine got to her feet, saying she wanted to get hers over with as she'd been struggling to learn it. She played a light, flowing, melodic piece by Schumann called *Kinderscenen* (Scenes of Childhood). It was perfectly pleasant, but as far as Rebecca could see, there was nothing different, no particular risk, although she reiterated at the end how tricky she'd found it. For once, Seth wasn't in raptures; in fact, Rebecca thought, he looked a little disappointed. Catherine hesitated as she took her seat again, not used to a lukewarm reception.

No one wanted to go next but Rebecca forced herself to her feet. She'd just treat it like any other audition. Like it was someone else's material.

```
It was just a short piece about... well about
losing my twin. It was called "Rachel".
```

"Come over here, she says.
Come and snuggle down, chest to back,
Back to chest, back to where we started.

"Come over here, she says,
Come and build a tower with me,
One brick each until it topples over both of us.

"Come over here, she says,
Pretend to be me to confuse the teachers,
Chase me at playtime.

"Come over here, she says,
Tell me about your first kiss,
Let me brush your hair
And you can brush mine.

"Come over here, she says,

Stand next to me on my wedding photo.
Come over here, I say,
Come and be my sister."

Her words ran into silence as she sat down, avoiding eye contact.

"You wrote it?"

She looked across at Seth watching her from the armchair. She hadn't wanted to get into that.

"I had a go. It's not really my thing, I'm better with a script."

"*Au contraire.*" His words were slow, intimate, as if she were the only other person in the room. "It's brilliant." Anna and José nodded on either side of her. "It's brave and honest and exactly the type of thing I was hoping for. On top of that, it's poetry."

Rebecca squirmed at the praise. Writing wasn't something she thought she could do well. But since talking to Seth about her sister, about Rachel, she'd been having dreams and this had poured out of her pen one morning.

Catherine didn't move, but the others leaned in, asking her what had happened, squeezing her hand. She felt held.

Michael went up to the stereo holding a cassette. "What do I do here?"

"Just switch the top button to tape."

He slipped in the cassette and turned. "As you know, I work at a school where most of the pupils have had incredibly tough lives and have had to grow up way before their time. This is a recording of these kids in assembly yesterday morning." He pressed Play and sat down again. The tape lurched and crackled, then sounds of scuffling, shuffling and whispered conversation catapulted Rebecca back to her school days. Sitting cross-legged on the floor, digging each other in the ribs, some poor sod standing at the end to find his shoe laces tied together. As she listened a distant piano started playing – what was that song? Seth had it:

"I'll name that tune in one."

And then the singing started, loud and distorted, and she heard what it was.

Consider yourself
At home
Consider yourself
One of the family

They looked at each other, struggling to keep straight faces. Broadway it was not. Too much special orange juice made Rebecca want to giggle and she looked away from Anna quickly. Jake coughed. "Don't give up your day job, mate. Oh, sorry, this is your day job." Sniggers. Michael seemed unperturbed, leaning back on the sofa and folding his arms. At least the kids had the accent right:

Always a chance will be
We will see some 'arder days
Empty larder days, why grouse?

And then at the good bit they suddenly went into harmony.

"Well, I never." Seth nodded and Michael nodded back. It was starting to sound rather good. And *Oliver* was the epitome of childhood cut short. As Rebecca listened she started to pick out individual voices; some gruff and broken, some earnest and squeaky, plenty out of tune, like someone was walking round with a microphone.

Maybe it was impossible for children's singing to be anything other than moving, no matter how rough and ready it was. Tears flooded her eyes unexpectedly. The song was about belonging, having a place in the world. How many of these kids had that?

How many of us have that?

There were bursts of laughter from the sofa at strange croaks and missed notes but she saw that other people's eyes were shining like hers. Michael had done something simple and yet wonderful. She saw Seth watching him as if he shared her thoughts.

For after some consideration we can say

Consider yourself...
ONE OF US!

No one spoke for a couple of seconds. Smiling eyes were wiped with the heel of hands.

"God, that really got me."

"That was amazing, Michael."

He smiled and bowed slightly. "Well, I didn't do anything really. All I did was let them have a voice. Sadly that may not happen very much for some of them."

Rebecca hoped he wasn't going to spoil the moment with a lecture. But she'd seen another side to him since volunteering at his school, which had softened her. He really cared about those kids and he was a good teacher. It was easy for her to breeze in, do something fun with them, but much harder to plug away day after day with the disruptive ones. Seth stretched an arm along the back of his seat and Rebecca was surprised at the fierce intensity of the look Michael shot back at him.

SCENE 19

We've been hearing people's accounts of the Childhood group, Mr Stanley. Apparently the word 'experiment' was used. Do you have any idea what Mr Gardner's experiment might have been? You're laughing, Mr Stanley?

I'm laughing because it was just Seth's usual shit, dressed up as an experiment so we'd waste pointless energy trying to figure it out. Like we're doing now.

So...

Seeing how far he could push us. That was his 'experiment'. Nothing like a bit of childhood regression to get us to lower our guard.

Is that what happened with you, Mr Stanley?

He should have stayed well away. Childhood cut short was never going to lead anywhere but a cold, dark trip down memory lane. Seth had drawn him, hadn't he, probed and asked the right questions. And he'd been too vocal about his job, talking about how the most vulnerable children were protected now at school if not at home. Other people wittering on about how this teacher and that teacher would never be able to get away with throwing blackboard dusters, caning or giving verbal abuse any more. And then he'd looked up and Seth was staring at him as the others continued with funny-but-disturbing teacher stories and he'd given it away, something in his face had given Seth the answer he craved. And then one of the others asked him a question and his mind went blank and he started stuttering, but Seth smoothly took the attention away from him.

Seth could have made him suffer but instead he was noticeably solicitous to him for the rest of the group. Barely any of the usual spikiness between them. And at the end he took him aside in the kitchen.

"You should talk to someone, you know."

"Talk to someone?"

"I think you know what I mean." That bloody group, the booze, the theme, because Michael discovered he had tears in his eyes. He looked away.

"I'm fine."

Seth's voice was low. "I'm sorry." That got Michael's attention. "If I'd known I would have been kinder to you."

They stared at each other.

"Look, I'm probably not your first choice but if you want to talk, you know where I am." It was a typically awkward male attempt to support, and reassuring for that. It made it seem genuine.

Michael nodded. "Thanks."

No, not at all. I didn't really talk about anything personal.

"Well – follow that, anyone?" A second's inertia then José sighed.

"I've been doing a bit of pottery."

"You had a bit of a thing about it at one point, didn't you?"

"Still do, in a way. There's something about the squelch of the clay under your hands…"

"Ooh, now I'm thinking Patrick Swayze and Demi Moore. Mmm." Anna closed her eyes and let out a pornographic sigh.

"Anna!"

"What's she on about?"

"The film *Ghost*. Sex scene with Demi Moore straddling a potter's wheel – need I say more?" Jake winked at Anna. "I'm with you there."

"Excuse me, does anyone want to see what I've done?"

"Sorry, José."

He took out a large, round plate, unwrapped the tissue paper and put it down on the coffee table. "Here."

Murmurs as they bent over it. Bars of watercolours in reds, orange and purple were, on closer inspection, clusters of houses. "It's the village where I grew up."

"It's beautiful."

There were two figures in the centre holding hands, labelled José and Carmen in calligraphic writing.

Rebecca smiled. "Just like the Royal Wedding mug my mum has."

"Exactly."

"Who's Carmen then?"

José didn't answer at first.

"And what about these two oldies here?" There were two small figures in the background looking at the young couple proudly. Surely they must be his parents.

"I'd say this is the key person."

Seth pointed to the dark figure of a young man Rebecca hadn't noticed peering out from a hedge. When she flicked her eyes back she saw the figure of José was looking at him. The significance began to dawn on her.

"This is a story of my life in Spain," said José quietly.

No one spoke for a minute.

"Carmen and I were going to get married. Our parents decided when we were children."

Charles blew out air in a low whistle. José shrugged.

"It was like that there. A small town, you did what was expected of you. She was lovely, pretty, kind, everything a boy could wish for. Except a boy like me. We dated for three years." His voice became harsh. "I went to the local park at night." He looked round. Rebecca dropped her eyes as she realised what he meant. "Of course I knew I had to get away. I was outed in National Service when they found me together with someone. It was hell. But at least my parents never found out."

Anna squeezed his hand and he flashed her a fleeting smile. "Anna's heard all this before."

"I don't mind hearing it again, though. It's nice to hear you talk about your old life."

"Nice." He shrugged. "My mother was heartbroken when Carmen and I broke up. I'd never even touched her. All the mothers thought I was such a good boy, such a gentleman." He laughed.

"How did she react when she found out?" The question was quite direct for Catherine.

José laughed again. "Found out? She has no idea I'm gay. It would kill her. My dad too. No, Mama phones up every Sunday to ask if I've found a nice girl yet. At first she insisted on a Spanish girl, then it was okay as long as she was Catholic... Now, I think she'd just be happy to hear I'd met anybody. Anybody female, I mean." His eyes moved over Seth.

"Do you think she's guessed?"

"I don't think so. I don't know if she can imagine such a thing. But my brother knows. He guessed five years ago."

"The brother who came over in June?"

224

"Yes, Juan. He wants me to tell Mama and Papa. But I can't. The shame would be too much. So I avoid going home and they can't afford to come here."

Rebecca ran her index finger over the plate. "That's really sad. Your hometown looks beautiful."

"It is. These are the colours I think of when I picture it. I tried to capture the light as it strikes the stone but I haven't really succeeded." He looked out of the window. "Sometimes the greyness here drives me crazy."

"I've got it." Anna's jaunty tone struck an odd note and everyone looked at her. She had two bands of smudged mascara under bloodshot eyes and was still on the vodka. A thick lycra-encased roll of flesh bulged above her pelvis. "Let's all go to Spain. This summer. We'll be your moral support – we'll stay in a local guesthouse and your parents will see what great friends you have, and we'll all wander around being inspired by the light and the colours."

José smiled and shook his head.

"Come on, it's a great idea. I'd love to meet your parents and I'm sure everyone would love a Spanish holiday – wouldn't you?"

People made vague, non-committal noises. Anna sat up in her chair.

"You *know* you've got to do it, José. What are you – twenty-seven? Do you want twenty-seven more years of lying to them?"

"Anna…"

She brushed aside the warning noises coming from Michael and Charles. "You need to get over your fecking Catholic guilt, man. And it might not be as bad as you think. They probably won't blow up so much if we're all there."

"And after that perhaps we'll all go over to Ireland and meet your family, Anna." Seth's voice was quiet but clear.

Anna put a hand to her face as if she'd been slapped. "What the fuck do you mean by that?"

"I mean that while we're talking about José facing his

demons maybe we should consider yours too. How's your father these days?" Seth's face was expressionless.

José put out a hand. "It's okay, Seth."

"You bastard. What do you know about anything?" Anna swayed for a second and ran out of the room, cape fluttering in her wake. The bathroom door slammed. Everyone looked at Seth.

"My mistake. Talk amongst yourselves." He left the room, closing the door carefully behind him.

They came back in fifteen minutes later, Anna sniffing and blotchy but smiling. "Sorry, everyone, too much vodka." She went to José and gave him a hug. Jake got up.

"Let's have a drink. I was thinking hot chocolate and marshmallows."

The suggestion divided the room. "Think I'd rather go for a beer, old chap. We can pretend it's ginger beer if that makes you feel better."

"Well, for real men like yourself, Charles, I was going to lace the hot chocolate with brandy."

Charles raised his eyebrows. "Brandy, you say? Go on, you've never let me down yet."

Rebecca took the first opportunity she had to go over to Anna. "You okay, love?" She touched her arm.

"Yeah, it's all been a bit heavy, this childhood stuff."

"I know what you mean. Saves on the therapy bill, though."

Anna smiled, not her usual smile. "Tell me about it. I've just yelled at Seth for trying to be my therapist." There was a slight pause. "Anyway, it's my turn for the couch now. Wish me luck."

Anna clutched an orange Sainsbury's carrier bag. "This is the first time I've ever joined in properly with the group. Now I know how nerve-wracking it is." Her hands shook slightly as she pulled out a furry bundle and opened it out. It looked like some sort of dog costume.

"I was going to make a surprise entrance in this, but I've spared you." Smiles all round. "School play, 1974.

Even then I acted the bitch." Her joke sounded rehearsed, forced. She fingered the floppy ears. "We love dressing up in our family. Me and my brothers would try to outdo each other. Pa too, sometimes. I was going to show you a load of cracking photos." A pause and no sign of photographs. "I wanted to make you laugh." She looked down and tugged at the costume on her knee. "My mam made this one. She died thirteen years ago. I suppose I was nearly an adult by then but – I didn't feel like it. At the time I said I wished it had been a Dalmatian costume. I remember that. I don't even think I said thank you." Her voice climbed. "Now I look and I see all these tiny, perfect stitches and all the hours Mam put into it. But it's too late to say thank you." She started to cry, burying her face in the costume. "I'm sorry, I can't do this."

José put his arms over her and rested his dark head on Anna's shoulder. Rebecca caught Catherine's eye and saw a film of tears that matched her own.

"I just can't bear it that she died. I can't bear it. We hardly noticed her and she did all these things for us and I wanted to show you how creative she was, making this costume..." It was hard to pick out the words. "I just miss her so much, I miss her and I'll never get her back."

There was a crescendo of sobbing that gradually started to ease. José kissed Anna's hair and wiped his eyes. Seth sat silently watching Anna. She lifted her head and looked for him; he held out his arms then and she went to him, sobbing again. Jake left the room and came back holding a glass of amber spirit. "Fuck the hot chocolate." Catherine frowned; for once Rebecca was with her. A glass of water would help more.

Anna gulped it down in one, gasped and giggled. "Hey, are you trying to get me pissed?"

He winked. "Not me. Though I have to admit there was a trace of vodka in the orange squash."

"Now you tell me!" A collective relieved laugh ran round the room.

Seth patted Anna's knee. "Well, by my calculation there's

only Charles and myself left. Unless you've got another surprise for us, Jake?"

"I have actually. But it will come out a bit later."

"What, after the watershed?" Anna grinned. She seemed to be loosening up towards Jake.

"In your dreams, love."

"Easy now, you two. Charles, shall we toss for it? *No, Anna, don't even think about it.*"

"Just a minute." Catherine had sat forward on her chair. "I was – well, I'd like to do something else if that's okay." She twisted her hands. "After seeing what other people have shared – well, I'd like to share something too." She looked for a second at Anna, then at Seth.

"Of course."

She walked to the piano stool and sat on the edge. "I haven't played this for fifteen years and I'm not even sure I can remember it. It was my dad's favourite piece. I mean, that makes him sound like he's dead." She swallowed. "In some ways it feels like he is. This was his favourite, before he stopped playing and everything went... bad in our house."

Rebecca felt a flash of curiosity as she watched the fragile-looking figure at the piano. When she started it was strangely tentative, childlike and unpolished. She made a couple of mistakes, but Rebecca had never felt more touched by her playing. As Catherine went back to the sofa, Anna stood up to hug her, then pulled her down next to her. The unexpected was certainly happening. She saw Seth watching them, leaning back with a cigarette. Perhaps this was something to do with his experiment.

SCENE 20

So Mr Gardner succeeded in bringing you all closer, would you say, Miss Laurence?
Yes, by stripping away the layers, the stuff we hide under. He did a beautiful thing. Charles told us about his sister.

"Forgive my amateur drawing skills." Charles put a pastel sketch on the coffee table. It showed an emaciated girl looking at her obese, distorted reflection in the mirror. The title was *Sarah x 2*.

"My sister. You've probably heard about her. She developed anorexia when I was twelve." His voice sounded as though it was coming from far away. "She still struggles."

The famous sister.

"She was in and out of hospital for years. I knew she needed to eat more but I didn't really understand. I used to make her sandwiches when we got in from school." He looked down at his hands, opened his palms in a gesture of helplessness. "I still do it. Try to feed her up."

Did Mr Gardner comment at all?
Seth? I don't really remember. I think he put a hand on his shoulder or something but I don't think Charles wanted that. He's a private person. It probably cost him quite a lot to tell us what he did.

"She's lucky to have a brother like you." Catherine echoed Rebecca's thoughts.

"Is she? I try my best. I try to make it all better, but I can't." He shook his head. "She's a perfectionist, that's what the doctors say. Apparently it's really common in high achievers. She was always twice as talented as me. And then this illness comes and strips it all away." His eyes were wells of sadness.

"Is she getting professional help?"

He cleared his throat. "She's had a fair bit. But I'd rather not talk about it because you'll probably all meet her at some point. And she's lovely, a bit shy at first but interesting and clever."

"She certainly is."

Charles jerked his head up at Seth's words and searched his face. Then he looked back at the picture.

"Anyway, the theme – childhood cut short – seemed so appropriate to her, to our family, and it was good to get out the pastels after so many years. I've been an architect for so long now it feels funny to draw anything that isn't in straight lines."

There was gentle laughter as people realised that Charles was drawing another type of line under the conversation and wanted the attention moved away from him. Seth stood up.

"Well, I wish I could say we've saved the best until last but I feel so moved and humbled by what you've all brought tonight that I'm strangely reticent about my own contribution, which I assure you is not a familiar feeling." He laughed dryly. "But here it is. It's a poem but not my normal type of thing. It's called *"Endgame"*." He cleared his throat.

"Orphaned in the lockjaw of
Elongated evening smiles
Dreaming of a death, the boy
Is watching his mother's slender hand
Peel away from the soap-smooth rock
Unable to scream as he
Sips bilberry juice."

No one seemed sure what to say.

"Can you read it again?" asked Anna.

"Sure. Or can you, Rebecca? I'd like to hear it read."

"Me? Okay." She felt his gaze as she lingered over the words, trying to make sense of them for herself and the others. She felt he was expecting something, but didn't know what.

Anna leaned to look at the printed paper. "Is the boy you?"

Seth smiled. "Ooh, what a question. I'll leave that up to reader interpretation. Anyway, now we're all finished with our childhoods, shall we crack open the Glenmorangie?"

It wasn't his smoothest segue but, barring a couple of

raised eyebrows, no one challenged him.

"Hang on a minute. I have one more slice of childhood to serve you." Jake leapt up towards the kitchen and returned bearing an enormous two-tiered cake flickering with candles, an intricately iced Magic Roundabout.

"Happy birthday, buddy."

Seth shook his head as Jake conducted the rest of them into a raucous "Happy Birthday". He had eight candles to blow out.

He looked at Jake. "How did you know?"

"I didn't. This was the cake that no one ever made me as a child. But seeing as it turned out to be your birthday…"

"You gave up your cake again." Seth waggled a finger. "Well, we can't have that. We'll share it. Which of little Jake's birthdays would this cake have been celebrating?"

Jake ran a hand through his hair. "Dunno really. Quite young, maybe my sixth."

"Right." Seth removed two of the candles and took out a silver lighter. "Sit there."

Jake half protested as Seth picked up the cake and rounded everyone else out of the room. They filed back in, singing as Seth led the way. Jake's hands looked huge and helpless and his face was a child's, lit by candle flame and wonder.

* * * * *

It won't come as a surprise to you that I didn't exactly have a silver spoon childhood. Bit of a correlation in your line of work, I would have thought.
Quite right, Mr Etheridge. It almost sounds like you're incriminating yourself.
I wouldn't go to the trouble when there are so many people happy to do it for me.
The other group members?
You're the expert, you tell me.
Let's go back to this particular Friday

Folly. The childhood theme. What do you think Mr Gardner was doing?
Well, I'm no psychologist but I get the feeling that Seth didn't have a great time as a child either. Despite the fact that he did have a silver spoon. Shoved out to boarding school, then losing his folks so young. Maybe he wanted to hear about other people's childhoods because his was pretty shit. And maybe he just wanted a laugh, have you thought of that? Why are you lot always looking for ulterior motives?

* * * * *

They were ending with party games. Rebecca voted for Murder in the Dark. She'd always loved it as a child; that frisson you get somewhere between fun and real fear. Seth took them all into the spare room and made them stare at the light before plunging it into darkness. She'd had a D on her card, a dancer, not that she was doing much of that. She hugged the wall, giggling like others around her. Anna swore at someone across the room. It really was pitch black. Shadows and jostling noises. The murderer was biding their time. A movement to her left sent her creeping in the other direction along the wall, heart racing. Suddenly a squeeze on the bum, causing her to whirl.

"Oi!"

"Shhhh"

Silence again. She tiptoed towards the door and didn't see the large body next to her until she'd bumped into it. She was screaming already before the hands went to her throat.

I was pretty freaked. But that's the idea, isn't it?
I wouldn't know, Miss Laurence. Not

232

something I play for fun, really.
No, I suppose not.
It was Jake Etheridge, the murderer?
I think so.
You think so?
He admitted to it. When the lights came on there were a few people close enough to me to have done it. He said it was him.
Was that it, then? You all went home?
A few more games first. Blind man's buff. Seth said it was his favourite but he was so good at finding us that we all decided he must be able to see under his blindfold. Things probably broke up soon after that. Oh...
Yes?
He gave me something. As I was leaving.
Another present.
Yes... a vintage brooch. Gold, an ornate rose design. It was his mother's. He said she was an elegant woman. He said... that I'd wear it well.
May I see it, Miss Laurence?
Well, that's the problem. I didn't wear it well at all. In fact, I lost it almost as soon as he gave it to me. Now it seems like a sign of what was to come.

SCENE 21

José propped himself up with one arm and pulled the covers over both of them. The figure beside him stirred and snuggled and slept on. It was like a miracle to see him there, his beautiful face naked with sleep. He wanted to lace his fingers into the thick, black hair but made do with running his palm over it as lightly as he could. Why now, after so long?

He brushed the sleeping head with his lips. Feelings so

long dammed began to burst and trickle out as tears, one plopping onto the shoulder below, making it twitch. He lay back and wiped them away with his wrists, then burrowed into the warm body next to him. He would have to stay awake to savour every heartbeat.

But he must have slept because he was awoken by kicking feet and pummelling arms. As he tried to sit up a piercing scream sliced through him and he turned to see Seth sitting bolt upright, eyes snapped open like a doll.

He wouldn't talk about it. He didn't touch the tea José made and sat blowing out smoke in silence. José's hand felt sweaty and unwanted sitting on his thigh, trying to make a connection. He drew it back and curled it round his cup.

"Do you often get nightmares?"

Seth continued to smoke, staring ahead. He looked cool and aloof but his hand trembled slightly.

"Oh, you know. Now and then." He flicked ash onto a coaster.

"Is it always the same one?"

"Usually."

José touched his shoulder. "Do you think it would help if you told me about it?"

For a long time they said nothing.

"She's stretching out her arms and slipping away into the water and I can't move, don't move."

José felt himself unable to move in case he snapped the moment. "Who is?"

"My mother." And then José remembered.

"The poem you read at the group…"

Seth stubbed out his cigarette and leant back, closed his eyes. José swallowed. "I guess it's not hard to understand the dream."

Seth looked at him. "No?"

"Well, losing your parents as you did. It must have been terrible."

Seth leaned back again. "Yes."

That was the extent of the conversation. A peephole into the inner world of the man he loved. José ran it through several times at home. Late at night he allowed himself to imagine Seth opening up properly, making himself vulnerable. Falling in love with him. And then there was the other possibility: that Seth might regret his moment of weakness and shut him out altogether.

Do you know why Mr Gardner let you get closer to him now?
No. It's funny...
Funny?
Well, I think some of the others felt they were getting close to him too.
Such as?

"I know shit about the acting world but it sounds to me like she's turning down an amazing opportunity."

José stirred his tea, puzzling over Rebecca's decision. From what he could tell, she'd been offered a fantastic part in some new play that would mean her being away from London for a few months. She'd decided not to take it because there was another part coming up in London that she really wanted.

Anna shrugged. "I'm sure she knows what she's doing. Becs is pretty career minded."

"Don't you think there's more to it?"

Anna frowned. "Like what?"

José paused. "I don't know. She and Seth have been spending a lot of time together. I just wondered if..."

"If she's got caught into his web?"

"Something like that."

Anna gave her friend a steady look. "Not jealous, I hope?"

The tea scalded his tongue as he gulped at it too quickly. "Of course not."

Anna exhaled. "Thank God for that. You were a pain in the arse when you used to moon round after him."

"Thanks." They'd rediscovered their equilibrium after all the heavy stuff a couple of weeks ago.

"He didn't give much away in that group, did he? While the rest of us were snivelling into tissues. At least in my case."

José shrugged. "You know what he's like."

Anna added two sugars to her cup. "Or maybe he did. Maybe it's all in that poem. Whatever it means."

SCENE 22

She is asleep on his bed, amber hair rippling across one white pillow case and caressing the other. He sits on a chair with his hands on his knees, stiff as a soldier. He matches his breathing to hers, except when she snuffles like an anxious animal and he holds his breath until she settles again. Sometimes she twists her body and thrashes her head; once she calls out and her voice is hoarse, trapped in her throat. He has never looked at her like this for so long. He sees freckles dancing along her arms and turquoise veins tracing the backs of her hands. He sees a film of powder dipping and hovering over the faint lines fanning out from the corners of her eyes and around her mouth. His mouth. She is all his. His right hand clenches and stretches but he does not go to her. He watches her breasts rising and falling under the sheet and concentrates on moving his ribcage with hers.

Some time later, when he is darting across the glass-lined room like a jittery fish, she appears in the doorway swathed in familiar towelling stripes. Sleep has stroked away some of the desperation from her face but her eyes moisten when she sees him and she stretches out a hand. He shakes his head. She starts to plead and he clenches his fists but keeps his voice steady as he tells her no. No. No. No.

When she has gone he collapses and howls like a dying dog.

SCENE 23

There is something I didn't tell the others.

I felt it was private, between Seth and me.
Please go on, Miss Jarret.
It was a couple of months ago. Late April.
A Saturday.

Election fever and bird song in the air. Exhaust fumes sweetened with cherry blossom. Sunshine in the breeze. The prospect of a walk with Seth, arm in arm through Hyde Park. She was stopping by his place first to hurry him up so they didn't miss the best of the day.

A woman was leaving his building when she arrived so she got into the hall without having to buzz. Catherine noticed her hair: flame-coloured tresses poking out of a raincoat hood that circled her face. People in London were so odd.

She took the stairs at a trot so only half heard the noise at first, under the scuffle of her shoes. She stopped. It was coming from Seth's door, a sort of deep, sustained moan, almost bovine, comical, a noise that didn't belong in his flat. She stood frozen, the hairs on her arms standing up. Maybe she should leave, phone him from round the corner, say she was running late. She started to back away but she heard a catch and a breath in the moan that sounded like someone in pain. She approached the black door and tapped with her fingernails.

"Seth?" A whisper, as if she was in a library. "It's Catherine."

Everything went silent. She cleared her throat, tried to make her voice sound normal. "We're having a walk, remember?"

Still nothing. Bubbles of panic rising from her belly. "Has something happened? Please let me in."

Moaning again, softer this time. "Seth?" She pushed against the door with her shoulder, expecting it to resist, but it shot open and she stumbled inside. The dark of the hallway made her blink. Something curled up on the floor like an animal.

"Oh God, what's wrong?" She pushed the door closed and

got down on her haunches, dropping her bag to the floor. It was Seth, but the only part of him that looked familiar was his striped dressing gown. Swollen eyes turned to her with no recognition. "Are you ill? Shall I get an ambulance?" He covered his head with his arms and started to cry. "Seth, you're scaring me. Here, come here." She put out her arms and he laid his head on her lap, sobbing, soaking her cotton skirt.

She held him until he started to quieten. Her legs tingled and her back ached but she could have stayed there forever. "Shhh. It's okay. You're safe. I won't leave you." She was Jane and he was Rochester. She was Cathy and he was Heathcliff. She stroked his hair over and over until he raised his head and sat up. This time his eyes focused.

"Catherine."

"I'm here. Let's get you somewhere more comfortable." She was calm, in control as she helped him to his feet. He let her lead him to the sofa like a cowed animal. She put a throw over him, tucking it down at the edges. "Can I get you something?"

"Water, please." He sounded parched. She brought two glasses through and sat next to him as he gulped both of them dry. Now that they had broken contact she wasn't sure how to touch him.

"What's happened?"

He turned his face to her and she tried not to shrink from the blood-stained eyes. His face looked broken. He searched her eyes as if they held the answer and she turned them over to him, offering them up if they would help. Then he sighed, put his face in his hands.

"I can't tell you."

"You can tell me anything." The words tripped off her tongue, a line she'd read so many times before. She knew the script. Soon he would open himself to her, reveal the deepest vulnerabilities that would make him hers.

And did he? Did he tell you the reason for

his distress?
No - he, he kissed me.

Kissed her like she'd never been kissed. Grasped her face with both hands, pressing so hard it nearly hurt, running desperate hands through her hair, his tongue silencing anything but a guttural sound from the back of her throat. She yielded as she knew how to yield, let her body dissolve against his, gave herself up to him. He pinned her down on the sofa with his full weight and she felt his need, the hard pressure bruising her thigh, the maleness that her books only hinted at. His eyes were closed but she forced hers open, trying to focus on him, to prove that this was real.

His eyes snapped open and he pushed her away, heaving himself to the other end of the sofa.

"What? What is it?" She struggled to a sitting position. He was facing away, towards the door. The sound of their breathing filled the room.

"It's okay, you know." She reached out to touch his arm, which flinched. She knew this scene too, where the man is overwhelmed by his feelings and the vulnerability he's shown. If she could just pull him towards her and comfort him they could carry on...

"It isn't you I want." His voice was ugly and his eyes, when they turned to her, were expressionless. She felt her own fill with tears.

"What do you mean?"

"It isn't you."

"But..."

"You were there, that's all."

That's a harsh thing to say.
But don't you see - he didn't mean it. What happened was real. He just couldn't cope with his feelings. In a funny way he was trying to protect me.

239

She tried to bring him round but he'd closed up like a clam. She gathered up her stuff, dropping it from arms that still shook. He lit a cigarette and his face relaxed a little. "Hey." She turned to him, a wisp of hope. "Thank you for today. You saved me from a dark place." Had she saved him? It didn't feel like it. "I'm sorry about our walk. But I think I need to be alone right now."

She swallowed. "I think… it's often helpful to talk in this situation. Even if you don't feel like it."

He raised an eyebrow. "Talking isn't exactly what we were doing just now, if I remember correctly."

She felt the blush erupt over her cheeks, chin, forehead. He held out a raised hand over her spluttered words.

"Catherine. I just need to be alone."

He dismissed you.
He was upset.

She scuttled towards the door like a woodlouse in the light, looking for a stone to hide her. Back she went through the sunshine, the cherry blossom, through the groups of chattering students until she was back where she began.

SCENE 24
He summoned me.

A text on a sunny April Saturday. *I need to see you.* Rebecca cancelled her plans. She was getting good at cancelling things. She'd turned down the West Yorkshire Playhouse two days ago. Her agent was bewildered. But London was more visible, and if she got the *No Exit* gig she'd be laughing. She'd get it. She had to get it now.

She hotfooted it to Notting Hill, worrying the words of the message over and over. Was he missing her? In trouble? Was there some big thing he needed to tell her?

He greeted her with a hug and a smile but his eyes looked odd, swollen, and she smelt alcohol on his breath.

"Are you all right?"

He led her to the drawing room and she was reminded of that first time, the first group, the way he'd held her hand.

"Not bad, considering I've just had a visit from Sister Catherine."

She laughed as she sat but there was an edge to him. "That bad, eh?"

A gesture like batting away a fly. "Let's not talk about her. Drink?"

That question from Seth only ever meant alcohol. "Um, I might start slow, just been to the gym for the first time in months. How about one of your coffees?"

"If you insist."

She stood by the locked patio doors, sniffing out a few molecules of grinding coffee beans from the kitchen. She called loudly to make herself heard over the kettle, "Mind if I let some air in?" The flat felt unusually stuffy and it was criminal to shut out a day like this. She opened the doors and turned her face up to the sun, eyes closed.

"The question is who's worshipping whom?" She jumped. Seth was lounging by the piano, head tilted as if admiring a painting. "I'd say you were sun-worshipped, rather than worshipper. Your hair is glowing round you like a halo."

She flicked it away from her face self-consciously. "I feel I should pout, like a model."

"Be my guest. Strike a pose. You know I love to look at you."

This was intense, even for Seth. "Is that why I was summoned? So you could look at me?" She felt her breath catch as she crossed one ankle over the other, mimicking his posture, also tipping her head to the side.

"Perhaps. Perhaps not only to look."

"Then that was a little... presumptuous of you."

241

"And yet you're here."

"I am." She felt silly suddenly, a little girl playing a part. She straightened up. "But only for the coffee."

"Ah, the coffee." He ran his eyes over her slowly and deliberately. She felt each part warm up as his gaze brushed it. "Well, you'll have to come and get it." He stretched out a hand and she saw the mug just behind him on the coffee table. "It's particularly good today."

"I bet it is." She walked past him, taking her time. He moved his head to follow her.

"Thanks." She put the mug to her lips and inhaled the vapour. "Whoa!"

He smiled. "As I said, a particularly good coffee. Go on, give it a go."

Typical Seth, lacing her drink. It was good, though. Warming her twice through.

Do you know what he put in your coffee? How did it taste?
Nice! A bit sweet, a bit aromatic.
Go on.

They sat on the sofa. Half of her wanted to suggest a walk, a shot of spring, but she was already warm and fuzzy from the drink and she lolled her head back. He leaned into her slightly and closed his eyes. "You're wearing it."

"What?"

"Your Christmas present."

She'd dabbed the nook of her neck before leaving the house. "Do you like it?"

Bloodshot eyes opened slowly. "I like it rather too much. Almost as much as I like this." He reached over and took a handful of hair. "Or this." He stroked the curve from her nose to cheekbone where the freckles were densest. She basked in his touch. "Or this."

I expect you can guess what happened
next.
**We tend not to deal in guess work, Miss
Laurence. I appreciate it's a sensitive
area but any details, anything above and
beyond what we might expect would be
appreciated.**

The first kiss. She tasted him hesitantly, the edge of his lips,
salt and whisky. An edge without a net to catch her, the edge
of her need, a precipice on which she was teetering. Hands all
over her hair, murmurs and mumbles, while she clung to him
only with her lips, hands at her side like a doll's, forgotten
and dumped. Body and soul distilled into a mouth. Tongues
twisted and twined, losing her balance, the drop below her
yawning rapaciously. She had already surrendered but she
wouldn't let him know yet. She would fall inch by inch like
a routed land, letting him plant flags on her throat, breast,
thighs.

Did you feel odd in any way, Miss Laurence?
A little. Like I wasn't connected to myself.
And I came round a bit, when…
When?
Well, he got a bit carried away, you know?
He was hurting me a bit, not deliberately
or anything, but - I knew I needed to get
a grip.

Fingers grasping her upper arm so hard that she'd have a
handprint of bruises the next day. Kissing her almost beyond
breathing point.

"Stop." He didn't seem to hear. He was on top of her,
suffocating her into velvety folds.

"I said stop." She struggled upright and shoved at his chest.
His eyes were wild and he was panting, they both were. They

243

stared at each other like two boxers who had been dragged apart. Her head pounded.

You had a headache?
Yes. He apologised and got me some water.

Passed it to her with a shaking hand.

"I'm sorry. I don't know what you do to me, Rebecca. I can't control myself."

She held the hand and squeezed it. It was her moment to say, "Maybe we should take it slowly." There was something strange about him today, something out of control. Something not very Seth at all.

But she didn't say that. Instead, when he started to move their joined hands up and down her thigh...

Miss Laurence?
Sorry. This is really difficult for me. I keep wondering if I did the right thing. If, somehow, this caused everything.
Take a moment.

"Not so fast, Ms Laurence. You want slow, you'll get slow." It was her rushing him now. Her body had woken up and taken advantage of her still-woozy thought processes. He was kissing her again but delicately, running the tip of his tongue along her teeth. One hand drifted down towards her breast, circling over her T-shirt like it had all the time in the world. She arched her back like a cat, an invitation. A request. A demand. Finally a thumb on her nipple, drifting backwards and forwards, a wire of pleasure down to her navel. Someone lifted her top, maybe her, maybe pulling at his spare hand until the other thumb obliged her too and he was grazing the black lace seams of her bra with his nails. It sent her crazy, of course, writhing on her back like a stranded insect. They stripped her, one of them, both of them, until she was laid out before him in her best underwear.

"So." He surveyed her, a customer about to make an important purchase, examining all particulars. "You are a sight for very, very sore eyes." He smiled at a private joke. Fingertips walked from her ankles up the insides of her thighs and skated lightly between her legs.

"Oh." She bit her lip, trembled.

"You are so wet. So very wet." Words slow and deliberate, like the fingers skirting the edge of her knickers. "Do we leave them on, or take them off? They are in a bit of a state." He was still fully clothed but her hands felt leaden again. All she wanted was for him to touch her.

"Please." A husky plea. He looked amused.

"What a good girl, remembering your pleases and thank yous at a time like this." His fingers probed. She closed her eyes, waiting for them to slip inside her.

"Or do we try something else?" His voice was low as he bent his mouth and started to kiss her stomach. She splayed her legs, willing him to go down. At last a finger sliding in as his tongue lapped the edge of the lace. Then two fingers and lace pulled taut to one side. Imperceptible licks, flicks, a lazy circling of the area before homing in for the kill. Loss of vision, thought, only currents of excruciating pleasure sparking between her legs. She put a hand on his head and started to rock her hips, thrusting towards him.

"Do something for me." He had pulled his face away and his voice was rasping. His mouth glistened and she saw her desire smeared over his face. She shuddered and forced herself to breathe deep, stop herself from tipping over.

"What is it?"

"Wear something for me."

"What?"

"I'll show you. Just say yes." He bent his head and ran his tongue lightly over her.

"Oh God. Yes." Her mind spun. Leather? Basque? Leather basque?

"Wait here." An erection pushing against his jeans as he got to his feet. She still hadn't seen him.

She felt drunk as she waited, as if it was the early hours and she was on her second bottle. The world tipped slightly as she closed her eyes. She opened them to see his arms full of white silk as though he were carrying a bride.

"This is it?"

"I know it's odd but – it would mean a lot if you would wear this. I've been imagining you in it." His voice was husky and he didn't meet her eyes. "I think you'd look amazing."

She was turned on then by the thought of his fantasies about her. "Okay."

He trailed it over her. "Put it on and surprise me. I'll be waiting in the bedroom."

She sat up and shook out the garment. It was an old-fashioned negligee, short and strappy. Like wedding underwear. She giggled to herself. Maybe he liked the virginal look.

She stripped off and slipped it on. It smelt old, a bit musty. A hint of mothballs. Had he bought it for her or did he ask all his conquests to wear it? She shook the thought away, fanning out her hair so it flamed down over the white ruffles. She liked how short it was. He would barely need to lift the hem.

She sashayed towards the bedroom, getting into role, enjoying the way it felt. Powerful. Her head was clearing as she took control. She stopped to look at herself in the hall mirror. As she twisted around for the back view she saw Millais' *Ophelia* through the open door to the study and stopped for a second to stare at the translucent skin and swirling hair. And vacant eyes. She shivered and a little of her power drained away.

Did he say any more about this garment and why he wanted you to wear it?
No. It clearly… did something for him.

246

An immediate and obvious effect when she went in. A naked man lying on the bed can't hide something like that. She liked what she saw. She wanted to get closer.

"No. Let me look at you first." His voice was thick with lust. So she preened and posed, turning her back on him and whipping up the edge of the fabric to show her arse. A strangled noise in his throat. She was enjoying herself now, swinging her hips and running her hand over her buttocks. Then she rounded to face him, tongued her teeth, did her sex goddess bit. He stared, mesmerised, and she saw how his breaths pumped his chest in and out. She approached slowly, seductively, until she was kneeling over him on the bed letting him drink her in. Let him slip his hands under the negligee and watch the ripples of silk he made. His cock barged at her thigh and she realised they hadn't had the condom conversation. Soon. She wanted to touch him, she'd barely touched him yet. Run her hands through a black fuzz of chest hair and feel the strain of the muscles underneath. She shifted down so she could see better.

He pulled her back to him and then they were kissing again, harder now, and he was whispering things she couldn't hear. Suddenly he threw her onto the bed and pulled the negligee up and tight over her face. She spluttered against its slippery folds as he nuzzled her breasts, playing with the nipples with the edge of his teeth.

"If you can't see, you feel more."

Jason had never done this. No one had ever done this. She thrust herself towards him as she gasped in mouthfuls of silk, glad to evade the gaze of the overhead mirror.

Were you frightened?
A little. But not enough.

She wasn't just blind, she was gagged too. When she moaned and thrashed her head from side to side he pulled harder to stop her. His cock rubbed her pubic bone and she opened her legs, unable to stop now. *Please fuck me.* But then she remembered. He slept with men too. She had to be careful. She pulled at the fabric and wriggled her face free.

Two eyes, more black than green, pupils dilated to mad villain proportions. He tried to re-cover her face but she shook her head. He pushed two fingers inside her. "Don't tell me you weren't enjoying that. I can feel for myself." He hooked them back and tugged. She writhed as he beckoned.

"Stop it. We need a condom."

"And luckily we have one." He nodded towards a shiny square packet on the bedside table. She threw her arms round his neck.

"Come on, you didn't think I was a total arsehole, did you?" She smiled. "Anyway, I'd say it's time for a little role reversal."

"Meaning?"

"You take charge." He lay back on the bed, pulling her on top of him. As they kissed he pulled her hair down over both of them. One hand squeezed her buttocks. "About time, wouldn't you say?" He came up for air and reached over. She hated this bit, didn't know whether to help or even to look as he ripped open the packet with his teeth and pulled out the rubbery prize. She stroked him as he put it on, trying not to notice that he was going soft.

"Sorry. Just give me a second. Better still, take that negligee off." She sat astride him and pulled it over her head. He caught it from her as she was about to throw it to the floor. "Do what I did to you. Over my eyes."

"This over your eyes?"

He nodded. She rolled it up and pulled it across his face. She'd never used a blindfold before, hadn't even tried those fluffy handcuffs. But she felt him becoming hard immediately as she held it tight. Her own arousal soared even as she wished she could see his face. He started murmuring and grabbed her hips. This was it. She lowered herself down. And down.

She was in charge. That was what he wanted and she

exploited her power, moving around, taking him deep, taking him shallow, pulling the fabric tight until he was calling out, pulling her hair.

You were okay with this?
Yes and no. It… turned me on, but it was our first time, I wanted to see his face. I thought about saying something but…

Her body took over, she was coming and it was too late. Her orgasm was violent. Noisy.

Solitary.

His turn now, holding the negligee to his face and crying out something weird that might have been "God help me." For a second he was still. She needed to see him, pushed aside the silk and his eyes flicked open, staring straight at her. "You're the closest." A whisper she wasn't even sure was meant for her. Then, "Down you get, baby."

She rolled off him and he bundled the used condom up in some tissue. He held out his arms and for a glorious minute she snuggled into him as he nuzzled her hair. Above her head a mirrored tableau of a perfect love scene. Then abruptly he got up, grabbing the condom. "Better get rid of this." She heard the toilet flush in the ensuite and then the shower. She burrowed under the covers, hugged her knees, trying not to feel dirty, disappointed. Tearful.

Ten minutes later he emerged, clean and whistling, newly shaven and swaddled in a stripy dressing gown.

"This is not very gentlemanly but I'm afraid I have an appointment in half an hour. It had totally slipped my mind." She stared, not quite understanding. He looked at his watch. "Unfortunately…"

"Sorry – I'll go." She sat up and looked for her clothes. Where were they?

"Ah, one second." He left the room and returned with them, turning away as she took them from him and went into the bathroom. Her knickers were unwearable. It should have been a funny thing to share but instead she fought the tears away. He was waiting by the front door when she emerged. Leaned over to give her a soft, lingering kiss – on the cheek.

"Goodbye, Ophelia."

Please stop calling me that.

SCENE 25

Moving on, Miss Carmel, I believe your next Friday Folly meeting was… one second… Friday 16 May.

Probably, if that's what the others have told you. Let me check my diary. Yes, that's right… oh, wait a minute. Yes, I remember. That was the plan, the 16th, but it ended up being rearranged. Why? What's so important?

Rearranged? No one mentioned this.

Well, they probably just looked back at their diaries and forgot we moved it. If it's José and Rebecca you've been talking to, they're both as disorganised as each other. I'm not sure Rebecca even keeps a diary.

Miss Carmel, it is absolutely vital that we clarify these timings.

I wish you'd tell me why. This is freaking me out.

The best way to help your friend is by cooperating fully.

Of course I'll cooperate, what do you think I'm doing now? It's Sunday morning, you know?

Thank you, we appreciate it. Please explain why the meeting was moved and exactly what happened.

Well, we all turned up at Seth's place on the 16th as planned. The theme was Secrets.

Mr Gardner was there?

Yes. But he was feeling off colour. He asked if we'd mind if we rearranged to the following Friday and just hung out instead. I was relieved, to be honest. I hadn't prepared anything.

Did he say what was wrong with him?

No, I thought maybe a stomach bug. The type of thing he wouldn't want to talk about. He's a bit squeamish about bodily functions. He was certainly pale. I remember that. He sat on the sofa while we all milled around. Probably hoping we would go, I guess. But we didn't, of course.

What about the others? How did they seem?

Um, hard to remember, really. Let me think. Michael was quiet, which isn't unusual. But he also seemed a bit less spiky towards Seth. I'm sure I heard them arranging to meet up, which surprised me. I didn't think they did things just the two of them.

Can you remember when or where they were meeting?

No idea. It was just a snippet I caught. You'd better ask Michael.

And the others?

Well – a bit weird, actually, now I think about it. José, Rebecca and Little Miss Uppity. Not Charles. He was trying to smooth everything over, as usual.

Little Miss Uppity meaning…

Sorry, Catherine. She's not exactly one for dancing on tables, but she was uptight even for her. Hovered over Seth, trying to wait on him. Nothing new there, I suppose. José was a bit the same, fussing around Seth like he'd had an operation or something, not a case of the Brad Pitts. To quote Jake.

The Br… ah, I see. Mr Etheridge was there then?

Oh yes, his normal self. Keeping up the patter and the bad jokes. Even Seth looked like he was getting fed up of it, which shows he was ill.

And you mentioned Miss Laurence?

Yeah, she looked a bit peaky too. Think she was pissed off with the other two fussing over Seth. I collared her to bitch about them – just mucking around, you know – but she wasn't really up for it. Seemed preoccupied.

What time did you all leave?

Dunno, 11ish? We had a Chinese, tidied up a bit before we left.

So food wasn't laid on? Wasn't that unusual?

Well, without Jake no one could be bothered…

One second. I thought Mr Etheridge was there with you.

Yeah, he was but he left early. So…

Slow down, please, Miss Carmel. What time did Mr Etheridge leave?

Maybe around 9? I'm not sure, to be honest. Think he had somewhere else to be. It wasn't a great loss.

I see. Thank you, Miss Carmel.

Have I given you what you need? I'd do anything…

You've been more than helpful.

SCENE 26

The theme was carried over from the previous week. Secrets. A postcard had gone out with a quotation from Robert Frost, something about dancing around a secret.

Was that what they were doing at these groups? Rebecca sighed and tried to halt her increasingly paranoid thought flow. She hadn't seen Seth since that day but they had spoken. It was the kind of conversation she used to love: teasing, lightly suggestive, familiar. Now it left her unsatisfied.

She was angry with him and in a state of constant arousal. She worried about him in a state of constant arousal. She washed the bloody dishes in a state of constant arousal at the moment. When she wasn't having flashbacks of the actual sex she'd see his eyes flick open beneath her. *You're the closest.* The closest to what, who? What did he want from her?

There was something else to worry about: she couldn't find the brooch he'd given her. She was sure she'd put it on her coat before setting off last week for the group that never was but when she looked for it the next day her coat was joltingly unadorned. Since then she'd turned the flat upside down, even got Shazia to search her room, but there was no sign of it. Had it slipped off her coat at Seth's? Had he found it, was he waiting for her to ask? But she daren't ask in case she'd dropped it somewhere outside. How could she admit she'd lost his dead mother's brooch?

She had her piece prepared: a monologue from *A Doll's House*. She'd always fancied playing Nora and Seth would love her so kittenish. Her belly lurched at the thought of seeing him. More flashbacks.

Take your time, Miss Laurence. I can see this is difficult for you.
I'm sorry.

Catherine answered the door, looking, even for Catherine, odd and distracted. She barely said hello, peering past

253

Rebecca onto the landing. Charming. Charles and Anna were standing by the coats talking quietly. Only Jake came up with his usual half-moon smile and enormous hug.

Rebecca hugged him back. "Hey. What's up? Why all the faces?"

"Oh, just ignore them. They're worried because Seth's not here yet."

"Not here?" Something bounced inside her.

"Hey, don't you start. He's got held up. He's keeping us guessing. He's also left us the run of his wine collection." Jake took her hand and led her into the kitchen. "So, what's it to be? Rioja or a New Zealand Sauvignon Blanc? I'd recommend the latter."

Rebecca smiled down her anxiety. "I'll be guided by you. Cheers."

They touched glasses as Anna joined them. Rebecca kissed her.

"So, no Seth, I believe?"

"Not yet. Keep trying his mobile but it's switched off. I missed a call from him earlier so maybe that was to warn us he was running late. Funny he didn't leave a message, though." She shrugged. "Cowardly bastard probably hasn't prepared anything and can't face us." It sounded like Anna had used that line a couple of times already.

"How come we could get in here then?"

"It was on the latch."

"Really?" Rebecca thought. "Surely that must mean he knew he was going to be late and didn't want us hanging around outside."

"Maybe. I always thought Seth was quite particular about locking up." They sipped their drinks while Catherine kept guard by the door like an anxious spaniel. Ten minutes later all the guests were present and the host still missing.

"We could at least make ourselves comfortable while we wait." They followed Michael's suggestion and spread themselves out in the drawing room, trying to chat about normal things. No one sat in Seth's armchair, which loomed large and empty.

"Hey, his cigarette box is still here. He never goes anywhere without it. Must mean he's not far away." José sounded puzzled.

"Could he have popped in on someone in the building, one of his neighbours?"

Anna snorted. "You must be joking. You should hear the things he says about them."

Charles coughed. "It's why he doesn't use the communal gardens at the back."

"*Swanky wanky Yankees*," chorused José and Anna.

The repartee subsided and people sipped their drinks. Rebecca looked round and pulled a face. "It's really strange sitting here in his house without him. I feel like we're burglars." She'd had a furtive look around for the brooch but there was no sign so far.

Jake smiled at her. "Not a bad idea, Becs. I've always fancied that hi-fi."

The laughter flared and died like a badly struck match. Someone said they should try his mobile phone again. It went straight to voicemail.

"Well, we could make a start. But…"

It didn't feel right to do that. Without any one of the rest of them the group could go ahead. But not without him. They couldn't do it without him.

They tried to chat about their weeks and work, braking mid-sentence if someone heard a noise, starting up again when it turned out to be nothing. They looked at their watches. At 9.30 Jake said he'd get dinner ready and Seth could join them when he got in. They had to try to guess the secret ingredients in the array of tapas. It didn't seem any fun without Seth but everyone tried to get into it.

Michael put down his plate. "He's playing games with us. This is all a bloody game and we're the losers."

Rebecca held her breath. This was not the time to start

arguing. But Anna seized the bait, almost gratefully.

"Why the hell would he do that, Michael? Has he ever done something like this before?"

Michael was silent but his suggestion lingered over them. Rebecca wondered if anyone else was thinking it too. Would he do such a thing?

At 10.30 it seemed pointless to keep waiting.

"Listen, I'm sure he'll call us in the morning and have some perfectly unreasonable explanation."

Michael and Jake stood up to go; the others hovered uncertainly.

"Do we just leave the door open? He might get burgled."

"Not in this building; you'd have a job breaking in downstairs." Jake sounded sure of his facts.

Catherine shifted. "I could lock up. I have his spare key with me." She looked at the ground. "I keep it on my keychain."

Just one second. Miss Jarret had spare keys to the flat?

Yes. Something to do with playing his piano, I think.

Or doing his ironing. Rebecca caught Anna's eye. "What if he's gone out without his keys?"

Jake checked the hall table. "That's where he keeps them, isn't it? No keys here."

"No hat either." The black Fedora, Seth's trademark, was not on its usual peg. "Bit warm for it today, you'd have thought." José pointed towards the bedroom. "See, his coat's here."

They peered through the open bedroom door. Seth's summer jacket lay on top of mussed-up covers. Rebecca was catapulted back to her last visit and turned away quickly.

Anna frowned. "That's really weird."

"What?"

"Well, have you ever known Seth not to make his bed? His

place is always immaculate."

A brief pause while they stared. The mirror above the bed waved indistinct reflections back at them. Charles cleared his throat. "This feels a bit intrusive."

"Yeah, what if he walks in and sees us staring at his bed?"

"Or his mirror."

They laughed and moved away. Jake nodded at Catherine. "Let's lock up then."

Anna hesitated. "It feels odd just leaving."

José picked up their jackets. "Anna, he's a big boy now. You can't wait up for him like his mother." The crack in José's voice betrayed him. He was worried too.

People gathered their music, scripts, pictures and headed for the door. Catherine said casually that she'd tidy up a bit and then lock up. It felt wrong leaving her on her own in Seth's flat, but there was nothing anyone could do to talk her out of it.

So Miss Jarret stayed behind?
She insisted.
Hmmm. Miss Laurence, I need you to think if there's any other detail of that evening you haven't told us.
I'm not hiding anything, you know.
No one's suggesting that you are. But we do need to run over the whole evening with you again. Just to see if there's any tiny detail we've missed.

ACT 3 – SCENE 1

José's phone spent an undisturbed night by his bed while he himself boomeranged in and out of shadowy dreams of orphans, running machines and red-haired prostitutes. At eight o'clock he texted Anna: *any news?* The reply pinged straight back: *no. tried home phone no answer. might get keys from c and go round later – u coming?*

Of course he was. But on his way to the Tube, after two cups of tea and a bowl of muesli, the glare of morning made him feel silly. Jake was right. They were all overreacting. Seth would probably be asleep and they would look like needy idiots. His phone beeped in his pocket: *c already there, no one home.*

What was going on?

What did you think was going on?
I don't know – I was worried, thinking about the way he was after that nightmare. I was wondering if there was something I'd missed, something I should have done. I suppose I just kept running over that day all weekend. And… other memories too. Then it was Monday and there was still no news.

Monday mornings were never José's strong suit. This was the Monday morning of Monday mornings. Work was loaded on him in the nine o'clock meeting, all the charity stuff, children with sallow faces looking out of grimy windows. Just what he needed to cheer him up.

At eleven he got an email from Anna entitled *Meeting Request*. It amused him that she still tried to make their emails look semi-professional.

Hey there still no word from s. Should we get together tonight? Shall I ask everyone? axxx

Like him, she had probably thought of little else since Friday night. He kept seeing Seth shooting up from his nightmare like a vampire from a coffin, hearing the echo of that terrible scream.

He typed back *Yes good idea, ask everyone xx*

* * * * *

It was oppressively hot in Anna's flat and the gentle odour of sweating flesh was seasoning the air. Anna kept saying "Hey, thanks for coming" as she answered the door, as if she was hosting a wake. *He was such a unique character, so full of life, we'll all miss him terribly.* Anna seemed nervous. The only flat they ever met at was Seth's. No one had ever questioned it.

Anna's flat was trendy with an unlived-in feel. She'd bought it last year, predicting that house prices would boom. She was already vindicated on that front – but not on what she'd done to it. Cream sofa, blinding white walls and precarious black candlesticks. Absurdly large TV and non-functional kitchen. Not a single personal touch he could see. People perched nervously on the sofa or sat on the laminate floor while Anna weaved her way round with a wine bottle, looking perhaps the most out of place of all. The 'minimalist' look had a lot to answer for. José had tried to make suggestions to her, small changes that would transform the room, but she said she was never in so what did it matter? Chicken and egg, he said, and if she made her living space more welcoming she might want to spend more time there. But Anna had always stopped listening by then.

She coughed for silence. "Well, I guess we all know why

we're here. And I take it no one's heard from Seth?"

No one had. Michael rearranged his position on the sofa abruptly. He could never sit still. "I was supposed to meet him on Wednesday. He didn't show up."

"Where were you meeting him?"

"South Bank. An exhibition and a drink was the idea. No message, nothing."

Anna frowned. "You should have said. He could have been missing for a few days then."

"Or he could just be an inconsiderate arsehole." His voice bit with venom.

Anna looked at José. "We thought we should meet to decide what to do. I for one am getting worried."

Jake swilled the wine round his glass. "Isn't it possible that he's taken off for a few days and didn't bother to tell anyone?"

"I guess. But it seems out of character. And what if something's happened to him?"

"We'd have heard."

"Would we?" Anna raised her eyebrows. "Why would anyone have contacted us? We're not his family."

José frowned. "Actually, do we even know if he's in touch with any of his family?" Everyone looked at Charles. There were glimmers of sweat on his forehead and he was pale despite the temperature.

"I don't think so. I never heard him mention anyone. The only person he ever talked about was his old nanny. Lucilla."

"Surname?"

Charles shook his head. "I got the feeling she brought him up to a large extent. I think his parents were away a lot. Anna, could you open the window?"

Next to him Catherine stirred as though she was going to say something but was still again. Anna wrestled with the window as Charles stroked his beard.

"And – well, he's done this before."

"How do you open this bloody thing? What?" Anna froze at the window as she took in his words. Charles shrunk back as if under attack.

"I didn't know whether to say anything at first. Didn't want to be... disloyal."

Jake forced the window up as Anna sat down. "So he's disappeared before? How long for? What happened?"

"At university. In the second year. He went AWOL shortly before exams. Came back a week later in time for his first paper. Got a first, of course."

José struggled through the jargon. "And when he came back – did he say anything?"

Charles opened his hands. "No – he was on blistering form, you know how he gets. Just said he'd needed some time out. He sailed through the exams and then I hardly saw him in May Week – he was drunk most of the time."

There was a short pause.

"Seth gets black moods, doesn't he?"

The quiet question from Rebecca pierced the room. Charles was still for a second before meeting her gaze.

"He's never really talked about it to me." He seemed reluctant to say more.

"And did he ever disappear again? What about after university?"

"Not to my knowledge. We – um – lost touch for a while." He coughed.

Anna frowned. "How long for?"

"Oh – seven years or so. Seth saw an article about me in an architecture magazine and got back in touch."

Seven years? There was another pause as they took in this unexpected information. José was full of questions but this was not the time. They had to stay focussed. Anna looked round.

"So what do we do now?"

The room was silent.

SCENE 2

When Seth had been missing for two days, Charles went to

their tutor. Seth would hate that but he didn't know what else to do. With other people you'd ring their parents. In this case he felt like the parent.

"So you have no idea where he could have gone?" Dr Hodgkins looked over his glasses, as every academic must.

"None whatsoever."

"Is it possible he's just staying somewhere else to concentrate on revision?"

Hardly. "Um – I suppose it's possible."

The tutor scribbled something in his notebook with a gold fountain pen. "I'll speak to his Director of Studies, find out if he's been turning up to tutorials. Of course I'll let you know if I hear anything. It's Charles, isn't it? I'd advise you not to worry. Tell him to come and see me when he gets back."

Charles rose from the chair more weighted with worry than when he'd gone in.

By day six he was falling behind with his work, unable to plan essays about The Visionary Artistry of Christopher Wren when he kept seeing his friend drunk in a gutter somewhere. That night when he'd picked him up from Ely – that phone conversation – Seth had sounded terrified. Was he in trouble? God, he sounded like his own parents. There was just so much he didn't know about him. And despite Seth's swagger, Charles had an instinct to walk beside him, protect him. He hardly fitted the mould of poor little orphan boy but he had still lost his parents.

The odd couple. That's what they were, really, he and Seth. He was Seth's foil, the straight guy, the gravity pulling him back after each adventure, each mishap. And from his side... he lived some of the adventure vicariously, had his blinkers ripped off and saw how different life could be. What people didn't always see was that Seth could be a wonderful friend, supportive – when he chose to be – and one of the most generous people he'd ever met, always the one to put his card down at the bar and just last week he'd surprised Charles by buying him a scarf. A rather nice one. That was it, he'd surprise you, keep you on your toes. But this surprise disappearance was starting to feel like one guessing game too far.

Charles meandered slowly from the library along the Backs, his heartbeat and footstep speeding up just a little when he saw the ivory stone of John's. There was always the chance, however small, that Seth was sitting in the armchair having a cigarette and afternoon whisky. Hope made his feet quicken up the wooden stairs to their suite. The door was ajar and he heard a loud voice and a gentle, familiar-sounding female laugh. Two beaming faces turned to him as he entered: Seth's and Sarah's. His sister. He stopped on the threshold, speechless.

"Charlie boy, it's good to see you. I've just been making a delightful new acquaintance."

"Hello, Chas." Sarah came over and kissed him on the cheek. "I was just passing and thought I'd see if you were in."

"Right. Gosh." He had no idea whom to address first.

"I just offered your sister a whisky but she's going for the traditional tea option. You couldn't knock the kettle on, could you?"

"Yes, sure. Sorry, Sarah, do sit down." He moved stupidly towards the kettle.

"Are you okay? You don't mind me popping round, do you?"

"Of course not. Sorry – I haven't seen Seth for a few days and I'm just surprised, that's all."

Seth poured a measure of whisky into a glass. "Yes, sorry about that, old chap. I had some business to take care of in London."

"Oh, I love London, don't you?"

Charles busied himself with the tea as Seth and Sarah chatted like old friends.

So what had Mr Gardner been doing in London?
Um, I never found out. He was evasive at

the time, and then, well, something else
started to bother me.
Oh?
It's nothing, really.

Just that Sarah started popping round more and more. And
never seemed to stay unless Seth was there. She was giggly
around him, the way all girls seemed to be, and even accepted
the odd glass of whisky. Sarah didn't drink: too many calories.
Seth in turn talked about his 'charming' sister, which sent
Charles' heckles rising.

You didn't like them becoming closer?
Seth was a good friend but when it came to
ladies he had a certain… reputation. The
Wolf in Chic Clothing was one nickname, if
I recall. I didn't want Sarah to get drawn
in. So I spoke to Seth.

He tried not to betray Sarah's confidence but it was impossible
to avoid telling Seth something about her history. Seth made
the whole thing as uncomfortable as possible, teasing him
about Sir Lancelot defending his lady against the villainous
Black Knight. But he did seem to tone down the flirtation
after that, even making excuses to leave when Sarah popped
round. As Sarah stared after him, Charles let little things
slip about Seth's womanising. He never quite knew what
happened, except that Sarah got thin and grey again and
stopped coming round. She often lost weight around exam
time and Charles put it down to that. But he did wonder.
Years later, when Seth got back in touch with him in London,
Sarah made it clear that she didn't want to be around when
Seth was there. It made things difficult.

**Is your sister still in contact with Mr
Gardner?**

No. To be honest she doesn't even like me
mentioning his name.
**All the same we think it might be useful
to talk to her.**
No! I mean, sorry, I'm not sure what it
will achieve. I can tell you everything
you need to know.

SCENE 3

**Miss Jarret, on the day Mr Gardner
disappeared you claim that you used your
spare key to lock up his flat immediately
after the others had left.**
That's right. Well, maybe not immediately
but not long afterwards.
**Did you use the key again in the days that
followed without telling the others?**
No. That wouldn't have felt right at all.

Catherine's heart provides the drumroll, the sense of
occasion, reminds her of the risk. She's like a tightrope
walker about to do a backflip while the crowd gaze up
from below. Perhaps seasoned criminals learn to switch the
drumroll off or at least ignore it, remind themselves that no
one else can hear it.

She freezes at every sound on the stairs like a ham actor,
turns the key in the lock as if the cops are after her. She
drops her alibi immediately, a scatter of books and papers
covered in dense black dots that skate across the wooden
floor. The drumroll is louder, distracting her, making her
vibrate to its rhythm. Start with the dining room, place the
alibi on the music stand, push the stool back, open the lid.
Not today, precious. Wander across the room with a frown
as if undertaking a barracks inspection. Everything in order?
What is she supposed to be looking for, anyway?

She's only here because she doesn't know what else to do.

If he's been driven away by his feelings for her she needs to be the one to find the clue that can bring him back.

Move slowly into the hall, take the first right turn into the study. Colonel Mustard with a candlestick in the study? She shakes her head to dislodge the running commentary. It's Seth's private space, the desk where he sits to do – what? Sift the papers, mark them with smears of sweat. Fingerprints. Bills, bank statements scattergunned with zeros, old newspapers, a couple of CDs. The invitation to the Secrets group, invested with a new significance. A laptop computer lying quietly. Do the ham actor bit again, look right and left before opening the lid and pressing the button. The computer purring happily, *look what I've got to show you, just give me a few minutes to open my programmes – you're not in a hurry, are you?* Sit down because your legs don't feel safe. Wipe your palms on your skirt. The computer telling you something now: *I just need a password and we can get started. Sorry, I'm sure I can trust you but you can't be too careful these days. Nope, not even close, I'm afraid. Can we get this bit over with so I can stop winking at you like a retard?*

The bang of the door downstairs throws her up from her chair like an explosion. She hits the keys, but can't find how to finish and shut the whole thing down. *Please stop banging my buttons. It's not going to get us anywhere.* Slow, heavy feet climb the stairs. **Fee fi fo fum.** Slam down the lid, make a break for the hallway, head for the alibi. **Fee fi fo fum**. Slow, heavy, slow, heavy. Wait for the rattle of a key in the lock. Perch on the stool, flip open a book of Chopin Preludes. Slow, heavy, slow, heavy.

Pause...

Sink onto the floor as the feet continue up to the next floor. Act the kind of relief that looks like despair.

After a minute, which is quite a long time in that position, she gets to her feet. She's had enough, isn't cut out for this type of thing. She needs to deal with the computer, shut it down properly so that Seth doesn't suspect when he comes back. Back into the study, open the lid...

Ah, it's you again. I'm still waiting for a password. No hammering this time, please. Oh dear, now you've frozen me by hitting all my keys at once. Let me think... No, NO, not that, please, we can work something out, NOOOOOOO...

She jams a pencil into the side of the machine and hears it choke into silence.

Back through the rest of the house, wipe away the traces. Then into the silence a foghorn blast, rising up through her feet like an electric shock and filling the house.

Her feet are rooted but she is not still. Even the tip of her nose trembles.

The noise assaults her again and she curls herself into a ball on the floor. Seth's entryphone. Someone wants to come in.

She stays like this, a stowaway child, until she can slowly unfurl her limbs. Crawl to the front window in Seth's room. Peer over the windowsill. Slowly straighten up, look down. Just an empty path and in front of it an empty pavement. Whoever wanted to come in has gone.

She bats the duvet automatically as she walks back past the bed. Then she sees it. A long, spiralling ginger hair on Seth's pillow.

SCENE 4

```
No, I didn't have keys to his flat at this
point. I did try his buzzer a couple of
times, I think.
```

The telephone box was the biggest stroke of luck. Best placed phone box in London. And, given its location, probably the best maintained. No graffiti or sharp smell of piss here.

Jake holds a silent receiver to his ear and watches through smeared glass as Catherine looks around her, locks the front door and lady-runs down the street, catching the heel of her shoe once on the kerb.

SCENE 5

```
Sorry, where was I? Oh yes, I started
working again.
```

Irony of ironies, the gamble pays off and Rebecca gets the part – Estelle in Sartre's *No Exit*. She has moved mountains, risked her career to stay in London and he has gone. Now she will be spending hours a day in a claustrophobic group situation from which there is no escape. Something out there is fucking with her.

But it's a new dawn, a post-election haze of smugness, a smog of twenty-somethings gathered in street corner cafes chattering about Tony Blair and Britpop. *Things can only get better*. They're right there.

```
We met back at the flat. Seth's flat, that
is.
```

One week PD, post-disappearance, as Anna had started referring to it. Even though he isn't there it's better than being somewhere else. They tell themselves he wouldn't mind.

Anna in charge again. "I think we should report him missing to the police."

No one raises any objections, not even Jake.

"Okay, I'll do that in the morning." She makes a note in her book and looks down at the next point. *Point 2: Seth's missing, Point 3: Seth's missing, Point 4…* Rebecca knows that she must speak up.

"The last time I saw Seth – he didn't seem himself."

Everyone turns to stare. Anna points her pen like a dart. "Go on."

"He looked shaken up. Almost like he'd been crying. His face was swollen."

The others exchange a look, or is that her imagination?

Anna frowns. "Crying? Seth? Are you sure? Could there be another reason for his face being swollen?"

Rebecca frowns in turn. "Like what?"

"I don't know... if he'd been hurt in some way."

Catherine crosses her legs across the room and looks down.

Rebecca shakes her head. "No, it wasn't like that. I think something had happened but he wouldn't tell me about it." She is nearly crying herself. "And I didn't really ask."

Anna looks her over like a detective.

José examines the cigarette box on his knee. They are taking it in turns to fondle it, rubbing their hands over the raised silver ridges as if Seth will appear in a flash of smoke. "I had a similar experience." All eyes are on him now. "He was thrashing around in his sleep. Then he screamed. I think it was a nightmare about losing his parents."

This sinks in. "So you were..." Rebecca's throat contracts and her voice squeaks silent.

"No – I mean, I was in here and he was taking a nap in the bedroom. I heard some noise and then found him like that."

They look at José, twisting and reddening, and they look at each other.

"It seems some people have got quite close to him recently." Catherine's voice trembles as she shifts her gaze to Rebecca and bites her lip.

"Or his flat." Jake is smoking, leaning back like Seth might have done, looking at Catherine, who jumps as if he's prodded her. Anna's eyes flick from one to another.

"Hey, chaps, this is all a bit intense." Charles laughs nervously, reaches for the bottle of wine. "Anyone need a top-up?"

Rebecca goes to the bathroom, taking her time to get there so she can peer at surfaces, windowsills, the floor, hoping to see an old gold brooch twinkling at her. Nothing. Her search for it has become superstitious, invested with extra meaning. If she can find it she'll find him. She sits on the loo with her head in her hands. Finally she sighs and flushes, keeps her hands under the tap until the water runs warm and heats them. As she passes the kitchen she spots the others in

269

a huddle by the sink. They stop talking when she sees them. She's surprised by how tight they look, Jake and Michael and Anna and Charles and Catherine and José. It reminds her that they were a group before she arrived. Jake reaches out an arm to bring her in and she smiles but still feels excluded.

Catherine starts rinsing glasses and Charles goes to collect more empties. Rebecca knows she should help, dry them up, but, let's face it, she's always happy to let someone else do this sort of thing. She feels vaguely guilty watching Catherine's busy shoulders. So it wasn't just to please Seth.

Jake has fetched his coat. He looks at them all for a second and cocks his head with a small smile. "Lighten up m'lovelies. We know Seth has disappeared before so he'll probably pop back up pretty soon. We can let the police know – even though I can tell you they won't be interested. Other than that, I don't mean to sound hard, but we should all probably get on with our lives."

Anna shakes her head. "No. There's something not right here. I can't just forget about Seth when he might be in trouble." She bangs down her drink. "I think we should search the flat." She eyeballs them. "It might give us an idea what the hell's going on. We don't even know if any clothes have gone. We don't know if he planned to go away, or did it on impulse, or – if something has happened to him."

Rebecca frowns. "Shouldn't we let the police do that? Won't they be annoyed?"

Michael half laughs. "Jake's right, they won't take it seriously. I'd be amazed if they came anywhere near this place yet."

Silence. Charles strokes his beard. "I don't know. I don't like the idea of going through his things." Murmurs of agreement but Anna bats them away. "I don't like the idea either but there's no choice."

Jake lights a cigarette. "What do other people think?" He swivels to his left, blowing smoke towards the sink. "Do you think we should search the flat, Catherine?"

Her shoulders tense in a haze of smoke and she puts down the cloth for a second. "I – well, I probably agree with Anna. Although it would feel awful." She doesn't turn round and her words are hard to catch.

Anna slaps her thighs. "Right – it's settled then." No one contradicts her. "When? It's a bit late now, how about tomorrow?"

The next meeting is fixed and no one stays for another drink.

SCENE 6

It was years ago. I told you, we got past it.

Things looked as bright as the June sky as Charles whistled his way through town, stopping at the off-licence to pick up a bottle of bubbly. Finals were over (and they hadn't been terrible – a 2:1, with any luck), the May Ball was tomorrow and for once he had a girlfriend to take. Bridget had started out as a friend and they'd got closer throughout the year as she opened up to him about school bullying and low self-esteem. She was shy in company and he liked that, liked being the one she could talk to. His sister had remarked – rather acidly, he thought – that Bridget was a clone of Amelia, who had dumped him for some Trinity lawyer last year. He had spent a lot of time listening to Amelia's problems and trying to be a caring boyfriend, only to be told that he was a 'lovely guy but'. In hindsight he should have seen that Amelia was bored; even at the time he suspected part of the reason she came round was to chat to Seth. Bridget didn't seem to like Seth; she shrank in his presence and looked uncomfortable. He could understand why. Seth was an acquired taste. Anyway, none of that mattered now – Cambridge was finishing and a whole new life awaited him. One where he would be solvent and independent and no longer a 'lovely guy but'.

On impulse he stopped off at the dry cleaner's to collect

his DJ; might as well save himself the queues tomorrow. There was still time to loop back to John's and drop it off. He was spending the afternoon at a rugby club garden party at Magdalene – not entirely his scene but Bridget had something to go to and you couldn't miss out on a garden party on a day like this.

Being laden down didn't stop him bounding up the stairs two at a time, energy sizzling from the soles of his feet. He imagined how Bridget would look tomorrow. She'd told him the dress was red so he could match his cummerbund. He pictured something floor length, maybe low at the back, with her fox-brown hair swept into a bun.

She was wearing red when he pushed back the door. A red camisole he'd never seen before that pushed her breasts into large, unrecognisable mounds. Below that a black suspender belt holding up fishnet stockings that tapered into crimson high heels. Her hair tumbled over her face as she looked down at the floor. Where Seth was lying, blazer-clad, between her legs.

He couldn't react because he couldn't comprehend it. So he stood clutching his dinner suit and his bottle of wine while Bridget whimpered and covered herself and Seth got to his feet. The two friends looked at each other, Seth moistening his mouth, trying out words.

"Not a great garden party then?"

He went for him then. He'd never attacked anyone before but his body knew what to do as he slammed Seth against the wall. Bridget may have been screaming as she tried to drag him off. He shook free of both of them and upended the coffee table, sending mugs and glasses pealing to the floor. The click of doors opening across the stairwell.

"I'm so sorry…"

"Get out."

He heard Bridget leave the room, clip downstairs in her ludicrous shoes.

"And you." He couldn't look at Seth in case he lost control again.

"Of course." It was as if he'd just asked him to pass the salt. Charles dug his nails into his palms. "I'll come back later and we can sort..."

"I'll give you half an hour to get your stuff out."

He heard Seth stop in his tracks. "What? You can't throw me out. Come on, Charlie boy, she threw herself at me, what's a man to do? Tell you what, I'll crash somewhere tonight..."

"I mean it." Charles pivoted round to face him with flint eyes. "If I see you here again, I'll kill you."

You threatened to kill Mr Gardner?
Well, I may well have said that in the heat of the moment but obviously I didn't really mean it. I just wanted to get him out. For all his… idiosyncrasies, Seth's my friend.

SCENE 7

I'm sure you appreciate the importance of detail here, Mr Sanchez. We've received differing accounts of this evening and we need you to make sure you remember as accurately as possible.
I'll try.

It feels as though they are in competition as they comb through the flat, on a treasure hunt, trying to be the first to spot the clues. It feels as if they are watching each other without showing it. Or maybe it's just him. Ever since he told them about Seth's nightmare he seems to feel eyes on the back of his head.

He's barely eaten all day and he feels shaky. Shaky on the inside, like his heart, his lungs, his blood vessels are all trembling. What are they doing here, rooting through Seth's flat? Each time Anna avoids his eye the shaking gets worse. She thinks he's been keeping things from her, can't bear to feel excluded. He can't bear the separation from her.

He wants to be the one to find something. He owes Seth that much. Just for once he would like to be the hero, to see the gratitude in Seth's eyes and the admiration in Anna's.

At the same time he's scared of what he might find. *Shake shake shake.*

We divided up the flat.

Anna is looking through a wardrobe where shirts and jackets are lined up and all the coat hangers face the same way. Michael is going through drawers, finding tidy folded piles of black Paul Smith boxer shorts. José focuses on the other wardrobe trying to remember any jumpers or casual shirts that aren't here. There isn't much talking. Anna directs all her observations towards Michael, who tries to include José in his response. It reminds him of fallings-out at school.

They have left Charles and Catherine searching the study while Rebecca checks the drawing room. Jake is supposed to be doing the kitchen but the smell of toast suggests he's found something else to occupy him.

Animated talking from the study prompts them to stop what they are doing, listen. Anna abandons ship first. José and Michael look at each other for a second and then follow. Rebecca enters from the drawing room. Catherine is in the study shaking her head.

"I'm positive it was here."

Anna looks at Michael. "The laptop isn't here. Catherine thinks it was here the other day."

People make token search efforts, wandering aimlessly round the room looking behind curtains as if it's a game of hide and seek.

"No, it was right here on the desk – I'm sure. He always keeps it here."

They look at the desk, empty apart from a small, tidy pile of papers on the back right corner.

Michael frowns. "Are you sure, Catherine? I mean, we didn't go into the study the other day, did we?"

She bites her lip. "No, but the door was open and I'm sure I saw the laptop on the way back from the bathroom."

"Maybe you're getting it mixed up with another time."

She opens and closes her mouth like a fish.

"Well, if it has been moved it was either Seth – or you, of course. No one else has keys." Only Anna would put it quite so bluntly.

Catherine scowls. "Well, it wasn't me. Why would I draw attention to it then?"

In the silence they listen to plates clattering in the kitchen. Jake sticks his head round the door.

"Anyone fancy a Scooby snack? You wouldn't believe what I found in Seth's freezer." He looks at their faces. "Right. I take it no one's hungry, then."

"Catherine thinks Seth's laptop's been taken. Since we were last here."

"Well, he's probably taken it with him, wherever he's gone."

Catherine slaps her hand down on the desk. "No, I'm sure it was here last week."

Jake narrows his eyes. "Sat down and did some work on it, did you? No?"

José looks from one to the other. Anna has always thought Catherine and Jake can't stand each other.

"Is it possible you're mixing it up with another time?" Charles turns to Catherine, who now has tears in her eyes.

"I suppose so. I just think there's more to it. Maybe we should tell the police."

"For God's sake." Jake glares at Catherine and José feels sorry for her. "Think about it. They'd just conclude that Seth has popped back home and strike him off their to-do list."

Light dawns on Anna's face. "Jake's right. They were already completely disinterested when I spoke to them yesterday. We don't want to make things worse."

Charles coughs, hand in pockets. "Uninterested."

"What?"

"One of Seth's little hobby horses. He was always putting people right on it."

There's a short silence. "Let's carry on for now, see what we find." For all of Michael's abruptness José can tell he's worried. People murmur agreement, get to their feet.

"Oh, there's one other thing I thought." Jake is leaning on the doorframe, feet crossed.

"Shouldn't we all have keys to the flat? It doesn't seem right that just one person has them. And if we all pop in and out we can keep an eye on things." Catherine shrinks under his gaze and says she'll get them cut tomorrow. There's some sort of agenda between those two that he doesn't understand.

"Right, back to work. Don't know about anyone else but I'm finding all sorts of exciting things. Come into the kitchen if you get peckish." Jake winks as he leaves the room. José feels an odd shiver run over his shoulders. Jake's probably trying to lighten things up but still it feels weird that he's just helping himself to what he wants and making a joke out of everything. Normally he'd say something to Anna. His eyes swivel over to her, but if she senses them she doesn't respond.

Back in the bedroom he finds a big box of green folders tucked away at the back of the wardrobe. As he looks at it, hesitating, Anna comes over and grabs the top folder. He and Michael watch her for a minute, furiously flicking through handwritten sheets of paper. If this was his moment, Anna's whipped it away from under his nose.

"Academic notes of some sort – poetry, I think."

She rifles through the other folders, all arms and intent, an industrious spider. He, the stunned insect, waits for her verdict. "They all seem to be on the same topic – metaphysical poetry or something. Isn't all poetry metaphysical?"

He shrugs and they call in Charles and Rebecca. Anna has found what looks like a draft thesis, typed up in a seriously dated font with scribbles all over it.

"Presumably he did a PhD?"

Charles looks flustered for the first time. "I don't actually know. We lost touch straight after undergrad, remember. He was always a bit vague about those years."

She holds the document closer. "Look, there's a tutor's name here – Dr R Cuddly. Cuddly – is that for real?"

They peep over her shoulder. Anna picks up her notebook and writes Dr R Cuddly.

"Seth never called himself Doctor, did he?"

They flick through some more papers and Michael points. "Look at that. It says Seth Basildon, not Gardner."

"What?"

"Yes, he did change his name." They all stare at Charles. "When we got back in touch he said he'd decided to take his mother's name. I'd forgotten all about it until now."

Anna writes Seth Basildon and underlines it.

What strikes them is how little personal stuff there is in the flat. No photos from childhood, adolescent scribblings, nothing to mark his parents' existence at all. Michael finds a folder of ideas about *Hamlet*, which Rebecca says she'd like to read some time. She goes round and round the flat looking under furniture, behind plant pots. José sees her slipping a book into her bag.

"What's that?"

She pulls it out, pink under her freckles.

"Just some of the metaphysical poets. I thought it might be interesting to reread them if Seth took such an interest in them." There's a brief silence and Rebecca puts the book back in her bag.

"He said he'd lend it to me anyway." Her voice falters slightly. José looks away.

Later he finds Anna in the bedroom, still digging her way through the box of green folders. Most of the others are there, sitting on the floor watching her, not sure what to do next. Jake has gone home with a final shake of his head.

Anna sits up a bit straighter.

"What is it?"

She flips over a piece of paper in her hand. "I don't... know." Her words crawl out. "What do you think?"

José leans in with everyone else. The page is titled *The Saturday Group* in Seth's loopy handwriting. Underneath, a subtitle: *Betrayal.* Below that a list of names.

A jolt. "Tell me I'm wrong, but this looks a whole lot like another Friday Folly to me." It makes him feel weird.

"Hey, so he set up a group like this before. Big deal." He knows Anna's feeling weird about it too.

"Look – one name's asterisked."

Michael straightens up. "Yes, and flip over to see why."

Overleaf, the twin asterisk and a scribble: *wind her up and watch her go!*

José stares. "Poor old Bridget Larson."

"What?" Charles' hand shoots out and takes the paper. His face changes colour twice.

"What is it?"

Charles backs away, letting the paper zigzag down to the floor. He holds the wardrobe handle as if for support.

"Charles? Do you know her?"

He is staring at the paper on the floor. "I did. Once. Just getting a glass of water."

They frown and shrug at each other as the tap in the kitchen splutters on. José mouths that he will go. He finds Charles leaning over the sink staring out of the window.

"Are you okay, mate?" He's never sure when the use of 'mate' is appropriate. Charles smiles sort of sadly at him; he's got it wrong.

"I'm fine. Just needed a breather."

José doesn't know which words to throw into the silence. Charles has turned back to the window.

"Look, m – Charles, I don't want to hassle you but – well, if you go back into that room you'll get the third degree. If it would be easier to tell one person, we could go sit on the sofa."

"Or I could always go home and not tell anyone." There's an

278

unfamiliar spike in Charles' voice. "Or is that not an option?"

"Of course it's an option. I just think that – if there's anything at all that might help us understand things better it would be good to know."

It is painful watching Charles tell his account of Seth's betrayal. To José's annoyance, Anna appears in the doorway to listen and the others follow behind her. Charles doesn't look at them but neither does he stop talking; he addresses the rubber plant in the corner. His voice is monotone but his hands jerk and twitch. He says they were young, that Seth was sorry, that it was one of those things. Looking at his hunched figure, José has no doubt that it is one of the worst things that has ever happened to him.

When he finishes talking, José reaches out and squeezes his arm, ignoring the ridiculous chorus in the corner, which has sat down in a huddle, trying to be unobtrusive. He wants to wave them away like an irritated stage director. But they get up and begin to disperse and he loses his chance to give Charles some quiet support.

"Well, I can't say I'm surprised." Michael's hands are jammed into his pockets, his mouth a narrow slit.

"It's amazing that you forgave him." Rebecca's voice is warm. Catherine nods and looks shell-shocked.

Anna cuts through, briskly. "So he clearly stayed in contact with this woman – Bridget."

Charles flinches and José wants to shake her. "When I first saw him in London – when we sorted things out – he told me it was a one-off. But, yes, it looks like they stayed in touch."

"So they could be in touch now." Anna is in full-on detective mode, with all the bedside manner. She appeals to the silent room. "Come on, guys, it's obvious we have to try to track her down. What other leads do we have? Now, I guess we could try the university?"

"I have her parents' number." Charles looks directly at Anna for the first time and she blinks. "I still have my college address book."

"Great."

"I knew her parents quite well. I think they rather hoped we'd settle down together." For the first time, his face flashes pain, and this time even Anna softens her voice.

"I'm sorry." She makes two steps towards him and touches his arm. "How would you feel about calling them?"

SCENE 8

There's a very long pause when Charles announces himself. He can't help stuttering.

"We were friends at Cambridge, I met…"

"I know who you are. I'm just wondering why you're ringing."

Charles can't account for the hostility in the other man's voice. He's waited till two o'clock so he knows they'll have been to church and finished their lunch. "I – I just wondered if you could give me Bridget's number. I wanted to say hello and – talk to her about something."

He hears a muffled snort. "After – let's see, fifteen years – you want to talk to her about something."

Charles doesn't know what to say. "If it's a problem…"

"Look, give me your number and I'll get my wife to call you. She's better at this sort of thing."

Mrs Larson phones back half an hour later. She sounds breathy and friendly, like she always did.

"I'm sorry if David was a bit short with you, Charles. He's been under quite a bit of pressure recently. We all have. I'm afraid Bridget isn't too well."

"Oh, I'm so sorry. I had no idea."

"That friend of yours has a lot to answer for." There's a sudden bite in her voice.

"Sorry?"

"Seth Basildon. She's never been the same."

Charles' heart speeds and swerves. "I'm terribly sorry, Mrs Larson, I'm not sure what you mean."

"You are in touch with him, aren't you?"

"I – well, actually that was part of the reason for getting in touch with Bridget. We've sort of – lost him."

There's a slight pause. "I think you'd better come over."

There's nothing of any significance in all this. Not to you, anyhow.
You may well be right, Mr Maslowe. But we have to be sure. Please go on.

He's only been to their house once before but he remembers the location almost photographically. That evening is stored on an index card in his brain. He seemed to stand six inches taller as he walked with Bridget's arm tucked through his, listening to her anecdotes of playing with her brothers on the street. Meeting her parents was the first step in a journey he hoped would never end.

Today there is no sense of anticipation, no looking forward. He is not where he should be. He longs for his flat, the 3pm pot of Earl Grey tea, settling into the Chippendale armchair and *Test Match Special*.

There's the house. Still nicely kept, hanging baskets by the front door. The door opens as he is about to knock and he almost stumbles into Mrs Larson, dressed in a frilly apron and dusting her hands of flour. Their slight muddle sidesteps the greeting issue – neither a kiss nor handshake seeming quite right – and she waves him through to the front room. Gold chintz curtains with elaborate tiebacks. Tea laid out on a circular coffee table, spotless white lace tablecloth presenting a cosied teapot and plate of scones. Just like his first visit.

"It's milk and one sugar, isn't it, Charles?" and he is touched by her remembering. She serves him taupe liquid in a rose china cup.

"Do help yourself to a scone – there'll be more ready soon."

He's not hungry but makes a show of appreciation, adding a blob of homemade jam from a tiny silver spoon.

"David sends his apologies – he's got a meeting at his golf club this afternoon. Besides," she looks at him and he isn't sure if the new severity in her face is an expression or due to wear and tear, "it might be easier to talk without him. He tends to find this type of thing difficult."

Charles isn't sure what *this type of thing* is exactly, but he can see why an afternoon at the golf club might be preferable.

"So. You wanted to contact Bridget to see if she was in touch with – him." Mrs Larson's mouth twists.

"With Seth? Yes. I – we – haven't heard from him for some time and people are getting worried. I thought Bridget might know something."

"And what made you think they might be in touch?"

"I, er, found her name on a piece of paper at his flat." Charles takes a sip of his tea to break an intense eye contact he is starting to find alarming. When he looks up, he is relieved to see Mrs Larson leaning back a little.

"We were very disappointed when you and Bridget broke up, you know. Both of us. David has always spoken very highly of you."

"Oh. Thank you." The words should warm him but they nibble at his heart like carnivorous fish. "It was a difficult time." He swallows. "But I forgave Seth years ago."

"That is to your enormous credit. I fear I shall never forgive him." She sees Charles' expression. "Oh – not for that, though it was most regrettable. Bridget was much to blame as well. But she lost sight of herself whenever she was around him."

A car suddenly speeds out of the silence, revving a juddering engine absurdly. Charles jumps.

"Those wretched kids. I've already written to the council twice." She dabs her mouth with a napkin. "I'm guessing, Charles, that you don't know what happened to Bridget after you two... ended things?"

He shakes his head. He doesn't want to know now.

"She went on to do a Masters and started a PhD. We were

so proud. Then we got a call in the middle of the night from Addenbrookes hospital." She took a deep breath. "Bridget was unconscious. They pumped her stomach of alcohol and sleeping tablets. Luckily she was found in time. But she's never been the same girl again."

The teacup starts to slip from Charles' grip and he rattles it down on the saucer.

"I'm so sorry, Mrs Larson. I had no idea. That's terrible. But – I don't quite see. Do you think Seth had something to do with this?"

She pours them a top-up and reaches for the milk jug. "My theory is that Seth Basildon quite calculatedly sucked my daughter in and destroyed her. When she told me what was going on in that house…"

"House?"

"Den of iniquity, more like. Under the guise of being some sort of club for the gifted few. Drink, drugs, sexual depravity – I can't bear to think about it. Bridget couldn't handle it. At some point, your friend seems to have tired of her and rejected her in a cruel, public way." *Wind her up and watch her go.* Mrs Larson is looking out of the window and he notices the tea quivering in the cup as her hand grips the saucer.

"When we found out the extent of it, we notified the police. I believe they raided the house. But knowing your friend he'll have wriggled out of it. I gather from Bridget that he just disappeared." She looks up. "Like he seems to have done now."

The *your friend* comments are derailing Charles, preventing him from hearing her words properly. It's almost as if he's to blame. Wasn't he the wounded party? She's talking again.

"…and after he betrayed her with that *Sarah*. Well, I suppose she should have seen that coming after their start together. But it wasn't just a case of cheating on her. It was like he wanted to take her apart."

Mrs Larson puts her cup down and he thinks she's weeping

but when she turns to him her eyes are bitter as jackfruit. "I know it's not your fault, Charles. But much as we liked you, much as you made Bridget happy, we can't help wishing she'd never met you."

There's a terrible ticking silence. Charles' breeding kicks in with the automatic response. "I'm sorry." He can't meet her eye. He wills another car to go past, but nothing occurs to distract them from each other.

"I think, given all this, you'll understand why I haven't handed you Bridget's number. She's terribly fragile and I don't want to risk unsettling her."

"Of course, I understand."

"At some point I may tell her about your visit and give her your number so she can ring you if she chooses. But not right now."

"No, of course." Charles stands up. Mrs Larson gets to her feet and looks him square in the eye.

"Be careful, Charles. You're a good person and that man is dangerous. I don't know why you choose to be around him, but if I were you, I would let him go now. Don't try and find him. You have a chance to break free."

He shivers when he gets out onto the street and dabs the sweat from his forehead. He has already dismissed her interpretation of events as coming from an overprotective mother. Not hard to believe that Seth was into all sorts but the idea that he would deliberately ruin someone... no.

He strides towards the evening sun, tailed by shadows, trying to focus on the client meeting he has first thing in the morning. But that line keeps coming back to him. *Wind her up and watch her go!*

You're a very forgiving man, Mr Maslowe.
Well, everyone deserves a second chance, I suppose.
Not everyone would see it that way.
No. I suppose they wouldn't.

They all chip in, questioning him endlessly. Anna is in full flow. "So she blames Seth for the demise of her dear daughter by introducing her to alcohol. Please!"

People smile but the atmosphere is subdued.

"And it sounds like she got Seth into trouble with the police. I wonder what happened. Did they find anything? That could be why he disappeared afterwards." Rebecca runs a hand through her hair.

"Do you think he got done?"

"Who knows? Maybe we should try to find out."

Jake stubs out a cigarette. "There's a fine line between concern and snooping. If Seth 'asn't told us any of this I'm not sure we have the right to start digging around in 'is past."

Jake's eyes look different without their usual smile crinkles. For a second Charles wonders what events in his past he might want to conceal. What secrets they might all be hiding.

SCENE 9

So you all had keys cut for Mr Gardner's flat. Did you ever use yours, Miss Carmel?

She tells herself it makes sense to try Notting Hill first. Hasn't someone from work mentioned a lamp shop on the high street? She could pop there and still be in time to meet Keeley at eight.

They don't have what she's looking for. She's only five minutes' walk from the flat and has an hour to kill. She feels the cold knobble of the key in her pocket and sets off, stopping and starting like the cars beside her in the evening traffic. She's a doing person, not one to sit around torturing herself about what she could have said and done. About what would have happened if she'd taken Seth's call on the day he disappeared instead of dragging home that bloke from PSN after having too much to drink over lunch. She's got enough guilt in her life.

From the outside nothing has changed; still the same shiny twists of the black balcony rails and the outline of the African vase behind net curtains.

"They're not net curtains."

"What are they then?"

"Lengths of the finest Turkish lace hung with great skill to create an atmosphere of tasteful opulence."

She smiles and closes her eyes for a second against the blast of missing him. When it passes she checks her watch. There's time for a quick cuppa.

She fiddles at the lock awkwardly. Thank God there's no alarm to deal with as well. Heading straight for the kitchen she fills the kettle and switches it on, anticipating the soothing shush that will make her feel better. She glances at the plate and cup in the sink and crumbs on the worktop; Catherine's not doing her job properly. But at least there's fresh milk in the fridge. It must be the steaming crescendo that blocks the sound of footsteps approaching the kitchen door as she fiddles around finding tea bags and the right cup for the moment.

"Hello, Anna."

She screams and drops the cup.

SCENE 10

I believe Seth's disappearance affected you rather badly, Mr Stanley.

Let me guess who you've been talking to. Anna? Catherine? Not telling me? I admit it was a shock at first. You don't — you don't know what to think. Not knowing is frustrating. But you have to stay logical.

"For fuck's sake!" Michael boots the silent hoover, which achieves nothing except to leave him one slipper down. He retrieves his slipper and bends down to push the plug back in at the end of its taut lead. As the machine yowls into action he grabs it by its long neck and continues where he left off, slamming sofa and skirting boards, ignoring the occasional crunch and scream as it slurps up something unsuitable. Before long it sighs to a halt again.

"Piece of shit."

He falls back onto the sofa and covers his face with his hands. Even a hoover can push him over the edge at the moment. A gargly, guttural noise emerges from the back of his throat. What's the point anyway? The carpet's so threadbare the hoover could swallow it whole. His left-wing, pot-smoking landlords are renting him this place at a good price – for London, of course – but draw the line at maintaining it. On a teacher's salary where else could he go?

Of course – he has relented, now vacuuming his room with grim gusto – people like Seth have their own reality involving trust funds and mortgages. Not even a mortgage in Seth's case. He grinds his teeth, picturing those high arched ceilings and dusk sweeping in behind the French windows. How did he ever become sucked into a world like that? His right arm aches as it jerks and retracts. Seth has his cleaners to do this kind of thing. Wonder if they've tried turning up for work recently.

You've spoken to the cleaners, I presume?
They're on our list.

Fifteen years of Tory government, soaring house prices and the gap between the haves and have-nots becoming irreconcilable. And it will take more than charm, smarm and a theme tune to sort things out. He stood with the others that sunny May morning, clapping and exhilarated, banishing his faint unease whenever Tony Blair spoke. It was too early to judge him. But something about his smile put Michael's teeth on edge.

Seth's hoover is one of those things with a face and a name. *Henry*. His body heats abruptly and he flings off a jumper. He doesn't want that memory now, would like to suck it up and throw the bag away. Things are unsettling enough without adding that to the mix.

He tries to clear his mind, running over a patch of carpet near the door as if ironing awkward creases out of a shirt. The roar in his ears is getting loader. What the hell has happened to Seth? What kind of weird game is he playing? Jake's right, they should all forget about him and get on with their lives. Why is it so hard to do that?

Because you opened yourself up to him and he ditched you. You let down your defences and believed him, believed his bullshit, and more fool you for falling for it. How long did you wait for him that Wednesday evening? How long before you had to admit the truth, that you'd mistaken the curiosity in his eyes for concern?

Trails of tiny fibres like fairy dust swirl on streams of sunshine pouring in through streaked windows. Michael squints and sees Seth turning mocking eyes and pursed matinee idol lips towards him. Sweat runs down his face and into eyes that already feel wet. He fumbles with the hoover, pushing buttons – panic buttons – as the snarl of the motor fills his head.

When he yanks out the plug he is panting.

SCENE 11

"I tell you, he was acting as if he owned the flat. Like he'd moved in or something. There were beer cans on the table, the ashtray was full – he'd probably had a few mates round too. What? I can see you looking at each other. It isn't funny."

José meets Rebecca's eye again. "Look, Anna, you went round for a quiet drink and found Jake doing exactly the same. I'm sure all of us have done it. Why have a go at Jake?"

"I don't know – it was like he tried to frighten me deliberately, sneaking up on me like that. And then he just laughed. He was so blatant about the fact that he was chilling out in Seth's flat drinking Seth's beer – you can guarantee he won't have brought his own. Maybe that's why he wanted everyone to have keys – so he could bloody move in."

She tips more wine into her glass.

José smiles. "Come on, he's got just as much right as the rest of us to go round."

"Has he? He hasn't known Seth for as long. Sorry, Becs – I know we met you later but it doesn't seem like it."

Rebecca squeezes Anna's hand and looks pleased. It's good to have the old Anna back, all of them on the same side again.

"And I can't help it, I just don't trust him. We don't know anything about him. The phone was on the coffee table too – he could have been phoning fecking Australia for all we know."

Rebecca shrugs. "Or a mate down the road."

But Anna isn't listening. "Worst of all," she leans in. "Seth's cigarette box was open on the table."

José runs a hand through his hair and tries to think. "So he wanted a ciggie. It's not a religious artefact or anything."

Anna flares. "It was to Seth. And you know it."

He sighs. "Look, I know what you're saying and I don't always know what to make of him but he's not done anything wrong that we know of, has he?"

"What about his watch? Have you seen his new watch? It's a fecking Rolex. Where the fuck does he get the money from to buy that?"

"I dunno, it's probably a fake or something. Come on, woman, drink some more wine and play spot the fit guy with me. God knows we could do with some fun."

* * * * *

Two hours later he's holding his hand over his glass as Anna tops up the other two. She's come round a bit. She even apologised for being off the previous week, said it was all messing with her head.

José leans back and grins at his friends across the table. "At least we're not in his bloody flat now."

"Yeah, it's starting to get a bit weird, isn't it? Maybe we should stop meeting there."

"I don't know, I find it vaguely comforting."

"Like people sniffing their dead husband's jumpers?"

"I suppose so. And he does have a good wine collection."

It's slightly feeble, but they're bantering again, doing a good impression of three friends having a normal night out. If the three of them can stick together maybe it will be okay.

José nods at the red, white and blue bunting fluttering over the bar. "And I thought London was up itself before. Now it's *Cool Britannia* this, *Cool Britannia* that. If I hear that phrase one more time I'm on the next plane back to Madrid."

Anna grins and takes another slug of wine. "At least we can choose where we want to go now. Seth was such a control freak. Always had to be on his terms."

None of them have ever spoken about him like this. They are saying the unsayable.

José spears an olive. "And let's face it, it was pretty bloody unhealthy, that group."

"How do you mean?"

"Well, him in control, the rest of us competing for his attention. He must have loved it."

The words surprise him, acidic like the house wine he's had too much of. He's admitted to something he didn't know he felt, put a card on the table. For a second's silence he wants to take it back. Then Rebecca nods.

"You're right, José. And I guess we're to blame too. But it's... hard to resist him."

"I've never met anyone with so much presence, charm – I don't know what to call it."

"Charisma." They lock eyes then Rebecca looks down and swirls her drink. "It's a dangerous thing."

"But you're setting him up as a manipulator and I don't think that's right." Anna's voice rises ominously in pitch. "Just because he isn't here we shouldn't forget all the great things about him. I've never met anyone so energising. And generous. Not just with his money, with himself."

"No one's saying he's a monster, Anna. And of course he's generous, great company, witty…" He stops, confused for a second, feeling around for more adjectives to pin Seth down.

"Like you told me, a one-off." Rebecca smiles, breaking the tension.

"I'll drink to that." They clunk glasses, sip a silent toast.

"Three weeks PD today, you know. And Friday the 13th on top of that. Lucky for some. Maybe he's back home as we speak."

They smile sadly at each other, eyes heavy again.

After a minute Anna sighs. "I know he's a bit of an enigma, and you're probably right that the whole group is dysfunctional and revolves around him." She looks around the table and sighs again. "But it doesn't change the fact that it's no bloody fun without him."

SCENE 12

[Enter all characters bar Seth, whose Fedora hat is spotlighted centre stage.
Characters walk round and round the hat.]

ANNA:	Where is he?
MICHAEL:	Where is he?
REBECCA:	Where i……………s he?
JOSÉ:	Who said anything about opera?
REBECCA:	Well, it's so dramatic I just burst into song. [*shakes head*] I'm wasted here, should have been on Broadway.
JAKE:	You're a doll, Becs, but no opera, aw-ight?
CATHERINE:	Would you please take that gum out of your mouth?
ANNA:	Am I allowed to agree with Jake, just this once?
CHARLES:	Come on, chaps. No opera, okay? We need to stay focussed… look for clues or something.
JAKE:	Uh-oh. Here they come.

[*characters peer out and sigh*]

ANNA: More feckin' questions.

REBECCA: Still in those sensible shoes.

JAKE: Like they're ever gonna work out what's going on!

ALL THE OTHERS: What makes you say that?

JAKE: Trust me, they're no match for Seth.

SCENE 13

This takes us up to last week. Could you
talk me through what happened next, Miss
Laurence?

The sun was streaming into Rebecca's eyes when she woke. Bloody curtains didn't meet in the middle. She caught sight of 6.48 on the bedside clock, groaned and buried her face in the pillows, knowing the game was already up. For a second the heat on her hair felt luxurious, as if she were lying on an exotic beach, sun shimmering above. Then she remembered Seth and the pleasure trickled out of her. It was like having something horrible hovering over your head all the time. Maybe he'd sent his black bird to keep watch over her while he was gone.

She sighed again and sat up in bed. The patch of sky between her thin beige curtains was dense cobalt. She could even pick out birdsong. The prospect of another glorious day had the equal and opposite effect on her, made her want to cry. Nothing seemed to mean that much now that he wasn't here, now that there was a huge bloody big question mark carved into her soul.

Always the drama queen. But the not knowing had infected her like cancer, taking her over cell by cell. It seeped out into conversations with the man reading the gas meter. It tightened her chest when she bought a Tube ticket, imbued her favourite American sitcoms with a bittersweet edge their creators could only have dreamed of. Every time she saw something glinting on the pavement she thought it was the lost brooch, made a grab for a chocolate wrapper or abandoned penny in the gutter. She lost her appetite halfway through a meal, staring suddenly at a tuna baguette as if someone else had put it into her hand. But the weight loss didn't even make her particularly happy, since there was no one to appreciate it. He tumbled round and round her thoughts on a rapid spin cycle until, at times, when she'd had too much coffee and solitude, she visualised her head starting to splinter like an egg hatching.

On those occasions, too many of them recently, she did the only thing she could think of to block it all out. The only thing that brought her a bit closer to him. Sometimes she imagined that he was there in the room, watching her, and on those occasions she took it slowly, revelling in the sensory distraction, playing to an audience. But more often the despair that powered her right hand made her hurt herself, using the handle of her hairbrush like a weapon, a scarf tied tight round her eyes, trying to bring him back. She'd given herself two urine infections and the doctor had lectured her on tampon hygiene. Afterwards it was always the same shame and loneliness but the next day she'd be doing it again.

She needed to find him. She had to know what had happened, where he was, she needed to talk to him and feel the warmth of his eyes on her face. Fuck it, she needed to kiss him, to hold him, to drown in the tide that had swept them towards each other. She needed to say *sorry and you bastard and I love you and don't ever leave me again and why?*

Why?

The trembling started between her legs and she reached for the hairbrush she now kept by her bed. Her hand locked around the ridged handle and paused. She could go to the kitchen instead and start her coffee-making ritual but nothing would change, no one would observe her plight and come to save her or give her the information she had to have. She was alone and it was terrifying.

On top of all that she had money worries. She'd tipped over her overdraft limit and needed to phone her parents to get her through until next week when *No Exit* rehearsals started. Of course they'd help her but they'd be worried, and she'd have to pretend.

She pulled the hairbrush under the covers. There was only one fantasy anymore and it wasn't a fantasy, it had really happened. It was the only thing that still connected her to him.

The phone started to ring and her eyes blinked open. For a second she listened. Then she ran for it. No one rang her at this time.

SCENE 14

"Hey Becs, sorry to phone you so early."

"Oh – hi, Anna." Rebecca's voice is hollow.

"Look, I've been lying in bed thinking about what we can do next to find Seth. And I think I've had an idea."

"Right." There's something like a sigh at the other end.

"I know what Jake said – about not snooping around – but I think we need to fill in as many gaps as possible. Look – can I come over and talk to you?"

Fifteen minutes later, Rebecca opens the door looking as jaded as her old green dressing gown. They talk over black treacly coffee that makes Anna grimace.

"So, are you up for it?"

"Today?"

"Yes. I've checked with his secretary that he's around. He thinks he's getting a visit from a couple of mature students."

Rebecca blinks. "So you've already set it up?"

"Yes. I'm going anyway. But I'd really like it if you came too."

A second's pause. "Okay, let's do it."

Anna grins. "Excellent. Get in the shower and I'll make us some breakfast. Where's your bread?"

The place needed a damn good clean. It would drive

her mad to be surrounded by so much clutter. She finds margarine, low fat, of course, in the fridge and little else, only a tub of cream cheese that instinct tells her not to open. Rebecca appears in a black T-shirt with something in-your-face printed on it.

"There's cream cheese if you want it. Here – oh shit. That stuff goes off so fast. Sorry."

She opens the bin lid and shoves the container down on a pile of rubbish. Anna wrinkles her nose at the smell of fish as Rebecca grins an apology. "Shaz's turn to do the bins."

"No worries – I'll bring your toast to your room, shall I?" Rebecca turns. "Sorry?"

"Well, you can't go like that – we won't stand a chance. Let's have a look through your wardrobe."

* * * * *

After a small scene Rebecca left the house in hip-hugging white jeans and stripy blue cropped top, finished off with a dusting of blusher and various things from black tubes that brought her eyes to life. Although she moaned about Anna's tactics, Anna could see she was amused and flattered too. Exactly what she'd banked on. Assuming Dr Cuddly was of heterosexual persuasion – and hopefully, being married, he was – she felt confident their double act could win him round. She glanced over at her passenger, currently resembling a mad Medusa in the head wind. There was something a bit fragile about her today. She needed to pull herself together for all of them.

"Hey – you okay? Do you want me to put the roof on?"

Rebecca shook her head and tried again to twist her hair into her top. She shouted something back that included the word 'banshee' and they both grinned and resumed their reveries. It was amazing how often the car had saved her from unwanted small talk.

"If necessary, you could always cry." Anna spoke casually

while she fiddled around with the roof in the car park.

"Cry?"

Anna took a breath, trying to stay patient. "Well, if he won't tell us anything. Say you're desperate, you'll do anything, that kind of stuff. You know better than me." She caught sight of Rebecca's indignant face. "Come on, you're an actress."

"Actor."

"Eh?"

Rebecca sighed. "Doesn't matter. Look, I'll do my best but I'm not promising anything." Anna had to bite her lip and be satisfied with that.

They emerged from a urine-streaked stairway into sunlight, cobbles and throngs of people.

"Blimey."

"Ever been here before?"

"Never. I visited Oxford once, when I was a teenager. Full of strange vampire-like creatures in black gowns. Some of my friends were Goths so I felt quite at home. Except for the strange hats."

Anna chuckled. "My brothers still go on about my gotholescent days. I'm sure I only lasted one bad hair dye but they make it sound like years. Ma's tears and Da's lectures were enough for anyone."

A silence settled after the mention of her mother. Then the King's College skyline reared up to their left.

"Wow."

"It's like a cathedral. Imagine going to university here."

They gazed for a moment at the blanched, parapetted silhouette gleaming on its azure canvass.

"Which one is this?"

Anna consulted her map. "King's, I think. As in cute choirboy sings 'Once in Royal David's City'."

"My mum's favourite." Rebecca blushed, as if she'd made a faux-pas. Anna kept talking to show she was okay.

"This is John's now, where Seth went. See that bridge?

Remind you of anything?"

Rebecca looked up. "Um... no, not really."

"It's a copy of the Bridge of Sighs in Venice. Look, we're being watched." Tourists stared down to the street through huge camera lenses.

"And this is where Seth hung out. Makes sense, doesn't it?"

They laughed. By the time they passed the porter, slagged off the tourists and circumnavigated three imposing courtyards, it had started to feel like a regular day trip. It was amazing how much better she felt just to be *doing* something.

Dr Cuddly was anything but. Anna realised her mental picture of some sort of academic-looking Father Christmas had been entirely based around his name. Faced with a beanpole with eyebrows she felt a little thrown. Maybe he kept himself chronically short of food so he could shatter people's preconceptions and gain immediate advantage.

He didn't come across as particularly cuddly by nature either, though the way his eyes were pinging back and forth between the table and Rebecca's midriff was promising.

"I'll cut straight to the chase, we're here to talk about one of our friends who's disappeared. He was one of your students and we're hoping you might be able to shed some light on it."

Dr Cuddly's eyes glittered. "I see. So your post-graduate interest in George Herbert..."

Anna tilted her head. "Let's call it... poetic license."

She returned his gaze until he relaxed into a smile. "Very good. So how can I help you, ladies?" His gaze took in Rebecca again. "I don't have long."

Anna sat up straighter. "Do you remember a PhD student called Seth Basildon?"

Dr Cuddly leaned back. "Ah, Mr Basildon, who could forget him?"

"He's been missing for about a month. We're talking to as many people as possible who know him."

"Knew him, Miss..."

"Carmel. And this is Rebecca Laurence."

The tip of a smile brushed his lips as he acknowledged Rebecca.

"As I said, I knew Seth Basildon but haven't heard from him in – sorry, one loses track of time in this job – well, I would have thought it was ten years. I'm not really sure how I can help you."

Anna crossed her legs. "We've found a lot of paperwork from his time at Cambridge. I believe he got into some sort of trouble, during his PhD? We're wondering if that might give us some clues as to his whereabouts."

Dr Cuddly folded his arms. "Lots of people get into trouble during their student years, Miss Carmel, and I doubt they want those 'clues' splashing about amongst their current friends."

His voice was vacuum-sealed. Anna told herself to stay calm.

"Dr Cuddly." Rebecca leaned forward urgently, surprising both of the others. "We are not here to snoop. We just want any information that could help us understand. Seth is a very dear friend and we're extremely worried about him. Please help us." A tremor rippled her voice. "We're just desperate."

The scoop neck of Rebecca's top pulled slightly as she leaned further. The professor seemed unsure where to look. Anna watched Rebecca in wonder. It was like a masterclass in how to get round a man. Dr Cuddly sighed.

"Well, if it helps I can tell you what I remember, which is not much."

"Thank you." They spoke in chorus, earnestly.

"Mr – Basildon owned a house which it seems was a bit of a meeting place for arty types. It had something of a reputation, if you know what I mean." Anna nodded to urge him on.

"At some point – maybe a couple of years in – one of the group had some sort of breakdown and recounted some rather disturbing stories to her parents, who tipped the police off. They raided it and found Class A drugs. In rather large quantities, by all accounts."

Anna's hands stuck to her trouser legs as she tried to move them. "So Seth was prosecuted?"

The professor paused. "Not exactly."

Anna and Rebecca exchanged a glance. "What happened?"

"Let's just say that someone influential stepped in and got him off the hook. But he left Cambridge, didn't complete. Damn shame actually – he had some fascinating, if undeveloped, ideas about George Herbert. Could have been an excellent thesis." Nostalgia settled around Dr Cuddly. "There've been one or two regrettable dropouts in the last few years."

Rebecca coughed gently and flicked her hair off her face "Do you have any idea who helped him?"

It took a second for the professor to turn a vague face towards her.

"Who? Oh – young Basildon. Or should I say Rothbury." He raised his eyebrows. "Well, his father, of course."

ACT 4 - PROLOGUE

The boy taps at the door, wanting his mother. The house is dark and there's a noise that has woken him up. He thinks it's a monster. He doesn't want the monster to catch his mother. He's not supposed to get out of bed in the night but he can't go on listening to that groaning noise anymore. He pushes the door, expecting dishevelled hair and sharp words. But the covers are pushed back and the room is empty. Maybe the monster has already got his mother. He hears its noise again, a bit louder now. It's coming from the Lilac Room. That's the room he's not allowed in, the room that is usually locked. He clenches his tummy to stop himself wetting his pants as he creeps past the room where Lucilla sometimes stays, to the other side of the house.

The door to the Lilac Room is clicked closed but there is a light on in the small study next door to it. If he angles himself correctly, he can peep into the small, bright gap where the door snags on the carpet without moving too close. A man glows under the overhead light, almost touching it because he's standing on his mother's kitchen stool. The man is his father and he is the one making the horrible noise. He is rubbing himself against the wall, wriggling, grinding his hips like he's disco dancing. Something tells him not to call out to his father. Something tells him he shouldn't be watching.

The next day, with the help of his bunk bed ladder, he discovers the secret black window from the study into the Lilac Room with a little door you can open and a perfect view of the inside of the room. He's pleased to discover that grown-ups like playing spying games too. In time he learns

300

that this type of window has a name. A peephole.

He's seventeen when he hears the noise again. Coming from the Lilac Room, or maybe the study. He's been waiting for this but he has to be sure. He lies still as a lizard, listening.

That's the creaky floorboard. Someone is moving around in that part of the house. He sits up, still foggy from alcohol, sees 2a.m, grabs a dressing gown but not slippers. Bare feet will be quieter. Even in this state he knows where to put his feet to make silent progress across the landing. He has practised many times. He stops to listen outside his parents' door. Nothing. They've been entertaining yet another of his father's business contacts tonight so he left them to it, sat in a pub, told them he'd probably stay with a friend. The door clicks. He doesn't need to push it open to know they're not inside.

The boy – although not really a boy now, not a man either – looks at his arms, streaked with black hair. He is old enough. The house is silent, slumbering like a bear in winter. But he knows. Each step is placed with exaggerated care as he progresses past the bathroom. Then he hears it, a groan, sickeningly familiar. Another step and he can see round the corner to the triangle of light in the study. The outline of his father's trousers.

He springs forward, smashing open the door of the Lilac Room. The dinner guest is tied up and gagged like a hostage on the bed, naked apart from black socks, eyes bulging as if they will burst. He knows this one, has seen him at the house before. Standing over him in black lace is his mother, facing the peephole, holding a whip in both hands, hair wild and tangled as a filthy gypsy. She screams and tries to cover herself but he is too fast, he has her by the throat and the only way to cope with the sight of her is to keep squeezing. The other man, stranded on the bed, writhes and groans in a parody of his recent pleasure. Hands seize his shoulders and he gives one final squeeze before letting go, hurling her towards the window. His father backs away, belt undone, moving to where his wife lies, retching in a heap.

The boy turns to the room then, tearing pictures from the wall, kicking over furniture. He must destroy it, smash it to purple pulp, or he will have to rip out his own eyes, rip the scene before him into bloody shreds.

When he opens his eyes again he too is handcuffed to a bed. Three men in white coats stare over their noses at him. He runs his eyes around the unfamiliar room, the curtain rail round the bed, the sink in the corner. His body is bound but his mind is now clear. Now he knows how to play it, now he has the leverage he needs to be free of them forever.

He smiles at the men. One of them opens a notebook and starts scribbling.

SCENE 1

"His father?"

Rebecca can still feel the tremors of her original shock as she watches the group reaction. How, with the blood banging in her ears, she told Dr Cuddly he must have made a mistake knowing suddenly, sickeningly, that he was telling the truth. It didn't take long to unravel.

"Oh, he spun you that poor little orphan boy line too? I'm surprised he's still using it after the truth came out."

Anna and Rebecca had barely been able to question him, their roadmap for the session now in tatters. Seth had both a mother and a father, alive by all accounts, or at least he did ten years ago. His father was some big shot in the wine trade. Seth had fallen out with them before leaving school and concocted the orphan story.

"Maybe he finds it creates sympathy with – young ladies."

They left then, stumbled into a jarringly picturesque courtyard. Idling tourists jostled them along King's Parade.

"His father is alive? He's not an orphan?" Michael's eyes are blazing. Catherine looks like she's going to faint. They are back in Seth's living room.

"That's what Dr Cuddly said. There's no reason why he

should lie." Anna's voice is flat and brittle.

"The lying, manipulating bastard." Only Michael seems able to muster a reaction.

Charles looks ill. "No – surely – he wouldn't lie to me all these years." His face is greyish-white, the colour of city snow.

Anna bites at her thumbnail. "There could be a reason why he's had to lie."

"Like what?" José's question sounds more hopeful than cynical. Everyone looks at Anna.

"I don't know, maybe his parents abused him or something and it was less painful to say they were dead."

"Oh, come off it, Anna, you don't believe that. It was just another game he played with us."

"I think Anna could be right. He told me some pretty strange things about his childhood." Catherine's voice is small and apologetic, as if it were she who lied.

"What sort of things?"

She shrinks further into her seat.

"I can't remember exactly."

"Sorry, you *need* to remember exactly." Anna looks almost as scary as Michael. "If you know anything, you have to tell us."

"It was nothing specific – well, he told me he found his parents – having sex on the dining room table," comes Catherine's whisper.

A heartbeat's pause as the others digest this. Charles is pacing backwards and forwards, muttering under his breath.

"Right. And?"

"Well, he implied they did other stuff, but we didn't talk about it. He did say he'd seen therapists over the years…"

"Just more speculation then." Charles shakes his head. Michael stands up and stares out of the French windows, his Roman profile accentuated against the blurring daylight. No one speaks for a while.

"We're sitting here in his house, like we always do, but

303

he's gone and it feels like we don't really know anything about him." José's voice bends in the middle and he puts his head in his hands.

Rebecca plants her feet on the ground and almost expects to feel it shifting. "Come on, José, that's not true. Okay, he's not an orphan but it doesn't mean that everything else about him is a lie too."

It doesn't come out quite right. Somehow words intended to give Seth the benefit of the doubt throw more shadow on him.

Anna looks at her. "So what do we do now?"

"I don't see that there's anything we can or should do." It's the first time Jake has spoken. "So he hasn't been entirely straight with us. That's 'is prerogative. Are you telling me none of you have secrets you 'aven't told the rest of the group?"

They must hear her heart thumping into the silence as she pictures herself in the white negligee kneeling over Seth. Then she notices that no one else is contradicting Jake either. She is afraid to look up and meet people's eyes until the cold snap in Anna's voice shocks her into doing so.

"I'm imagining there's plenty *you* haven't told us." For a second she thinks that Anna's eyes will be on her. Then she sees them fastened on Jake, the colour of summer sky before a storm. She needs to stop this before everything unravels.

"Anna."

"What? Don't tell me you haven't wondered?" She looks round the room. "We may not know everything about each other, but we know almost nothing about him. Do we, Jake?"

Jake's face is weirdly still. No winks, no naughty grin. He spits out his chewing gum and rolls it into a wrapper. Rebecca tastes acid at the back of her throat.

José glares. "Leave him alone, Anna."

Jake holds up a hand. "No, it's fine. Let's get this done with. What is it you'd like to know, Anna?"

The room watches.

"Nothing to say now, eh?" They are circling each other.

Anna looks only at Jake. "Far from it. What did you do before you met us?"

"Before I met you?" He laughs, hard, letting his head roll back for a second. Then the smile is gone. "I had a whole life, Anna, believe it or not. People do exist away from your cosy little bubble, you know. Maybe they don't go to Sunday School or Boy Scouts, maybe they don't come from a nice, respectable family unit, maybe they make some mistakes and get into trouble. But it doesn't mean you can treat them like shit on your shoe." He laughs again. "Especially when you're not so whiter-than-white yourself."

What do you think he meant by that?
I don't know. He said it meaningfully, though. Looking at all of us.

Michael steps forward and speaks quietly. "Anna shouldn't have said that. You don't have to explain yourself to anyone."

Jake looks at Michael for a second then releases his breath in a soft hiss. He looks at the wall. "When I met you lot I'd recently got out of prison."

Anna folds her arms but Jake ignores her. "I was running a stolen car racket. A young father was killed driving one of my cars. Brake cables were chewed through."

Stifled gasps. Even Anna looks like she got more than she bargained for. Jake looks right at her.

"So there you go. Feel better, knowing you were right?"

Anna says nothing. Jake smiles but his eyes don't crinkle. "Do you think I should've told you? Do you think you'd have given me a chance if I had?"

His questions now address the whole room. Rebecca wishes she could push off this precipice and plunge down into the wind, her clenched, hurtling body arcing and twisting through white sound.

"Of course you wouldn't." Jake's voice drifts into her

shutdown. His words are light and singsong. She sees movement and realises that he is walking to the door and other people are getting up.

He turns on his way out. "Seth did, though. Seth gave me a chance." For a second she catches his eye and she wants to say something, but the wind is still rushing in her ears and all she does is watch him leave. She does catch his parting shot, though:

"It's Jack, by the way."

Quite a day for you, Miss Laurence.
Yes. It's hard to believe it was only a week ago. So much has happened since.
Have you seen Jake Etheridge since that night?
Er, no. No I haven't. I've just realised, by the way, when we reported Seth missing, we said he had no next of kin. Obviously that's not true.
Don't worry, Miss Laurence. We'd figured that one out for ourselves.

"There you go, then." Despite its harsh timbre, Anna's voice wobbles. Rebecca knows she wants contact, reassurance. But no one looks at her. "We needed to know."

"Did we?" Charles sounds unusually keyed up. "Seth knew. And it didn't matter to him."

"And that's just it. Seth's not here now. Is he?"

"Exactly what do you mean by that?" Michael speaks slowly, enunciating each word.

"Well, maybe Seth was a bit too trusting. There was clearly something weird going on. I don't mean like *that*. But we all know that after Jake shagged his boss' wife and lost his job, he never really worked, and he never seemed short of cash. We also know how generous Seth was. Is."

Catherine nods. "I do think Seth was helping him quite a bit financially."

Michael shrugs. "So? Seth can give his money to whoever he likes. God knows he has enough of it."

"It's not just that. I don't trust him – Jake, Jack– I mean, look at what he's just told us. And his whole reaction to Seth's disappearance has been odd. You know it has."

Michael smiles. "I see. So because Jake has a record he's now – what? Murdered Seth and taken his money?" He looks round the room for backup but most people are looking at their feet.

Anna raises her voice. "It's not just a record, Michael. He didn't get done for nicking a wallet. He basically killed someone. Who knows what he's capable of?"

José looks up. "I'm not accusing Jake of anything but it has always felt like we don't know much about him. And now, after this..."

Michael surveys the room and snorts. "Well, you've got your scapegoat, haven't you? The big, black villain comes after poor little innocent Seth." People try to interrupt but he holds up his hand. "I'll tell you what's going on here, he's just not middle class enough for you, is he? Can't join in discussions about philosophy and art history. How can you trust someone without a degree?"

Anna gets to her feet. "Don't be so fucking ridiculous, Michael."

He continues as if he hasn't heard, pacing in front of the fireplace. "You turn nasty insinuations on Jake when your darling Seth has lied to us and toyed with us and fucked off without a word. It's not Jake who's phoney. It's Seth. He's played us and he's still doing it now. Can't you see that?" He bellows the last bit and Rebecca is back at school, chided in class.

Suddenly he turns and addresses them full on. "Have you ever wondered what really happened last year? Now that we know he lies? Or is that all forgotten in favour of this new, perfect version of Seth?"

Rebecca frowns and looks at the others. What is he talking

about? She's glued to her seat, doesn't dare to ask. She sees alarm on the faces around her.

Anna moves towards him. "Michael!" Charles and José are on their feet too.

"Oh, don't want to get that one out at the moment, right?"

"Michael, please!" Everyone stares as Catherine comes towards him. "This is not going to help."

"Fine, have it your way. Your dirty secret is safe with me."

She flinches like she's been hit.

Could you wait one moment, Miss Laurence, while I note this down? Thank you. Do you know what Mr Stanley was referring to when he said, 'what happened last year'?
Not exactly. Something before I met them all. They said it was nothing. Just Michael over-dramatising. When I pressed them, Anna said Seth had got into a fight in a bar one evening and then the police had shown up and they'd played the whole thing down. No one was hurt so no big deal.
A fight? From what I know about Mr Gardner, that doesn't sound like his style. No one else has mentioned it.
I'm sorry, I can't tell you any more.
Of course, carry on, Miss Laurence.

Michael still holds the floor, waving his hands by the fire no one has bothered to light. He's on one now. "Look at us. We're just like stupid little lapdogs still meeting in his house and drinking his wonderful fucking wine like he's going to walk through the door any minute. Well, he's not. He's not coming back. Get over it!"

No one says a word. Catherine might be crying. Rebecca knows Michael is right, she does expect Seth to walk back in any minute, they all probably do, and he'll get out his whisky and an explanation to satisfy them, make them laugh even. But what if he doesn't come, what if he never comes?

She looks around for something to hold onto but all she sees is a disintegrating cluster of friends without the glue to keep them together.

Michael slams the door as he leaves. Charles offers to drive Catherine home. Anna, José and Rebecca kiss each other at Notting Hill Tube barriers and say they'll talk tomorrow. Hot, viscous air floods the train, flinging Rebecca's hair over her eyes. She gets off one stop early and walks through the windless night.

SCENE 2

Catherine suspects Charles would like to be asked in but she longs for the cool greeting of her empty flat. It is the only thing that can soothe her. Work, friends, even talking to the man in the corner shop strains her mind to breaking point, or at least a migraine. But here, at home, she doesn't have to pretend. Here she is free to run over the horror of it all endlessly, paraphrase the same old questions. There are new questions now. There must be a reason for his deception. His parents must have hurt him. She aches with the not knowing.

She closes the door on Charles and pushes scraggy, pallid limbs into summer-weight pyjamas her mother bought her for Christmas. She's withering like a plant without sunlight. Her only scraps of sustenance are tucked away in memory and fantasy. She lies down under her pastel-striped duvet knowing she won't sleep for some time. It is her time with Seth. She rolls onto her left side and picks up the fantasy easily from where she left it yesterday. In two minutes he is in her lounge, buried in her arms. He has come to her because he knows no one else can help him. He is a broken toy that she must lovingly mend. She holds him as he opens up to her, tells her things he has never shared with anyone else. She strokes his face as he clings to her. He cannot face the others, begs her not to tell them where he is. She is all he needs. She is his angel.

SCENE 3

It must have been the breeze that took her back so vividly, almost three years in a *whoosh* of chilly air. A June breeze that belonged in early autumn, in September '94 to be specific, bringing people to life as she and José and Seth walked briskly along the Cromwell Road looking for the Institut Français. It was Seth's idea, of course, just like everything else was Seth's idea. He had decided he wanted to improve his French and took José along for backup. 'You're a continental, aren't you? You're bound to speak good French already.'

Anna got wind of the plan and decided to tag along. Partly for a laugh and partly...

"It's a good way to meet men, don't you know?"

Seth's eyebrow shot up and José shook his head despairingly.

"Seriously, now. I read this article about where to go to meet men. Language classes are right up there with car maintenance courses and singles' nights."

"Car maintenance courses?" Seth roared with laughter. "My God, and we men sit there declining our verbs and twizzling our screwdrivers obliviously. Somebody shoot us." Then a wolfish grin. "I'm looking forward to this class more and more."

Anna wasn't far wrong. Rows of young women turned to look at Seth and José when they walked in. Even José stood up taller and puffed out his chest. Bridget Jones clones, or 'Bridgets' as Anna referred to them. Black knee boots, low-cut cardigans and Sloaney ponytails. José got out his sketching pad and started some cartoons with a wink. He'd have a field day here. He did a couple of quick, caustic caricatures, which Seth leaned over and labelled Elouise and Annabel. The three of them dissolved into giggles and were glared at by Madame.

That pretty much summed up the evening. They were still laughing when they hit the pub afterwards.

"Madame and the Sloanes – great name for a band, don't

you think?"

Seth lit up. "I didn't pull, though. Should have left you two at home."

Anna nudged him so hard he spilt some of his pint. "Oi. You should be grateful. We saved you from the Bridgets. They would have had you tied up in a Fulham basement by now – with their Scrunchies."

They all hooted again. Seth wiped his eyes. "They sound like Doctor Who monsters... We will exfoliate. We will exfoliate."

They rolled around, helpless with laughter. And so it continued. At some point during the evening, José spotted a table of blonde ponytails studiously ignoring them but close enough to have heard much of it.

```
Needless  to  say,  we  never  progressed
further with French.
```

The memory of that laughter has an equal and opposite effect on Anna now, nearly three years later, walking into the wind. A stabbing pain in her abdomen so she has to stop, clutching her waist, and wait for the pain to subside.

```
I still see him, you know. And hear him.
Sometimes I think he's right there in
the room with us. Other times I remember
something  so  vividly  it's  like  it's
happening all over again.
```

All she can do is straighten up and keep walking, past the people sipping their drinks in pavement cafes, past the people laughing like she used to laugh.

SCENE 4

She misses Jason. Finally she misses him. Or maybe she misses the idea of him: steady, straightforward, sticking

311

around. It seems a long time ago.

There must have been a reason for Seth to lie. Something had traumatised him, the tear tracks she saw on his face before they slept together, the way he'd shut down afterwards. What could she have done to reach him? If she hadn't gone over that day, would he still be here?

She let him down. No, he has let her down, all of them, making them need him and then abandoning them. She rings his mobile phone every day but his voice has gone. Now a machine tells her *this voicemail box is full.* Full of her worry, her questions, her pleas.

And now Jake has gone too, or Jack or whoever he is. Why didn't she stick up for him, go after him? Because she suddenly didn't know what she thought and who she could trust. Seth would never have allowed Jake to be cast out like that.

Panic rises like a tide. She squeezes her legs together, feels it hovering there, distilled stress manifesting as arousal. She has moved her hairbrush across the room. She could orgasm her way to brief relief in seconds just by continuing to squeeze but now only penetration will do. Hard, rough penetration to blot her out. She opens her bedside drawer and finds the Ann Summers box.

She feels sordid afterwards. And sore. She's never had the urge to hurt herself before, only since he disappeared. Like she needs to feel the pain of missing him in her body.

She thinks again of Jake and a faint light glows in her head. If she builds bridges with him she'll be doing what Seth would want. And if – when – Seth comes back he'll be pleased with her. There is at least this small thing she can do.

She pushes away the image of Jake's strange, waxen face last night, replaces it with his usual mischievous flicker and gets out her phone.

* * * * *

They are meeting somewhere obscure that involves her

getting off at Liverpool St. She steps out into high buildings, heat and humidity. City boys in pin-striped suits shouting into mobiles. Tourists blocking the steps, jaywalking along the main drag. She wishes for winter, possibly for the first time in her life.

The bar is underground, a cellar with tables. She thinks she sees Jake near the back, head buried in the *Evening Standard*. A huge close-up of some bloke's face leers at her from the front page.

"Jake?"

He looks over the paper and grins at her.

"Or, should I say, Jack? Which shall I call you?"

"Whichever you prefer, m'darlin'. I've been called both for long enough not to care now." He points at the newspaper as she removes the bag from her shoulder. "Some poor bastard murdered in a basement. 'Opefully not this one."

He rolls his eyes and she laughs nervously while glancing around, feeling suddenly far from home. Jake looks her over. "Now, you're a sight for sore eyes. Take a pew. What are you drinking?"

She sees his beer and orders the same even though she'd planned to stick to fizzy water. She watches him at the bar having a joke with the waitress. The same old Jake.

She thanks him as he sits down. "So, how are you?"

"Oh, you know – all right, in an ex-con sort of way."

She lets out some air and smiles, remembers why she's always liked him.

"I'm sorry about all that." She goes into her prepared speech. "I don't think Anna meant to fly at you quite like she did. She was probably in shock about the orphan thing. We all were."

He nods slowly. "I kept meaning to tell you – about being in prison – but it seemed to get 'arder the more I got to know you all. Seth knew pretty much from the beginning and he was great. But people generally don't look at you the same once they know. That's why it's so difficult to find work."

She swallows and tries to meet his eye. "We wouldn't see you differently, though."

He raises his eyebrows. "Wouldn't you? Chances are I'm responsible for a man's death. I didn't sell on 'eaps of junk but I didn't do the proper checks either. That's got to change the way you see me."

She looks at his right ear. "But – you're sorry, aren't you?"

"Yes, I'm sorry. Prison alone makes you sorry. But I can't spend the rest of my life feeling sorry. I 'ave to move on."

There's a hardness around his voice that makes her want to back away. He seems to sense it. "Look, I wish it hadn't 'appened, course I do. But there's no point in ruining another life – my life – by feeling guilty all the time. Guilt's pointless. It wears you down and gets you nowhere." His eyes don't flicker from hers but there's a catch to his voice. Can he really feel no guilt? It reminds her of something Seth might say.

She needs to say her piece before she loses her nerve. "Will you come back to the – group, or whatever it is now?" She attempts a laugh. "I'd like you to."

"Thanks, Becs, you're a sweetheart but I don't think so. Don't get me wrong, I think you're great, but with Seth gone – I just don't feel like I should be there."

She nods and lowers her eyelids to pull a blind over the relief she feels. At least she can say she tried. They both take a drink.

"Anyway, 'ow's things on your side, gorgeous?" He narrows his eyes. "Don't mind me saying but you look a bit washed out – in an appealing way, of course. Are you okay?"

She starts to say *fine, thanks* but to her horror she feels tears gathering like clouds at the back of her eyes. He is still watching her.

"I'm fine, just worried about Seth." Her voice gives her away. Jake puts a hand over hers and the clouds burst and her face is deluged. "I mean – is he hurt? Is he dead? Is he just a heartless bastard like Michael says? I can't stand not knowing." It's a relief to blurt out and she looks up at him

314

for the answer like a child. "It's driving me crazy. How can someone just disappear?" Jake retains her hand but glances around him. People are looking at them.

"Sorry." She hunts in her pocket for a tissue.

"Here." He hands her a napkin. "Poor Becs. I had no idea it was affecting you so badly."

She controls her response. "Of course it is. Aren't you worried?"

He shrugs. "Not so much. I just think he must 'ave his reasons and he'll be back when he's ready."

"How can you be so sure?"

"Just a hunch." He looks at her. "Trust me, Becs, Seth is fine. He probably just needs some space." He drains his glass. "Another? And some chips to build you up?"

She agrees and he brings her a portion to herself. He watches her for a minute. "Eat them, for Christ's sake. You're waving them around like they're little cigarettes."

She dips one in ketchup and pops it in her mouth. "Sorry. I seem to do this a lot at the moment. Lose my appetite as soon as the food comes."

"I'm worried about you, love, I really am."

It touches her. He bites his lip as if he wants to say something. "Have you seen much of Anna and co then?" He grins. "Sounds like Legs & Co, remember them on Top of the Pops? Anna & Co – that'll be the new name of the group, new leader and all."

She forces a weak smile.

He cocks his head. "Although Becs & Co sounds much better. You'll 'ave to organise a coup."

She shakes her head, can't keep up with the banter. "I've seen them here and there." Several times, in truth.

He leans in. "You need to be careful. They're not as squeaky clean as you think. Don't trust 'em, Becs."

"What do you mean?" She pushes the plate of chips away.

"I've known them for longer than you have. Stuff 'appened before you came on board. You're a trusting person, Becs, but don't lower your guard too much."

She tries to smile. "Okay, you're really freaking me out now." This is a mistake and she needs to get out.

"And while we're on this subject, I have to say that maybe it's for the best Seth's taken a leave of absence, or whatever."

"What?" She stares at him in the semi-darkness.

He reaches out a hand and she tries not to flinch from it. "Look, Becs, you know I like you. Not like that – well, yes, like that, but that's not where I'm coming from right now. Believe it or not I have your best interests at 'eart."

"I don't know what you mean."

He lights a cigarette. "Sometimes people need a little time out when things are getting on top of them." He puffs out a mouthful of smoke and leans in. "And sometimes it's best just to let them."

Her eyes widen. "Do you know something? Are you in touch with Seth?"

He shakes his head. "Nothing like that. But I've been around a bit. A bit more than you, maybe."

And then he changes the subject until she gathers up her things to go. Outside the bar he squeezes her hand. "Look after yourself, Becs. You've got the chance to really do something with your life. Be selfish. Forget about the group. Forget about all of us."

SCENE 5

[*A disused warehouse*]

PC 1:	Fuck. Fucking hell. What the fuck is this? Oh God.
PC 2:	Whoa. For fuck's sake. Check this one out, Rob.
PC 3:	Jeez. What's with the eyes?
PC 1:	Fuck. [*staggers away; vomiting noises heard offstage*]
PC 2:	[*tuts*] There he goes again. Did exactly the same with the girl they found under the

	arches.
PC 3:	No stomach for it.
PC2:	That's some sick fucker did this... Backup's on its way.
PC 3:	I thought I'd seen it all but... the eyes... poor bastard.
PC 2:	At least he can't see Jono blubbing like a little faggot in the corner. Oi, Jono, get a grip, mate.
PC 3:	I mean, what's that about?
PC 2:	[*shrugs*] Probably some arse banditry that went wrong. Looks like it. You'd be amazed what sort of stuff goes on.
PC 3:	Jesus.
PC 2:	Right, backup's here. Hope they've got a stretcher for Jono.

SCENE 6

[Police station]

DC 2:	Your bunch of weirdos is here, Suze.
DC 3:	No wonder they put a woman on the case for this one.
DC 2:	Yeah, you're so much better at *picking up dynamics* than the rest of us.
DC 1:	Fuck off the lot of you. Taylor, over here. You're in with me.

Finally they were called in. It was excruciating sitting there in the waiting area, all of them with Jake. Michael and Charles went to talk to him, wandering over with hands in pockets trying to look casual. Catherine sat as far away from him as possible. Anna glared at him. Jake winked back at her and said, "Long time no see." Rebecca had barely dared to look at him. If Anna found out they'd met up last night...

"So, thank you all for coming in at such short notice. There have been some developments in the case that you

317

need to know. As the press has already got hold of it, some of you may know already." The detective turned expressionless brown eyes on them, one of which was partially covered by a flop of lank brown hair. The other detective looked like someone you'd want to avoid late at night. Thick neck, grey buzz cut, narrow eyes. Rebecca shrugged and shook her head along with the rest.

"Okay. You may have read about a murdered man found in a basement two nights ago. That man was Clive Rothbury, a successful wine importer and father of your friend, Seth Gardner."

That brought them to life. Rebecca gasped and involuntarily looked at Jake, chewing gum with his arms folded. That headline in the *Evening Standard*. José had his hand over his mouth. "Not the one…"

"I'm afraid so. It was rather a brutal murder. You can read the details yourself when you get out of here, but suffice to say that the victim had his eyes gouged out."

"Oh God." Rebecca felt her empty stomach heave. The detectives watched them impassively, the woman making a note in her book.

"Clive Rothbury had been reported missing some time ago, at around the same time we started to question you all."

"Why didn't you tell us?" Anna's voice was almost a squeak.

"There was nothing to tell at that point. People go missing all the time, especially people with a complicated home life." Her face was bland as a news reader's.

"So Seth – is he in danger? Could the same person who killed his father have him as well?" Anna's question wrenched a choked sob out of Catherine. Charles put an arm round her.

"We don't know, Miss Carmel. It's a wealthy family, as you know. We're looking at the possibility of a money-related kidnapping but there has been no demand for cash yet. We're doing all we can."

"Do you have any leads on the murder?" Michael's lips

barely moved.

"Nothing concrete. We may call some of you back for more questioning – just to tie up loose ends, you understand. Incidentally, we believe that Clive Rothbury disappeared on May 16th. That's the date you were originally supposed to be having your Friday Folly meeting, I understand. Secrets."

Jake shifted in his chair next to her. "In the meantime," the detective caught her colleague's eye quickly, "if any of you receive any sort of contact from Seth Gardner it is absolutely essential that you notify me immediately before responding in any way. Is that clear?"

SCENE 7

Anna grabs them on their way out of the police station, as unsubtle as ever. Nods towards Jake and hisses *let him leave first*. Michael wants to say something to Jake to make up for the other night but doesn't know where to start. He's no good at this sort of thing. And with Anna acting like they're in the Secret Seven or something…

Jake waves as he leaves and looks amused.

"Come on." Anna pulls them towards a café. "You get the drinks in and I'll get a newspaper."

He needs to get back to school but Anna is having none of it. Her eyes are shining as she sits down. She leans in. "Listen. That date, May 16th. Remember, we were supposed to do the Secrets group and Seth wasn't well?" Nods. "Well, the police got very excited when I told them Jake left early that night. Remember?"

Michael scrunches up his eyes as if that will bring it back to him. "Nope."

"Well, they did. They kept asking me what time he left."

He can see where this is going. "So?"

"Well, they must suspect him, mustn't they?"

He stares at her. "Why would Jake abduct, murder and mutilate Seth's father?"

Her shrug makes him snap louder than he intends. "For

Christ's sake, Anna." A couple on the next table glance over and he lowers his voice. "You're like a dog with a bone. These are wild accusations. Dangerous accusations. And I strongly recommend you don't go to the police with them. We don't want to alienate Jake any more than you already have." It's as much as he can say in front of Rebecca. Jake knows too much. And Anna needs to remember that.

She casts a deathly glance at him and they open the newspaper, poring over the details. He remembers Seth that day, slumping on the sofa between bursts of sudden animation. A horrible suspicion is beginning to take shape inside him. He feels it as a dark mass in his belly starting to seep into his veins.

Rebecca leans over Anna. "How long had – the body been there?"

"Over a month, they think."

"Do you think they suspected us? Is that why they've been questioning us?"

Anna shrugs. "They certainly kept the Clive Rothbury thing close to their chest. Him being missing like Seth."

A shaft of sunlight is attacking half of Catherine's face. She dodges away and Michael sees that her eyes are wet. She looks like she'll lose it any second. Her face is bloodless. Charles shuffles up to let her move towards him and bends closer to the newspaper. "They think the cause of death is stabbing."

Anna leans forward. "He must know something. Jake, Jack, whatever." She sees Michael's face and drops her eyes. "Look, this is serious. We thought it was bad before but – this? We all have to rack our brains. Is there anything we can think of, anything we've overlooked?"

The dark mass in his belly is rising to his throat and he needs to hiss it out. "Well, yes, Anna. Perhaps we've overlooked the possibility that Seth's disappearance and his father's murder are connected in another way."

She frowns. "You don't mean?" He says nothing. "If you're saying Seth had something to do with it, how do you explain the fact that he was with us that night?"

"A most convenient alibi." His jaw is clenched so that the laugh barely escapes. Rebecca shakes her head at him over and over again. Catherine turns towards Charles but he doesn't meet her eyes. Anna opens her mouth but José gets there first.

"Listen, all of you." It's the first time he has spoken. "I've just remembered something. When I did up that house of Seth's in Shepherd Bush there was a cupboard up in the attic that was always kept locked. Seth said he stored some of his stuff there. He was a bit weird about it. Maybe there's something in there, something that could lead us to him."

Anna nods. "It's worth a look."

"Do we tell the police?"

She hesitates. "Maybe we should check it out ourselves first."

"Or maybe we should leave well alone." Michael can't help raising his voice again. They're getting sucked in deeper and deeper. "How would we get in anyway?"

José sighs. "That's the thing. I might still have a spare key, but I've not seen it for ages."

"It doesn't matter." Charles sits up in his seat. "It won't be a problem. I've broken into enough of my flats in my time. You'd be amazed how many clients lose their keys."

"Charles – you dark horse." And they can't help laughing at his mischievous face. Charles, of all people. He leans over to José and raises his eyebrows.

"So, José, you and me? Let's play detectives."

SCENE 8

They are sitting next to each other in Charles' car, watching the house with the red front door. They've been there a while. Charles has just fetched them pizza from the high street. He seems to be rather enjoying himself. "Look at us, sitting here like Starsky and Hutch."

"Hardly." José is not enjoying himself.

Charles ignores him. "Think we should ring the bell soon.

Just to be sure there's no one home."

There's no car outside the house and there's been no discernible movement from the windows while they've been there. But they do need to be sure. Charles fumbles in his briefcase and pulls out a laminated restaurant menu.

"Here you go." He coughs and there's that mischievous look again.

José stares. "What's this?"

"It's a prop for when you ring the bell."

"When I ring the bell? No way, mate, this is your idea. You do it."

"But I don't look Turkish." He strokes his beard. "You're opening up a new Turkish restaurant and want to tell people about it." Charles ignores his spluttered refusal. "Come on, ham up the accent: *please I am wanting to let you know new café...*"

"Charles! This is outrageous. So because I'm Spanish... God, you're as bad as Seth."

Charles just winks at him.

* * * * *

Luckily there's no answer. José returns to the car and thrusts the menu at Charles. "Go and have a kebab on me."

But Charles becomes suddenly businesslike. "Okay, we'll go to the back door. There's a path down the side. Hope none of the neighbours are about."

They knock on the back door too, just to be sure. The terrace is deserted. Charles leans on a screwdriver and the door gives way almost immediately.

The place is squalid. Saucers full of cigarette ash, pizza boxes, beer cans all over the work top. It smells like a hamster cage.

José blinks. "What a mess." He can barely stand to look at it, his baby, roughed up and ruined. "It was beautiful when I'd finished it."

"Come on." Charles is already halfway upstairs. "Show me this cupboard."

The cupboard is much harder to break into than the house, but between them they force the lock. José used to wonder about this cupboard quite a bit, when he was living here. Sometimes he'd try the handle, knowing it would be locked but wanting to turn it all the same.

"Shit. It's pitch black in there."

"Which is why we'll be needing this." Charles has thought of everything. The torch flicks on a large cardboard box full of papers. "We'll have those for a start."

"What, all of them?"

"Unless you fancy flicking through them until whoever lives here comes home and finds you." Charles pulls out the box, dragging it with both hands, then crawls in. "It goes all the way back."

"What's in there?"

"Boxes of books. Records." There's a clattering sound. "Photos. I guess this is where he keeps them all." Charles' voice is a muffled echo. José feels a shot of panic.

"Let's get going, Charles. We'll take the papers and go." He suddenly pictures Seth appearing at the top of the stairs. "Jesus, Charles, hurry up."

Charles crawls back out. He's holding something and his face is white around the smears of dust by his nose. They look down at it. It's hair. Long, ginger hair.

"It was in a carrier bag."

"Oh my…"

"Don't worry, it's a wig. But – you remember?"

Of course he remembers. He has never stopped remembering. "Put it back, Charles. Put it back now. Rub your fingerprints off it or something."

Charles stares. "I can't."

"For fuck's sake." José grabs the wig with his sleeve and starts rubbing it on his jeans. One or two hairs detach themselves and cling to his thigh. "We should never have

323

come here." He flings the wig back inside the cupboard. "Let's get out now."

They are so focused on getting the box down two flights of stairs that they don't notice Jake waiting for them at the bottom.

SCENE 9

He is leaning against a wall in the kitchen, arms folded, chewing and grinning. "Well, if it isn't Cagney and Lacey."

They are halfway down the last flight of stairs. José screams; he can't help it. They stop and stand for a second, gaping down at Jake.

"Ah," mutters Charles.

"Down here will be fine." Jake points to the corner of the kitchen as if they are removal men. They shuffle the box down and drop it in the corner. On top is Charles' screwdriver.

"Don't even think about it, buddy." Said cheerfully as he sees the direction of Charles' glance. "Why you don't you come over here and we can chat."

José cringes, waiting for the blow. But Jake gestures towards the table. "Have a pew. Beer?" He shakes the remains of a can of lager and laughs. José sits on his hands to stop them shaking.

Charles coughs. "What are you doing here?" José has to admire him, going on the offensive at a moment like this.

Jake sits opposite, trowel hands laid on the table. Two silver rings and the flash of his watch.

"You see, Charlie boy, that's what I need to ask you. But I don't mind going first. I'm living here. I've been living here since I lost my job last year. And you, my friends, have broken into my home."

They gape.

"Is it really so amazing? Seth asked me to keep it quiet. You know how he is. Believe he did the same thing for you once." He looks straight at José. "Nostalgic for the place, were you?"

José's mouth is too dry to reply. Charles clears his throat.

"We were looking for anything that could lead us to Seth."

"Were you now?" Jake leans in. "Well, having never been nosy enough to force open the lock to a private cupboard, I don't know what you found up there – apart from this nice fat box which is, of course, staying right here. But whatever you've seen, I'd advise you to keep quiet about it. You don't want to add breaking and entering to whatever else you might have done."

Charles stands up. "You've made your point."

Jake remains where he is. "Attempted burglary too. Hmmm. First offence, let's call it – eighteen months? Out in a year with good behaviour. And I'm sure your behaviour will be very, very good." His eyes slide over José.

"That's enough, Jake. Message received."

"And while we're at it, you'd better keep a grip on Miss Carmel. Wouldn't want her saying anything that could get the rest of you in trouble."

"Come on, José." Charles pulls him to his feet. José isn't sure which will give way first, his heart or his legs. They collapse into the car.

Charles bangs the steering wheel.

"What are you doing? Let's get out of here."

"Okay, okay. I need to think this through." He looks across. "You know we can't mention the wig to Rebecca."

José nods. "I know. But can we just go now? He might come after us."

"He's not going to come after us. He's got us just where he wants us." Charles shakes his head with a dry little laugh. "And now there's Anna to deal with. God knows what she'll say about this."

José isn't looking at him. He's looking at the large, muscular man coming out of the red front door. Charles follows his gaze as the man starts to walk towards them.

"Bugger." He starts the engine and slams the car into first gear. "I guess it's home to Anna then."

SCENE 10

[Michael and Anna pacing; Rebecca, Charles, Catherine
and José milling around]

MICHAEL: Nice one, Anna. Making an enemy of Jake. Just what we need.

ANNA: It wasn't just my idea. And, anyway, he is our enemy. He's living in Seth's house. What the hell's he done to him? I told you it was him.

MICHAEL *[laughs]*: He's done nothing, Anna. Except, maybe stay in touch with Seth. And we don't even know that.

CHARLES *[coughs]*: It does seem possible that Seth has chosen to – er, take some time out, let's say. Perhaps his disappearance is nothing more than that.

JOSÉ: But you saw Jake yesterday. Why was he so threatening?

MICHAEL: Because you'd broken into his house? Just a wild guess.

JOSÉ: Seth's house.

MICHAEL: Where you also lived when it suited you.

JOSÉ: He even came after us.

CHARLES *[coughs]*: Hardly, old boy. He was probably just popping out for some milk.

CATHERINE: He's a bad man, a bad man.

ALL: Who is?

CATHERINE: Jake. I never trusted him. I can't deal with this.

CHARLES *[comforts Catherine]*: Where is Jake supposed to live, anyway? I mean, where did we think he lived?

ALL: *[murmur that they have no idea]*

REBECCA: I thought he said Ealing way.

ANNA: Shows how upfront he was.

CHARLES: Shows how much interest we showed in him.

MICHAEL:	And now he has two things on us.
REBECCA:	What do you mean?
ANNA:	Who knows what he means?
REBECCA:	Is there something you're not telling me?
ALL THE OTHERS	[*to audience*]: Surely not!
MICHAEL:	The time has come to accept that Seth has gone. He's chosen to walk out on his life, on us, and the only thing we can do is move on. Like him.
CATHERINE:	Move on?
MICHAEL:	Yes. We can still do things without him, you know. Fun things. Hell, we can even carry on the Friday Folly if you want.
REBECCA:	It wouldn't be the same without him.
CATHERINE:	This is ridiculous!
MICHAEL:	It wouldn't be the same without him, I agree. [*sighs of relief*] It would be a lot better! [*gasps of horror*]
ANNA:	He's losing the plot.
MICHAEL:	I'm not joking, I really believe it would be better. No one in control – except maybe you, Anna, but we could deal with that. No divide and rule. And, let's face it, what did he really contribute?
ANNA:	You can't be serious.
MICHAEL:	Yes, I am serious. What did he bring? A lot of fancy spiel about art. The odd half-baked poem here and there.
REBECCA:	[*spluttering*] Half-baked? He's a published poet.
MICHAEL:	Ever seen any of his poems in print? No, me neither.
CHARLES:	Aren't we getting sidetracked here? Ah well.
MICHAEL:	You know what I think? I think that Seth is a parasite, feeding on other people's creativity.

Bleeding them dry while he gets fatter and more self-satisfied.

[shocked silence]

REBECCA: That's the biggest pile of crap I ever heard. Seth is the most... inspirational person I know. And he's generous with it. He catalysed us all into doing stuff we wouldn't have done otherwise.

MICHAEL: *[laughs]* Really? So he catalysed you into taking that part for West Yorkshire Playhouse? Oh, wait a minute, you turned it down. Your biggest break yet. Funny, that.

REBECCA: *[shouts]* That had nothing to do with him. I turned it down because there were better opportunities in London. Like the play I'm doing now.

MICHAEL: Horse shit. You turned it down because he was in London. At least be honest with yourself.

REBECCA: How fucking dare you!

ANNA: Ignore him.

JOSÉ: *[to audience]* You may recall me saying something similar at the time.

MICHAEL: Can't you see? Can't any of you see? He took us in, sucked us dry and spat us out like pips. Just like he did to that poor Bridget girl. He's lied to us from day one, oh poor Seth the orphan, poor little rich boy with no one to take care of him. Next thing he'll be setting up a Sunday Soiree in Southamp –

CATHERINE: *[covers ears]*: SHUT UP! SHUT UP SHUT UP SHUT UP!

MICHAEL: *[shocked]*: Catherine?

[Catherine rocks. Charles approaches but she shakes her head]

ANNA: Quit the character assassination, Michael.

328

	It's not helping anyone.
MICHAEL:	Fine. I'll keep my opinions to myself. If the rest of you want to wait around for the second coming, that's your choice. I'm out of here. I'm done with you.
	[*looks out to audience*]
	I'm done with all of you.
	[*exits*]
JOSÉ:	And then there were five.

SCENE 11

José leans against the smeared steel pole and tries to keep his balance with a series of near-constant weight shifts. The train is rattling furiously towards Clapham Junction, where he hopes his precarious position will pay off. People always stand near the doors, but the only chance of grabbing a seat at this time is to hover like a hawk between the parallel rows of fanned-out newspapers. As the train brakes – unnecessarily jerkily, a sadist driver again – he is forced to handle the pole to stop himself charging the carriage like a battering ram. The metal carries the warmth of someone else's grip. He must remember to wash his hands before he dips into the fridge at home.

He's in luck: the twenty-something P.A. on the seat in front of him (you have to make assumptions about people on the Tube to pass the time) glances up as the train stops and gets up in a bit of a fluster. José bumps down heavily and closes his eyes for a second. It's moments like this that make it possible to go on living in London. He mentally scours his fridge, putting together a pre-dinner snack. Damn, he's out of olives. The Indian shop only sells the crap jars and he'll have to detour at least ten minutes to the deli to get decent ones. Crap olives will do.

He's left work early again. One or two raised eyebrows, he's sure. He can't even face going to the gym. It's been ten days now. He's so tired he wonders if he's got glandular fever.

He picks up today's *Evening Standard* from the ledge behind him. More lurid details and speculation about Clive Rothbury. He skims the article… *disused building… recently separated from his wife… socialites… benefactor of the arts.* There's a photograph of Clive and Julia Rothbury together, taken at some party or other, with a *Tatler* photo credit. She's as tall as her husband in heels, red haired and glamorous, pouting like a model. It's the first time he's seen a picture of Seth's mother, and the first time he's wondered where she could be in all this madness. Clive Rothbury is dark, like Seth, handsome but not as arresting. Normal brown eyes, for a start. A sudden surge of sickness. Not anymore.

When he gets home there's a letter in his mailbox, typed and unstamped. He's curious, slips a finger under the seal and brings the opened jar of olives over to the table before unfolding the paper inside.

And that's when he ends up with bits of half-digested olives splattered at his feet. The opened letter falls to the floor to join the briny green gunk. José calls to a God he no longer believes in and sits with his head in his hands.

SCENE 12

Michael wakes from a night of underwater dreams to the trill of his alarm. For a minute he lies still, waiting for the reverberation running through his body to still. What day is it? Monday, of course. Another Monday of double lessons and post-weekend backchat. And not just in the classroom. He sags at the thought of his colleagues with their matey laughter and staffroom cliques. Is this really what he wants to be doing? After all his grand dreams of social justice, is this all he has amounted to? A secondary school teacher?

He can put a radical spin on it – deprived kids, minority kids – but is he really making a difference? He pictures the slouches and smirks of his Year Tens. Like hell he is.

The clock says 7.11 which means he can have ten more minutes and grab his breakfast on the way. The phone rang at least five times yesterday. Catherine, no doubt. They'll patch things up in the end but he doesn't want to talk to her now. It's better to stay away from the lot of them. He needs to go cold turkey on anything to do with Seth. Especially with the latest Jake fiasco.

He steers his thoughts back to teaching. It's a meditation technique Rebecca told him about when she was doing those workshops, something she uses to get into role. Acknowledge the thought that's troubling you and then move it aside. Like brushing a hair off your face.

He knows things are never as bad as they seem on a Monday morning. He has done some things he's proud of, connected with a few kids. He's even been getting quite busy at parents' evenings, less likely to be treated as a joke. Trelawny is a pain but basically rates him. Still there's a thought that he doesn't want but he can't brush this one aside. It's forcing its way into his head more and more these days, forcing him to acknowledge it.

After everything that happened he's following in Mr Fleming's footsteps.

He turns the shower onto red, cranking the dial clockwise until all he can think of is the heat of the water. Tiny jets fly out from the top of the shower head and pepper him in the face. As he leaves the house he grabs the same battered black bag he's been using for years.

SCENE 13

Charles sighs and puts his briefcase down in the hall. Another long day. He puts a hand to the small of his back and stretches. As usual the kitchen cheers him, light and orderly and, dare he say, rather well designed. The cleaners have been and there's a neat pile of post waiting for him on the granite breakfast bar. He sifts through it: bills, pizza flyers and an odd typed envelope without a stamp. Probably some local councillor trying to get his vote. He grips it with both hands to rip it down the middle and throw it in the recycling.

But it won't tear.

Cursing mildly he takes the silver paper knife from the shelf above and slits the envelope. To his surprise he pulls out a photograph. The girl is red haired and scantily clad. He shouldn't really, but he looks more closely. She's young and skinny, but a little too skinny. His eyes move up to her face. She's his sister.

Sarah pouts back at him, a little self-consciously, from beneath a red wig.

SCENE 14

Rebecca is being reckless. She laughs, throws her arms out and whirls.

Midnight shakes the memory
As a madman shakes a dead geranium.

She wouldn't normally walk down by the canal late at night. But the good thing about having Big Worries – a missing lover whose father has been maimed and murdered – is that Small Worries such as personal safety don't make it to the starting blocks anymore. And she's been drinking. Anna met her after her rehearsal and they both seemed to need to hit the bottle. She was surprised to see Anna turn up alone – it was always two for the price of one with her and José. Rebecca, for once, didn't probe. She had enough on her plate.

She'd met Jake again yesterday. She didn't really want to but nor did she want to break a potential connection to Seth. She'd chosen the venue this time – somewhere central and well-populated. Not a word was said on either side about the fact that he'd found Charles and José breaking into the Shepherd's Bush house. While never dropping his cockney charm, he quizzed her about they were all saying to the police. She twizzled clammy hands under the table and tried to change the subject.

He asked her a lot about the job too, where she was rehearsing, her schedule. Two months ago she'd have been touched by the friendly interest and encouragement. Now she gave cagey answers disguised as modest deflections.

It's dark on the canal, patchy light from the street barely illuminating the tow path, and now and then she stumbles. But she likes the cool, slightly sweaty smell of the water and the sense of rebellion. She is partner in crime with the wind which tickles her ankles and lifts the sticky hair from her neck like a lover. *Rhapsody on a Windy Night*, she thinks, and lifts her head to follow the streetlamps. There's even a moon, three-quarters full, blurry round the edges like her mind. *La lune ne garde aucune rancune.* She's saying it for Seth, in case he's out there, listening. He would appreciate the reference.

And of course hot on her heels is the dreadful Andrew Lloyd Webber version, "Memory", chasing her towards the next streetlamp.

There's something strangely appealing about a power ballad at this moment and she joins in at the key change, giving it her best Elaine Paige. If Seth was here she'll have driven him off now. She laughs because she can picture his expression. And because, despite the fact she's clearly falling apart, rehearsals for *No Exit* are going well. Never before has she been able to channel her life so effectively into her art. He's still inspiring her from wherever he is.

Or is it what Michael said, that he was feeding off her creativity and now she is free? Seth the vampire. She tilts back her hair to expose her throat. *Come and get me then. Make me yours.* She closes her eyes and imagines his teeth sinking into her neck.

It turns her on, which isn't surprising because everything does at the moment. She exists in the sweet spot where anxiety and desire and fear meet. Ahead of her there's a bridge. If she slipped under it no one would see…

Snap. A sound like a twig underfoot behind her. She whirls and listens. Only the wind riling the litter-strewn edges of the tow path. But the moment is broken, the bravado gone, and she sees herself as she is: all alone by a canal after midnight. She starts to walk, upping the pace with each step. Another crack behind her. She turns as she runs, flings a glance into the shadows, a shape perhaps, moving, but her right foot twists and she has to face forward, search for the next exit. Steps are on the far side of the bridge. She stumbles into them, up them, the back of her mules slapping each step and giving her away. Up onto a deserted street, not enough breath for tears. Sporadic street lamps and dark houses. *Keep running.* The main road in sight. Another glance over her shoulder. She sees the shadow, coming for her, stretching a giant finger along the ground to hook her back.

SCENE 15

She's never fought with José before. Nothing more than a barb or two that touched a nerve, and of course that thing at the Childhood group, but that was over so quickly. He's her buddy, her touchstone, her pocket rocket. And she's just said some terrible things to him. It was the shock, the fact that he hadn't told her before. The way that she suddenly felt she didn't know him.

She doesn't want to think about him doing that, being that. A rent boy. It's too much of a reality check and it makes the end of her fingers curl. No one wants to imagine their friends having sex. And maybe this sort of sex is worse. Men on men. Men in men. Her chin retracts as if someone's stuck something smelly under her nose. There it is, her latent homophobia. Maybe it's in everyone, like racism.

She frowns as she weaves through the post-work ruckus, stepping off the pavement to overtake a pushchair and feeling the breeze from a bus sailing too close to her. This fecking city. And now José's being threatened, blackmailed, and stands to lose everything. Poor José, she thinks, and then remembers she's angry with him.

She bangs straight into someone coming the other way, so hard it nearly knocks her off her feet and the briefcase slides from her hand. It's instantly kicked into the gutter by the oncoming surge and papers start to spill into puddles. *Fuck*

fuck fuck. She steps down to grab the papers but is beaten to it by an unseasonal black Fedora hat.

Time stops.

People carry on pushing past her as she stares at the hat at her feet. "Seth." The name leaves her mouth before she can stop it, a squeak, instantly absorbed and carried away by the Tube-bound multitudes. She stands with outstretched arm as he rises to his feet and lifts his head.

Jake raises his hat and winks down at her. "Well, if it isn't the lovely Miss Carmel." People carry on pushing past. There's a tingling behind her eyes. She tries to back away but he takes her arm. Tightly. Her legs won't move.

"Careful, now, you look like you've seen a ghost. Let's get you somewhere quieter."

He steers her into a side street, holding her briefcase with his spare hand. She leans against a garden wall. "I can scream, you know."

He chortles. "You disappoint me, Anna. Resorting to such feminine tactics already? And all I've done is pick up your briefcase for ya."

She holds out her hand. "Give it back to me."

He shakes his head. "Anna, Anna, Anna. Needs to learn some manners."

She can't help staring at the hat.

"Oh, this." He takes it off and examines it. "I've always 'ad my eye on it. Does it suit me?"

"You fuck…" She tries to snatch it but Jake's too quick.

He pops it back on his head. "And I thought you liked dressing up. Now, listen, seeing as you're 'ere, I just wanted to check that you've not been letting your mouth run away with you to Mrs Plod. I know what you women are like when you get together. Wouldn't want things to get unpleasant for you, would we?"

"Don't threaten me. I know it was you who sent the letter to José."

He raises his eyebrows. "Nope, you've lost me now. I

335

prefer to do my business in person."

"Liar. You're a coward."

He shrugs. "Sticks and stones. You know, I used to think you were a right laugh. Until you got so serious. Lighten up, love, and do us all a favour. Here's your business-woman briefcase." She grabs it from him. "I'll be seeing you around. And don't forget what I said." He taps the side of his nose and winks. "Ciao, baby."

SCENE 16

José has called in sick again. Then the phone rings straight back and he picks up to brief whichever colleague about whatever client but it's his mother. He's angry with her straight away because it's the working day and why would he be at home anyway, and then he has to say he's sick and that's all the entry point she needs for her favourite subject, her only subject, the handkerchief to her eyes, the sniffle in her voice as she wishes he had a *chica bonita* to mop his brow and make him soup.

"Mama…" He can't shout at her when she's crying. But he can't hear this, not today. He pretends the office is calling him and hangs up.

Back in bed he's shivering like his body believes it really does have a fever. He needs to eat, but food feels like an indulgence he doesn't deserve. A salt spray of shame stings his eyeballs and the back of his throat. He's lost everything. Even Anna. The flare of memory: Seth holding him, forgiving him, redeeming him. Wiping out his past and making him whole. But isn't this Seth now, threatening him, punishing him? He remembers the pantomime, the sense of being toyed with like a captured mouse. What is Seth doing to him? Why?

The door to his flat bangs suddenly, three times, and his heart hammers a response. Father Christmas come to claim him. He sticks his head under the duvet. He's not here, why should he be here, it's a Friday morning. The door bangs again, repeatedly. Then a female voice calling, nasal and no-nonsense.

"José. Open the door, for feck's sake. I know you're in there."

He shrinks from the sound of her. The things she said to him.

"José. We need to talk. I have your feckin' key, you know."

Fine. Let her use it then. He turns his face to the wall like a sulking child.

She rattles around and finally gets the door open. "José?" It's a one-bedroom flat and it doesn't take her long. He feels her standing over him, hands on hips. "It's ten o'clock, man. Are you ill?" He stays put, looks at the wall. A touch to his shoulder over the duvet. He shrugs it off.

"You need to get up, get some air into here." He knows she's taking it all in, the scattered clothes, unwashed cups. "Look, I need to tell you something. Why don't I wet the tea while you put some clothes on? Come through when you're ready."

He doesn't expect to move but her restlessness has permeated him. He puts on his dressing gown and finds her ransacking his kitchen. "I'll do it."

She turns and grins. "Knew that would get you up." But her grin fades as she takes him in. He knows he looks rough, hasn't shaved since Monday. He tells her to sit down while he makes the tea. He takes a tray to the coffee table and they both perch on the sofa like nervous guests.

"What's wrong with you, then?" Always so direct, so insensitive. He shakes his head, looks out of the window. She can try a bit harder than that. She jumps up. "Got any sugar?"

"Sure, on the worktop." It's his cue to tease her about her latest, evidently abandoned, resolution, giving up sugar in hot drinks. But he doesn't take it. She brings the sugar over and puts it on the coffee table, but stays on her feet, twisting her hands.

"I bumped into Jake yesterday. Literally."

He looks up at her but says nothing.

"I don't think it was an accident." Her voice wavers a bit. He sees now that she doesn't look too good either. Like she hasn't slept. And he realises she's not in work herself.

"He threatened me. The stupid bastard threatened me."

He feels himself softening so he grabs something hard, the edge of the table. "What happened?"

There's an appeal in her voice as she tells him. She needs him now, needs some reassurance. She's frightened. Like he was on Monday when he needed her. The things she said to him.

She sits next to him. "I'm sorry." He knows what it costs her to say sorry. The next second her face melts into a gush of tears. "Those terrible things – I don't know why I said them. I just felt like I didn't know you anymore. It was the last straw, to lose you. I couldn't bear it."

He wants to cry too, surrender to the wave pushing up from his chest, but it scares him. Instead he dams it with his lips and puts a hand on her knee. "I should have told you."

She looks up at him with her child's face. "Why didn't you?"

"Because I didn't..." and he feels the wave now, rising to the surface as he shudders, "Because I hate myself for that bit of my life and I didn't want you to hate me too." The words spew out along with the sob, detritus washed ashore in a storm. He reaches out his arms and she's there, clinging to him.

"I could never hate you, José. You're my best friend. I love you."

He loses it then, making noises he doesn't recognise as his. "What am I going to do, Anna? What am I going to do?"

She holds him until the wave passes. Then she lifts his head and scrapes the tears away with her palms. "Listen. All you've received is this note. There's nothing really in it, no specific threat. It's just to scare you."

He gazes at her, desperate for her words to be true.

"No prizes for guessing who sent it, of course." She sees his face. "No. Seth would never do that. Remember how he helped you?"

He nods, runs a tongue over his lips, wanting to believe.

"It's Jake. Look at the way he threatened me yesterday. He's dug around a bit and found out. He's rattled by you and Charles breaking in. He's just warning you off, nothing more."

José nods again. He can't even think. Anna sounds so sure he agrees with her like he always does.

"You can't let him take you apart like this. He's playing with you. You have to hold it together and tough it out." She sighs and he catches a look he isn't meant to see. "God knows what else we can do."

SCENE 17

Michael notices his sweaty palms again with his Year Nines. What is this strange awkwardness that has infiltrated his teaching? It seeps through his clothes and into his conversations with colleagues. He struggles to make eye contact, fluffs his standard classroom jokes. The boys sense it too and give him pitying looks. He has a sense of being stranded on a precipice, leaning out and looking down, drawn to the glinting rocks below.

He feels dizzy and his eyes hurt. He rubs at his glasses with a hanky; maybe he needs a new prescription in his lenses. It's 4.30 and he should be at home but he has to supervise detention. Scott Mullen bends his blonde head over the question paper, the only one in today. He's usually a good boy but he's started hanging out with the wrong crowd, trying to be popular. Michael looks at the thin shoulders and feels a tingle of pity. He sees himself there, fourteen and friendless. With any luck Mullen has more of a family life than he did.

He rises and paces the room, looking at the wall displays. A project on rural development in South America, cartoons from Year Seven depicting the founding of Rome. He treads the old parquet floor until he finds himself directly behind Scott Mullen. He can see the speckles of black fluff on the back of his shirt that need batting off, the wiggling of muscles as he writes. A thought rises up from his feet. He could find out once and for all what it meant. The thought enters his lungs, stops his breath. He may never have this opportunity again.

Like a mime artist Michael stretches out his right hand until it is splayed in front of him. He expects the boy to look round but for once the detention exercise is absorbing. He watches his hand, as though it belongs to someone else. What would happen if he placed it on the boy's back, just beneath the shoulder blades, making a greasy handprint on the grey polyester?

Little by little he extends his right arm. He sees his fingers tremble like an alcoholic's. Strands of sandy hair graze the edge of the boy's collar, just beyond his reach. If the boy turns round now he will be caught with a face as frightened as Mr Fleming's.

The boy shifts his weight and looks up, sees the teacher's empty desk in front of him. As his head turns, Michael's hand is safe in his pocket and he is looking at a wall display of geometric drawings. He meets the boy's glance and nods at him to carry on with his work.

SCENE 18

Jake pops another piece of gum in his mouth and looks at his watch. He likes to look at it as often as possible. He presses the tiny light switch with his huge finger pad: 1.30am. No sign of her. It's getting pretty uncomfortable hanging out by this tree. About the only tree in sight of her flat. It'll probably flourish with all the pisses he's taken on it.

At last, the faint clip of heels from a side street. He sticks his head out but sees at once it's not Rebecca: short legs, flared hips. Nice for a change, though. A few yards away she spots him and immediately crosses the road, starts to run. Her arse bustles fetchingly from side to side. Now and then she throws a worried face back at him. He shakes his head and smiles, leaning back on his tree, and pulls out the silver cigarette case. He lights up and is just about to take a drag when he hears more footsteps, uneven and stumbling. He stubs out the ciggie and peers out. This time it's her. She looks drunk, vulnerable. Easy pickings. She takes a good minute to open her front door. He lights another cigarette and smokes it slowly. She's getting more and more reckless and it's not good. Luckily he's decided to take matters into his own hands.

ACT 5
PART 1 - SCENE 1

Rebecca blew a kiss to her flatmate when she saw the pot of fresh coffee on the worktop. It was a relief to have Shazia around again, especially now *No Exit* was finished. She'd forgotten what it was like to hear someone else's voice first thing in the morning, someone who wasn't Chris Tarrant. Shaz took a little of the emptiness away just by being there.

She sat down at the table with coffee and a bowl of Special K, batting the crumbs from last night's pizza to one side. Her ripped-out reviews were still stacked unwisely next to the ketchup. *Extraordinary power. An Estelle whose cruelty comes from inner desolation.* Seems it was her best thing to date, even better than *Hamlet*. And at the Orange Tree again, in the round. What better demonstration of the catch phrase of the play: *L'enfer, c'est les autres.* Hell is other people.

Some days that's exactly what she thinks. Other people leave you when you need them. They keep secrets from you. They follow you at night. Several times in the last few weeks she's had the feeling of being watched. Could it be Seth? Paranoia? God knows she doesn't trust her own mind anymore. She's feeling paranoid about the group as well, wondering if she's only being told half a story. But she needs them. Just like the characters in *No Exit*, they torture and depend on each other in equal measure.

She still thinks about him first thing every morning. His voicemail is still full. Nothing has changed.

But then there's the pot of fresh coffee and Shaz coming in, grinning at her in Minnie Mouse pyjamas, and small

342

things like that might just keep her sane.

Shaz nods at the cafetiere and smiles. "I hope you've left me a bit of that."

"A bit is probably the word. I'll make some more in a tick."

"Okay, I'm off to see if the shower fancies heating up this morning." Shaz bangs the radio on and leaves the room.

Rebecca reads the back of the cereal packet, looking at lithe women in red swimsuits cartwheeling across the words. Then she stops, mid-mouthful, and stares at the radio.

"Shaz, come here!"

A distant response from the bathroom. Rebecca swallows her cereal and shouts louder. Her flatmate appears, tying a peach satin dressing gown round her waist.

"What..."

"Shhh!" Rebecca waves at the radio. "I think Princess Di's dead."

"What?"

SCENE 2

It was ridiculous what was happening. Anna found herself unable to catch her normal district line train to work because it was packed with foreigners clutching bouquets. The whole world was suddenly in mourning. People kept saying *Can you believe it?* and *Where were you?* She wanted to say *Having a shit, as it happens* but the hushed reverence of these conversations inhibited her normal bluntness.

It was a distraction of sorts, she could give it that, a break from the mundane reality of wondering where Seth was and trying to get on with life without him. No more questions from the police, no more visits from Jake; the trail seemed to have gone cold. Even the *Evening Standard* had toned down the coverage. And now it had this, of course.

It was Saturday morning, *The Day of the Funeral*. God knows what she would do all day. She should have arranged to get out of London, although all exits had probably been sealed. It was pointless to go into town, nothing else was being shown on TV and apparently music was banned on some radio stations. Luckily she had a week's supply of chocolate and liquid refreshment that should last her until the evening. If she was under siege, she was damn well going to find the silver lining. And with that she broke open her first Kit Kat.

At ten thirty she gave in and flicked on the television. Rows and rows of people and a constipated royal correspondent whispering as the hearse approached. She boiled the kettle again. Could she ring anyone? No, that's all they would talk about. She wished Seth were here. He probably would have hosted an alcoholic parody of the occasion. At the very least she and he would have sat and laughed and wondered at the stupidity of it all.

José had some friend over from Spain who'd hopped on a plane to catch some of the atmosphere or something. Unbelievable. She gurned at the telly. Was that Westminster Abbey, lurking modestly behind ten thousand people? The camera panned in on the coffin being borne aloft towards the doors, and a single white envelope on top of it. *Mummy*.

Delete. Her index finger jabbed around for a second until the image disappeared and she stood up, started putting newspapers away until the room looked like an Ikea brochure again. How much longer till this farce was over? She broke open a Yorkie bar at the table. Raisin and biscuit – not bad. Surely it was reasonable to open a bottle of Chardonnay now.

The pop of the cork was the best sound she'd heard all day, puncturing the swelling silence of her flat. Music – of course, that was what she needed. Something subversively upbeat. *Graceland* would do it: lots of smiling African faces instead of miserable white ones. She whirled her glass of wine round as a dance partner, singing her own approximation of Paul Simon's kooky lyrics.

She was half a glass down by the second song, the one about losing love. So much for upbeat. She'd never liked this track much so she flicked it forward. And forward again.

Come to think of it she just wanted a quiet drink without Paul Simon babbling on in her face.

She found herself in front of the television again. The service had started. Prince Charles looked like he had a holly bush shoved up his arse. The princes – *her boys* as everyone referred to them – sat in suits and brave faces too old for them.

The sob started as a gagging cough at the back of her throat. She was too surprised to stop it, too slow to switch off the television. Tears rained over her vision but the boys' faces loomed in front of her and tore up chunks from her gullet. She bawled through the whole service, even to the revolting Elton John song.

Just three chocolate bars, half a bottle of wine, a state funeral and the tears of a nation for her to say a proper goodbye to her ma.

SCENE 3

The newspaper images should have prepared her but they didn't come close. The smell hit first, a thick fragrant sweetness that gave her goosebumps. Rebecca stopped still at the first glimpse of white, upsetting the steady procession behind her. People in front were staring rapt as if a host of angels had settled on the grounds of Kensington Palace. As she shuffled forwards the same *Oh my God* dropped from her open mouth as everyone else's. This wasn't a few bunches of flowers but a glistening ivory ocean that swelled and rose before her like the taffeta skirts of a giant bride. She thought of an inflated, goddess-sized Diana on her wedding day. As the waxy horizon continued shifting and expanding she gasped and her eyes watered. It was the feeling of tininess in the presence of something extraordinary. But this was also a fixed moment in time. She would never see anything like this again.

She spent a little time moving amongst the bouquets, where she could. Sometimes they were thigh-high. She was silent, lost not just for words but for thoughts, a way of processing what she was seeing. She laid her own modest clutch of freesias next to an old-fashioned teddy bear with a note round its neck. *Sleep well in heaven.*

It was easy to cry because everyone else was. The British upper lip was down and drooping. They were crying for Diana, they were grieving their mothers, spouses, old lives, lost dreams. Finding comfort under this shared blanket of sadness. Standing shoulder to shoulder, just for this moment, to better bear the weight of death and debris grinding them down.

I've lost him she said, to her surprise. The woman next to her nodded and took her hand. For a second there was peace and acceptance. Everyone here had lost someone. Then the certainty came. *He's here.* As soon as she said it she knew it was true. He'd followed her again. The woman stared as Rebecca broke away and tried to back up, knocking into mounds of plastic-wrapped lilies. He was here and she had to find him.

She was making a stir now, pushing forwards then stopping suddenly to stand on her tiptoes. People tutted as she disturbed their reveries. She didn't care. He was here, she could feel it.

"Sorry, sorry, excuse me..." She fought her way along a floral corridor, struggling for breath. Bloody bouquets everywhere like the last night of a performance. She wanted to hurl them out of her way.

"Have you lost someone, madam?"

She looked at the hand on her arm with its navy cuff and up into the spectacled eyes of a policeman. Relief flooded her.

"Yes, a friend of mine. I have to find him, it's urgent."

"Okay, madam, let's just move this way." He was guiding her, his hand firm on her elbow. "When did you last see this friend?"

"Oh, er..." She couldn't exactly say two months ago. And he was moving her too fast. She pulled back, twisting her head around.

"Sorry, I know he's here, I just have to find him." She looked at her escort. "You couldn't make an announcement or something, could you?"

The officer regarded her evenly. "Perhaps it might be easier if you called his mobile phone, if he has one?"

"Oh – no, it's switched off. I have to find him. Please can you help me?" She wanted to clutch his sleeve, drop to her knees and beg the kindly policeman to make everything right.

"Let's get you out of these crowds and we can talk about what to do."

She submitted for a couple of minutes until a jet head of hair jumped out from the blurry hush.

"That's him!" She pulled away from the hand on her elbow and lunged forwards, shoving a middle-aged woman so hard that she toppled over. "Sorry." Gasps around her, the woman spluttering. She was vaguely aware of the policeman stopping to help the woman up and pushed harder through the crowd: there he was, twenty people ahead of her. The policeman would catch her any second. She had one option left.

His name circled once, twice, three times around the arena of flowers before her scream was sucked silent into the waiting foliage. Everything seemed to stop. A magpie called overhead. The distant rumble of a bus from the road. And then the black head turned.

It was a woman.

"No." She said it aloud, backing up now, bumping more people, more flowers, more teddy bears. "It was him. It was him." Someone grabbed hold of her upper arm, hard, until the policeman forced his way through. She pulled free of the new hand but the policeman took her by both shoulders.

"Forwards please." His voice was harder now. "People are trying to pay their respects. Please restrain yourself."

Tears rushed to her eyes as he propelled her along. "You don't understand. Please slow down. Please slow down or we'll miss him."

The hands on her shoulder were implacable. She twisted

her head frantically from side to side, trying to pick out a face. Her nose sought for oxygen in the thick, sweet air. The tips of her fingers started to tingle and gratefully she closed her eyes.

There was movement around her when she opened them again. And voices, perhaps in the next room, talking about her.

"Up you sit." She was pulled up under her arms like a child.

"Put your head between your knees."

She did as she was told, breathing rapidly. Then a woman's voice and a hand on her back.

"Are you feeling better, love?"

The kind words kick-started the tears.

"Come on now, lift your head and have a bit of water." A bottle was pressed into her hand. She sat up straighter and took a sip, letting the tears slide into her sticky mask of hair.

"Is there anyone you want us to call?"

She cried harder, put her head back on her knees. The voices were talking about her again.

"Look love, we've got your mobile phone here and we're going to call someone. How about Anna? Or Catherine?"

"No no." She sniffed up into a thudding headache. "Call Shaz, my flatmate. Shazia." She parted her hair and saw a short-haired policewoman crouching by her side. She was at the edge of the gardens and the sight of the ghostly tableau in front of her reminded her.

"I have to go." She clambered to her feet, wiping her face.

"Not so fast." The policewoman had also stood up. "You're in no fit state to do anything. We'll go across the road and wait for your flatmate to come."

* * * * *

"He was there, Shaz, I know he was." They were drinking musty herbal tea at home that Shaz had found at the back of the cupboard. "You don't believe me either, do you?"

Shazia looked down at her chipped Birmingham City mug.

"He was there and I missed him. And I don't... I don't know if I'll ever find him now."

SCENE 4

Catherine finds herself at Seth's flat more and more. She's always ready with an excuse, leaves the Jif on the worktop in case someone else turns up, but she's never disturbed. Seems like everyone's lost interest in him, including the police. It's just Diana, Diana, Diana at the moment. The person she really fears meeting is Jake. That phoney smile – and now, knowing what he's capable of – makes her jumpy as she sips camomile tea. But even he isn't a big enough deterrent. This is the place where she's closest to Seth, and it pulls her back over and over again.

She was always happy here, practising her scales, waiting for him to get home. For some reason she can't play anymore. Some people pour their heartbreak into music or writing but she can't begin to start. She feels guilty seeing the piano lying there dormant, its closed lid reproaching her. She dusts it regularly, though, runs fingers along its back. She doesn't play but she does wait for him to return, telling herself that today he'll be back at five after visiting his accountant and stopping by Selfridge's food hall. She makes up outings and errands for him, realising that she never really knew what he did when he left the house.

She's at her own flat at the moment, on her tightly sprung little sofa, slipping into her other world. She takes his face in her hands and he clings to her and tells her why he had to go, how he couldn't handle his growing feelings for her, how he's terrified of trusting but realises he can't manage without her. They are kissing now and the savagery of his need overwhelms her. Tears scorch his eyes when he looks at her, seeing into her as no one has before.

The shrill ring of the phone shatters their moment together. Her mother's voice on the machine, again. Wondering if she's alright, why she isn't calling, saying her sister Suzanne's worried too. Catherine nearly laughs at the reversal. She isn't trying to worry anyone but there are more important things to think about at the moment. She doesn't want to be disturbed when she's feeling so close to him. Now it will take a moment to get back to where she was.

A thought leaps up, licking her like a stray flame. She could go to his flat and stay overnight, go straight into work in the morning. She could be with him all night, in his bed, surrounded by his things and his smells. For one whole night she can leave her life and inhabit this other world, the real one.

Her heart dances as she packs her bag: best underwear, body spray, clothes for tomorrow. She thinks of sliding into his bed, nestling the pillow that has cradled his face. She can have him all to herself for one night.

SCENE 5

Not a single taxi – and there were many, sailing gaily along Ladbroke Grove – had its light on. Charles waved anyway but wasn't even treated to a glance by passing cabbies. Bloody London. If public transport was going to shut down at midnight the least you could do was have a decent supply of taxis.

He carried on walking, repeatedly craning his head backwards in search of a yellow light. Nothing. Autumn had leapt in suddenly like a matador with a chilly swish of its cape. A suit jacket was no longer adequate at one in the morning. He stopped and pulled out his blue inhaler, turning out of the wind. It was the first time he'd let his hair down since the photo arrived and now look at him. Smashed and stranded with work tomorrow. Just for one night he'd wanted to forget, down pints like a twenty-year-old, flirt with some of the sassy girls in dark blue jeans and maybe even take a telephone number home. But who was he kidding? Charles Maslowe didn't get to be a selfish ass. Charles Maslowe didn't get the girl. Charles Maslowe was not allowed to forget.

His mind had been on overdrive since the photo, searching

and surmising and making connections even in his sleep, insidious connections in deep, dark neural pathways. At three in the morning he'd ping suddenly awake with a perfect recollection of something Seth said, a put-down, an obscure reference, a hint. Stuff he'd forgotten, or tried to forget. He was re-evaluating everything he thought he knew about his oldest friend.

He'd said nothing to Sarah, of course. Something like that – well, goodness knows what it could trigger. He tried to be natural around her but he kept seeing her in a red wig and unsisterly pout. A child playing dress up. The shock of ribs under her taut skin. The Bridget connection came to him in one of those midnight epiphanies. Sarah, Mrs Larson had said. Seth had betrayed Bridget with Sarah. He had pushed it out of his mind and now it was staring him in the face. Looking at the photo, the timing fitted. Sarah would have been doing her Masters. He'd no idea they'd stayed in touch. And now she couldn't even bear to hear Seth's name. What the hell had he done to her?

This was no longer playboy Seth, hedonistic Seth, notching up conquests for fun. This was completely personal. Seth, his oldest friend, his best friend, had tried to ruin the two most important women in his life.

But why?

Was he jealous?

That seemed ludicrous. But the only other explanation was a terrifying malice. Or it wasn't Seth at all. Someone else was behind it, someone who wished them all harm. His hands trembled as he put the inhaler back in his pocket and surveyed the quietening road. A tiny bulb of panic started to flash in his head, faster and faster. He couldn't even get himself home, let alone figure out how a mind like Seth's worked. His friend's laughter blew around him like the accelerating rain and spray from passing cars.

He gripped his keys in his pocket. That's when he remembered. He pulled them out and checked. There it was,

a single gold key, never used. He laughed back into the wind.
Seth may as well help him out for once.

SCENE 6

She burrows down into wrinkled white cotton, one pillow
nuzzled by her face, the other hugged hard to her chest. She is
awake and asleep, drowsy and alert, suspended in dreams and
duck down duvet. She knows he will come to her, summoned
by her whispered calls like Jane Eyre to Rochester. She hears
his key in the lock. *Honey, I'm home*. Rolling through ripples
of darkness towards the chink of light she sees a silhouette
above her. He tries to speak but she puts a finger over her
mouth and holds out a hand. He takes it wonderingly as she
pushes back the covers to let him see her. Any second now she
will feel his hand on her, first fluttering then frantic, then the
weight of his body drowning her out, crushing her to rubble.
His neck is wet and she closes her eyelids against his tears.

* * * * *

"Catherine, please talk to me."

How can she talk when she cannot look, cannot meet his
tender confusion and fired hope, her mirrored image in his
eyes?

"I don't want you to feel embarrassed about what
happened. I don't. It was beautiful."

She's in a nightmare. That's what it is. She's in the misted
kingdom of changelings and dark magic where betrayals are
undone upon waking.

His hand tries to evoke a response from her rigid body.
"Please. Please look at me. I know I was – I'd had a few
drinks, but I knew exactly what I was doing and I don't regret
it for a second. To be honest I don't think I've ever had such
a nice surprise."

He means to lighten the atmosphere, make her feel better,
but she curls up as if he has released a swarm of cockroaches

to crawl over her body. "Please leave." She has too little power to be polite. Her voice is a whisper and she knows he will make her repeat it. The second time she manages to say *sorry*.

Nothing moves in the room for a second. Then the creak of the bed tells her that he is getting to his feet. Still she cannot turn her head.

When the door has clicked closed she flies into sudden life, stripping stained sheets and cases and covers until they are safely scrunched behind the snap of the washing machine door. For the first time in weeks she takes a shower instead of a bath, twizzling the nozzle until it stings and pummels. She gets dressed in the swirl of steam, brushes her teeth without a glance at the obscured mirror.

By the time she has smoothed down the tumble-dried bedding it's eleven o'clock and people will raise eyebrows at a doctor's appointment taking so long. For a second she thinks of making an excuse and going home, but there is something in that choice that frightens her even more. On impulse, she nearly posts the key back through the letterbox after locking the downstairs door. In the end she slips it back into the breast pocket of her jacket and hurries onto the street.

SCENE 7

Charles skips work. He's never done it before – thirty-three years old and never taken a 'sick day'. Sometimes he thinks he hasn't lived, not like other people. Responsibility is sewn into his DNA. Always taking care of other people, trying to do the right thing, good old Charles picking up the pieces of other people's adventures.

Never having his own.

But today will be different. Today he's breezing around Hyde Park in yesterday's clothes and unbrushed teeth. He's had a pastry and cappuccino for breakfast and intends to have another coffee stop soon. Flashbacks break over him, disrupting his stride, his train of thought, flushing him with stunned pangs of arousal. The directness of her desire, her creamy skin, the vice-clasp of legs wrapped around him. He has to stop for a second and grasp something solid, something to tell him it wasn't a dream. Rust from a grilled fence rubs into flakes under his fingers while a man and his dog stare. Charles laughs.

She was mortified this morning. He knows women can feel tremendous embarrassment, even shame, at taking the lead in bed. With her sensitive nature, Catherine would feel it even harder. The thought that such passion, such abandonment, is simmering under the still waters of her public face, that it was he who unleashed it... he has to stop again until his vision clears. She is embarrassed now but if he gives her space while remaining attentive, she will surely unfurl like a snowdrop in the sunshine.

He needs a plan. The thought buoys him towards another coffee stop, where he finds his reveries punctured by the waitress. She's impossible to ignore, especially since his table almost adjoins the counter. She has a strong regional accent – northern of some description – in which she booms 'nice one' in response to every transaction. At first he finds it amusing, even charming, but halfway through his coffee he wants to throttle her. She's chatting to some supplier or other who's leaning on the counter in a familiar way. Charles tries not to listen but the bawdy laughter cuts through his would-be daydreams.

"By the way, if you see Jonny, tell 'im nice one."

He's about to leave when she's called through to the back; now the slow rotation of his hand stirs up sugar and memories. He's had a soft spot for Catherine for some time, an Achilles' heel that Seth used to kick at when the mood took him. He always flatly denied it, which made it hard to pay Catherine any particular attention in a group situation. And they were always in a group situation.

Back then, Catherine never looked much further than Seth. She was dazzled by him, like all women, maybe like everyone. So dazzled that when she looked at Charles she probably saw dancing spots in front of her eyes. Maybe since Seth had gone her eyes were readjusting. Last night, for sure, she had seen something that she wanted. What incredible luck that they had both needed somewhere to crash out for the night. Was it luck? Or fate?

His heart beats to the rhythm of the generic Latin American soundtrack. He thinks of her pulling him down onto her outstretched nakedness. Then he thinks of the sweetness of her smile and the line of her spine like a pencil at the piano. How could he not have known he was in love with her? Why had it taken Seth leaving to see clearly?

The thought comes so rapidly that he doesn't have time to deflect it. He doesn't want Seth to come back. His breathing is jagged as he stares at his coffee.

He thinks of Mrs Larson and her warning. Ever since that visit he's been batting away memories of what happened with Bridget. Sometimes he can't help revisiting that moment, those black suspenders and ludicrous heels, the red haze that descended over his vision and said *kill him*.

He thinks of Sarah, wrapped up in jumpers too big for her, and pictures Seth strolling back into their lives, broad smile, flashing energy like an electric storm.

Then he sees Catherine's face crumple into euphoria, her bare arms reaching for Seth.

And his hands twitch and start to sweat.

* * * * *

He's back at Seth's flat. He could rather get used to it here, especially with no one in it. He sips his Earl Grey and smiles. Catherine has made the bed but he prefers to think of it rumpled. Hopefully she'll return later and this time he can surprise her. He's got them some supper in. Seth can provide the wine.

At five o'clock he pops on some Schubert and starts to potter. He sticks his head into the bedroom a couple of times.

That's when he notices the door to the wardrobe slightly ajar. He goes over to close it but finds himself pulling it open. All those shirts lined up, awaiting a wearing that may never come. It makes him shiver. He sees the boxes of folders where Bridget's name was buried. Did they ever finish going through them?

He drags a couple of boxes through to the drawing room and opens a bottle of red wine. *Rioja Reserva, good choice, Charlie boy.* He flips and sips, flips and sighs. It's all academic stuff, notes on sexual imagery in the metaphysical poets, detailed analysis of some George Herbert poems. He starts to feel overwhelmed and a little light-headed.

Halfway through the third folder down he sees that the handwriting has changed. It's tidier, smaller, like a child's. There's some more poetry but this is definitely not George Herbert.

He must die
And I must do it.
Shake him up like a
table cruet.
Knife his heart like a
fillet steak,
Teach him not to
fork at the table.
Swill him down with Wolf Black Label.

Something flashes, something Catherine had said about Seth catching his parents having sex – was it on the kitchen table? And is this a poem about his father? He reads on.

Wipe the debris, slip outside,
Illegal smoker, patricide.

Charles stares at the poem. The word is there in black and white, cementing his worst suspicions onto paper. *Patricide.* He skims the papers underneath. Death-laced images jump out like pop-ups from a children's story. Poems about patricide.

He puts down his wine and goes to the kitchen to make more tea. His hands shake like an old man's but his mind is agile, leapfrogging to make sinister connections. But he needs to be careful. These are adolescent ramblings. What teenager hasn't wished their parents dead? Well, maybe not dead – and maybe not enough to write several poems about it – but then he had a decent upbringing. It seems fairly clear that Seth hadn't. Maybe he's just processing his feelings.

Rapid, staccato knocks at the door jump-start his heart and set it pumping in synch. His first thought is the police. Who else could bypass the entry phone? He runs to the lounge, starts stuffing papers back into folders as the knocking comes again, just as urgent. One of the others? Catherine? He cranes his head towards the front door as he loads up the box, sees it move inwards slightly as if someone is pushing against it. He calls out, *just coming, won't be long,* hauls the boxes to the corner and closes the drawing room door behind him.

As the knocks start up again he twists the catch, his smile prepared to greet Anna or Catherine or the lady detective.

It would be rude to drop the smile immediately just because he doesn't recognise the caller so he lets it hover inanely for a second. The woman's eyes are darting, trying to see past him.

"Is Seth here?"

She speaks quickly with the cool, deep tone of authority. Charles finds himself gripping the doorway as if she will try to push past him.

"I'm afraid not, no."

"I see." The woman appraises him, top to toe, in a blink. She is as tall as him with long, rust-coloured hair. Her face is ageless; she could be anything from thirty-five to sixty. "Are you expecting him back soon?"

He coughs. "I'm not sure. May I pass on a message?"

The woman's eyes are flicking again. Something resonates with him.

"Are you sure he's not here?"

He strengthens his voice. "I'm sure. I'm his friend, Charles. Can I help you in some way?"

They weigh each other up for a second and then the woman says *Christ,* and runs her hand through her hair and she too grasps the doorframe.

"Can I wait inside for him?"

He takes a deep breath. "I don't know when you last saw Seth but he's not been here for quite a while. We don't know when he's coming back." It's the first time he's had to break the news of Seth's disappearance to anyone. The woman makes a small moan and leans on her hand as if she's about to collapse. Should he ask her in? Something tells him not to. Her face is hidden by swirls of hair as thick as Rebecca's. Slowly she lifts her head and turns sea-coloured eyes on him, watery pools that harden as she stands upright.

"If you speak to him, please tell him that – Julia was looking for him. Tell him to come – to go back to Burnholme."

She turns so swiftly that he gets an eyeful of hair.

He sees her a second time that day. When he turns on the TV for the evening news. Her face is taut despite the frown and the tears. She's making an appeal for witnesses to come forward. Witnesses to the abduction and murder of her husband, Clive Rothbury.

SCENE 8

"What thinks you, fair Ophelia?"

They are enacting a light-hearted lunch, the three of them, plus Charles, who's on rather good form. He even seemed cheery as he told them about his run-in with Seth's mother.

Anna looks up. "Yeah, what was all that Ophelia business anyway?"

"How do you mean?"

"Well, Seth was obsessed by you as Ophelia for a while, wasn't he?"

"Was he?" She remembers achingly well. *Good night, sweet Ophelia.*

"Maybe he's just got a penchant for mad, badly-treated, suicidal women." Charles again, making them laugh. Rebecca sees José purse his lip. He's joining in the chit-chat but seems preoccupied. The shadows under his eye look almost blue. He cried when he told her his secret a couple of days ago and she held him, hiding her shock. Seth did something good there, getting him out of that life; no one could take that away from him. But who sent the letter?

They measure his disappearance in months now, rather than weeks, rather than days, an ever-more robust baby whose presence is no longer marvelled at continually. Four-and-a-half months, give or take.

José looks across. "What's *Hamlet* about anyway?"

She blinks. "Oh – er, well Hamlet's father, the King of Denmark, is murdered by his own brother, who then marries Hamlet's mother, but the King's ghost tells Hamlet what happened so he spends much of the play agonising over how to carry out his revenge, in between dallying with Ophelia's feelings, who then drowns herself. In the end he kills his wicked uncle and dies himself."

Charles smiles. "Basically it's about revenge, old boy." He sounds thoughtful.

"Revenge served cold with a large side order of procrastination." Rebecca winks at José. "What's all this? Are you doing English lit A-Level or something?"

Anna nudges him. "Lots of cute foreign students?"

He gives her a saccharine smile. "Just trying to understand your cultural heritage better."

"Ah, that's what they call it these days." The laughter ebbs as they go back to their plates.

Charles dabs his face with a napkin and addresses Rebecca. "She looks like you, you know."

"Who does?"

"Julia Rothbury. Seth's mother."

She remembers the conversation. *You remind me of someone.* "Makes me feel a bit weird, really." She flicks hair from her face.

Anna snorts. "Yeah, good job you didn't, you know, sleep

with him or anything."

It isn't just Rebecca who looks embarrassed. Anna's trying too hard today, her one-liners constantly overshooting like stray arrows.

Rebecca coughs and changes the subject. "So, where's Catherine then?"

They all look at Charles, who is chasing an errant potato around his plate.

"Oh – think she's busy with her sister or something." There's a studied casualness to his response. Rebecca exchanges a look with Anna.

"Did you tell her we were meeting?"

He succeeds in getting his fork into the potato. "I texted her but didn't hear back. I'm pretty sure her sister is around."

The women share more silent communication and continue eating. After a minute or two, José carefully lays down his cutlery.

Anna raises an eyebrow. "'Ey up, more Shakespeare analysis coming."

"Ha ha. I was just going to say…"

"You can't bear to look at the spinach between Rebecca's teeth anymore."

"What?" Rebecca falls straight into Anna's trap and puts her hand to her mouth. They laugh at the slight break in tension.

Anna points her knife at him. "Don't tell me. You're really straight and have had a crush on me for years."

"Anna. For God's sake."

Rebecca doesn't blame José for snapping. No matter how hard they try, they're just playing at having fun. The banter is as dry as firewood and goes up in flames with a single stray spark.

"Sorry," Anna mumbles.

José sighs. "It wasn't very interesting anyway." He pulls an *Evening Standard* out of his bag and puts it on the table. "There's some stuff on the murder. Speculation, mostly.

They're thinking it might be someone known to him. Old business contact maybe. Reading behind the lines he screwed over a fair few people."

Between the lines, my dear Manuel. But no one says it. They pore over the newspaper and look up at each other.

Charles strokes his beard. "Seth disappears and not long afterwards his father is killed. Does anyone else keep wondering…" No one helps him out. "Well, could Seth have had something to do with it?" Silence. "Has no one else even thought it?"

José runs a hand through his hair. "It went through my head. But if he did it, then he's…"

"A monster." Anna's voice is rock hard. "Clive Rothbury's eyes were fuckin' gouged out. Do you seriously think Seth could have done that?" She sticks her neck out, hissing at him like an angry goose. "And he was with us on the night his father disappeared. How many times have we been through this?"

"Like Michael said, a water-tight alibi." Charles doesn't drop his eyes. He takes a breath. "What if he used a hitman?" The words pop from his mouth, splatter into their faces.

Rebecca draws back. "A *hitman?*"

Anna laughs. "Have you ever heard of a hitman gouging someone's eyes out?"

Charles nods slowly. "Suppose that was done later?" He rushes in to fill the silence. "And, yes, maybe it is possible Jake helped him in some way, Anna. He did leave early that night."

Rebecca stares at spirals of congealing fusilli on her plate, bound for the dustbin.

Anna has found her tongue but Charles speaks over her. "There's something else."

Charles lowers his voice. "When I was at his flat, before that woman came – his mother – I looked through a few more folders. I found some poetry that looked like his own stuff, written a long time ago, judging by the handwriting."

Anna stares at him. "And?"

"And… they're about killing his father. Patricide."

"*Mierda!*" José topples his glass, sending sparkling water frothing down the table. They all grab for napkins as Charles apologises. Rebecca dabs vaguely at dark blotches on her skirt and the waitress brings over a cloth. No one even cracks a joke. They all resume their positions, looking at each other.

Charles leans in and lowers his voice. "Also, talking about his parents having sex on the kitchen table. Like Catherine said."

Rebecca swills the information around like a wine she's trying to identify, but her pallet is saturated, numb. She feels nothing except for the white negligee pulled hard across her face.

Anna throws her napkin down. "It's mad to speculate like this. Come on, let's go and look at the feckin' poems. I bet they're nothing more than adolescent fantasies."

Rebecca looks up. "What, go now?"

"Better than sitting here getting worked up. I'd rather be doing something. Why don't Charles and I go and get them and bring them back here? We'll only be gone half an hour or so."

Rebecca thinks of insisting on going with them but the thoughts don't reach her mouth.

* * * * *

"Whoops, I seem to be buzzing." Twenty minutes later, José twists to reach into his pocket. Rebecca realises she's left her phone on the kitchen worktop. José frowns as he reads.

"What is it?"

He lifts his head, an odd expression hovering but not quite settling over his face.

"Anna says they can't get into the flat."

"Why not?"

"She says the locks have been changed."

SCENE 9

The big guy in sunglasses ducks into the red telephone box when he sees them approach. Best-placed telephone box in London: has he said that before? They're in a hurry, far too anxious to notice him smiling as he watches them. Anna marching half a stride ahead, as ever. They glance around like extras in a cop film before unlocking the downstairs door. As they disappear from view he imagines the scene unfolding inside and his smile broadens.

Four minutes later and they're back on the pavement, looking around again. He can't see their expressions but imagines them perfectly. As they stumble off in the other direction, his mobile chirps a cheery tune. He drops the big black receiver and any pretence to be on a call, looks at the name flashing up on screen. For a second he lets it ring. Then he presses the green button.

"Hello, buddy. Yes, all sorted. Yes, I've cashed it – thanks for that. No worries. Just let me know. I'll be on standby."

SCENE 10

José looks at his watch. It's only 5.30 but he can't continue the pretence to be working any longer. Eyes follow him as he gathers up his stuff and mutters goodbye. He made another mistake yesterday, got confused about a deadline and the whole team ended up having to work late to bail him out. His boss yelled at him in front of a couple of colleagues and José nearly lost it. His chest tightened in a way that was becoming frighteningly familiar and he had to run to the bathroom.

The first time it happened he was at home, thank God. He thought he was going to die. He collapsed to his knees by the front door, jacket half on, clutching his chest. How long would it be until they found him? He was surprised not to lose consciousness, to be able to crawl to the hall shelf to reach his phone. He called Anna, whispered, "I think I'm having a heart attack." How telling that he'd called her rather than an ambulance. He's increasingly dependent on her, his only compass point in the foggy shadow-land he inhabits. She arrived before the ambulance she called and by the time the paramedic had rushed in with a stretcher he was drinking tea on the sofa.

Panic attack, they said. Is there anything you're particularly stressed about at the moment? Anna laughed at that. Since then it had happened three times. And once was at work. He had to endure a dozen sets of eyes on him when he emerged from the bathroom. Eyes that may or may not know about his past. He's no idea if his boss has been notified by the anonymous hand that is squeezing the life out of him. Or if the hand is biding its time, waiting to resume its onslaught of block capitals.

He bangs the door on his way out and stands for a second, gulping at air that tastes of autumn bonfires – or, as it turns out, a newly stubbed-out cigarette smouldering on the ground. He moves away and his eyes catch on the *Evening Standard* billboard across the road.

SCENE 11
Business man: Wife arrested.

Rebecca grabbed the paper and bumped people on her way out of the door. As soon as the pavement started to widen she stopped against a railing and started reading as the fine drizzle came down and umbrellas poked her shoulder. Clive Rothbury's wife had been arrested that morning in connection with his murder. She skimmed quickly – *separated... other woman... millionaire.* Her phone rang: Anna.

"Have you read it?"

"Yes, I..."

"Can you believe it? His mother, after the way she cried for the cameras."

Rebecca shuffled closer against the railings. "I know, she looked so – genuine. But Charles had a funny feeling about her."

"Well, he was right. So all the time it was her. Seth had

nothing to do with it."

I told you so was in there somewhere. Rebecca looked upwards as flimsy fingers of sunlight wiggled out of the clouds. Anna was still talking.

"I knew it wasn't him. He wouldn't be capable of something like that." Her voice sounded high, manic.

"She hasn't been found guilty yet, remember."

"It won't be long, I bet you. And guess what – the funeral is on Friday. I think we should go. Seth must be going – it says here that police have spoken to him."

"*What?*" How had she missed that?

"*It is believed that police have also spoken to the couple's estranged son.*"

"God." Rebecca felt her throat closing as she made arrangements with Anna. It was being held near the family home in Buckinghamshire. Would she see him again, after all this time? What if it was him, changing the locks, shutting them out of his life? How would he respond to them turning up? Anna was convinced Jake had changed the locks to get his hands on Seth's stuff but now that the police had spoken to Seth that didn't seem likely.

The arc of a rainbow was brushing the sky. She plunged underground, gripping the rail tightly, as if her feet would slip from under her.

SCENE 12

Cars lined the main street of the village, encircling the church like a giant metallic garland.

"Worse than Chelsea on match night. We'll have to park outside and walk in."

The rain came from a clear sky, fine but deceptively wet, streaking Anna's mascara at the corner of her eyes. Rebecca kept wiping her own face, grateful she'd brought a cap to keep some of the frizz out of her hair.

A crowd had already gathered outside the church gates, a very English assortment of multi-coloured cagoules and black umbrellas.

"Obviously more used to the weather than we are. It was gorgeous in London."

Rebecca grunted, scanning faces in the crowd. No sign of him yet. But then he'd probably arrive in the funeral car. Her stomach lurched.

"It's not quite Princess Di's funeral but I bet the village has never seen so many visitors."

José looked across the square. "Pretty, isn't it?"

It was. But she couldn't quite picture Seth in this picturesque place, with its thatched doll's houses and rose bushes.

"Do you think we should try to get in the church?"

"Are you kidding? Do you think all these people would be waiting in the rain if there were places inside?" Anna's hair was sticking to her cheek.

"Well, we'd better bag our spot then. Bloody hell, the press are out in force."

She hadn't noticed the group of photographers at the other side of the gate.

"Big news, isn't it? Even the nationals are following it. And TV, by the look of things."

They positioned themselves in a huddle as close to the front as possible, umbrellas grazing them like the wings of giant black birds.

José got up on his tiptoes and craned his head. "So Julia Rothbury will be coming? Even though she might have killed him? It's like upper-class *EastEnders* or something."

Anna nodded. "She's been bailed so I think that means she can do what she likes. Within reason." She nodded towards a policeman and woman patrolling the edge of the churchyard.

"Do you think the mistress is coming?"

"Dunno. Maybe that's why the police are here."

José stamped his feet and shivered. "I feel a bit bad that we didn't tell Charles and Catherine."

Anna shrugged. "Charles would probably have been against it. And Catherine's just dropped off the radar."

Rebecca waved her friends into silence. She was eavesdropping.

"Serves him effing right if you ask me. Lording it around like he owned the place. But who would have thought it was her, Miss Butter-wouldn't-melt?"

"Butter-wouldn't-melt my arse. That woman's as brassy as her hair. Probably getting her hands on his money before he frittered it all on his new fancy woman."

The conversation was directly behind her and Rebecca didn't want to alert them by looking round. Two middle-aged women by the sound of it.

"It's him I feel sorry for, the boy. What was his name – something a bit odd. Seb? He wouldn't stand a chance with parents like that. Though my Nathan said he was a right prick." Rebecca stopped breathing for a second.

"Sent away to boarding school, poor sod, which is a prick-making factory if you ask me."

"A prick production line." Slightly muted cackling, followed by a "Shhh."

"Look, the hearse is here. Do you think she'll be in it?"

It was like a moment from *The Godfather*, a shapely calf appearing from the door to a collective gasp and the frantic click of cameras. The rest of Julia Rothbury appeared slowly, a cascade of hair emerging last like a bride's train. Except this bride was head to foot in black, complete with enormous sunglasses. She clipped a few brittle steps, holding onto the arm of a tall, grey woman. No one else came out of the car.

"Well, that's a pair of killer heels." The women sniggered and spluttered. "Trust Long-faced Lucy to come out of the woodwork. She was always sweet on Mrs R if you ask me."

Four suited men came forward to lift the coffin out of the car.

"What, you mean like that?"

"I'd say. Look at her."

The tall woman guided Julia Rothbury as they walked behind the coffin and up to the church. People started chattering and moving away. Rebecca turned round but her comic informants must have slipped off, gossip over for one day. She noticed a woman with streaked blonde hair, dabbing at her face with a tissue. They caught each other's eye and the woman smiled slightly. "Did you know him?"

Rebecca moved a little closer. "No – I, we, know his son, Seth."

The woman nodded.

"Do you know the family?"

"We're neighbours. Didn't know them very well but said hello over the gardening, that type of thing." She looked to her husband who nodded and leaned in.

"Terrible business."

They had a reassuring burr of local accent. Rebecca could feel Anna's eyes on her, waiting to be invited into the conversation. She ignored her and pressed ahead. "Actually we were rather hoping Seth, their son, would be here today. We haven't heard from him in a while. I don't suppose you've heard where he might be?"

The words sounded stark and direct, even to her. She tried not to look too hopeful.

"Oh, I see. No, there's been no sight of him round here for many moons. No one's seen young Seth for years, have they, Bill?"

"Not for years. Let me see, it would be – when did we move in, Joan? '79? Not since a couple of years after that, probably. It was no good asking about him – they just changed the subject."

Rebecca wiped rain spatters from her face. "Oh well, not to worry."

But Joan was still thinking. "And there's no point asking Julia, I should think she's got a lot on her mind at the moment. If anyone knows stuff about that family it's Lucilla Hargreaves."

"Who?"

"Family housekeeper. She moved away a few years ago but I think she's come back. You saw her just now helping

Julia into the church. I believe the boy – your friend – was close to her."

Before Rebecca had finished her thank yous Anna snatched her arm. "What was all that about?"

"I'll tell you over a coffee." She marched her friends towards a little tea shop on the square overlooking the church and filled them in while José had four cups of tea and Anna two scones with jam and clotted cream. Half an hour later it had stopped raining and they were back at the railings. Anna stiffened next to her.

"Holy shit! You'll never guess who's over there."

For a second Rebecca's guts turned inside out. Then she saw what Anna meant: Charles and Catherine standing further along the railings looking their way. Charles smiled awkwardly and raised his hand, shunting Catherine towards them. It was excruciating, how pleased they sounded to see each other, double kissing and muttering that they'd meant to mention they were coming. The group – or what was left of it – had snapped in two.

Rebecca told them what she'd found out, gabbling and tumbling over her words. People started to file out of the church and they all turned, glad of the change of focus.

"There she is, the tall one with the grey hair... What the hell?"

Some sort of scuffle had started between Julia Rothbury and another woman. The crowd around them buzzed and surged. *That's her. The other woman.* The women started to scream at each other, necks at full tilt, *bitch, whore, murderer,* cameras flashing, until Lucilla Hargreaves got in between them and raised her hands. Belatedly the two police officers ran into the churchyard and pulled them apart.

Rebecca whistled. "You weren't joking about *EastEnders*. This is nuts."

The policewoman accompanied Julia Rothbury to her car while her colleague led the other woman, still gesticulating, in the direction of hers. Photographers surged around both

369

vehicles. Lucilla stood for a second like a lost child before scurrying towards the gate.

Rebecca saw her chance. "Excuse me, Ms Hargreaves, isn't it?" Lucilla stopped as she eyed the group blocking her way. For a second it looked as if she might dart off left like a cornered sheep. Rebecca lifted her hands. "I'm not a journalist. We're friends of Seth."

Lucilla looked even more wary. "We haven't heard from him for a long time and we just want to know he's okay. I don't suppose you've seen him recently?"

Quick glance around her. "No, I'm afraid not. I haven't been in touch with Seth for years."

"We assumed he'd be here today, we were hoping to see him."

She shook her head. "I'm sorry I can't help you. I must go now."

"Please." Rebecca instinctively stepped forward and put a hand on her arm. "We're desperate for news. Can you at least tell us if he's safe?"

People were starting to look now. Rebecca felt a tremor run along the woman's arm as she brought it closer to her body.

"Please keep your voices down." She sighed. "I saw him briefly. He stayed with me for a couple of days."

It took all Rebecca's self-control not to cry out. She felt Anna's breathing stop beside her.

"When was this?"

"A couple of months ago. Around the time his father died."

They had moved in on her like curious cows. Rebecca tried to signal to the others to draw back. "And you haven't seen him since then?"

"No."

"Was he okay? Did he say why he'd left?"

She shook her head. "He was tired. He needed to rest." Her eyes swept Rebecca's face, brows drawing into a frown. Then she looked away. "I don't know anything more."

Her hand made a stop sign as they rushed in with more questions, and she straightened her spine. "This family has been through a terrible time. I will not be answering any more questions, not now and not in the future. Please let me pass."

Rebecca rummaged in her bag, pushing a card into her hand as she turned. "Please call me if you hear from him. I just want to know he's safe." Lucilla took it without a word and stalked away. As Rebecca watched her go she noticed a tall man at the end of the street looking in their direction. He pivoted immediately and disappeared round a corner with a loping, familiar gait.

Rebecca turned back to the others. "I could have sworn that was Jake."

SCENE 13

This morning, José can barely dress himself. As soon as he lifts an arm to fasten a shirt button it slumps back down to his side. His body is an empty bottle, all its energy glugged away. He sits like a half-dressed school boy, legs kicking the side of his bed then giving up, like the rest of him.

He's taken as much as he can take. His body can no longer sustain the surge and crash of misguided adrenaline. He isn't in a Hollywood thriller; there's no obstacle to overcome or heroic task to fulfil. He's been clinging to a frayed lifeline all these weeks – Seth is in trouble, Seth needs rescuing – and it's finally snapped. And, unlike a film set, there's no one to call *Cut*.

He thinks of yesterday, how his heart nearly smashed its way out of his chest when that strange woman said she'd seen Seth. In a flash he had fast-forwarded to the happy ending and rolling credits. But Seth has slipped through their grasp again; turned with a little wave before vanishing into thin air. And now they must face the fact that Seth hasn't been kidnapped, that he's okay, and that he has no apparent intention of coming back.

He was with another man last night. His third visit in

a week. He's doing all he can to feel bad about himself, to self-destruct. He thinks of the man's chewed fingernails, the wart under the pubic hair. His shoulders slump lower, producing small ripples of flesh over the line of his boxer shorts. He stares at them loathingly. Even his flat stomach is an illusion, created by holding in, being constantly watchful. His nostrils flair into a sneer. After all those years of pretty, serious-eyed girls and his mother's nudged innuendo, he is still living a lie.

SCENE 14
Thank God.

Charles lets the relief rock around him. He buries further down, feet propped up on the end of the too-short bath. Seth is not coming back. Only now can he feel what that means, now the fraught emotions of the day are draining away.

Thank God. He means it; he is offering thanks to a real God, a white-bearded God left over from his childhood. Perhaps he should also be asking forgiveness for giving up on his friend, betraying him in his heart as Seth has betrayed him in deed. He closes his eyes but it is Catherine, not Seth that he sees. Her voice on the phone yesterday morning, asking him to drive her to the funeral, was thrillingly tentative, gentle and grateful like her usual self. But then she hardly spoke to him all day. Of course it was difficult for her, it was difficult for all of them – and bumping into the others like that. His toes curl and he bends his knees to allow them back into the water.

Still, he'd expected more. He'd allowed his hopes to billow like her beautiful raspberry-coloured skirt that allowed a glimpse of shy, tapered ankles. But he has to curb his eagerness, wait for her to come to him in her own time. Perhaps today will mark some sort of closure for her. Seth didn't turn up, he isn't going to. Charles breathes into the relief again but finds it diluted by uncertainty. There is no telling what Seth will or will not do. He flexes his fingers and watches their distorted reflections grapple under the water. The only thing he can do is to be prepared to fight.

SCENE 15

Curtain opens to reveal Michael sitting at his desk holding a small bottle. The room is dingy, badly lit. A pile of photographs and papers lie on the floor. The fingers of one hand tap rhythmically on the desk while he clutches the bottle with the other. He shakes the bottle and we hear the rattle of tablets. Slowly he pours a large glass of clear liquid from a larger, squat bottle on the desk. He smells it and closes his eyes, remaining like this for some time. With no warning he tips a handful of pills into his mouth and drains the glass. He lays his head on the desk. The lights go out and the curtain falls.

SCENE 16

Rebecca crunches along the gravel like an advert for autumn. Crimson coat, looped red and orange scarf, matching hat snuggled over hair that bursts into flames in the October sunshine. She watches her boots mark out the path that Seth showed her. She's retracing a walk they took together earlier in the year on a sudden urge to get out of London. It turns out to be only a few miles from his childhood home – not that he told her at the time. Just a little further is the cluster of rocks where they sprawled and talked and offered themselves up to the early spring sun. It's a Sunday and her route is punctuated by families like knots on a rope that she must leapfrog in order to progress. She wonders if he is here, following her. She has never mentioned it to the others, that scalp-pricking feeling of being followed. It's something she keeps for herself.

And it gives her hope, alongside the fear. There's still the knife in the gut that he didn't show up on Friday, but there must be a reasonable chance that he's in the vicinity. Was it March they came here? Yes, he'd quoted Emily Dickinson to her:

March is the month of expectation, the things we do not know.

There was so much she didn't know then. But at the time she'd taken his arm and felt a thrill of anticipation for what lay ahead. Now, seven months later, she revisits the places they went together like a grieving spouse. But she must play detective too, still looking out for clues, for a glimpse of a face behind the wall, a shadow in the trees.

An unseen bird coughs and stutters like an old car trying to start. Faraway voices move in and out of the gush of river. What if he's here, watching her? She quickens towards the rocks, picks out the centre one where he sat, lit to perfection by weaving strands of sunlight. If this were a film the camera would cut to her now, wheedling in for a close-up of the distraught heroine with head in hands. *Hold it now. That's good.* Then, after half a minute, it would zoom out to reveal the dark-haired man stepping out from the bushes and going to sit beside her. *Lovely. Look up at him now.* She raises her head to blurred acres of silent woodland. She is alone.

The film crew has left her stranded, bottom hardening into the cold stone seat. Dead leaves drop sporadically from the sky with a log fire crackle as they brush and nudge each other down. The forest is burning itself up in a last act of defiance, igniting its own funeral pyre as the shroud of winter closes in. She keeps to her spot like a loyal bride and does not struggle.

SCENE 17

I'm a little surprised to see you again, Mr Maslowe.
There's something I didn't tell you. We didn't tell you. A missing scene in our account.
I'm curious as to the relevance now. As you're aware, we have made an arrest in connection with Clive Rothbury's murder. With regards to your friend, he's off the missing persons' list. He came in to see me shortly before the arrest of his mother.

374

Oh... I see.

You look surprised, Mr Maslowe.

I suppose I am. We still haven't seen him. But, yes, I think it's become increasingly obvious to us that Seth is staying away because he wants to, not because he's in trouble.

Do you still wish to proceed with your statement?

I think I do. I want this on record. Just in case.

Just in case?

I don't know. We didn't tell you because we didn't want Seth to look bad... and because we were worried about being implicated. Myself, Anna, José, Michael and Catherine that is. Rebecca and Jake weren't on the scene then, though Jake knows about it. We don't come out too well from this episode. But it's not really about us. It's about Seth. And the possibility that he may be... dangerous.

I see. Please go ahead, Mr Maslowe.

It was Sunday 22nd of January, 1995. I've checked the date. We were all due for Sunday lunch at Seth's.

He was going to cook them a roast. Something spectacular, he said, a big bird with every imaginable trimming. He'd built it up all week, dropping culinary hints and thumbing cookbooks ostentatiously. Charles thought it was probably a goose; Anna said she wouldn't put it past Seth to nab one of the Queen's swans. José was kept sweet by the promise of some vegetarian delicacy. The email teasers and cryptic text messages bouncing around amounted to a full-on marketing campaign. They were ordered to fast from midnight on Saturday.

They were ordered to dress up, too. It was the first time Charles had donned a DJ at 10.30 in the morning, shining his shoes and adjusting his bowtie with an indulgent smile. Seth was like an overgrown kid at times like this. But his excitement had rubbed off on him, on all of them. With Seth around, weekends were to be looked forward to all week. Occasionally Charles imagined a mundane weekend, listening to the radio and sorting through his admin, with a slight wistfulness. Mundanity, Seth's nemesis, conveyed a certain comfort to him: everything in its place, no surprises. Seth held no truck with that view whatsoever. *Carpe diem, Charlie boy. One day I'll abandon you to your pipe and slippers. But not yet. There's plenty of time to get old.*

He arrived on foot at 11.23, just as Anna was pulling up with José in her MG. Round the corner came Michael, replete with cagoule and cycling helmet. Catherine arrived a couple of minutes later, slightly flustered, clutching a foil-covered glass dish; her bus had been late. Seth was very particular about punctuality but all of them were well in time for the 11.30 kick-off. They giggled at each other, all dolled up on a Sunday morning. Catherine in particular looked stunning, hair swept up from a neck he rarely got the chance to see. He found himself wondering what her dress would look like.

Anna grabbed José. "Come on, it's feckin' freezing out here. And I'm feckin' starving."

José raised his eyebrows. "Don't tell me you feckin' fasted?"

"Too feckin' right I did. And I won't be doing that again anytime soon, I can tell you."

Turns out they'd all followed the instructions and refrained from eating all morning.

Shows you the power he had over us. He could even control us remotely.

So it seems, Mr Maslowe.

Michael bent to remove the clip from the leg of his trousers as he locked up his bike. "This had better be something special. I'm not in the mood for silly pranks today."

Anna snorted. "I'll take any prank if someone feeds me first. What've you got there, Catherine?"

Catherine blushed slightly. "Just an apple crumble. I said I'd bring pudding. I probably should have done something a bit fancier..."

"You're kidding? Apple crumble's my absolute favourite."

Catherine blushed brighter at the unusual compliment from Anna. Charles resisted the sudden urge to skip up the path.

Seth buzzed them in and they sauntered up the stairs, still debating what was on the menu. The door to Seth's flat was closed.

"It'll be on the latch. Give it a shove."

Michael rapped hard, giving them all a sideways glance. "What did I tell you? God knows what he's got up his..."

The door opened onto Seth. Charles noticed the striped dressing gown first; so, things were running late. The smell of smoke hit him next, making him wince and recoil towards the clean, cold corridor air. Only then did he take in Seth's face. Bloodshot eyes, dense black stubble. And two deep, bloody scratches down one side of his face.

He smiled slightly. "Thank God you're here."

His breath reeked of whisky. They stared like wide-eyed dolls. Charles thought of Michael's words outside. Could this possibly be a prank?

Then Anna took a step forward. "What's happened? What's wrong with your face?"

A raised eyebrow, pulling at one of the scratches. "I'm in a bit of a mess. Come in and see for yourself."

They stumbled after him, exchanging worried glances that were caught by the hall mirror. Empty beer cans lined the skirting boards. Cigarette butts on the polished floorboards. It smelt like there'd been a house fire. Charles felt in his hip pocket for his inhaler. He'd need it in a minute.

As they approached the drawing room they heard a husky female voice, a voice that didn't belong in this flat. *Oo the fuck is that?*

Michael stopped short so that Anna bumped into him. "What's going on, Seth?"

But he didn't answer. The first thing Charles saw from the doorway was an overturned chair. The curtains were closed and the air thick with cigarette smoke, almost unbreathable. He pulled out his hanky and held it over his mouth. His dinner jacket would never be the same again. As he swivelled in the doorway he saw a half-naked woman appear through the haze, dressed in a short, ruffly white nightie and clutching handfuls of clothes to her as she turned away. The back of her long, red hair was matted and wild.

What the bleedin' 'ell? came the voice.

Even Anna was silenced. It was rude to stare but what else could they do? Michael muttered an obscenity as Seth extended an arm. "This is – sorry, I don't think I caught your name, pet."

"Pet? I'll bleeding pet you." The woman turned and they gasped now as she loomed out of the smog like something from a horror film. Her middle-aged face was contorted and smeared with blood. Her right eye was half closed and her upper lip swollen. A thin, red stream ran out of her left nostril towards her chin. *Drip drip drip*, plopping rhythmically onto the cream carpet, splattering crimson into abstract patterns. Dark smudges of bruising or make-up criss-crossed with the blood. Catherine let her dish of crumble slide to the floor, dropping it clumsily by the wall, but no one even looked down. They stared, mesmerised.

```
It might sound odd but even then part of me
wondered if it was a set-up, a trick.
```

"For God's sake. Use this." Seth pushed his own handkerchief at the woman and waved an ineffectual arm at the smoke. "Look, can you at least get dressed? We'll give you some privacy."

They were rooted, gawping; he had to push and pull at them to herd them out.

Michael's face was ashen. He grabbed Seth's arm, hissing, "What the hell's going on? Is this some kind of sick joke?"

"If only." Seth gestured them into the study and ran a hand through his hair. "I don't know. I don't know what's going on."

"What do you mean, you don't know?"

"Just that." He pulled his dressing gown tighter around him and Michael looked away. Seth cast his eyes round the room. "Where the fuck are my cigarettes?"

"Leave it, Seth. Just tell us what happened." He nodded at Anna and they all gathered round him, squashed like children sharing a secret. "Look, a few chaps came back here last night." Charles reads the looks around him, hurt and jealousy that he hadn't asked any of them to join him. "It was pretty full-on." José folds his arms. "I must have passed out about two o'clock. When I came round this morning the place was empty apart from the charming lady in my drawing room, whom I assure you I had never seen before. I presume someone got a little over-excited at some point and ordered her in, so to speak."

"Ordered her... what, like a Chinese takeaway?" There was disgust in Michael's voice.

"Precisely. Late night appetites and all that. Don't shoot the messenger, old bean." He held his palms up in appeal. "Anyway, when I got up I found this woman spitting like a wild cat and bleeding all over my cream carpet." He put a hand up to the side of his face. "Don't think she was particularly pleased to see me either."

Michael frowned. "She just attacked you?"

"Oh, it gets worse." He lowered his voice and they leaned in further. "She claims she's been drugged."

379

"Sweet Jesus." Anna.

"I know." He looked at them with an expression of bewilderment, lingering on Catherine who reached out a hand to him. "Let's just say I could be in a lot of bother. I didn't do anything but it's my house, of course. Who would believe me?"

"Can you get hold of the other people who were here?" José asked.

Seth blew out a sigh and shook his head. "Not a chance. Casual acquaintances, at best." He looked at Catherine again. "Sorry, I've been a bit stupid." She had red rings around her eyes and hadn't spoken yet.

Michael was still frowning at Seth. "But we have to call the police. We have to find out who did this. Just because she's a... sex worker doesn't mean she should be beaten to pulp."

Anna stepped closer. "But, Michael, Seth's right. He'll get done for this. It's him who'll be locked up, not the nut job who did this."

Michael made a guttural sound through clenched teeth. Seth looked from one to the other, eyes wide, throwing himself on their mercy.

"I'll be guided by you. If you think we should call the police that's what we'll do. I know I can't do anything without your help..."

His voice petered off and José squeezed his arm. "We'll help you. We'll help you in any way we can."

Michael glared at him. "Will we? How?"

Everything was unfolding in its normal way, other people debating and deciding and he, Charles, watching from the edge, unsure of what he thought and what to do. Embarrassingly, his stomach let out a long whine.

Seth laughed a little through his nose. "Yes, sorry about that, chaps. You must all be famished. I haven't exactly got very far with lunch yet."

No one replied. They were all still standing in their winter coats. Anna suddenly threw hers off and began to pace in a black shift dress. Her bracelets clanked as she turned. "Okay, this is what we're going to do." She turned to Seth. "How much cash have you got on you?"

"Cash? Oh, I see. One second." He opened the door and reached his wallet from the hall shelf. "Ah. Empty. I presume that was her friend."

"*Friend?*"

"She claims another girl was here too. Never mind, there's always my secret stash."

He returned from the bedroom with a wad of notes. "I reckon this should cover it. Good thinking, Anna." He winked at her. "Come."

"What? You're just going to pay her off?" Michael made to bar the door.

Catherine spoke for the first time. "It may not be a bad outcome for her. It's probably not the first time she's been hurt. At least we can give her some money to help sort herself out."

Charles noticed the *we*, the fact that they were suddenly very much part of this. But still he did nothing, waited for the others to make a decision. Seth inclined his head and Anna, Catherine and José left the room with him. Michael and Charles looked at each other and followed on.

They hung back in the doorway while Seth went into the drawing room. The woman, now clothed in fishnet tights and a short skirt, was sitting on the edge of a chair dabbing her face. The white negligee lay bloodstained at her feet like a bandage.

Seth coughed. "Look, I'm terribly sorry this has happened."

She looked up and there was hatred in her disfigured face. "You won't get away with this. I'll call the pigs."

Seth raised an eyebrow. "I doubt that very much."

She scowled. Seth moved towards her. "How about this, to help you forget?" She looked at the money in his hand. Charles held his breath. *One elephant, two elephants, three…* She lunged for it. Counted it, quick, like a bank clerk. Then looked up at all of them, face by face.

"Scum."

She stood up in tottering heels and they jostled each other trying to clear her exit. On her way past Seth she grabbed at her head and a cascade of tangled red hair hit him in the eye. She was blonde, black roots to match the black chequers across her cheeks.

Seth's eyes opened wide. "Lord, it's one surprise after another today."

She spat in his face. A shimmering glob of saliva landed near the corner of his mouth.

For the first time he lost his cool. "You stupid bitch."

Charles saw a flash of fear in her good eye as she flinched like a startled rabbit. Then she smirked slowly and extended a hand. "Want your hanky back?"

Charles watched Seth's eyes harden into bottle green glass, the saliva starting to dribble towards his chin, and instinctively reached out to hold his arm. He felt the muscles flexing under his fingers. Then Seth snorted, threw off his hand and reached for a tissue from the coffee table. The woman pushed past them and the door banged shut in the hall.

So you just let her go? How hurt was she?
Well, that was the other thing. She passed right by me as she left and I saw some marks on her neck.
Marks?
Like a band of bruising.
Like she'd been throttled?
I think so. Yes.
And did you mention it to anyone else?
Er, no. I don't know if they noticed. I was in shock, I suppose. We all were.

They spent the next two hours cleaning up, light-headed and white-faced. The party aftermath wasn't too bad once the furniture had been righted, just a few empty bottles and full ashtrays, beer cans and softening peanuts. Seth said he'd done some clearing up before going to bed. Catherine got down on her hands and knees in a burgundy ball gown tied with a sash at the back and scrubbed at the bloodstained carpet for an hour. Charles felt bad seeing her like that, as though she was Seth's scullery maid. He stationed himself by her side, changing the water in her bucket when it turned dark and cloudy, mostly feeling useless. None of them really spoke to each other. They worked in silence like a team of cleaners with a mission to accomplish. All of them did their bit, even Michael. Only Seth breezed from room to room, offering coffee and light refreshments.

"Imagine waking up to find *that* in your house. Christ, it was like *Jane Eyre* with Bertha Mason on the loose." Catherine jolted and stared up at him.

"What is it, my little honeypot?"

"Nothing. I just know that book very well."

He closed his eyes and put his hands out. "Jane, come back to me, Jane."

"Stop it."

But he must have heard the smile in her voice because he carried on, moving towards her and stubbing his toe on the bucket, which sloshed a warning. "Ouch." He opened his eyes and stared down at the carpet and its new coat of murky brown splodges. "Not much good as a blind man, I'm afraid. I'll leave you to it."

But he was back minutes later with a handful of garish takeaway menus. "Sorry about the roast, chaps. I know it's not quite the same, but would pizza do you? On me, of course. Order as many toppings as you like."

Anna was holding up the white, frilly negligee at arm's length as a pizza menu landed at her feet. She kicked it aside. "What shall I do with this? It's covered in blood."

They all stared. It looked as though someone had been shot in it.

"Um. I suppose we'd better get rid of it. I'll fetch you a bin bag."

Anna bagged it up and stuck it in another bin bag full of rubbish. Charles felt his stomach turn. But still he found himself an hour later eating pizza on the sofa. He started by nibbling tiny mouthfuls, revolted by the idea of food, but halfway through the second piece realised how hungry he was, how easily the salty, slippery triangles slithered down his gullet. All eight pizzas disappeared, plus most of Catherine's crumble. The dark blotches on the carpet watched them like bloodied eyes.

Next time he went round the carpet was gone and the floorboards sanded and varnished. Seth slung an arm over his shoulder. "Just fancied a change, Charlie boy. Knew you'd approve."

Thank you, Mr Maslowe. I will try to look at the incident records from that time to see if any complaint was made, or similar incidents recorded, but it seems unlikely.
I know. I don't really expect you to do anything but I wanted you to know.
Will that be all?
Yes. Well, there is one other small thing. When I was tidying up that day I opened Seth's fridge.
What did you find?
Well, it's more what I didn't find. There was no sign of a bird for roasting, no vegetables, it was in its usual half-bare state. It's as if…
Yes?
Well, as if Seth never planned to make that roast. Of course, he could have just decided he didn't want to bother. But he made such a big thing of it. So I wondered

if there was a reason why Seth wanted us there that day. If he wanted to drag us into something so that… so that we couldn't speak out against him later on. Or perhaps to test our loyalty.

Mr Maslowe, if I understand you correctly, you are proposing that Mr Gardner deliberately beat up a prostitute, brought you over to implicate you all, and then murdered his father knowing you wouldn't refer any suspicions to the police.

I know, it sounds mad. Forget I said that. And of course he didn't murder his father. Sorry, I just want to be completely open with you now.

One small observation, Mr Maslowe.

Yes?

To a dispassionate onlooker it might appear that you almost want to indict your friend. Has something happened to prompt this?

No, no, that's not it. Nothing's happened. Of course I don't want to indict him. I'm just trying to do the right thing.

SCENE 18

Despite the early mornings and late finishes, the boulder-like black files she lugs home, the sherbet-coloured romance novels she keeps for the Tube or bath, something is forcing Catherine to think about that night. It's not the gasping memories that wake her at four a.m, nor the throb in the pit of her body that starts from nowhere, nor even the taste of shame when it hiccoughs onto her tongue. It's much more prosaic. It's the fact that her period, never late, is now ten days overdue.

Good sense has been drilled into her from head to toe like writing in a stick of rock (*swot! teacher's pet! goody two shoes!*) and is not easy to evade. She buys a ludicrously priced do-it-yourself test with a hazy mother-and-baby picture in blue. Hazy, presumably, so as not to parade a positive result in case that's not what you're looking for. What is she looking for?

Not this, not this absurd reaching between her legs on the toilet seat. Not this wait where she should put the stick down and do something else but instead clutches and stares at it like a tarot card. What will it be? The Lovers? Death?

The Abandoned, she thinks. The Limping Boy, the one left behind by the Pied Piper. The one who survived. Survived in a clinical sense with all his friends, his joy, the magical music, gone.

Gone. Such a short, innocuous word. Gone with the wind. Gone to the shops. Gone swimming. Gone mad.

All gone.

The second blue line creeps along its window like a caterpillar. She hears the drawing of a blind, the soft closing of shutters. The line completes its journey and stands straight, a bookmark in a discarded book that she will never finish now.

She stays on the cold toilet seat to gaze at the card fate has dealt her. The Fool.

SCENE 19

In the end it was Green & Oldthorpe who hammered the final nail into the coffin. Or rather into one of their For Sale boards. Advertising an elegant two-bedroom first floor apartment that had once been home to a Steinway grand piano, restored Italianate sideboard and weekly gatherings of would-be artists.

Anna was so upset when she called that Rebecca went over to her flat straight away, unable to hear past the gulps and panted stutters. When she arrived, Charles was there too, a strange light in his eye. Anna's face was patchy but dry.

"What is it?" She didn't want to be here. She'd just heard she'd got the part of Abigail in *The Crucible* for a new production that was going to be touring. She wanted congratulating, wanted to talk through her mixed feelings of leaving London, of moving on. Something told her she wouldn't be moving on just yet.

Charles patted the sofa next to him. Why did people always make you sit down when they had something bad to tell you? She preferred to stay on her feet, poised, ready to react. She didn't move.

Anna nodded, seemed to understand. "He's put his flat up for sale." Her voice shook slightly.

Charles was right, she should sit down. Sink into black leather as the words sank deep into her heart. She looked at Charles for clarification. He spoke gently, like a doctor delivering news of a terminal illness.

"Anna saw the For Sale sign and phoned the estate agent. It's his flat. He's selling up."

There had to be another explanation. "What if it's not him who's put it up for sale? What if he's being defrauded by someone – Jake, maybe – or his mother is selling, or something awful has happened to him..."

The first stage, denial. Even she could hear it.

Charles shook his head. "I phoned the estate agent to find out more, asked if I could be shown around by the owner so I could ask specific questions. They said it was all being handled by a third party."

"There you go then."

Now Anna was shaking her head. "I don't think so, Becs. Only Seth could sanction the sale of his flat. His father's dead and his mother's awaiting trial for murder." She breathed. "I think we have to accept that, for whatever reasons, Seth wants to make a fresh start."

Her voice was as harsh as the white glare on the walls around them. Rebecca thought of the embers glowing in Seth's drawing room, the dark wood furnishings, the cosiness that wrapped you up like a fleece blanket despite its size. It belonged to them, all of them. Now she would never see it again, never see Seth blowing smoke from the armchair or Jake emerging from the kitchen with plates of food. The door buzzed.

"That'll be José."

She said nothing as they told him, didn't even watch his reaction. *It's over.* The words filled her head like a mantra. *It's over.* That was all anyone could say.

But it wasn't. She tuned into Charles talking to Anna, his eyes still lit from behind like a computer screen. "He's been pulling our strings all along. Michael was right. And we've been covering for him, making excuses for him. He's got us right where he wanted us." He paused and there was a new hardness in his voice. "That woman – it was him all the time. And we covered for him."

Three sets of eyes turned to her and she knew that they were ready to answer her question. If she was ready to ask it.

* * * * *

"Becs. Talk to me."

She feels a hand on her arm and faces looming towards her.

"I'm sorry, Becs, we promised him we'd never breathe a word. We wanted some new blood in the group so that we could put it behind us, move on."

"New blood?" She pushes the hand away, struggles to her feet.

Anna looks away. "Sorry, that was a bad choice of words."

"New fucking blood? That's all I was? Your next plaything? To distract you all from… God, you make me sick." And she thinks she might be for a minute, has to grab the back of the chair and bend her head.

"I'm sorry, I didn't mean it like that." Anna sounds as if she might cry again. She stands too, tries to make eye contact. "After it happened there was this huge shadow, this *blight* over the group. Nothing was the same. Seth said we needed to bring someone else in to re-energise us."

A curdling noise from the back of her throat, like someone has slit it. Tears start to tumble down Anna's cheeks. "We all loved you straight away, Becs. You shook things up, brought us together again. Seth said you'd be a breath of fresh air and you were."

Rebecca feels her mouth hanging open. She looks at them, each in turn. One by one they drop their eyes. She waits for words to come to her, the right words, the last word. But in the end she just runs for the door.

SCENE 20

Some time later, when the soothing emptiness of her flat has shrivelled to a bone-aching loneliness, when she is staring out of dead eyes at the blank television screen, her doorbell rings. Even now she thinks it might be him, come to explain, to claim her. Hope heaves, propels her to the front door. She can see at once by the shape behind the glass that it isn't him, but her neighbour has come out of the flat opposite and she can't run back now. Two swipes under her eyes must suffice.

"Hey."

It's José. He's never been to her place before. Why not? Why has she never invited him? He looks strange in north London, stranded at the wrong side of the river. Once she would have teased him about it.

"Why are you here?" She can sense her neighbour behind her trying to catch the conversation. "Did they send you?" She sounds crazy, paranoid. She wants to scratch at his face, leave marks on his perfect olive cheekbones.

"Please let me in."

"Why the fuck should I?" Her voice rises and she can't keep the tears down. But she can't make a scene here. She sighs and lets him past.

He looks around him as he goes into her flat. He finds the kitchen and pulls out a couple of streaky tumblers. "Let's go and sit down."

She follows him through, watches him move things from the sofa and pat the seat next to him. He still has his coat on. He pulls out a bottle from his man bag and pours caramel liquid into each glass. This is so unlike José that she wants to laugh. She also wants to throw the liquid in his face but the urge to drink it is too strong. She sits beside him as he shrugs off his coat.

"Nice place."

This time she does laugh, a quick nasal scoff. "I'd say you're a hopeless liar. But clearly you're not."

She can't help being pleased with this line, and the effect it has on him. She inhales the fumes rising from her glass and takes a quick, burning sip.

He fingers his glass. "I'm sorry we lied to you. We should have told you. We'd all tried so hard to forget about it."

She takes another drink, a gulp. "I knew there was something." Her mouth twists. "I told myself I was being paranoid."

José shakes his head. "He had such a hold over us." His voice is thick and phlegmy. "And me particularly. All that stuff in my past. I always felt I owed him something."

Is he looking for sympathy? She hardens herself.

"And we didn't believe he'd done anything to that woman, we really didn't. But now... if he did... then we owe you much more of an apology. Much more."

His voice quivers and she looks at him, not sure what he means. His eyes, when they meet hers, are tormented. "We found a red wig, Charles and I, when we broke into his Shepherd's Bush place. He obviously likes red-haired women. But maybe he likes to hurt them too."

She breaks eye contact and stares at the wall ahead of her. She thinks of dressing up for him, the blindfold, his fixation with her hair. José puts a hand over hers and she feels the tremors as his shoulders shake.

"We put you at risk, Becs." Her brain starts to make the

same links as his. She thinks of the footsteps tracking her at night.

She gets to her feet. "We don't know any of this is true. We don't know he deliberately hurt that prostitute."

You don't understand the connection we had. You're sullying everything I have left of him.

She turns to him as he wipes his eyes. "I hate you. All of you."

Her words spin around them, echoing over and over. There's a long silence, which she will not break. But her brain is busy and questions are forming.

"What was she wearing?"

"Sorry?"

"The prostitute."

"Oh." He blinks. "When she left, the usual, I suppose. Short skirt, high heels. But, when we arrived she was in some sort of nightie thing, short. And... bloodstained."

The brandy has dried the roof of Rebecca's mouth. "What colour was... the nightie?" She knows what he'll say before he answers.

"White."

She clamps two hands over her mouth, runs to the bathroom and heaves over the sink. Nothing comes up. Even her eyes are dry, staring at her like assassins in the mirror as she raises her head.

She goes back to tell José to leave, but he doesn't even look up when she enters the room and she finds herself slumping back onto the sofa again as her legs buckle. Still he stares at his shoes, hands clasping the glass between his knees. When he speaks it's not what she expects.

"I slept with him, you know."

She flinches. "I know."

He swills the brandy in his glass round and round, staring down at it. "Not just two years ago. In April. Just before he disappeared."

She blinks against the waves rolling in towards her. Why

391

is he telling her this? Hasn't she endured enough?

"When he had that nightmare we – we'd been together."

She thinks back to the blush and the shifty look.

He raises his eyes. "Did you sleep with him too?"

She closes her eyes. "Once." The same questions, *What if I'd said no? Would he still be here?*

José sighs out a long breath – relief or pain, she can't tell. "Was it recently?"

They both colour at the question. "It was…" She stops, it's hitting her now. "April."

The kitchen clock ticks louder and louder into the silence. Rebecca sits forward, hair flooding her face. She hears the clink of his glass on the coffee table and expects him to leave. Nothing happens. She raises her head and he's looking at her, waiting to talk again.

"After you left, Michael came over."

"Michael?" Surprise lifts her voice.

"Anna invited him. I think she wanted to reach out in some way, maybe let him know he was right. She's – I don't know – quiet. I don't know what that means."

Rebecca raises her eyebrows a fraction. "What did Michael say?"

"Not much. Not even 'I told you so'. But then some more stuff came out."

Something about his face gives it away. In a flash, a puff of smoke, she sees it all and laughs like a pantomime villain.

"Don't tell me – he was having an affair with Seth too. In fact everyone was, we all were."

He recoils from the pitch of her voice. "Not everyone. Seth made a pass at Michael three years ago. He says it didn't go further than that. He looks awful Becs, really thin and pale."

Rebecca's eyes are hard. She has no sympathy left, not for Michael, not for herself.

"Catherine went a bit mad and ran off pretty much like you did."

So this is Seth's legacy. This is what he has left them with.

Rotting remains to pick over before turning teeth on each other. "She's been sleeping with him too?" Her voice is dead and bears no relation to what's going on inside her.

José shrugs. "She didn't say but from the state of her it wouldn't be hard to believe. She's in love with him, but we knew that already."

Rebecca looks at him and knows there's more. She winces as she swallows. "Anna?"

He drops his gaze. "You know Anna, she said it was a drunken snog that went a bit too far and they both realised it shouldn't happen again. I believe her. She adores – adored – Seth but I think it's more like a brother. Or maybe a father."

"Jesus Christ." She looks across at his curved shoulders. "Aren't you mad at her?"

Two hands open. "Why should I be? What point is there in being mad at Anna or you or Michael or Catherine?"

She twitches, bristling like a hound on a lead with the scent of blood. He meets her eyes, reads them. "It's not me you should be angry with, Rebecca. Or Anna."

She is gripping her glass so hard the ends of her fingers blanch.

"He messed us around, Becs. Michael's right. He used us for idiots. I don't know why, but he did." For the first time there's a growl in his voice. "He toyed with the lot of us, manipulated us, and we just sat around and let him."

No. She wants to shake José, shake him empty of these vicious words. She needs to think clearly but thoughts are rushing at her like rain in the wind. She hugs herself and rocks slowly, backwards and forwards. The sofa sags as José moves up next to her.

"I didn't come here to turn the knife, Becs." *Twist*, she thinks. "I just thought you deserved the truth. Maybe we've all been sitting around thinking we're the special one he'll come back for."

She closes her eyes, an admission.

"But the only person special to Seth is himself. I don't

believe he can love anyone." His words move in on her, jostling and poking her and she needs him to stop so she can put things together for herself.

"He..."

"Please. Stop." She is on her feet, facing him. "No more, not now. I just need time to get my head round it all."

He nods and his eyes are pools of molten chocolate. "I know. I'll go now. I'm here if you need me."

After the door has clicked she goes to Shazia's bedroom window and watches the leather jacket until it has disappeared.

SCENE 21

Catherine hasn't been to work for three days. Maybe she will get used to the feeling of something brewing in her belly, giving off strange vapours that rise up to her throat and fill her mouth with metallic flavours. Maybe she will stop being afraid of stepping outside onto streets where the elbows of strangers are internal injuries waiting to happen – not to her body but the other body, the Russian doll tucked away inside her. Maybe she will lose the feeling that something supernatural was at work that night in Seth's flat. She felt him, absorbed him and now she is pregnant. It's as if Charles was a conduit, summoned out of the empty night by her longing for Seth. As something was taken away, something else has been given. The new life inside her is bound up with Seth, almost as if it is his baby.

Now her aching belly has something to fill it, something that will kick and suck from her and make demands. She runs her hand over it, willing the thing inside to grow and be strong. A week ago, she had even considered the unthinkable, found a telephone number. But she has forgiven him now. For everything. He is troubled, confused, and he needs her more than ever. Now she takes folic acid capsules, drinks peppermint tea and feels a part of him growing inside her.

A flash of Charles' face, lop-sided and crinkled with kindness. She's barely seen him since Clive Rothbury's funeral.

He leaves her messages and yesterday a card arrived, a Turner print he thought she'd like. So thoughtful, so dependable. Perfect father material. But he's all mixed up with the sweat and dampness of that bed, stripped of his crew-neck sweaters, adorned with soft clumps of carrot-tinged hair.

She stands up quickly, too quickly, and steadies herself against a chair. It's Seth's face she sees now, sparkling with school boy mischief. She stretches her hand to cup his cheek but her fingers curl and drop to her side as they always do.

"Please come back. Please." Her soul is a windswept wasteland, her body a tree bowed and broken. She closes her eyes and feels the terror of the void hurtling towards her, a black hole where even fantasy cannot survive. The sounds from her mouth are pre-verbal now, her baby's sounds, and she rocks on her heels.

It reminds her, and her hand moves to grip her belly. She breathes, her belly breathes with her. He is still here. He has given her this. His last, and best, gift.

PART 2 – SCENE 22

Rebecca feels clumsy and out of practice, stumbling on loose paving stones, squinting at street names, dizzy with the constant flow of human traffic. If she could step back from herself for just a second she might find it amusing, but that would risk losing concentration and getting under someone's feet. Instead she finds herself propelled along by currents of energy, not fully in charge of her own legs. It's a good seven months since she's been in London and, half an hour after arriving, there's a tingling at the ends of her fingers and a tightness around her ribcage. Stressed already. She isn't late this morning and she doesn't have to rush, but she still finds it hard to persuade her heart to revert to normal rhythm. Maybe this is the normal rhythm for London. Fast rock instead of the easy ballad she's been getting used to.

She decides to leave the pedestrian motorway at the next junction, Kensington Gardens. From here she can saunter down towards South Kensington along sunlit side streets and gleaming ivory walls. She's aiming for a posh coffee somewhere in Knightsbridge. No real reason – just because she can. She's flush again and has a week off before the London rehearsals start.

The Crucible has been 'a triumph' (*The Times*). It's collected such good reviews around the country that it's coming to the West End. In two weeks' time she'll make her West End debut as Abigail. Three years ago that would have seemed impossible. She quickens her stride, making ground on a mac-clad young woman in front of her. She deserves this. She's been through shit but she's survived it, thrown every bit of herself into her career. And she's even made some new friends along the way.

She's not forgotten her old friends, of course. For a while she wanted to, tried her hardest to. Shaz forwarded on a letter Anna wrote to her after she went on tour – apologising, hoping she could forgive them. She didn't reply. She needed a clean break. But she's found herself softening as the months go by. At some level she knows that the person to blame is Seth, pulling the wool over all their eyes. So she's agreed to meet Anna and José for lunch in Soho.

Her stomach gripes but she decides to put it down to lack of breakfast. A coffee stop soon would be welcome. She turns off the main road, immediately relaxing and breathing into the slower pace, the beauty. She smiles and feels like a local now, confident under the serene smiles of towering Georgian terraces, finding her London legs. She sniffs the sunshine and smiles.

A couple of things of note since she got back. Firstly, Mornington Crescent station has finally re-opened, halving her walk to the Tube. Secondly, she's had an email from Jake. She barely ever checks her account but a flicker of curiosity yesterday prompted her to borrow Shaz's machine. She didn't even realise he knew her address. It seems that's not all he knows; he mentioned that he might pop along to see her in

The Crucible. Since when has he become a theatre follower? She's puzzled but touched. He writes as he talks and she realises she's missed him too. He says he's been doing okay, was working as some sort of PA for a while for a lucrative client but knocked it on the head because of moral scruples. *Imagine that eh Becs?* Then he asked how she was, said he knew she'd been in a bad way and left a phone number, saying she could call him at any time – the last three words underlined. Again, she's touched and a little puzzled by his protectiveness.

This leads her to the third thing. She'd changed phones when she left London and left the old one behind. It was time to upgrade but it carried the added benefit of forcing her to cut loose. She hadn't given her new number to anyone connected with Seth or the group. It turned out to be a huge relief, not having to check her phone all the time or jump when she saw an unknown missed call.

But back in town she couldn't resist turning on the old phone. At least twenty texts came through, most from Anna and José, one from Charles, and one even from Catherine, wishing her luck with the tour. There was a single voicemail message. Rebecca jolted when she heard the low, clipped voice of Lucilla Hargreaves and had to strain to hear the words. *Don't try to find Seth. Leave him alone. It's for your own good.* Even after repeating the message three times she wasn't sure if it was a warning or a threat. She shivers again now, pulls her jacket around her and tries to put it out of her head. It's all pretty irrelevant now. Seth is gone and she's finally accepted it.

She assumes no one has heard from him. The trail stopped after his mother was convicted of murder. It seems she hired a hitman to kidnap her husband and tie him up in a basement. A few days later he was stabbed to death and his eyes removed. One of her hairs was found at the scene. All the papers were mad for it. They dragged in the mistress, the woman from the graveyard, a plain-looking widow sitting on a fortune.

But mostly they just focused on the sex. Lurid allegations and rumours were reported daily, most of them claiming that Julia Rothbury slept with her husband's business contacts to seal deals, some reporting that he liked to watch. Lucilla Hargreaves, looking even taller and greyer in the courtroom artist impressions, testified that on many occasions Mr Rothbury brought back clients to stay overnight, which seemed to create tension between husband and wife. It made you wonder what kind of mess Seth had been brought up in. As far as she could tell, his name hadn't come up at all throughout the whole proceedings. At one point she was desperate to sit in on the trial, binge on revelations about his family, try to understand who he was. Then self-preservation reappeared like an errant genie. She knew she needed to let him go. Such a self-help book expression, as if he were a butterfly between her hands, as if she had caught him rather than the other way round. A more accurate term for what she needed was exorcism.

She thinks of *The Crucible*, of people who believed they could be possessed by spirits. This was something different, more like an addiction. Human heroin. They should call their group Sethoholics Anonymous; God knows how many fellow sufferers would crawl out of the woodwork.

People like us, Rebecca. People who wring every last drop from life.

She starts as if he's whispered it in her ear. A slow, cold tremor makes its way up her back and into her hair. She can't help turning round. Only a middle-aged man behind her, tutting slightly as he has to swerve past her. This was always the danger of coming back. He is getting into her head already.

The sun ducks behind a cloud and the ivory walls around her darken abruptly as if someone has turned out the lights. No. The fear, the ache, the yearning, she can't let it happen. Away, in cheap rentals all over the country, locked into gruelling schedules that gave her little time to herself, she could survive. She did more than survive, in fact. Perhaps she has something to thank him for there. The deep vaults of her suffering have improved her art, given her new fathoms to draw on. It's a time-honoured equation, after all.

Or perhaps it's what Michael said, that Seth was feeding off her like a parasite and now he's gone she can unleash her full creative potential. She shakes her head, fed up with the same thought loops and looks at the road ahead. She doesn't recognise the street and can't cut through as she expected. It's only ten o'clock and she's worn out. Hungry. Tense. Suddenly the whole return to London doesn't seem like such a good idea. She could have stayed with her parents, got up late, eaten her mother's lentil shepherd's pie. Instead she's lost in a deserted, white-walled maze.

She needs to cut her losses, retrace her steps to Kensington Palace Road and then make her way down Gloucester Road, fight her way past the tourists, the coach parties of children heading for the National History Museum.

At the T-junction back into the fray she stops for a second to watch the step, stride, scuttle passing in front of her. The weather has divided people. Some are hopeful, coatless, ducking their heads against unpredictable gusts that frisk them like pickpockets. Others are still in scarves and hats. Rebecca's somewhere in the middle: linen trousers and mules, a pale brown jacket she wears about three times a year but can never throw away because it's the only thing she has for days like this. By next week the jacket will be too heavy and will go away until September. She stops for a second, puts a hand to her throat and tries to breathe. What should she do now?

* * * * *

Three hours later Rebecca is back in the London stride, swinging customised carrier bags in a Ginger Rogers sort of way. It would make a good nickname for her. How could she have forgotten that shopping is always the answer to any question in London? She peeks again at the tan leather trousers and funky body warmer all wrapped up in embossed tissue paper. Wrong season but that's why she could afford them.

She has the feeling she's turning a few heads. She feels light as she walks. Ready to meet Anna and José, ready to deal with her demons. A different person from the brittle wreck they saw last time. She can handle this.

She sees them at once, at the usual table in the corner. For a second she feels like the new girl again, like at her first lunch with them all that time ago, snaking her way past feet, bags, knees, chairs. But then their faces light up and they're on their feet and she is hugged hard for the first time in too long. The smell of them is a hug in itself: José's lightly spiced aftershave, the hint of sweat and garlic at Anna's throat. José and Anna. Anna and José. Much is silently said in those hugs. Wine is poured, drunk in gulps. Minutes pass while all they do is grin at each other, saying *So!* and *Wow!* and *You look great!* Whatever she expected, it isn't this. She wants to laugh and cry at the same time.

They both look a little different. José has colour back in his cheeks and newly conditioned biceps bulge out from the sleeves of his tight green T-shirt. Rebecca notices both men and women checking him out. Anna has grown her hair longer, and she looks softer for it, a bit 1940s.

She tells them about her time on the road, warming to her theme, rediscovering familiar ways of interacting, grinning at the sparring between Anna and José. She tells them about the people she's met, exaggerating character quirks when her audience howls with laughter, glowing when they say how well she's doing. Everything is exorcised in the telling: the shitty hair-covered bathrooms, the drunken director with a wandering right hand, the first night panics, the last night snogs (only two but it was good to know she still had it.) How had she coped without this? For the first time she isn't looking for Seth to appear. It's enough to be just the three of them.

Better than enough. She has hardened herself to them in the past year, demonising them in their absence – her absence, Seth's absence – and she sees she was wrong. Maybe she needed to, maybe everything and everyone got tarnished by Seth. But her barriers have crumbled into dust at the sight of these friends, these dear friends, and there's something surrounding them, winking in the sunshine, a glimmering prism reflecting between them. Love, she thinks and she squeezes it back into their hands.

During the second bottle there's a gratifying flow of gossip, mainly from Anna. No one has had contact with Jake and it's safe to conclude that he was only interested in Seth's money – although Anna does appear to accept that his crimes might go no further than that. Rebecca doesn't mention the email. It's too soon to wade into tricky waters. And Anna has moved onto Michael, recounting that she'd tried to get in touch with him in connection with work; a client who wanted to fund something for the community in North East London. When he didn't return her calls she phoned the school and discovered he'd left a few months previously.

"Presumably to move to another school?"

"I don't know, they were a bit mysterious really. Said they couldn't comment on his reasons for leaving. I was left with a slightly strange taste. Teachers rarely leave in the middle of the school year, do they?"

"Weird. I can't imagine he got into trouble – he was dedicated to his job."

They muse on this for a minute until Anna bumps her glass down. "And now for the really juicy stuff. You'll never guess."

Rebecca laughs. "I've missed you."

They clink glasses. "That's not all you've missed, sweetie." She raises an eyebrow. "Charles and Catherine."

"What? No!"

Anna's face is the clue, eyes bulging expressively.

Rebecca mirrors her. "You're kidding. I can't believe it. What about her dedication to Seth?"

It's the first time his name has been spoken, and Rebecca feels a ripple fan briefly and die away.

"Well, clearly she's moved on. In a pretty major way. You're never going to believe this." Anna licks her lips, drawing out the moment. "The Virgin Catherine is with child."

Rebecca's squeals and facial contortions delight Anna. "See – I told you she'd be gobsmacked. What about that then?"

Rebecca can only just speak. "Well – good luck to them, I guess. Do we presume it was an, um, accident? Ouch, the mind boggles."

"Tell me about it. Well, I'm hardly in her confidence but I can't imagine they'd plan it like this. I had lunch with them last week. Quite the doting couple."

Rebecca frowns. "And is she…"

"Fat?"

"Well…"

José shakes his head like a despairing parent.

"I wasn't going to say that – but is she?"

"'Fraid not, love. She has a compact but quite impressive bump that she fingers constantly and otherwise looks pretty much the same. Pale, pained, vaguely disapproving."

They cackle over José's remonstrations.

"That's just unbelievable. I guess Charles is pleased?"

"Over the moon, his little smile was practically cracking his face. She's harder to read, of course. What was interesting is that the subject of Seth didn't come up once."

Rebecca sips her wine and takes a breath. "I suppose we have to be careful it doesn't become that way for us." A sudden hiatus, as if she's pressed Pause in the middle of a song. The dialogue resumes immediately but the rhythm is more stuttering.

"You're right. But it's also good to have a break from talking about him."

Rebecca nods. "That's true." But she knows she has to say her piece or it'll be left forever inside her, a shred of shrapnel in her heart. She looks at both of them. "It hurt so much that you were keeping secrets from me."

José lowers his eyes. Anna fiddles with her glass. "I know. It was wrong, like I said. I'm sorry. We both are."

José makes a slight head movement, a nod.

Anna puts her glass down. "But we were all keeping secrets from each other, weren't we? You too, Becs."

Rebecca feels a flush of anger across her cheeks. "It's not the same."

"Isn't it? Isn't that the way he wanted it? Divide and rule, all of that." Rebecca is amazed to hear Anna talking like this about Seth. "It's what he did. Look, I understand why you cut us off, Becs. When it all came out I didn't even want to talk to José for a while."

He manages an uncomfortable smile. "That was pretty mutual, actually."

"Yeah, I know. We've all been through this. We all made mistakes. The question is, can we move on? And I think we can."

Rebecca nods but looks at the table. She can't put it all away quite so easily.

José shifts in his seat and speaks quietly. Rebecca leans in to hear him over the increasing clatter of the lunchtime rush. "I was in his debt. I was so grateful to him, you know about all that stuff now. And whatever motives he had, whatever he's done since, he did save me." He looks at her. "I would have done anything for him."

Anna's voice is soft too. "I think you'd have done the same, Becs. Covered for him if he'd asked you to."

Another flare of anger. Because it was the truth. "Maybe. But after he'd gone you should have come clean with me."

Anna shrugs. "We were also protecting you. Have you ever thought of that? With all the police questioning it was safer and easier for you if you didn't know anything. Otherwise you could have been dragged in too."

She can see that. Suddenly, as if a curtain has been raised, she can see another interpretation for their secrecy. The surprise of it takes her words away. Instead she feels the burn of tears behind her eyes.

"Hey." Anna takes her hand. "Don't get upset." She nods across the table at José, whose nose has turned pink. "Or you, Josie. Come on, we're not gonna get dragged down by this again. Let's order another bottle."

Both Rebecca and José reach to cover their glasses in identical gestures and everyone giggles. Rebecca takes a breath. "You're right. So, tell me about you two. How's work, José?"

He blinks and rolls his shoulders as if to shrug something away. "Okay. Much better. I feel like I've got into my stride again, which is a relief. Life at the moment is pleasantly... non-eventful."

They smile at each other. Anna shoots him a sidelong glance. "Of course that will change soon."

"Will it?"

She leans back in her chair. "Spoken to your *Mama* recently, darling?"

"They're away."

"How convenient."

Rebecca grins at the ping-pong dialogue. "Now now, you two. Play nicely please. What's this about?"

José scowls. "Playing nicely with her is impossible."

Anna blows kisses across the table. "It's just that José has finally decided to tell his parents the real reason why he hasn't found a nice girl yet and I'm encouraging him to do it as soon as possible."

Rebecca looks at him. "Wow. That's pretty big."

José grimaces. "You have no idea how big. I'm not doing it over the phone, Anna, as I've told you before. I'll go home after the summer and do it then. My brother has offered to be a human shield."

Anna eyes him. "Fair enough, I suppose. I'll nag you about booking your flights until you do it."

"I bet you will." He turns to Rebecca. "After... everything, you know, I just wanted life to be simpler, cleaner. More honest."

She feels her ribcage swell. "I can relate to that. Good for you, love." She squeezes his hand. "If positive things can come out of all this…" She trails off. "Sorry, that's such a platitude."

"Oh, I don't know." Anna speaks lightly but looks out of the window. "I can't say I regret meeting Seth, knowing him, having that experience. We had some amazing times. Well, I did." There's a pause. For the first time Rebecca feels the empty seat at the table, his absence. Anna sighs. "He has a seductive power over people but it was also our responsibility how we reacted." She flushes slightly and turns back to the table. "I've been having therapy, in case you can't tell."

"Cool." Rebecca keeps it light in return, hides her surprise.

"Yeah. There was a point a few months ago when I thought – well, anyway, I wasn't in good shape. I started seeing this counsellor, Laura, and it was amazing what came out. I thought I was there just to talk about Seth but she showed me all these connections I hadn't made before. Between Seth and my dad. In some ways they are quite similar – the charisma, dominating a group, that sort of thing. Although my dad isn't a complete nutter." They share a smile. "I ended up talking more about my family than anything else. I suppose that's the usual thing with therapy. My mother's death, all the unprocessed stuff there." She smiles. "Listen to me, with my therapy-speak."

Rebecca smiles back. "It sounds like it really helped."

"It did. And of course we did spend a fair bit of time talking about Seth, analysing him. I still needed answers, needed to understand."

Rebecca knows she should keep the focus on Anna but the kick of curiosity is sudden and intense. Familiar. "And did you?"

Anna pauses as if deciding whether to respond. Then she sighs. "It was interesting to hear her perspective. She thought

405

he was probably very damaged as a child, which I doubt anyone would dispute. She talked about narcissism and how that can mask feelings of emptiness and self-hatred."

Rebecca shrugs. "Sounds like more therapy-speak. And a lot of guesswork."

"Yes, and she said that – said we had to be careful about looking for a label to give us an explanation. Which makes sense." Anna drains her glass and looks hopefully around for a waitress. "We're all individuals after all, and Seth was more of an individual than most. Some of the narcissism stuff fits though – charming, manipulative, needing to be adored." She catches the waitress' eye and orders another bottle. "I'll drink it, even if you two don't."

"So – why did he disappear then?"

Anna shrugs. "That's still the million dollar question. She said maybe in pretending that his parents were dead he'd split part of himself off, repressed it so that he did almost believe he was an orphan. Then if something happened to challenge that version of reality, like his mother showing up at his flat, for instance, upset about her husband leaving her, it could have totally unhinged him."

Rebecca thinks of him on the day they slept together, swollen-eyed and brittle.

Anna looks at her. "She said it was possible the collision of the two realities, as she put it, could push someone like that over the edge."

"Meaning?"

"Make him delusional. Maybe even dangerous."

Rebecca thinks of Seth – suave, sardonic, self-assured. "No, I can't see it." But other images are filtering through: Seth at the dinner party, Seth holding the negligee over her face. Footsteps following her at night. Goosebumps hatch like flies along her upper arms.

Anna lines her cutlery up in the middle of her plate. "She did actually warn me, you know. She said the main threat would be towards his parents or anyone he identified closely with one of his parents – but that I should still be careful."

There's a connection here that Rebecca doesn't want to make and she shivers, reaches for her cardigan. José makes the more obvious connection. "And, of course, after he disappears his father is mysteriously killed."

"But…" Rebecca frowns. "His mother's been convicted for it."

Anna shrugs. "And she had a fair old motive. We'll probably never find out the truth about that one."

Rebecca doesn't want to go any further. She runs a hand through her hair. "He's sidetracking us again. You didn't finish telling me about you, Anna. Sod it, give me some more wine."

Anna grins and passes it over as José shakes his head. "Well, I suppose the therapy has set a few wheels in motion. You know I'd lost contact with my pa?"

Rebecca nods.

"I think I transferred some of my feelings for him onto Seth. That's what my counsellor said and it makes sense. When Seth left – I just lost it. Sorry. I know I was hard work."

"Nothing new there then."

Anna gently prods José with a fork. "I couldn't handle it. I had to find him so I didn't have to face up to all these other feelings that were coming up. Losing my pa, losing my ma. Too much losing."

Rebecca rubs Anna's arm. "Do you feel better now?"

Anna nods and a smile widens slowly across her cheeks. "I'm going home next week."

"Home? To Ireland?"

The smile doesn't fade but tears start to well. "Yes. God, sorry, I'm as bad as you two."

"Oh, Anna, that's wonderful." Rebecca gets up and goes to hug her, fighting tears herself.

When she sits down José winks. "And what about the rest of your news, Anna?"

"There's more?"

"Go on – tell her."

But there's a sudden tap on Rebecca's shoulder. She turns into a smiling Charles, who wraps her up into a bear hug as she gets to her feet. They step back and look at each other while José grabs another chair.

"Charles! I had no idea you were coming." She's so pleased to see his lop-sided smile, eyes twinkling at the surprise he's given her.

Anna pinches an empty glass from the table next to them. "Sorry, that's my fault. I completely forgot you might stop by. Here, have some wine."

He perches next to Rebecca. "I can't stay. I've just nipped out of a job to grab a few bits of shopping." He coughs and the corner of his mouth twitches. "Pickled gherkins and grapefruit, I think it is today."

Rebecca laughs and grabs his hands. "Congratulations, they've told me. That's incredible news. How's Catherine?"

He colours a little but his chest puffs out like a pigeon. "She's... wonderful. Doing really well. A bit tired of course, a bit of indigestion, but, well, blooming, I suppose."

Rebecca resists catching Anna or José's eye. It's hard to take it in. She nods as if pregnancy is something she knows all about.

He sips at his glass. "It was a surprise, I won't deny it, but... well, it feels like the best thing that has ever happened to me." He chuckles into his beard. "Crikey, I sound like a delinquent teenage dad on Jerry Springer."

Everyone laughs. "I can't think of anyone less like that, Charles."

"Well, let's hope so. But how about you, Rebecca? You look wonderful. All glowing and... glamorous." More laughter. "When's your opening night?"

They talk pleasantries until Charles makes a sudden grimace at his watch. "Bugger! Told them I'd only be half an hour." He stands and bends down to kiss both her cheeks. "You must come over to dinner this week. Catherine would love to see you." He grabs his jacket and apologises left and right as he squeezes his way through the clutter of tables to the exit.

Rebecca whistles. "Blimey. Was that really Charles?"

Anna smiles. "Amazing, isn't it? It's like he's finally stepped out of the shadows."

"Out of Seth's shadow."

They consider this for a second. Then Rebecca remembers. "Hey, you were about to tell me some more news before Charles showed up."

"Was I?" Anna makes a non-committal face.

José coughs. "I'll tell her, if you don't."

Anna sighs. "You win. It's nothing really. Okay, I'm seeing someone."

It strikes Rebecca that she's never heard Anna say she's seeing someone. She watches her squirm in her seat like a bashful toddler.

"My God!" She looks at José who nods and grins. "This is too much to take in. Tell me all. Where did you meet? What's he like?"

"Hey, don't get all excited." But Anna's face betrays her. "It's all quite boring really. We met at a work do. He's the marketing director for Hackney council. He's… he's cool."

Rebecca and José exchange meaningful expressions. "And what's his name?" She sees José bury his face in a wineglass. Anna squirms again.

"Well, that's one of the problems."

"What, his name? I'm sure it can't be that bad."

"Don't bet on it. It's…" Anna takes a breath, "Grenville."

"Grenville?" Rebecca sees José's shoulders shaking and it starts as a little splutter, then a snort, and within three seconds they are all choking in waves of delirious laughter.

SCENE 23

Michael hitches his rucksack back onto his shoulders and lengthens his stride. This is what he has missed. The give and squelch of earth beneath his faded brown walking boots as he tramps up the track. Bird song – sparrow and mistle thrush. The whir of a distant lawnmower. And, like a miracle, no traffic noise at all. He stops for a second to feel the rapid thumping of his heart and breathe the clear air until it fills him to the brim. The first day of spring, his father said at breakfast. It's come late this year. Dew glinting on snowdrops at first light. Faint footfalls of the army of winter darkness retreating steadily, marching on empty stomachs and icy toes.

In the city all of this would pass him by, drowned in discord and diesel fumes. Here his senses are flexed to seize the waft of woody incense snaking down the valley, tiny leaves pitter-pattering like a child's bare feet on polished floorboards, the cold, sweetening taste of air inside his mouth as he climbs. He knows what waits for him at the top, or he thinks he knows. It's ten years since he has been here; things change, even in the places of childhood, even when the need to reference yourself demands they stay the same.

He hasn't told his parents what happened, of course. All they know is that he's taking a break from teaching and London. He's let them think that his dad's stroke has got something to do with it. His dad is surprised by this, maybe a little pleased. His mouth turns down now at the left-hand side and some of the anger seems to have dribbled out along with the milk from his morning breakfast cereal. His eyes are cloudy, lack conviction, rest on Michael more and more. Seeing him for the first time. Perhaps it's not too late for them to learn to be father and son.

His mum flaps around him, alarmed by his lack of employment and structure, tutting when he comes back with muddy trousers and ruddy cheeks. She wants to know what's going on but doesn't know how to ask. There are no family templates for this sort of discourse. He knows he's partly to blame, having made it clear from his teens that he would make his own decisions. He has never granted her a visa to enter his internal world and she has never requested one.

He pushes upwards, the last part of the track curling

before him like a tabby's tail. He resists the temptation to look backwards at the patchwork hills fanning open, wanting to preserve the surprise until the last possible moment. As he reaches a grassy plateau he sees it's just as it was; two sets of swings, still flaking and wonky, with a pock-marked red slide like a witch's nose in between. Only now, stepping out onto the grass, does he let himself turn and behold. It stops his breath. A magical storybook of miniature trees, roads and rooftops is spread out below him. Ancient creviced hills stoop over it, skirts adorned with a giant jigsaw of rush-green fields, faces still streaked with morning mist. This is no false grandiloquence of childhood memory. More than ever it deserves its name, the name he gave it nearly a quarter of a century ago. *The playground on the edge of the world.*

He wishes he could broaden his eyes, pan back like a movie camera, but instead they have shrunk, squinting in awe, reminding him of how tiny he is. How is it possible that this enchanted lookout has remained unspoilt? He inhales pine and feels the answer prickle deep in the pit of his stomach. Fingers interlock in front of him and he allows his eyes to close.

At first there are no words, just presence, his presence in this moment. No reflecting or regretting. It's a technique they showed him, a way to switch off the jet of his mind, or at least turn it down. He presses his fingers together and breathes all the way from his toes to his scalp. Once he would have mocked such an image, made sarcastic observations about the function of lungs. But it's a different sort of breathing, and this air is purified energy streaming in to fill every molecule of his being.

There's another presence now, expansive and orange, buffeting him in buoyant waves that take his weight and lift him off his feet. His body is surrendering but his mind holds on. Always holding on. One day he will let go completely and allow the waves to sweep him away, body and soul. He breathes up from the soil again, leans back into the waves, but the tug of his mind still resists like the rope anchoring a hot air balloon. It's okay, this is good, this is enough for now.

His lips twitch into murmured words once alien, now familiar: *Thank you, help me, Lord.* At this his mind, straining in the wings, bursts back onto centre stage. *Thank you for helping me make this decision, for showing me a new path.* And, more burningly, *Thank you for saving me.*

You could call it a coincidence, of course. A year ago he would certainly have named it such. A neighbour who'd locked himself out came banging at the door, wanting to use the phone. The neighbour's knocking swelled and dipped like waves of sound, each one trickling a bit closer to him until something in him woke up in air too viscous to breathe. Realisation dawning on him. A groping hand found the phone and they traced the 999 call when his voice wouldn't work. He was pumped full of salt water and shame.

It's the shame he needs to excise now. In his head he knows he is forgiven. But he can't always feel it. The Devil pops up at every unguarded moment, springing from the ground or hanging from the rafters like a bat, leering and laughing, cajoling and carousing, until at times he covers his ears and tries to shout over it. Meditation is a better defence but harder for someone so primed for conflict. He has a lot to learn.

He thinks of the others, Catherine, Charles, Rebecca, José, Anna, and regrets his harshness. The heat is gone, the fire left unstoked to fade into gentle warmth, an occasional flicker and glow. But the other one, the missing one, is too closely bound up with the leering sprite, the sprite who still holds out his hand from time to time to draw him back. There is too much fear for forgiveness yet.

He tries to focus on his breathing. Deep peace is ultimately what he's after but he's sure God will also smile on this hopping excitement as his mind veers off again. He has a new purpose, one that is born out of the crisis he survived. Teaching is not his vocation, or at least not teaching in schools.

"It's all very well to trust in God but He's not going to give you a monthly pay cheque, is He?" This was his mum over lunch yesterday. Well, maybe He will. It's only two months since he found faith and yet conviction burns inside him that he is meant to share it, that the restless animal in his belly can at last be harnessed and put to use. He will spread the flame, ignite others with passion and purpose. Reveal to them the true meaning of passion; how much more it is than the modern definition of sex. He shudders slightly, drenched again with relief that he can leave this issue behind, dedicate himself to higher things.

And when the Devil had ended every temptation, he departed from him until an opportune time.

Smiling, he opens his eyes and sees the world almost as he left it. The haze over the valley is starting to thin; dense clumps of conifers have moved into sharper focus but the sandy, mottled moorlands above them are still in the clouds. A car potters by behind him, followed by quick, tripping footsteps. He turns to meet the curious gaze of two little girls who giggle like dormice and run off to the slide. Someone is clipping his hedge a few houses down and he hears distant sounds, a village starting to wake.

It's time to make a move.

SCENE 24

Rebecca exits the restaurant into a different London. At first she thinks it's the light. There's a late-afternoon haze floating over the city, blurring its edges into commas and question marks. The people passing her are meandering rather than striding, or maybe she's slowing the whole thing down in her head, so their bodies bob like puppets.

The magic portal. Follow me, Alice. Maybe Seth has disappeared into this alternative universe. If he even existed at all.

She smiles as she joins the pottering throngs, floating along where only hours before she was jarring and jolting. A couple of people smile back, confused at the warmth of greeting from a stranger, wondering if they know her. Despite the wine, she feels lucid for the first time in months, years, seeing the world pass in slow motion, its beauty revealed to her in a series of urban freeze-frames. Girl with a bandaged arm, a new tattoo. Three Japanese tourists on the way to Piccadilly Circus. Butch man carrying a tiny, trembling Yorkshire terrier. Lights of all hues guiding the weak and weary inside, offering food, drink, massage. She sees it all and embraces it.

Is she dead, an angel, in the world but not of it? She laughs. If this is dead, she's never felt more at one with her body. She breathes into its solidness, holding her like a bear hug. The hungry ache she's learned to live with is gone. She feels sated for the first time since Seth disappeared.

No, for the first time since she met him.

It's a light-bulb moment that stops her in her tracks just off Oxford Street. She's been associating the restlessness, the gnawing hunger, with his disappearance rather than his arrival into her life. How long was it before she was constantly craving more? Living for the next fix and never satisfied?

Because that's what Seth did, made you want more. More from life, people, yourself. That line again: *Oh, I know there's more. For people like us, people who know how to feel.* And she was flattered but she'd felt it too. It was as if he shone a light into the cracks and dark spaces within her until he'd unearthed a bellyful of gaping yearning. But sometimes she wasn't sure if the hunger belonged to her or to him, if she was vibrating with his unrequited desires or her own. She had believed this was due to the special connection between them. But more likely this was the effect he had on all of them, the deep hole inside of him sucking them in.

They were never going to be enough to fill his emptiness. That's why he would need to move on to more people, more experiences, more more more.

She starts to feel sombre. The streets have closed in again and everything has sped up, *normal service is resumed.* She's not far from her old flat but scuttling back immediately would feel like a defeat. The wide avenues of Regent's Park are only ten minutes away, benches where she can sit and make sense of it all without interruption. These are important revelations and she needs to hold onto them before they fly away.

She sits upright, serious, the holder of knowledge, flung out of Eden and newly self-sufficient. She knows the dark side now, the dark side of her, she has traced its snaking paths and found her way back again. She can take care of herself. Empowerment swells like an orchestra inside her but there's an underlying shimmer of sadness, a single violin. She thinks of beating her parents at Scrabble for the first time, feeling thrilled and triumphant and then, later, after the packing away of the tiles, the feeling that one had dropped to the pit of her stomach. *Sadness, eight points.* A rite of passage moment, the beginning of independence, maturity. Aloneness.

But she isn't lonely, that's the distinction. She has people, friends, more than she needs, even. She doesn't even need a boyfriend; she can be by herself and enjoy the space. She has a vocation she loves, something precious and life-affirming. She thinks of Catherine, drudging away in her firm of accountants, narrow shoulders bent over a task she doesn't care about. *Poor Catherine.* Compassion takes her by surprise, sprinkling tears that make the picture run a little, so that Catherine and her desk start to melt and slide towards the ground. *I've been a bitch.* She closes her eyes. She won't dodge it, she'll stay with this, *take responsibility*. It was rivalry for Seth's attention that made her put Catherine down. She swallows. She can fix it. Right now anything seems possible. She'll buy a present for the baby, something nice.

She barely notices that she has got to her feet, zigzagging like a drunk, veering towards the dwindling dapples of sunlight. The wind takes the weight of her hair in delicious bursts and the goosebumps on the tops of her arms are stroked away by the next patch of sun. Something is lifting, loosening again. The ache has left her legs and each long breath draws in rippling energy. She thinks again of Anna and José and her unexpected discovery that they could still be friends. In a different way, a better way. Perhaps she is ready to base herself in London again, persuade Shaz to rent a new place, somewhere a bit nicer, where they could have dinner parties of their own. Then she'll have a big break, get famous, do photo shoots for magazines. At the point where she's moved into one of the mansions on the edge of the park she smiles, reins herself in. But not too much. Anything is possible, just as her parents always said.

She inhales to the perimeters of her new solidness, where something is perched, fluttering like a bird back from a faraway summer.

Hope.

SCENE 25

Catherine lifts her voluminous white blouse so that the baby can sunbathe a little while she reads. She's got at least an hour to sprawl across the sofa like a Rubens painting before Charles gets home. In her one brief foray outside it had been quite chilly, but inside the window serves as a solar heater and she basks in it.

Rebecca is back. Charles is seeing her today, with Anna and José. He invited her along but she isn't ready yet, not willing to wheel out her pale, veiny, distended body and spread it out next to Rebecca's long, lean, lovely one. Not ready for the feelings that seeing her may unsettle.

She has a pile of papers in a green folder and she lies back to read them one by one. She does this quite a lot. Charles doesn't know, in fact none of the others know that she has copies of Seth's poetry, at least the stuff he chose to share with her and the group. And maybe a few other bits she found for herself and copied down when she'd finished her piano practice and he still wasn't home. It comforts her that part of him is still in her hand. Sometimes she reads aloud to the baby, although a lot of it isn't suitable.

The baby is big now, protruding from her small frame in

comical fashion. Sometimes it tries to push its way out of her stomach, pummelling her with tight fists, looking for the exit. Charles reassures her she looks more beautiful than ever. She has breasts for the first time in her life and suspects that's part of her new-found beauty. She's got no experience in finding supportive bras so goes to a maternity shop where the sales assistant straps her into a beige number with plenty of lace and no wire. Her bras used to get lost in her underwear drawer. Now they take up most of the space like granny girdles.

She rifles through to the last of the poems, appropriately called *"Endgame"*. This one isn't good to read to Baby, isn't really suitable reading for her either, but she's drawn to it over and over, his last message to them. She scans the familiar words, absorbing more than reading.

Endgame

Orphaned in the lockjaw of
Elongated evening smiles
Dreaming of a death, the boy
Is watching his mother's slender hand
Peel away from the soap-smooth rock
Unable to scream as he
Sips bilberry juice.

Then she stares. How could she not have seen it? Her heart bangs against her raised ribcage. She doesn't know much about poetry, but isn't that the oldest trick in the book? The first letter of each line, read vertically.

Oedipus.

She racks her brain through school classics lessons. Killed his father, slept with his mother. Her hand trembles and she sits up straighter to try to pull in some breath.

She sees the narrowed, darting eyes of Julia Rothbury as they looked at each other through a glass screen. The smell of prison, layers of bleach with something rotten underneath.

Her last-ditch attempt to find out where he was.

She knew she had made a mistake almost at once but she was shut in now, guards stationed all around to catch her if she bolted, as if she were the guilty one.

It was him, of course, who killed Clive. You know that, don't you? Of course you do, you wouldn't be here otherwise.

She clutches her stomach, trying to reassure Baby, cover its eyes and ears. Julia Rothbury was a liar. She'd felt it through and through; those fidgeting hands, that whine, those crocodile tears.

He was trying to protect me. He'd always do anything for me. Afterwards he went to Lucilla, raving and delirious, calling out for me. A sudden cloud of confusion passing over Julia's face. *But he wouldn't have set me up, he'd never do that. God knows who he was, that man.*

What man?

The one who taped me saying I'd consider using a hitman to kill Clive. Entrapment, they call it. Big man, broad London accent. Funny blonde streak like a racoon. Of course I didn't mean it, I was angry, he was buying me drinks and flattering me. Goading me. Chatting me up. I would never really have done it.

Catherine is starting to hyperventilate, like she did at the time, and it's bad for Baby, robbing him of oxygen. There's some lukewarm camomile tea at her side and she takes a ragged slug.

Feeling queasy, by any chance? When's it due?

Too sharp to be deceived by a big jumper. *July.*

Not his, is it? My boy's? You're not expecting me to become Grandma?

A violent blush. *Of course not. I haven't seen him – Seth – for nearly a year.*

Nasty laugh, high pitched and nasal. *I was kidding. You're not really his type.*

Even in navy prison clothes she drips disdain over Catherine. And lies, dreadful things about Seth, her own son, so she wants to press her fists into her ears to stop the poison seeping into them. But the next minute she calls him *my boy*, claims she would do anything to protect him. *And isn't he handsome, doesn't he break hearts?* Her mouth twists as she takes in Catherine's ankle-length skirt and shapeless jumper. *I suppose you're in love with him too.*

Tears of anger. *What makes you think you know anything about him?*

Touched a nerve, have I?

Whatever you did to him, it was bad enough for him to tell people that you were dead.

That takes the wind out of her, for a minute. Then she lifts her head. *I made some mistakes. But he'll come back to me. And he'll get me out of here.*

Catherine shook all the way out, like she's shaking now, terrified she might shove the guard as he led her back to the entrance and end up being locked up herself. Outside the gates she put her hands on her knees and breathed the clean air.

She takes another sip of camomile. Julia Rothbury has been tried and convicted for her husband's murder. There had been no doubt. She stabbed him, took out his eyes and was incriminated by one of those long, coarse red hairs. The judge had said something about a terrible crime planned meticulously. So of course she'd been lying. It was sick, trying to implicate your own innocent child.

She takes the copy of *"Endgame"* that she has allowed to drift to the floor, battling to reach over her own stomach. It's a fantasy, of course, another fantasy from a traumatic childhood, like the poems Charles found. *Killed his father.* Well, he might have thought about it but he hadn't done it. *Slept with his mother.* She shudders, thinking of the curling wisp of ginger she'd found on his pillow. It must have been Rebecca's. Hairs like hers got everywhere; she'd even found one on her own jumper once. No, the whole Oedipus thing is poetic licence, a joke even – that sounds more like Seth.

She lies back and flips to another poem.

Charles finds her fast asleep on the sofa. She's curled on her side, one hand cradling her bump, the other tucked under her head. He's late and she's conked out. Her mouth is open and she rasps and heaves like his own, adorable beached whale. He'll start cooking supper and let her sleep. He notices a piece of paper on the floor and goes to pick it up. A quick, sharp twist of his guts when he sees what it is. His hand itches to rip it into shreds, bury it in the kitchen bin under junk mail and potato peelings. Instead he places it carefully back where he found it. He must be reasonable. He can't expect her to forget about Seth straight away.

Which poem is it, anyway? He glances down, barely interested, he's seen too much of Seth's poetry recently. He misses the title but letters jump out and arrange themselves vertically and he blinks. *Oedipus*. Of course, how very Seth, an obscure reference to Greek mythology, an in-joke between him and Sophocles.

But… someone did kill Seth's father. He frowns as more details of the story come back to him. Oedipus blinded himself. Clive Rothbury had his eyes gouged out. Surely, though, it should be Seth being blinded in that case?

He shakes his head. This is just more dust being hurled into their face by a gleeful, departing maniac. To keep them hooked in, wondering, forever trying to solve the mystery of why he disappeared. They are the blind ones and they always have been around him. He will not get sucked back in.

The next night, after Catherine has gone to sleep, he creeps to the living room and reads the copy of Oedipus he has picked up in Waterstone's. Oedipus kills his father at a crossroads. He starts tugging at papers in the magazine rack. Catherine's kept everything, all the press coverage, he knows she has. There it is, a green folder at the back of the rack with newspaper pages neatly filed, in backwards order, unfolding a story of violence and speculation. He thumbs through them until he finds the location of the disused basement, on a street corner near Hackney. He grabs the A-Z from the shelf and finds the page reference. His index finger traces the crossroads down and across, down and across. It doesn't need to mean anything. There are many crossroads in a city like London. But it takes him two attempts to swallow.

The painting, the bloody painting. Oedipus on his knees. He's always hated it, always wondered why Seth would sully a spectacular room with a look of such crazed anguish. He puts away the folder and paces the room, thinking of the play. Oedipus gouges out his own eyes with a brooch. As far as he knows, no details have ever been released on how Clive Rothbury's eyes were removed.

His throat tightens. They know Seth is violent. He thinks of the woman, her half-closed eye, the marks round her neck. He thinks of her red wig, of the red wig that Sarah was wearing, the red wig they found in the Shepherd's Bush house and the bile rises. Everyone dressed up to look like Julia. Everyone he fucked made to resemble his mother.

For a second he closes his eyes and the room swirls around him. He clenches the back of a chair with white knuckles. A picture of Rebecca, red haired and radiant at lunch yesterday, pops like a bubble over his head.

It's a good job that Catherine is no longer light on her feet because he hears the creak of the bed long before she comes squinting into the lounge.

"I need a wee. What are you up to?"

He has immersed himself in a file of drawings and measurements. "Still a bit of work left to do here. You pop on back to bed and I'll be in soon. Do you need anything, darling?" It thrills him to call her this. She shakes her head and shuffles out and he exhales.

He pours himself a large whisky from a crystal decanter. A certainty is settling over him. Seth did it. He killed his father, maimed and mutilated him, and then disappeared. He paid a hit man, possibly with Jake's help, and then gouged out his eyes in a sick nod to the Oedipus story, his own private joke.

He slugs at the whisky so hard it makes his eyes water and his airways tighten. Seth's still out there somewhere, crouching in the shadows, planning who knows what. But what can he do about it? Catherine would never forgive him if he went to the police, and who's to say they would take any notice anyway? There's no new evidence, only a theory born of ancient Greek drama.

And Julia Rothbury is clearly a nasty piece of work who quite possibly deserves to be in prison. Did she seduce her own son? Do all Seth's actions spring from the damage his parents wrought on him?

He reaches to the coffee table for his inhaler. The shock of the sucking noise punctuates his inner dialogue, a sharp intake of breath. He thinks again of Rebecca. She's a big girl. There's nothing to suggest that Seth will get back in touch with her, no reason to warn her, alarm her. Nothing really to suggest that Seth is a danger to anyone else, now his father is dead.

He sleeps without covers that night but the weight of knowledge pushes on his chest like rubble.

EPILOGUE

For the fifth time this week he is watching her scream. Watching and listening. The voice has caught his attention tonight, swooping over their heads like the screech of an owl. *Sarah Good, Goody Osburn, Bridget Bishop.* All those people she saw with the devil.

Is that what she's been shouting about, night after night? They draw back from her, the whore who cried witch, and she laughs as she pulls off her bonnet and flings her hair into flame. She is basking in the warm gaze of the eyes on her, his eyes, too absorbed in her own revenge to remember that others might be planning theirs. Offstage, away from the glare of the audience.

In a disused basement, for example. Something of the sewers, perhaps a rat or two. Just one player, an old man, both victim and voyeur in a perfectly staged set-up. No one to applaud him, not like here, a full house ready to ejaculate its appreciation. A smile slides across his face, at odds with the scream before him. That luscious mouth still agape as she sways and swoons and splatters her deceit across the stage. He is starting to shut off from the sound again, just as husky pleas in the basement faded into mime. The smell of fear or the old man shitting his pants.

No slugging oozing drops
But a black rain and bloody hail poured down.

The plot had been worked out years ago; all he needed to do was press the button. And change the script just a little. The punishment was passed on, the sins of the father placed squarely where they ought to rest, but can the gods be

423

cheated so easily? Will their thirst for revenge be quenched or enflamed by his sleight of hand?

No doubt time will tell. It's a good job he has no plans to have children. They might well feel the need to complete the circle and dispose of him, their father, their millstone and curse. *Patricide*. A word to be tried on the tongue until the pallet is ready and the taste is first normalised, then craved. *Patricide*. He knows from the sideways glance that he has tasted the word aloud, his lips kissing the 'p' and his teeth releasing the 's' like the hiss of a snake.

His hand goes to his pocket where he can feel the hard, round object, fluted at the edges. He runs his thumb along the pin tucked behind it. It's not like him to take back a gift. She will understand when he returns it. An act must be completed in the proper way, even if some details have been changed. And the act itself is another gift for her, laid at her feet like the dead mouse a cat brings its owner.

Her white dress is sliding down one shoulder. His hand twitches to straighten it, to tear it off. It's the same scene as always, arm outstretched as she slips away. But this time will be different. This time he must rise and go to her. This time he can save her and save himself.

This time…

Do it for Daddy, darling. Just one poem

… he will rip…

Many a man before you, in his dreams, has shared his mother's bed

… away the layers…

You remind me of someone

… that hide her face…

You're staring at my hair

… one by one…

Please take me back. He's left me for someone else

… until he learns…

Goodnight, sweet ladies

… her truth.

Her hand is taut, there for the taking. A rush of hair tips over her face and strokes the ground. Splitting sounds, the crack of thunder.

The dark-haired man rises from his seat and makes his way to the exit.

ACKNOWLEDGEMENTS

Thank you to my lovely editor, Lauren, and the whole Legend Press (dream) team. Thank you to everyone who has given me practical support with this book, including advice (Greater Manchester Police, Jo Mitchell, Katy Peden), space to write (Laura Tunbridge, Mark Holtom and Catherine Putz) and feedback (Lee Bullman and Nigel Tordoff). Thank you to my wonderful local friends and to all my friends who have supported me along the way. Each time you said something encouraging about my writing, I tucked it away to savour later.

Thank you to Liz Flanagan, my dear friend and writing buddy, always on hand with ideas, brilliant advice and backup whenever I most need it.

Thank you to my family: to Mum, Dad and Dae for believing in my creativity, and to my fabulous network of uncles, aunts and cousins cheering me on. Thank you to my gorgeous girls, Leela and Evie, for putting up with a mother "always in front of a screen": I might not get picked for *Strictly Come Dancing* quite yet, but I still hope to make you proud. Thank you to Dave for your unique and galvanising blend of support and brutal honesty – and for the tantalising kitchen smells that keep me going through long nights of editing.

Finally, a huge and heartfelt thank you to Elaine Hanson and the Luke Bitmead Bursary for giving me my break. It's a wonderful thing to support unpublished writers and, Elaine, I am truly grateful for your enormous generosity in the face of personal loss. I wouldn't be here without you.

Untouchable Things was the
Winner of the 2014 Luke Bitmead Bursary

The award was set up shortly after Luke's death in 2006 by his family to support and encourage the work of fledgling novel writers. The top prize is a publishing contract with Legend Press, as well as a cash bursary.

We are delighted to be working with Luke's family to ensure that Luke's name and memory lives on – not only through his work, but through this wonderful memorial bursary too. For those of you lucky enough to have met Luke you will know that he was hugely compassionate and would love the idea of another struggling talented writer being supported on the arduous road to securing their first publishing deal.

We will ensure that, as with all our authors, we give the winner of the bursary as much support as we can, and offer them the most effective creative platform from which to showcase their talent. We can't wait to start reading and judging the submissions.

We are pleased to be continuing this brilliant bursary for an eighth year, and hope to follow in the success of our previous winners Andrew Blackman (*On the Holloway Road*, February 2009), Ruth Dugdall (*The Woman Before Me*, August 2010), Sophie Duffy (*The Generation Game*, August 2011), J.R. Crook (*Sleeping Patterns*, July 2012), Joanne Graham (*Lacey's House*, May 2013), Jo Gatford (*White Lies*, July 2014) and Tara Guha (*Untouchable Things*, September 2015).

For more information on the bursary and all
Legend Press titles visit:
www.legendpress.co.uk
Follow us @legend_press